For Bobbie Birk

. . .who encouraged me all the way.

One

There's an old saying in the Pacific Northwest that if you can make it through winter, the rest of the year's a piece of cake. The only problem is that winter in the Pacific Northwest too often begins in October and lasts into May, bringing with it months of raw winds and pelting rain, hail, snow, and flash floods. It's especially hard on the homeless, many of whom have no choice but to huddle in doorways and alleys, trying, if not to keep warm, at least to keep dry.

On a typical early morning in the middle of February, a stone's throw from the docks of Port Hancock, Washington, Jason Lightfoot was asleep in the alley behind The Last Call Bar and Grill, in the tarpaulin-draped box wedged into a thick stone wall that he called home, snoring loudly and dreaming that he was really in a front row seat at the fights, close enough that he could grasp the metal guard rail, feel the spray of sweat from the boxers' bodies across his face, see the concentration in the sparring duo's eyes, and hear the shouting of the crowd and the sound of the bell -- so loud that it made him jump. He was close enough that it felt almost as though he were right there in the ring with the fighters, and the punches being thrown were coming right at him.

Jason awoke with a start to realize that this was no dream -- someone really was, if not punching him, certainly kicking him. He opened his eyes into the glare of a flashlight. It had been a long time since anyone had rousted him like this. His head was throbbing, as was his bum right leg, and, with the light shining directly in his eyes, it hurt to look up.

He had no idea what time it was, but he could tell it was still more or less dark, which meant it wasn't anywhere near time yet for him to be awake. He didn't have to be at the dry dock until mid-morning. He wondered if he might have drunk a bit more last night than he usually did, or maybe taken more of his medication than his doctor recommended. But, fuzzyheaded though he might have been, it didn't keep him from realizing that it was two uniforms that were standing in front of his box.

"What the. . .?" he muttered, blinking. Having become more or less a permanent fixture in the alley after fifteen years, the cops had pretty much stopped hassling him. Or to be more precise, the one mean son-of-a-bitch cop who used to get off on making his life miserable had got himself promoted and was no longer on the hassling detail. He squinted up at these two.

"What's the matter, officers?" he asked.

"That's what we're looking to find out," the taller of the two replied.

"Come on out of there," the shorter one said.

Under the circumstances, Jason decided there wasn't really much point in arguing. He was already crawling out of his box, slowly because of his bum leg, which ached all the more in damp weather, when his knee knocked against something hard. It skittered out from under him and onto the pavement. Even the pre-dawn darkness, compounded as it was by a thick fog, didn't stop him from seeing it was a gun.

The two officers saw it, too. They jumped back, caught off guard, and quickly reached for their own weapons.

"Don't touch it," Paul Cady, the shorter one, barked, pointing his Sig Sauer P250 directly at Jason's head.

"Don't even look at it," Arnie Stiversen, the taller one, ordered.

Jason didn't intend to. It wasn't his gun. He didn't even know what it was doing in his box. He moved away from the weapon. It lay on the ground until Stiversen inched forward and snatched it up.

"Now I want to see you flat on your face, mister," Cady instructed, "arms straight out to the side."

The lanky Indian's brain might have been a bit soggy, and he might not have been thinking too clearly, but he wasn't dumb enough to argue with two men with guns. He lowered himself to the damp pavement, turned his face down, and stretched his arms out. There was nothing to see, so he closed his eyes. He could sense the two policemen hovering over him, checking him out. Then he could feel them searching through his shapeless jacket and frayed shirt, running their hands around his waistband, and patting up and down his baggy trousers. When they were satisfied he had no other weapon, they told him he could get up.

It was as he was scrambling to his feet that he spotted something, maybe fifteen feet down the alley. He couldn't make out much, but it sure did look like someone was lying there where no one should have been.

"Uh-oh," he said. "Is somebody hurt? Does he need help?"

"No, he's not hurt," Cady snapped. "He's dead, you son-of-a-bitch!"

Jason Lightfoot blinked. "Dead?" he echoed. "Well now, I'm right sorry about that. But I sure hope you ain't thinkin' I had anythin' to do with that. Because if you are, I can tell you, right out, I ain't had nothin' to do with that. I been in my box, mindin' my own business."

The two police officers had rousted the Indian thinking he could be a witness to the crime they had just discovered. It didn't occur to them that he might be involved until they spotted the gun, and the oversight made the shorter one angry.

"And what exactly *is* your business?" he asked with a sneer in his voice.

"I clean up over at the bar," Lightfoot told him, gesturing across the alley at the back door of The Last Call. "And I do odd jobs. I got no reason to kill no one." He squinted in the direction of the body. "Besides, I don't even know who that is."

"Well, I'd say it's a little late for introductions," Stiversen said, "but his name is -- was -- Detective Dale Scott."

Jason had his mouth open to reemphasize his point, but suddenly closed it. Because he did, in fact, know who Detective Dale Scott was. He was the very same son-of-a-bitch cop who used to get off on using him for a punching bag.

He tried to remember if he had run into the policeman last night, and if there had been an argument of any kind, but his head was throbbing so much, it was making his mind all the more muddled, and he came up blank. The only thing he could recall, and not even that was very clear anymore, was his dream.

"You ain't sayin' I killed him, are you?"

"Sure looks that way," Cady replied.

"But I don't remember doin' nothin' like that," the Indian protested. "Why would I have done that? That ain't even my gun."

"No, it isn't," Stiversen agreed, having examined the police issue semiautomatic weapon that was exactly like his own. "It's his."

"What's your name?" Cady asked.

"Lightfoot," the Indian mumbled. "Jason Lightfoot."

"Lightfoot. . .Lightfoot. . ." the officer repeated. "Don't I know that name from somewhere?"

Jason shrugged. "You might," he conceded. "It's not such an uncommon name around these parts."

The Indian wasn't exactly clean with the law, but his offences were years old and mostly about being drunk and disorderly, which is why he knew the dead cop with the mean streak. Even so, their encounters had never amounted to anything really serious -- a broken nose, a couple of split lips, a few cracked ribs, assorted cuts and bruises, and then the usual overnight accommodation, courtesy of the city. He tried to think. He barely recalled leaving The Last Call, dumping the garbage, and crawling into his box. He didn't remember seeing Scott, and other than that, there was nothing, nothing except his dream, until these cops had kicked him awake.

"But I got nothin' to do with that."

"Maybe no and maybe yes," Cady said. "Not for us to say." He leveled his gun at the Indian. "But right now, we're going to take you in for questioning regarding the murder of Dale Scott."

From the corner of his eye, Jason saw Stiversen starting to move around behind him, unhooking a pair of handcuffs from his belt. In spite of the weapon pointed directly at him, in spite of his bad leg, the Indian bolted. It was the instinct of a cornered animal, of course, because there was nowhere to go. The alley was narrow, with the police car blocking one end of it and the two policemen blocking the other.

He froze for an instant, trying to decide what to do. It was just long enough for Cady to whip out his baton and deliver a blow to the back of his bad leg. Jason collapsed like an accordion.

But the officer didn't stop there. Blows began to rain all over his body as he lay there on the pavement. He managed to roll over onto his bad leg, and tried as best he could to protect it, only it didn't help much.

"All right, all right," he heard the other cop say. "You don't want to kill the guy."

After one more blow, the beating stopped. Jason felt Stiversen grabbing his arms and pulling them tight behind his back, and he heard the snap of the handcuffs as they locked securely around his wrists. Then the cop began reading him his rights about being under arrest and his right to remain silent and his right to have an attorney.

"There's gotta be some kinda mistake here," he mumbled through a bloody lip.

"Yeah, and you made it," Cady said. "But look on the bright side. Think how lucky you are that we found you before the guy's partner did."

"How do you mean?" the Indian asked.

"I mean our getting to you first guarantees you get a trial and then years of living off taxpayers like me before you hang."

• • •

Port Hancock was the largest city on Washington State's Olympic Peninsula. It sprawled across a thrust of land that jutted out into the Strait of Juan de Fuca -- that strip of watery highway defining the northwestern border of the United States.

The seat of Jackson County, Port Hancock boasted a population just short of 25,000, in a county that, added all together, came in at just under 105,000. A good public transportation network brought the major city of Seattle and the state capital of Olympia within a three-hour journey. A reliable private ferry system regularly transported Canadians and Americans back and forth across the border. And the Pacific Ocean was a mere ninety minutes away.

Arguably one of the most beautiful cities to be found in the Pacific Northwest, or anywhere, for that matter, Port Hancock was dominated by architectural masterpieces, crisscrossed by tree-lined avenues, and dotted with exquisite parks and gardens. Its location was no drawback either, nestled as it was between the scenic Strait on the north and the magnificent Olympic Mountains on the south.

The city's spectacular deep-water harbor had led early settlers to believe that Port Hancock would one day be the largest seaport on the West Coast and, as a result, a great deal of money had been invested in the fledgling town. However, when the railroad failed to extend west onto the peninsula, despite all the pressure that was put on politicians, those dreams were dashed, and many of the investors simply wrote off their losses and deserted the place.

Port Hancock was, perhaps more accurately, two cities in one, with the residential sections to the south referred to as New Town, and the predominantly commercial district that stretched along the waterfront to the north known as Old Town. It was a misnomer, really, considering that a good part of New Town was just as old as Old Town, but nobody, except perhaps the historians, seemed to care.

And not even the historians seem to take much note of the fact that, over time, the cultural divide, that had been wide to begin with, only grew wider.

For several hundred years, the area had been a stable home for half a dozen Indian tribes. But by the late 1700's, their populations had been almost decimated, thanks to territorial wars among the tribes themselves, and strange new diseases brought by white explorers and missionaries -- small pox, measles, syphilis -- that wiped out a whole generation.

Their livelihoods were systematically destroyed -- settlers logged the massive stands of cedar trees that the natives relied on for basket weaving and clothing, using only downed trees for shelter and warmth. For little more than trophies, hunters slaughtered the wild game that had sustained generations of Indians, and fishermen overharvested the salmon, killed seals for their skins and shellfish for pearls, and polluted the waters.

By the middle 1800's, little more than a thousand natives were around to greet the colonizers. By the end of the century, only a few hundred remained, swindled out of most of their property, removed to reservations, left to eke out meager livings off the land that remained, if they could, or work on the docks or as servants, if they were lucky, and get drunk in the bars along the streets of Old Town. Once a proud and independent people, they had come to be regarded in their own community as second-class citizens.

Named not for John Hancock, as most people quite naturally assumed, but for Commodore Edward Hancock, a relatively obscure seaman who had plied the waters of the Pacific with George Vancouver back in the late 1700's, the town was officially settled in 1854, incorporated as a city in 1862, designated the seat of Jackson County in 1863, thrived until the 1890's, and was then essentially abandoned until the late 1930's when a resurging logging industry took hold, and the Port Hancock Paper Mill opened. Even then, a great many of the grand buildings remained uninhabited for another thirty years, until budding entrepreneurs stumbled into an essentially untouched utopia for business opportunities, young people began to migrate in search of work and a good place to raise a family, and old people came looking for a comfortable place to retire. What they found was an incredible collection of Victorian, Edwardian, and Romanesque structures that had been preserved, almost as time capsules, for nearly a hundred years.

The Jackson County Courthouse was one such building. The fabulous Romanesque structure, begun in 1888 and completed in 1894, was constructed of red brick and sandstone, and replete with arches, gables, and turrets. Four stories high, not counting the clock tower, it sat on the edge of New Town, overlooking Old Town, presiding over both. It had withstood earthquakes, floods, abandonment, a rare lightning strike, and countless renovations with amazing grace and fortitude.

Built at a time of enormous promise, the interior of the building was finished in nothing but the finest materials, walls paneled in mahogany, floors of polished marble, and furniture that had been hand-carved out of rosewood, walnut, and oak.

The first floor of the courthouse held most of the county's offices. The second floor, accessed by a grand marble stairway as well as an elevator, contained four courtrooms of varying size and grandeur. And the two upper floors housed the quarters of the prosecutors, the public defenders, the judges, and their staffs.

By contrast, the Port Hancock Police Department, an unremarkable two-story concrete building with a daylight basement, circa 1975, sat just across the plaza from the courthouse. Within its austere confines of bare plaster walls and cement floors, one police chief, one deputy chief, two lieutenants, three sergeants, six detectives, and some eighteen officers worked diligently to keep the city safe.

While Jackson County, as a whole, had a slightly higher than average crime rate, Port Hancock's crime rate was reasonably low -- just the way everyone in town liked it. Vandalism was, of course, the most common crime, attributed mainly to teenagers, and there were the typical number of assaults, burglaries, arsons, DUIs, and drug-related episodes, and even the occasional rape got reported. But in the past decade, there had been only four homicides.

The city's main sources of income had changed somewhat over the last fifty years. The paper mill was still in business, and fishing and tourism were still important, but the economic focus was now on professional and related occupations. Despite the setbacks caused by the fiscal disaster of 2008, service jobs were still available, financial operations were regaining ground, and most of the corporate firms were holding their own. Even small business owners were seeing signs of a brighter future.

· · ·

Lily Burns walked quickly down the fourth-floor corridor of the Jackson County Courthouse, her high-heeled shoes tapping smartly against the polished marble, looking neither to her right nor to her left, and neither stopping nor even hesitating until she reached the door at the far end, the door with the small brass plaque affixed to it that read: Presiding Judge.

Lily always walked quickly, as though she didn't intend to waste so much as a minute more than was absolutely necessary to get where she was going.

At the age of thirty-five, she stood a trim five-foot-seven inches tall, with light brown hair that waved more than curled and fell just below her shoulders, her mother's prominent nose, and hazel eyes that were either green or gold, depending on the weather, her mood, or the clothes she had chosen to wear.

Lily had pretty much grown up in this building, scurrying behind her father from the time she was eight years old, sitting on the floor of the Jackson County Prosecutor's office, spinning stories with crayons, picture books, and imagination. Then, as she grew older, she had been allowed to sit behind her father in the courtroom and watch, totally enthralled, as he spun his stories for a jury. And finally, after graduating from law school, she had worked from an office of her own, just down the hall from his.

For almost thirty years, her father had occupied the big corner office on the third floor until, at the age of sixty-seven, a stroke cut short his tenure. But Carson Burns remained a legend in Port Hancock, for settling his family in the economically turbulent city of the late 1970s, and for taking on the prosecutor's job when no one else wanted it. Much of the respect that the people of Jackson County still held for the law today was due to his quiet, steady influence.

The youngest of three daughters, Lily went through the Port Hancock public school system, graduating near the top of her class, and then off to the University of Washington for a degree, with honors, in English. While her sisters opted for marriage and family -- one now lived in Oregon, the other in Colorado -- Lily was her father's daughter, through and through, and there was never any question about what she would do after college.

She was accepted to half a dozen of the country's top law schools, but because she had no particular desire to journey too far out of her comfort zone, she chose to go to Stanford, just down the road, so to speak, in California, to graduate third in her class, and then return to her hometown.

"You could make it big in any city of your choice," several of her professors told her. And in fact, she had been heavily recruited by a number of law firms up and down the West Coast.

But Lily only smiled. "It isn't about fame and fortune," she told each of them. "It's about doing what's right."

Althea Burns had died of breast cancer in the autumn of her youngest daughter's final year in law school, and what was right for Lily was to go back to Port Hancock, immediately after she had graduated, to live with her father in the Morgan Hill home she had grown up in, and to go to work for him at the courthouse. She was good enough at her job that many believed she would one day be elected the county's first female prosecutor. But a year after her father's stroke -- and with his blessing, Lily had made the switch across the aisle to private practice.

There were two firms in town that tendered her excellent offers, partly because of her ability, mostly because of her name. But, in the end, Lily elected to hang out her own shingle, in front of an Old Town Victorian, a block and a half from the courthouse. In the five years that had passed since then, she had earned a reputation for being smart, honest, dedicated, and a tenacious adversary. Which was why she was fairly certain of the reason she had been summoned to the presiding judge's office on this particular Friday morning. Port Hancock was, in many ways, a small town. And word had a way of getting around.

"With all due respect, Your Honor, I know why I'm here, and I don't want the case," Lily declared before the judge could even get her mouth open.

"I know you don't," Judge Grace Pelletier acknowledged pleasantly. "But your number came up." The county kept a list of private attorneys and, when necessary, rotated them through the system to offset a frequently overworked public defender's office.

"I knew the victim," Lily informed her. "I grew up next door to his wife. I was in their wedding."

"I know that, too," the judge responded. "But then, this is a small town, and I expect you'll find you grew up knowing someone related to someone in just about every case you'll ever handle here."

"But I see no redeeming value in this defendant." Lily declared, falling back on an old legal ploy.

"And do you honestly believe that would prevent you from protecting his rights to the fullest?" the judge inquired.

"Well, no," Lily had to admit. "But as long as you're asking, I'd prefer to be the one protecting the *people's* rights -- by making sure the noose gets put around this guy's neck." Washington was one of only two states in the union that still used hanging as an official method of execution.

"One job at a time," Grace Pelletier suggested.

"Oh come on, Your Honor, the bastard killed a police officer," Lily exclaimed.

"All the more reason, then, why he deserves the best representation we can give him, wouldn't you agree?"

"There are at least two other attorneys right here in town who don't have the personal connection that I have with the victim's family, and who I'm sure would be more than happy to give him far better representation than he deserves," Lily argued.

"As it happens, I know all the attorneys in town," the judge reminded her. "All fine, dedicated people. I also know that, considering the controversial nature of this case, it has to be tried with the utmost integrity."

In other words, put an unimpeachable attorney on the case so that, when the defendant got buried, no one would be able to cry foul. There were times, she had learned, when being her father's daughter could be a major drawback.

Lily sighed. "I'm not going to win this argument, am I?"

The judge shook her head. "If I thought you couldn't be objective, we wouldn't be here, having this conversation," she said. "But I've known you since you were a baby, and like it or not, you're the right attorney for this case."

Grace Pelletier was sixty-three. She had been privileged to work for Carson Burns for ten years before being elected to the bench, the youngest jurist ever to serve conservative Jackson County, and the first woman.

"Only way to get you out of my hair," the prosecutor had explained when she discovered that he had been the one to put forth her name. In return, she had spent the last twenty-three years making sure he would not regret it.

Now she picked up the Lightfoot file to give to his daughter. "It can't be anyone but you," she said.

"Why?" Lily asked in defeat.

"Because this is the first capital case Jackson County will be prosecuting during my tenure, and I need someone who's up to the challenge."

"Of course, you know I've never defended a death penalty case before," Lily reminded her.

"Well then, here's your chance," the judge said, handing over the file.

Lily accepted it with a heavy heart, and more than a tinge of resentment. "I assume you're presiding?"

"Yes, I am," the judge declared. "Is that a problem?"

"On the contrary," Lily responded. There were currently two other judges who heard criminal cases, and neither of them held a candle to Grace Pelletier. There were also three public defenders that worked for the county. "And which one of our overworked public souls handled the arraignment?"

Grace Pelletier shrugged. "He hasn't been arraigned yet."

Lily was genuinely startled at that. "You mean he's been sitting in jail since Monday without an arraignment?"

"Apparently, it took John Henry a while to decide what the charges were going to be."

"I'll bet," Lily said with a scowl.

John Henry Morgan -- for some reason, he was always referred to as John Henry -- was the Jackson County Prosecutor, promoted in the wake of her father's stroke, and elected to the office a year later. Lacking both the stature and the charm of Carson Burns, he retained the position as much because of his name as his ability, the Morgans having been original settlers, and one of the few families that had never totally abandoned Port Hancock.

However, knowing John Henry as she did, Lily also knew that the charge against Jason Lightfoot was never going to be anything but first-degree murder -- with special circumstances.

"His seventy-two hours came and went," she muttered in disgust, "and because the poor bastard didn't know any better, they got away with it. Whatever happened to due process?"

Grace hid a smile, seeing Lily engaged in spite of herself. "I understand it was an oversight, and I apologize," she said. "But he never asked for an attorney."

"How convenient."

The judge ignored that. "We can schedule the arraignment for today, if you like," she offered.

"I would most definitely like," Lily declared. "I'm available at three o'clock."

"All right then, three o'clock it is," Grace said, clasping her hands in front of her, which was her way of signaling that the matter had been dealt with to her satisfaction, and it was time to change the subject. "So, how's your dad doing?"

Lily shrugged. "He has his good days and his bad days," she confided, because Grace Pelletier was a family friend and could be trusted with the truth. "I'll tell him you asked."

"No," the judge said with a twinkle in her eye. "Just tell him I'll see him on Sunday." Whenever she could, Grace stopped by on Sunday afternoons, to chew the fat, as Carson called it, fill him in on all the courthouse gossip, let him win at Scrabble, and give Diana Hightower, his caregiver, a few extra hours to herself. Even in his healthier days, Carson Burns was nothing if not ornery, and the judge had plenty of reason to know he was not the easiest person in the world to please.

• • •

Lily made her way out of the courthouse, climbed into her dark green Toyota Camry, and drove eight miles east on the highway and then two miles south on back roads to the Jackson County Jail. The solid three-story complex was within hailing distance of the Olympic foothills, surrounded by scrub brush, and enclosed by a two-foot-thick, ten-foot-tall cement wall topped with strips of barbed wire. Not to be confused with the maximum security Jackson County State Prison some seventy miles west, this facility was used for those who were serving misdemeanor and low felony time, and those who were unlucky enough to be awaiting trial without bail.

She found Jason Lightfoot in a cell on the third floor of the jail's west wing. Renovated in the late 1990's, the typical space was now eight feet by twelve feet, and contained a steel bunk that was bolted to the floor, a lidless stainless steel toilet, a stainless steel sink, a small steel storage cabinet bolted to the wall, and a horizontal slit of steel-reinforced window too high to see much of anything but sky, and an occasional bird flying by.

The Indian lay across the bunk bed, staring up at nothing. There was nothing to see but a gray ceiling that matched gray walls. He was thirty-eight years old and looked fifty. He smelled bad, the orange jumpsuit they had made him put on when they took away his clothes was filthy, his long brown hair was matted, his normally ruddy complexion had lost most of its color, there were purplish bruises all over his face, arms and torso, and blood was oozing from a swollen lip.

An untouched breakfast tray of greasy eggs, sausage and cold coffee sat on the floor by the door. It was ten past eleven on Friday, he had been in the cell since Monday morning, and he had just lived through the worst four days of his life.

First, it was the pain from the beating he had taken. Then it was the shakes. Then it was the nightmares. Then it was as though he was coming right out of his skin. His brain was so messed up, he couldn't think straight. He didn't know what was going on. All he knew was that he needed a drink. He needed a drink so bad, he could almost feel his insides drying up worse than a creek bed in a drought.

Jason Lightfoot lived on the fringe, and had done so for most of his life. A bright enough kid, he was just about to enter the ninth grade when the county abruptly shut down the reservation school on the rather contradictory pretext that there was not enough attendance to keep teachers there, and too much violence to keep them safe.

He had the option of going to the white high school in town, but it was ten miles away, no bus service was provided, and he didn't have a license to drive the old Ford pickup that was rusting away in his father's front yard. Besides, he knew some kids from the reservation who had gone to the white school because their parents wanted better things for them, and he had heard how they were treated. He certainly didn't want any part of that.

His two older sisters had left the reservation as soon as they married, his father was dead, and his mother, well, she might as well have been -- lying around the house, drinking up what little money there was. So at sixteen, Jason went to work.

He tried farming for his uncle, but there wasn't enough money in it to support one family, let alone two, so he headed for Port Hancock and the docks. He had grown up tall and tough, and he was willing to put in an honest day's work for an honest day's pay. So he lied about his age and hired on as a deckhand aboard a deep-sea charter boat called the Seaworthy.

The captain was a crusty, hard-drinking, fifty-something loner named Barney Cosgrove who took a genuine liking to the kid. He couldn't afford to pay him much more than the minimum wage, but he was willing to let Jason live aboard. And many a comfortable evening was spent by the two of them, in the aft cabin, over a bottle of rum, with Barney chain-smoking cigarettes and spinning tall tales about his younger days on the high seas.

In truth, Jason wasn't all that interested in the fish stories or the tobacco, but he developed a real liking for the smooth Caribbean liqueur.

It was an arrangement that suited them both quite nicely for more than six years, until the day that Barney collapsed on deck and was rushed to the hospital, where he was diagnosed with both cirrhosis of the liver and stage-four lung cancer. It was too late to do much about either, and Barney was not a man to tolerate a slow, painful demise. So one morning, not two weeks later, he sent Jason off to town on some pretext or another, and set out to sea alone. As soon as he was well clear of the harbor, and far enough out in open water, he blew himself and the Seaworthy to smithereens.

Which left Jason without a job, without a home, and without the man who had had a whole lot to do with how he had grown up. He moved from boat to boat after that, taking on jobs when they were available. He liked some of the boats he worked on better than others, but none of the captains treated him as well as Barney Cosgrove had.

In down times, he helped out over at The Last Call Bar & Grill, one of the bars that populated the lower Broad Street area just off the docks. Instead of a paycheck, Billy Fugate, the owner, paid him in food and rum and a little cash on the side. Jason preferred it that way.

He appropriated a large cardboard box from a dumpster behind an Old Town warehouse, fastened a waterproof tarp around it, and for further protection, wedged it between one of the breaks in the thick stone wall that ran along the alley behind the bar. For a dollar, he bought a big dog bed at the local thrift store. For another dollar, he got an old army blanket. After that, whenever he wasn't at sea, the box was his home.

"You got a bit of money in your pocket, so why don't you go get yourself a nice room over at Miss Polly's?" Billy suggested. Miss Polly Peterson ran a boarding house on Bayview Avenue, just two blocks from the bar.

"Don't need a room," Jason told him. "Not around that much."

And that was true for several more years. Then, two days before he turned twenty-eight, as he was climbing the main mast of a visiting schooner -- a beautiful boat poorly treated by her master -- it suddenly snapped beneath him, sending him hurtling to the deck, fracturing his right shoulder and crushing his right leg. The doctor who treated him at the hospital told him he was lucky -- that he could have fractured his skull or severed his spine, or not even survived the fall at all.

But Jason didn't feel particularly lucky. The shoulder eventually healed well enough, but the leg, put back together with steel rods and pins as best the doctor could when Jason refused to let him amputate, never really healed properly, causing him constant pain and balance problems and leaving him unfit to go to back to sea.

After that, Jason pretty much drifted. He was good at fixing things, so people hired him to do odd jobs -- there were always odd jobs that needed doing. But the people that hired him were frequently those who couldn't afford to pay him, and more often than not, didn't.

Still, it wasn't so bad. He didn't need much. He collected a little money, here and there, and Billy Fugate gave him regular work. He would show up at The Last Call a couple of hours before closing, clean up the kitchen, wash out the latrines, sweep up the floors, and wipe down the tables and the bar.

He was allowed to eat whatever food was left over, and then he would sit at the bar, sipping on the rum liqueur he had come to like so much, before taking out the trash, and heading back to his box.

Along the way, he built a better box, from some scrap cedar and insulation instead of cardboard. With the tarp fastened around that, and a heavy plastic flap he found to cover the opening, it was as snug as any place out in the open like it was had to be.

Miss Polly was a nice lady, and he knew he could have gotten a room over at her place. She had told him as much on any number of occasions. But the truth of it was, he kind of liked his box, he definitely liked his privacy, and he especially liked being able to come and go as he pleased, without having to answer to anyone. And as long as no one hassled him, he saw no reason to change anything. That was, until early one morning in the middle of February.

• • •

Lily entered the cell, knowing she could have requested an interview room, but deciding it wasn't worth the bother for this initial meeting.

"Mr. Lightfoot," she said pleasantly enough, "my name is Lily Burns. I'm an attorney, and I'll be representing you in the matter concerning the death of Detective Dale Scott, if that's acceptable to you."

Jason looked her up and down, from the edge of her high-necked jacket to the hem of her knee-length skirt. "Don't got much hope of nothin' if they're sendin' a girl to do a man's work," he muttered irritably.

Lily looked him straight in the eye. "I suppose that's one way to look at it," she said crisply, plunking her briefcase down on the metal bunk beside him. "Another way is -- I may be the only hope you've got."

"If you say so," he said indifferently.

"You've been sitting here for four days," she observed. "Why didn't you ask for an attorney?"

"What for?" he replied.

"Because it was your right," she explained. "Didn't anyone tell you that?"

"Yeah, they told me," he said. "Didn't figure it would make much difference."

She had to admit he had a point. Arraigned or not, this was where he would likely be staying until trial. "Maybe not," she said. "But if you have another attorney you'd prefer to handle your case, now's the time to say so."

He scowled up at her. "Lady, I don't know what you're talkin' about. I don't got no other attorney."

"Do I take that to mean you are prepared to accept me as your attorney, then?" she asked, realizing just how much she was hoping he would say no.

He shrugged again. "Guess so," he said.

"All right then, let's get to work," Lily said.

After listening to the Indian's account of what he remembered about the night of the murder, which wasn't much, and the morning after, the first thing Lily did was to call a photographer friend of hers to come over to the jail and photograph every inch of him.

"And I mean every inch," she instructed the man she had known for years, and then she stepped out of the cell so as not to embarrass her client any more than necessary. "Every cut, every scratch, every mark on him."

The second thing she did was to insist that a doctor be called in to see her client, and the two of them waited in the cell together, more or less silently, for him to arrive. The examination confirmed that, in addition to a number of bruises and lacerations, the Indian had sustained several cracked ribs.

"What happened?" Lily asked, after the doctor had treated the lacerations and given him some pain medication for the ribs.

"I tried to run," Jason admitted, although he couldn't really remember what had happened all that clearly.

"He didn't complain of nothin' when they brought him in," the floor guard for the west wing of the jail said with an indifferent shrug when Lily confronted him.

"How convenient for you," she replied. "And I have no doubt that the lighting around here is so bad that you just weren't able to see the cuts and bruises all over him."

"Look lady, the bastard Injun killed a cop," she was told. "If you ask me, he's gettin' a hell of a lot better than he deserves."

"Can I quote you on that?" Lily snapped, hearing her very own sentiment coming back at her, and not particularly caring for the sound of it. "I'm sure there are still some reporters outside. They were there when I came in. Not to mention the warden. I'm willing to bet he's in his office, as we speak." She glanced at the guard's nametag. "So what do you say, Officer Crandall -- shall we have them come in? And shall I explain how, if so much as a single hair on my client's head is disturbed from this moment on, I'll have your job?"

The guard backed off then, but not before giving her a singularly malevolent glare.

• • •

Jason Lightfoot was arraigned an hour later, but not until after Lily had suggested, when nobody else had apparently bothered to, that he could take a shower and change into a clean orange jumpsuit, courtesy of the county.

And then, on the advice of his attorney, he pleaded not guilty to a whole list of charges, from assault and battery to first-degree murder with special circumstances, whatever that meant. After which, as Lily had told him to expect, he was denied bail and remanded back to the jail. An October trial date was set.

"Why ain't nothing' gonna happen until October?" he asked uneasily. "Why can't we just get this whole thing over and done with?"

"I'm assuming it's because the court docket is full until then," Lily explained, thinking that eight months to trial on a capital murder charge was ridiculously fast.

"I don't like that place they're keepin' me in," the Indian said. "It's too small. I can't breathe. I can't see nothin' out the window."

"Well, I'm afraid there's nothing I can do about that," she told him, thinking he would be lucky if he got to spend the rest of his life in such a place. "You'll just have to make the best of it."

"You don't like me much, do you?" he asked.

Lily stopped for a moment to consider his words. "I don't know yet whether I like you or not, Mr. Lightfoot," she replied after a moment. "We'll have to see how our relationship goes." And then she smiled, an ironic smile. "But don't worry. I'm not being paid to like you. I'm being paid to represent you."

Two

Carson Burns had been a dominating presence in his time. Standing over six feet tall, with a thick shock of hair that used to be brown, he towered above both witnesses and juries, his courtroom voice often reverberating off the walls. But no one, except perhaps a defendant, ever felt intimidated by him. Rather, people felt protected.

Now he spent his life confined to a wheelchair, having lost control over the whole right side of his body. There were some who felt sorry for him. There were some who resented that he was no longer there to protect them. And there were some who, having once taken him for granted, were now hesitant when they encountered him, as though they were afraid that, if they got too close, some of his misfortune might rub off on them.

He supposed he understood. In any case, he made the best of it. Each morning, he read three newspapers, from front to back -- the local *Port Hancock Herald, The Seattle Times,* and for good measure, *USA Today.* After lunch, he would turn on the television. He liked to joke that he finally had time to watch cable news. And then, he would pull out his computer. He had taught himself to both write and type with his left hand, and he used the computer to research anything and everything that caught his attention.

But far and away, his favorite part of the day was the afternoon hour when, rain or shine, summer or winter, in shirtsleeves or beneath a blanket or an umbrella, he was wheeled out onto the back patio of his Morgan Hill home and left by himself, with a glass of his favorite Bordeaux, to breathe the fresh air, and listen to the birds, if he were lucky, or to the chorus of neighborhood dogs barking, if he were not, and contemplate his life and circumstance.

He was, on whole, reasonably satisfied with the way things had turned out. Oh, he wished he still had a sound body, of course, but he was thankful he hadn't lost his mind. He wished he had had the comfort and companionship of Althea a lot longer than he had. And he wished his two elder daughters and their families lived a lot closer than they did. But at least Lily still lived at home. And he had Diana Hightower, his faithful housekeeper and caregiver, who catered to his every whim. In truth, irascible and demanding as he knew he could be on occasion, his needs were simple and his wants few.

There had been years when he had felt cheated at not having a son to carry on his name and work, but not any longer. He was more proud of Lily than he could ever put into words. She had not only grown up in his image, she had, to all intents and purposes, exceeded him.

He shrugged off the idolization the community held for him. He knew what his limitations were, even if no one else did. He was a good attorney, to be sure, and he had brought all the fervor and righteousness to his work that he could muster. Lily, on the other hand, had no limitations. She had a love for the law and a mind for the nuances and ambiguities that he had never had patience for, but that often won cases. And now, being there for her whenever she needed him had become his primary focus.

The Lightfoot case was going to be a challenge, Carson knew. Never mind the death penalty, just the effort to change the perspective of the community was going to be a giant mountain she would have to climb.

"I can't believe Grace dumped this in my lap," she had fumed when she got home Friday evening.

"If I were Grace, I'd have done the same thing," Carson had told her.

She probably wouldn't get the fellow off, he knew, but everyone in the county, right down to the last Native American, would know she had left no stone unturned in trying -- even if she didn't yet know it herself.

Carson pulled the blanket that covered him a little tighter against the raw Saturday afternoon and sipped at his glass of wine. He loved his daughters dearly, all three of them. But if truth be told, perhaps he loved his youngest just a little bit more.

He glanced across the expanse of manicured lawn that separated his property from that of his next-door neighbor. It was the home of Helen and Maynard Purcell, the in-laws of the slain police detective, and things had been bustling over there for the past several days, as people from town had come to pay their respects, and people from out of town had made their way into town to attend the funeral. It was quiet now, the house was empty, the limousines had come and gone, and Carson hoped there was enough room in the church for all the people he suspected would want to be there.

The man in the wheelchair sighed deeply. He should have been at the church, too, he knew, and then gone on to the cemetery afterwards. The Purcells had been more than neighbors -- they had been good friends for decades. He had watched their daughter grow up right alongside his own.

But he was fighting some sort of a bug, and he had been told in no uncertain terms -- by Maynard Purcell, himself, no less -- that he was not to go out and potentially catch something worse, that he was instead to stay at home and keep warm.

That was the real price he was paying for his stroke, he thought with a scowl, not the loss of half of his body, but the loss of most of his independence.

• • •

The Port Hancock Presbyterian Church on Parkland Avenue in New Town was indeed overflowing at two o'clock on Saturday afternoon. It looked as though a good part of the community had turned out for Dale Scott's funeral. There was a steady drizzle, which some might have thought appropriate for the occasion, and a sea of dripping umbrellas filled the church foyer.

One of the few buildings never completely abandoned, even during Port Hancock's darkest days, the church had been built in 1872 and carefully preserved into its third century. With all but two of its original stained glass windows still intact, the graceful stone building was considered, especially by the Presbyterians, to be the crowning symbol of the city's perseverance. Its single spire boasted a bell that had been faithfully ringing every hour, without fail, for over a hundred and forty years.

Inside the church, the choir sang a selection of Dale Scott's favorite hymns, revealed by his widow, several of his fellow officers got up and spoke -- the most poignant eulogy coming from the dead detective's partner for the past three years, Randy Hitchens -- and the minister waxed eloquently about a good life cut tragically short. The Chief of Police, Kent McAllister, announced that, by declaration of the mayor, city flags would be flown at half-mast for the next week.

In the first pew, Lauren Scott sat with an arm around each of her two daughters. She was dressed in black, from neck to toe, and a thick black veil covered her head and shoulders. From her position in the fifth pew, Lily eyed the veil. Lauren had the face of an angel, and this was the first time Lily could ever remember seeing it completely covered.

"She must not want anyone to see her with her eyes all red and puffy," Amanda Jansen murmured from her seat beside Lily.

Amanda and Lily had been friends since kindergarten. Lily had been the maid of honor at Amanda's wedding that had ended in divorce only two years after it began. And Amanda had been the first person Lily told when she lost her virginity her senior year in high school. There was little about either of their lives that the other didn't know.

"She'd be gorgeous even with puffy eyes," Lily whispered back.

Lauren, who had been Harvest Ball Queen and Senior Prom Queen and voted Most Beautiful in the school two years running, could have been a top model or even a Hollywood actress. Everyone said so. But though she had been an active member of the drama club in high school, she had never had any serious interest in doing anything professional. She claimed she was born to be a wife and a mother and nothing else.

Lily Burns and Lauren Purcell had grown up right next door to each other on Morgan Hill, one of the nicest residential areas in Port Hancock, with lovely homes, winding streets, well-tended lawns, and spectacular views of the Olympic Mountains. Lauren's father, Dr. Maynard Purcell, was the Burns' family physician. And Lily had been one of six bridesmaids to march down the aisle at Lauren's extravagant wedding, in this very church, thirteen years ago.

Over time, the two girls drifted apart. Lauren hadn't lived on Morgan Hill since her marriage, and Lily had opted for the professional life that Lauren had eschewed. They saw each other occasionally, and still traveled in more or less the same social circle, but they were no longer what either of them would call close friends.

It was at least an hour before the ceremony ended and the procession made its way slowly up the main aisle and out of the church, the pallbearers with the coffin, followed by the minister, Lauren and the two girls, her family, Dale's family, and then an assortment of friends and coworkers who had been excused from their jobs to pay their last respects. Once outside, the sea of umbrellas reappeared as people scurried to their vehicles for the half-mile drive out to the Holy Family Cemetery where Dale Scott would be laid to rest in the Purcell family plot.

Dale was not Port Hancock born and bred. He came from a small town near Yakima, and his parents had wanted their son to be buried in their church cemetery. But Dr. Purcell had convinced them that it was bad enough for Dale's children to have to grow up without their father, it would be unconscionable for them to have to grow up without ready access to his grave. The Scotts were simple people, who had loved their son and now loved their granddaughters, and they were no match for the impressive, persuasive physician.

For Maynard Purcell, it was little more than a practical matter. The detective had not been his choice of a son-in-law. Good-looking though he may have been, and smooth, in a cocky sort of way, there was something about him -- a bravado, a roughness, an edge -- that might have been well suited to the police force, but bothered the doctor. Still, Lauren was his only child, and he had never been able to deny her anything.

From the moment the two of them had met, in church, as a matter of fact, it was clear that the thirty-year-old police officer had swept his twenty-one-year-old daughter off her feet. As a result, she resisted every effort her father made to discourage the relationship. And after all these years, he had more or less resigned himself to the situation. But he had no intention of making matters worse by pretending to support what he knew were sure to become all-day family pilgrimages to some remote little cemetery in the middle of nowhere. Let the man be buried where he had lived, Purcell had decided -- whether he deserved to be or not.

The mourners reassembled at the cemetery, beside the freshly dug grave at the Purcell plot. The rain had let up, and by the time this second ceremony was over, the umbrellas were closed. People filed slowly out of the area, pausing for a word or an embrace as they went.

"I'm so sorry," Lily murmured when it came to her turn, bending down to kiss each of Dale's girls on the cheek, and then reaching over to give Lauren a hug.

But Lauren stiffened and backed away from the embrace. "I can't believe it," the widow cried, and everyone within earshot stopped and turned. "I can't believe you had the audacity to come here today."

"Why wouldn't I have?" Lily asked, perplexed.

"Oh my God, what a hypocrite you are!" Lauren shrilled from behind her heavy veil. "How can you possibly show your face here? How can you pretend to be my friend and mourn my husband -- and at the same time defend his killer?"

Lily didn't know what to say. Word certainly did have a way of getting around. She had had the Lightfoot case for barely more than twenty-four hours. She opened her mouth to say something -- anything, and closed it again. There was no point in telling Lauren that defending the Indian had certainly not been her choice. Besides, all around them, people were beginning to stare at her with curiosity -- in some cases, mixed with resentment.

It was at that moment that Randy Hitchens stepped out from beside the widow. "It would probably be best if you left," the dead detective's partner said softly, putting his hand firmly on Lily's elbow. "She's already on the edge, and this wouldn't be a good time for a scene."

"No, of course not," Lily demurred. "Tell her I'm terribly sorry for her loss."

"Wow," Amanda breathed as the two women exited the cemetery and headed for Amanda's car. "Are you really defending the guy?"

"Looks like it," Lily replied with an unhappy sigh.

"Not exactly the best way to make friends and influence people, huh?"

"I didn't have any choice in the matter -- the damn case was dumped in my lap," Lily snapped, really not appreciating having to defend herself, much less Jason Lightfoot, especially to her best friend. "Would you prefer if I walked home?"

"Don't be silly," Amanda said with a chuckle. "If the truth must be told, I never really cared for Lauren all that much. And to be honest, I don't think I particularly liked her husband, either. So, come on, let's go have a drink."

• • •

Lily let herself into the Morgan Hill house just before six. She could hear Diana Hightower in the kitchen, humming to herself as she went about preparing supper. Nothing seemed to faze the live-in caretaker, housekeeper, cook and bottle-washer.

"Hi Sweetie," she said, seeing Lily. "You look cold and out of sorts. But that's all right, because you're just in time for supper. We're having yummy crab bisque tonight. I know it's one of your favorites, and I have a big bowl right here that's got your name on it."

Diana was fifty-four years old. Given to her husband at the age of thirteen, as was the custom of her tribe back then, she was the mother of five and the grandmother of nine.

Despite some pretty stiff resistance from her husband and the tribal elders, she had seen to it that all five of her children graduated from high school, even when she had to drive them to and from the white school herself. And then she had made sure that all of them acquired a trade. Most of all, it pleased her enormously that neither of her two sons or any of her three daughters wed before turning eighteen.

She had come to work for Carson Burns four months after he had had his stroke, and eight months after her husband had been killed in a drunken brawl outside the tribal center on the reservation.

To be honest, she didn't know what she would have done without Carson and Lily Burns. In turn, Carson and Lily didn't know what they would have done without Diana Hightower.

"That sounds great," Lily said, and she meant it. Despite two glasses of wine with Amanda, she was still irked by her encounter with Lauren, and Diana's delicacy would more than help take the edge off.

"Your dad's in the library," the caregiver told her. "And supper is in fifteen minutes."

Nowadays, Carson passed most of his hours in the library, a large mahogany-paneled room with a great stone fireplace, a giant-screen television, and floor to ceiling shelves crammed with a collection of books, forty years in the making.

"At least I've still got my eyesight," he would say out of the left side of his mouth, his tone light. There was never a shred of self-pity in Carson Burns. His body may have betrayed him, but his mind was still as sharp as ever.

"How was it?" he asked, after she had changed out of her funeral clothes and joined him in the library.

"It was fine until we got to the cemetery," she replied, kissing him lightly on the top of his full head of white hair, and choosing the chair that was closest to the crackling fire. "Then Lauren just about up and had a seizure when she saw me."

"Word does get around in a small town, now doesn't it?" he observed.

Lily made a face. "I can't believe anyone in his right mind thinks I took this case because I wanted to," she declared.

"Doesn't matter why you took it. All that matters is you've got it, and now you have to do right by the fellow, guilty or innocent."

"Guilty," Lily muttered.

It wasn't that she hadn't represented her share of guilty clients over the years. She certainly had and, sometimes, quite effectively, too. But none had involved as blatant a crime as this, or a client as unpopular as Jason Lightfoot.

"Well then," her father said, "you do whatever you can for him." It was what he always said when she had a case she knew she wasn't going to win.

"Yes, well, I might not keep him from hanging, but there is one thing I can do," she said with a sigh. "I can get him a sponsor."

"A sponsor?"

"He's a drunk," she explained. "And I suspect he was so drunk that night, he just doesn't remember what he did. But he's going to be sitting in that jail cell, detoxing, for eight months. I saw what he looked like after four days. I'm not sure he can make it through that alone. I'm going to ask Greg Parker to help him, and maybe, if he can get his head clear enough, he can tell me what really happened."

"Good idea," Carson said. "And if you can prove he was drunk that night, it might just give you a mitigating circumstance."

"Yes, it might," she agreed.

Greg Parker had been one of Lily's first clients. He had joined the army right out of high school, and four years later had been deployed to Iraq. He survived, but came back with a stress disorder that had turned into alcoholism. Five years ago, mere months after Lily had hung out her shingle, he came knocking on her door. He had been involved in a traffic accident that had seriously injured a teenaged boy on a bicycle.

By doing some digging, Lily learned that the teenager had a drug problem his parents were trying to conceal, and she was able to get both parties to agree to share the responsibility. In turn, a newly elected John Henry agreed to drop the felony charge of aggravated vehicular assault against her client, and instead negotiated a fine and probation for the misdemeanor of driving under the influence.

On the day he walked out of the courthouse, Parker vowed to quit drinking and, as far as Lily could tell, he had stuck to it, going to local AA meetings at least three times a week, and working with others -- teenagers, in particular -- to help them avoid what he, himself, had not been able to avoid.

Although she had just been doing her job, Parker proclaimed her his savior. "If there's ever anything I can do for you," he told her, "don't waste even a minute thinking about whether you should call me."

Lily decided her last phone call of the evening would be to Greg Parker.

Diana appeared at the library door just then and beckoned them into the dining room where the table was set with steaming hot bowls of crab bisque, a basket of her irresistible freshly baked corn muffins, and a platter of winter fruit.

A mitigating circumstance, Lily thought, wondering if it would really make any difference -- and deciding it probably wouldn't. "I'll talk to John Henry on Monday," she said with a sigh. "Maybe we can find a little wiggle room between having to go through a trial and taking the death penalty off the table."

• • •

John Henry Morgan stood almost eye-to-eye with Lily, when she wore low heels, and she made certain to do just that on Monday morning. She knew from experience how much the Jackson County Prosecutor resented having to look up to anyone, much less an adversary, either figuratively or literally.

He had once been a bit on the scrawny side, but by the age of fifty-two he had developed quite a paunch, due perhaps to too much time spent on his butt and not enough on his feet, or as some put it, trying only those cases that he was sure he could win, and win him reelection. He thought the extra weight made him look successful, even distinguished. And no one thought it wise to disavow him of the idea. He favored dark gray three-piece suits and starched white shirts, winter or summer, which caused others, both in and out of the courthouse, to liken him to a penguin -- behind his back, of course.

"Let me see, I'll bet you're here this morning about the Lightfoot case," he said when his assistant had ushered Lily into the third-floor corner office that had once been her father's. And then he smiled, a little cat-and-mouse smile around teeth that were just too perfect to deny some serious orthodontic intervention.

"I always said you were sharp, John Henry," Lily said lightly.

"You must want something pretty bad," he countered smugly. "It couldn't have anything to do with a plea deal, now could it?"

"Just looking to save the state some time and money," Lily said sweetly. "I haven't talked to my client about it yet, mind you, but if I can get him to plead to, say, murder two, and a sentence of thirty to life -- I assume you'd be willing to bump the death penalty?"

John Henry crossed his arms over his chest, leaned back in his oversized desk chair, and pursed his lips as if he were actually considering the offer.

"No can do," he said after a moment of letting her wait. "Any ordinary killer can get thirty to life, even life-without. But this one killed a police officer, a veteran police officer -- and a decorated one, to boot. No, we're going to go all the way on this."

"Like it or not, there are mitigating circumstances here," Lily reminded him. "If the Indian was as drunk as I suspect he was -- and I'm sure I'll find enough evidence to back that up -- I can argue diminished capacity. Besides, you know as well as I do that Dale had a reputation for being, let's say, a bit of a bully. So I might even be able to convince a few jurors that his death may somehow have been provoked. But I'm willing to compromise."

"Nice try," John Henry said. "But no deal."

"Without even taking two minutes to consider it?" Lily countered. "A trial is months and money. I'm giving you the chance to put this guy away for a long time and save the taxpayers a bundle in the process."

"Lily, I'm going to level with you," John Henry said. "As you know, next year is an election year, and I'm going to run for reelection, because I like my job -- I like it a lot, and I'd like to keep doing it a while longer. Now, cutting a deal for Lightfoot might save the county some money, it's true, but how would it look to my constituents? I'll tell you how it would look. It would look like I was weak, not strong, like I was skulking around making backroom deals because I was scared I couldn't win in open court. The people of Jackson County want to know that they've got a strong prosecutor protecting them. And the truth of it is, the people of this county want something else, too, in case you haven't noticed -- they want Jason Lightfoot hung by his neck until he's dead for what he did. And that's exactly what I'm prepared to give them."

Lily had indeed noticed. And the idea of that frenzy potentially poisoning the jury pool was one of the reasons she had come looking for a deal. "Now, John Henry, you wouldn't be using my client to play politics, would you?" she inquired.

"Well, can't say as I'm proud of it," the prosecutor replied. "But then again, look at your client -- at his record. For most of his life, what has he been but a bum, a drunk, and a drain on society?"

"I suppose that's one way of looking at it," Lily conceded.

"Sure am sorry you got stuck with the case."

Lily cocked her head. "You know, that's exactly how I felt about it," she said, "until just now." She smiled at him, and the smile was radiant. "I'll see you in court, John Henry."

Then she was gone. And John Henry frowned. He had a solid case against the Indian, and he knew it, but it always made him uneasy to go up against Carson Burns' daughter. He doubted that she realized it, but even during the year that she had worked for him, after her father had his stroke, there was something about the way she handled herself in a courtroom, a comfort level, an air of assurance she had, that always made him feel, well, inadequate. It was even worse now that she was on the other side.

. . .

It was a bluff, of course, and Lily would have been the first to admit it. She had no case. She had nothing at all. But his smugness had gotten to her. If she had to name the biggest reason why she had left the prosecutor's office for private practice, it was John Henry Morgan.

She exited the courthouse and walked the short block down Meridian Avenue to Broad Street, which marked the beginning of Port Hancock's business district. It didn't look much like the financial center of a twenty-first century city, filled as it was with block after block of nineteenth-century dwellings, featuring gingerbread facades, Corinthian columns, and old-fashioned porticos, rather than the more typical glass and steel skyscrapers one expected to see, but few in Port Hancock were much bothered about it. Everyone knew that what went on behind those vintage walls was every bit twenty-first century.

Lily crossed Broad Street, turned left, and headed for a building in the middle of a row of similar buildings, a vintage Victorian rumored to have been a popular brothel in its more illustrious days, but had since been converted to accommodate other kinds of professional services.

With Carson's assistance, Lily had bought the place after a year of renting it. She had then kept the two bathrooms and the kitchen more or less intact, but proceeded to turn the first floor -- or parlor floor, as it was referred to, into a reception area, a conference room and a computer room. The second floor became three offices and a library, and the third floor was used as a storage area that, after only five years, was more than half-filled.

The sign outside the front door said simply: Law Offices.

And just below that, there was a sign that read: Private Investigations.

Three years ago, Lily had given one of her offices, and all that came with it, to Joe Gideon, in exchange for first dibs on his expertise.

Like Lily, Joe had been born and raised in Port Hancock. And like Lily, Joe had followed in his father's footsteps, in this case, to the Port Hancock Police Department, rising from officer to detective to sergeant. Then, after twenty-five years, with one bullet having blown off half his left ear and another having splintered his right shoulder, and amid some serious talk of a promotion to lieutenant, the fifty-year-old came to the conclusion that management didn't really suit him, and it was time to retire.

"Let's just say, I want to go out while I'm still mostly in one piece," he liked to joke, whenever he was asked.

There was a big ceremony, with memorable accolades from the mayor on down, a touching speech from the Chief of Police, and a lot of shoulder pats -- on his left shoulder, of course -- from his fellow officers. His retirement even made the front page of the local newspaper. And for a while, the celebrity made him feel pretty special.

But it didn't take long, barely a matter of spring passing through summer into autumn, for him to realize that, as enticing as it had first seemed, retirement didn't suit him any better than management. He wasn't ready to sit on his back porch for the rest of his life, massaging his shoulder and watching the Canadian geese fly by. He decided there had to be something he could still contribute, on perhaps a more flexible and less demanding level. Or maybe it was Beth, his wife, who decided.

In either case, the timing couldn't have been better for Lily. Her practice was picking up steam, she and her paralegal were too often working sixty to seventy hours a week, and she needed to add a seasoned investigator to the team, especially one with connections. Because among the things she had learned from her days in the prosecutor's office was that you couldn't always trust the police to get it right.

And for the last three years, whether it was because he knew the Port Hancock Police Department so intimately, or simply because he was a really superb investigator, Joe Gideon had been getting it right.

As if the point needed emphasizing, Lily marched up the front steps of the Victorian, pushed open the big front door, and just about collided with him.

"Oh my," he observed, catching her expression. "You look like you just met with John Henry."

"The man's a moron," she stated, tossing her head.

Joe chuckled. "Then why do you let him get to you?"

She shrugged. "I don't know," she muttered. "Guess I can't help myself."

"The moron just left you a message," Wanda Posey, the receptionist, file clerk, schedule-keeper, and coffee Meister said from behind her desk.

The grandmother, who was sixty-six years old and recently widowed, had retired from the Port Hancock Public Library after thirty years only to discover, not unlike Joe had, that she was too young to sit at home and do nothing.

"The body might be slowing down," she liked to say, "but the brain is still speeding."

While at the library, she had taken advantage of the opportunity to read almost every legal thriller that came her way, so there was never any doubt about what sort of job she would look for when she decided she was going to rejoin the workforce.

"It hasn't even been ten minutes," Lily said irritably. "What did he want -- to rub it in?"

"Actually, he said that he's thought your offer over," Wanda replied, referring to the careful notes she always took. "And he admits that he might have been a bit hasty. So, in the best interests of everyone involved, he wants you to call him back."

Lily was stunned. "I don't get it," she said. "Ten minutes ago, he was salivating over a public hanging. I wonder what changed his mind so fast."

"I'd say it was realizing that he has to go up against you," Megan Fleming said, coming down the stairs carrying two heavy folders.

The twenty-eight-year-old had been Lily's paralegal, sounding board, and right arm since the attorney had first opened her practice. The wife of a Marine sergeant who had been stationed at Joint Base Lewis McChord, and the mother of an adorable little girl named Amy, she had lost her husband to the war in

Afghanistan before he had even had a chance to meet his daughter.

Megan had gotten her legal certificate as something to do to fill the void, without having any real idea of what, if anything, she was going to do with it, much less where she was going to do it. Then, on a pure whim, she answered an ad placed by a female attorney who was about to open a brand new law practice, and barely a month later, she and two-year-old Amy had landed in Port Hancock, where the people were friendly, the skies were blue, and she was going to be paid enough to rent a cute little ground-floor apartment on the edge of New Town, and enroll her daughter in a delightful daycare, a mere three Victorians away from her new office.

"Not with the case he's got," Lily declared. "Not to mention the rather cloudy climate of the community." In addition to her conversation with the prosecutor, the scene at the cemetery was still fresh in her mind. "There's got to be something else going on here."

"Well, whatever the reason, I wouldn't look a gift horse in the mouth," Wanda advised.

Lily didn't intend to. "Joe, before I talk to John Henry again, I need to know what changed his mind."

Joe Gideon wasn't any happier about this case than he knew Lily was, and if he could have declined to have any part of it, he would have. But his loyalty was to the lawyer, not to the client.

"I'm already out the door," the investigator said, making his exit.

"And I'm right behind you," the attorney said.

"Wait a minute -- where are *you* going?" Megan cried, as Lily started after him. "You just got here, and there's a bunch of stuff on the Wicker case you have to look at."

"There's someone I need to talk to first," she replied.

• • •

Even after three years, it felt strange for Joe Gideon to park his van in a visitor's spot, rather than in the police employee parking lot, and enter the station through the front door instead of the back. And sometimes, he even had to remind himself that he was visiting and not coming in to work a regular shift.

"Hey there, Sarge," the duty officer at the front desk greeted him. "How you doing?"

"Hi, Manny," the retired police sergeant replied. "Can't complain. How about you?"

"Can't complain, either," Manny Santiago said. "You here about Dale's case?"

Joe chuckled. Even a city of 25,000 was a small town when it came to how quickly word could get around.

Like what attorney was representing what client, and what private investigator worked for the attorney who was representing that client. And to be honest, Joe realized when he thought about it, he wouldn't have wanted it any other way.

"You bet," he said.

"I think Stiversen and Cady are in the back," Manny told him.

"Thanks."

Indeed, Arnie Stiversen and Paul Cady were in the big squad room that, along with interview rooms and holding cells, took up the rest of the first floor.

"Hey," Stiversen said, coming forward with a big smile and an outstretched hand.

"Hey, yourself," Joe replied, grasping the hand. "How's it going?"

"Okay," the ten-year veteran who was still a friend said. "So what is it with you? You just can't stay away from the old place, can you? Still can't figure out why you hung around as long as you did. Not sure I'm going to make it another fifteen."

"A wife who wanted me out of the house, and two kids to put through college," Joe told him with a chuckle.

"I can relate to that," Stiversen said with a nod. The thirty-two-year-old had a wife and two kids of his own at home.

It was more or less the same opening banter that the two of them liked to engage in whenever they met, which, for the last three years, if not at the department, had been once or twice a month, over drinks at The Hangout, a trendy bar on Broad Street that was regularly frequented by Port Hancock's finest, past and present.

"He talks about quitting all the time," Cady, the twenty-five-year-old who had almost five years in so far, said. "But I don't believe him anymore. He's probably going to make detective pretty soon, and then, you just watch, he'll outlast all of us."

"And I can relate to that, too," Joe said.

"So, let me guess," Stiversen speculated. "You're wouldn't be here about Dale's case, now would you?"

"It's for sure that no one's ever going to accuse you of being a dumb cop," Joe responded with a chuckle.

"I can't believe you're trying to help Dale's killer," Cady declared.

"Well, you know how it is -- we don't always get to pick and choose our clients," Joe reminded him. Working this case had definitely not been his idea. "And between us, I can tell you Lily's not too happy about it, either."

"Your boss may be good," Cady conceded. "But she's not good enough to get Lightfoot out of this one. We got means, we got motive, and we got opportunity --

not to mention the murder weapon. In other words, we got him dead to rights."

"All documented?"

"You bet," Stiversen declared. "Fingerprints, GSR, DNA -- the works."

Joe nodded. "And how about results from the breathalyzer?"

The two police officers looked at each other. "Well, we got results, but we didn't get to test him until a while after we brought him in," Stiversen said reluctantly.

"How long a while?"

His former colleague sighed. "Five hours," he had to admit.

"Five hours?" Joe exclaimed. "What the hell happened?"

"Look, you got to appreciate, things were a little crazy around here," Stiversen replied. "It's not every day we lose one of our own, you know."

"Okay, so when you did get around to it, what were the results?"

Cady shrugged. "The results showed he wasn't drunk. In fact, his reading was zero."

"Zero?" Joe was frankly surprised.

"That's right," Stiversen said. "And we took him right in for a blood alcohol test after that, just to make sure. It came up the same."

"And that was how many hours after you figure the murder went down?" Joe asked.

"According to the M.E., twelve hours or so," he was told.

"So, we have no way of knowing if the guy was sober or drunk at the time of the murder," Joe said. "And if Lily can come up with any evidence of the latter, she could put one giant hole in a murder-one case."

"Yeah, well, if it comes to that," Stiversen replied, taking the cue, "I don't think either one of us would be able to testify one way or the other when we arrested him."

"I sure wouldn't be able to," Cady confirmed.

"Anything else I should know about?" Joe inquired.

"We'll keep you posted," Cady told him.

The former cop nodded. "Appreciate it."

"You know we wouldn't do this for anyone else but you," Stiversen said, almost under his breath. "I mean -- talk about an investigation that's still ongoing."

"I know," Joe said. "And I appreciate that, too."

"Hell, you're a better cop than most of us will ever be, and you know it," Stiversen told him. "That's why we'll continue to talk to you. If there are any holes in this case that need to be plugged, we want you to find them. Make our work easier."

"Happy to oblige," Joe said with a smile.

• • •

This time, Lily met with Jason Lightfoot in one of the Jackson County Jail's interview rooms, a small space with wide barred windows, gray walls, and a metal table and two-chair unit that was bolted to both the wall and the floor.

Jason sat across from her. His hands and feet were shackled and then fastened to a waist chain for added security. He was shaking so hard the chains rattled.

"What's the matter?" Lily asked.

"Nothin'," he told her. "I get the shakes from time to time is all."

"Are your ribs bothering you?"

He shrugged. "That stuff the doc gave me seems to be workin' okay."

"Well, I have good news," Lily said. "The prosecutor might be willing to take the death penalty off the table if you plead out."

Jason blinked. "What does that mean?"

"It means that you stand up in court, you admit to killing Detective Scott, and then you tell how and why you did it. And after that, the judge will sentence you to spend between thirty years and the rest of your life in prison."

The Indian stared at her for a full minute. "Thirty years?" he croaked finally. "Maybe the rest of my life?"

"That's right. It saves the county the cost of a trial. And it saves you from having a noose put around your neck."

But instead of the look of relief she expected, Lily got a stubborn squaring of his jaw. "Sorry," he said, "but I don't think I can do that."

"Look, Mr. Lightfoot, I'm your attorney," she told him. "I'm not only here to represent you, I'm here to advise you. That means I'm here to lay out your options, and then tell you which I think is your best one."

"And you think my best option is to live the rest of my life caged up like an animal?" He shuddered. "I'd rather be dead."

"Well, if we go to trial, that's quite likely how you'll end up."

"Look Lady Lawyer, I can't stand up in front of a judge and say how or why I killed that cop," Jason declared. "'Cause I don't know how or why I killed him. All I know is I was asleep in my box, mindin' my own business, just like always, when these two cops come along and kick me awake, and then start tellin' me all about what they think I did."

"I doubt that story will play very well with a jury," she told him.

"I thought you were supposed to be on *my* side," he said, glaring at her. "If you ain't, then maybe I should be thinkin' about gettin' myself another lawyer."

"I *am* on your side," she snapped. "And whether you like it or not, I'm trying to save your life. So listen to me, carefully. Their case is a good one -- you were there, you had a history with the victim, you had his gun in your possession -- which just happens to be the murder weapon, and which they can prove you fired, and you can't say how you came to have it, or why you fired it."

"But that's the truth," he argued.

"The police are theorizing that Scott may have been hassling you for some reason and there was a confrontation, during which you managed to get his gun away from him and shoot him. Now it's possible you were drunk -- so drunk you didn't know what you were doing, and if that's true, I can argue that. But I can tell you right now, it isn't going to make much difference to a jury -- not when a decorated police officer is dead."

Jason shook his head slowly. "Don't you think I wanna remember?" he told her earnestly. "Don't you think I wanna know why I killed him, if that's really what I did? Especially if I killed him for no reason other than that my brain was bombed out on booze." He punched at his head with the heel of his hand. "I just can't remember. It may not seem right to you, but it's all just a blank to me. I think I remember leavin' the bar, I think I remember puttin' the trash out, and I think I remember gettin' into my box, but after that -- nothin'. Not that it's gonna make much difference. I'm not stupid. I know how this is gonna go down. I'm gonna die anyway." He looked around him. "And, while someone like you might not be able to understand this, as far as I'm concerned, I'd rather be dead than have to live the rest of my life in a place like this."

Lily sighed. "I take that to mean you want to go to trial?"

"Yeah," Jason replied. "Yeah, I guess so."

"All right," Lily said, getting up. "Before I go, though, there's one more thing. I've asked a friend of mine to come see you. I think he can help. Try to be nice to him."

"A friend of yours?" he said warily. "Why would you wanna ask a friend of yours to come see me?"

"He's an alcoholic," she said flatly. "Well, he's a recovering alcoholic, actually, who now works with other alcoholics. He'll to try to help you get over the hump."

"The hump?"

"You're going to be in here for a long time, for at least eight months anyway, until we get to trial. That's eight months without a drink. Do you think you can handle that on your own?"

"How'd you know?" he asked.

"The shakes, the irritability, the problems with your memory," she said. "I'm afraid you aren't my first client with a drinking problem, Mr. Lightfoot."

He looked at her for a long moment. "Jason," he said at last.

"What?"

"I guess you can call me Jason."

• • •

"I certainly appreciate your willingness to reconsider," Lily told John Henry Morgan over the phone an hour later, "but as it turns out, my client has decided he wants his day in court."

There was a noticeable silence at the other end of the line. "Did you try to talk some sense into the man?" the prosecutor asked finally, his voice perhaps a trifle more strident than he intended. "Did you tell him his chances of an acquittal are slim to none?"

"I did my best," Lily confirmed. "But apparently, he wasn't listening. So, I guess we'll be going through the motions, and you'll be able to put on a show for your constituents, after all."

• • •

"I did my best," she told her father that evening as they took their after-dinner coffee in the library, a reassuring fire again crackling in the hearth. "I tried to get him to see that a plea was the only way I would be able to save his life. But he didn't care."

"Know the person you're representing," Carson Burns told her. "There are Native Americans who can't be incarcerated for life. It's like trapping a wild animal. They're free spirits. They need to come and go as they please, breathe fresh air, feel the sun on their faces, and the dirt between their toes. Hanging is a quick death. Life behind bars is a slow death. For your client, there really may be no choice."

Three

Jason Lightfoot was not Lily's only client. But, from the amount of mail that began arriving at the Broad Street Victorian within days of the Indian's arraignment, and word getting around that she was defending him, one would think he was. And there was nothing ambiguous about what the majority of it said.

Born and raised in this community, and having lived in it all of her life, except, of course, for her time away at school, the viciousness took Lily completely by surprise.

It was one thing to read the odd Letter to the Editor printed in the *Port Hancock Herald*, or to hear someone rant and rave on the local talk radio station. But messages that were sent to her place of work, calling her every name in the book, threatening her with all manner of bodily harm, were different, and she couldn't help but take them personally.

"I had no idea so many people in the community would feel this way," she said. "I didn't think anyone could hate me so much just for doing my job."

"You can't let this go, you know," Joe told her. "You're going to have to file a complaint."

"With the police?" Lily countered. "And what would I tell them? That I'm being harassed because I'm defending a man for killing one of their own? That ought to be good for a laugh or two."

"Let them laugh," Joe said. "That's not your concern. Taking care of yourself is."

"This is still a free country. Everyone is entitled to his opinion."

"That may be so," Wanda Posey, the savvy ex-librarian, added. "But it seems to me that someone is trying to scare you off this case by threat, and using the US mail to do it. Now, I'm not the lawyer here, but that doesn't sound exactly legal to me. In fact, it sounds downright criminal."

"You have such a logical way of putting things," Lily told her.

"Good," Wanda said, picking up the phone. "You want to make the call, or should I?"

She talked it over with her father first. "I agree with Joe and Wanda," he said. "Sending threats through the mail is illegal. You have every right to file a complaint. And it's important that you do so. Not that it will get you anywhere, but at least you'll be on record."

"You mean, if anything happens to me?"

"Well, we certainly don't intend to let it get to that," Carson declared firmly. "But I think dropping this nice little ball in Kent McAllister's lap is the right first move."

• • •

"I sure am sorry about this," Arnie Stiversen said when he and his partner responded to Lily's complaint. "It isn't appropriate, and we'll certainly do our best to find out who's responsible."

"Although this kind of case, you know -- a murdered police detective and all -- I guess it was bound to bring out the crazies in the community," Paul Cady put in. "Of course, being crazy doesn't mean being stupid. We'll check for fingerprints and DNA and all, but don't be too surprised if we don't find anything."

"Cut the bullshit," Joe said bluntly, because he had been senior to both of them, and he still had some clout in the department. "You take this as seriously as you would take any threat of this kind, or I'll go over your head."

"Don't worry," Stiversen said, stepping in before his hotheaded partner could respond. "We don't take this sort of thing lightly, Joe, and you know it. We're on it one hundred percent. And I'll personally keep you updated on whatever we find."

· · ·

"What's the matter with you?" Stiversen barked at Cady as they exited the Victorian. "You know damn well she didn't ask for this case -- it was dumped on her. So now you want to make her pay twice?"

"Defense attorneys -- they're all alike," Cady sneered. "They start crying foul the minute the going gets tough."

"Oh, come off it," his partner told him.

"Why should I?" Cady countered. "Dale was my friend. I thought he was your friend, too. I don't want some smart-ass lawyer getting his dirty Injun killer off on some screw-up technicality."

"Dale *was* my friend," Stiversen confirmed. "But that doesn't make Lily my enemy. She's only doing her job, and you know it. So maybe you better start thinking about doing yours."

"Yeah, and who are you to be telling me what to do?" Cady snapped.

"Well, I don't know, partner," Stiversen said. "You want me to think the reason you're dragging your feet on this is because you know who sent those letters to her?"

"Now that's loyalty!" Cady exclaimed. "Whatever happened to cops sticking together?"

"I've got loyalty," Stiversen told him. "But just so you know, I've also got ethics."

"All right, all right," his partner grumbled. He looked at the plastic bags containing the threatening letters. "I'll get these over to the lab. They can run their tests. They might even find us a perp or two, although I won't hold my breath. But who knows, maybe they'll luck out, and we can go waste time hunting down some otherwise law-abiding citizens who aren't doing anything but letting off some steam. And why? Just because they have the balls to say what the rest of us are thinking!"

• • •

There were no usable fingerprints on the letters. There was some DNA on the envelope flaps, but other than confirming that there was no match in any of the national databases, nothing came of the complaint, and the offensive mail continued to come to Broad Street.

And, as if that weren't enough, Lily was becoming *persona non grata* around town, as well -- at the local supermarket, the beauty salon, her favorite restaurant, the JCPenney store in the Port Hancock Mall. Acquaintances glared at her from a distance. Casual friends did their best to avoid her. Close friends didn't discuss it. And on one Saturday afternoon at the end of March, courtesy of a complete stranger, a rotten tomato found its mark.

"Wow, you're getting downright dangerous to be around," Amanda Jansen exclaimed, she and Lily having gone to the market together. "Anything harder than a tomato could do some real damage, you know."

"I'm really very sorry, Ms. Burns," the store manager said. "If you tell me who threw the tomato, I'll have the person removed from the premises."

"I don't know who it was," Lily told him.

"Oh, I see," the manager said. "Well then, I hope you won't hold it against the store. After all, we can't be held responsible for our customers. Legally, I mean."

"Don't worry," she said. "My calendar is full. I have no plans to sue."

Twice in the next month, she walked over to the courthouse in the middle of the day, only to come back and find her Toyota Camry adorned with crude graffiti. Once, she was parked at the mall for half an hour, but it was long enough for the driver's side of her car to be keyed. And another time, she came out of the local movie theater to realize that not one, but two of her tires had been slashed.

"I guess you could say there are pros and there are cons to living in a small town," Carson Burns told his daughter.

"Yes, but this is ridiculous," Lily said. "And you know what bothers me the most? No one reported it. No one even tried to stop it. And it didn't happen in a vacuum. My car was either parked right out on the street or in a public parking lot. There had to be witnesses."

"Well, you can always talk to Grace," her father said.

"And tell her what? That I'm representing a killer that nobody -- including me -- thinks should get away with what he's done, and I'm being demonized for it?"

• • •

But Lily mulled over her father's suggestion. She wasn't a quitter, and the last thing she wanted was to let these crackpots chase her off a case, even if it was a case she didn't want and wasn't going to win. But there were other considerations. Her livelihood, for one, and what any serious community protest could mean to her practice. She certainly didn't need to lose any business over someone like Jason Lightfoot. In the end, she decided a conversation with Grace Pelletier couldn't hurt.

"I know it's been tough, and it's likely to get tougher before this whole thing is over," the judge told her frankly. "And I will take you off the case, if that's what you want. But you know how would it look. It would look like you were weak and the hate-mongers were tough. Which would only embolden them to ratchet it up a notch or two against whatever hapless attorney I might appoint in your place. Not to mention what quitting the case might very well do to your reputation going forward."

Lily sighed. Either way, she knew, she was screwed. "Well, just as long as I don't end up dead before we get to trial," she said, and it was only half in jest.

"If you're that worried, the one thing I can do is arrange some protection for you," Grace said immediately.

"And how would that look?" Lily countered.

"I don't care one whit how it would look," the judge declared. "Certainly not if you're going to be looking over your shoulder every minute from now until October."

But Lily tossed her head. All this nonsense was starting to get her dander up. "Never mind," she said, preparing to leave. "I may not like the case, and I definitely don't like the odds, but I'm not going to give anyone the satisfaction of making me quit."

Grace Pelletier watched her go, with her eyes narrowed and her teeth clamped on her lower lip. After a moment, she picked up the Rolodex that sat on the side of her desk and flipped quickly through the cards until she found the one she was looking for, and reached for the telephone.

"The problem is you're too damn good at what you do," Joe told her. "And I think maybe there are some who are scared out of their minds you might actually find a way to get Lightfoot off."

"Sure," Lily said. "As if there's a chance in hell of that happening."

In the past five years, she had defended her share of unlikable clients. It went with the territory, so to speak, and in truth, she had even found an occasional loophole that either got charges reduced or altogether dismissed. But she sensed this case was very different. That it wasn't any great love for the police that was motivating the people who were coming out of the woodwork here -- that it was about something else entirely.

Lily knew what prejudice was, she supposed she had grown up with it all around her, but it had always been something that had never really impacted her, until now. Of course, that may have been because she had never defended an Indian accused of murdering a police officer before.

In truth, other than Diana Hightower, she really didn't know any Indians to speak of. They weren't a significant part of the Port Hancock society that she traveled in. Oh, there had been a few of them back in high school, but they hadn't been friends, they'd had nothing in common, and she had never visited their homes or invited them to hers. Only now, she was being painted with the same brush they had been, and it was coming a little too close to potentially putting her life in danger for comfort.

"Maybe you should take the judge up on her offer," Joe suggested.

"Just what I need," Lily said in distain. "To be escorted around by Port Hancock's finest, so everyone will know I can't protect myself. I can't wait to see who among Dale's co-workers would step up for that duty!"

"If you're sure you want to look at it that way," Joe said. "As for me, I wouldn't care who it was, as long as I stayed in one piece."

"I agree," Wanda put in.

"But what if all this nonsense is about nothing more than a handful of disgruntled citizens blowing off steam, and I make a big fuss over it?" she argued. "Like the judge says, if we give them legitimacy, who knows what they might try next."

Two days later, shortly after one o'clock, a tall, slender man who looked to be in his early forties entered the Broad Street Victorian. He was dressed in khakis, a T-shirt, and cowboy boots. He was clean-shaven and his long brown hair was neatly caught up in a rubber band at the nape of his neck.

"Hello, my name is John Dancer," he said in a soft voice. "And I'd like to see Lily Burns."

"I'm afraid she's not in the office right now," Wanda told him politely. "I don't expect her back for at least another hour."

"That's okay," he said pleasantly, taking one of the comfortable visitor's chairs that were arranged around the reception area. "I don't mind waiting."

"Suit yourself," the receptionist said, but she kept a careful, and somewhat curious, eye on him as he sat there calmly, quietly, with one leg balanced across the other knee.

• • •

Lily left the courthouse just before three o'clock and headed back toward the Victorian. She was in the middle of a sticky domestic abuse case that wasn't going very well at the moment, it had started to rain -- for which she was unprepared, and she was not in a particularly good mood.

As a result, she hardly noticed the red pickup truck stopped at the corner of Broad Street and Meridian Avenue, its engine gunning impatiently for the traffic light to change, nor did she see the driver hit the gas as soon as the light did change, skidding around the corner just as she was crossing, neatly sideswiping her, and knocking her off her feet.

"You should watch what you're doin', lady -- and who you're doin' it for," the driver, whose cap was pulled too far down on his face for recognition, jeered as he gassed the truck and sped off. "You never know -- you could get hurt."

Lily lay on the road, shaken and confused.

"Oh my word!" an elderly man, who had been standing at the intersection, exclaimed, as he came hurrying to her aid. "Are you all right, Miss -- are you hurt?"

He wasn't anyone Lily knew. "I don't think so," she told him, as he helped her to her feet.

"Maybe you should see a doctor, just to make sure," the stranger suggested.

"Thank you, but I think I'm okay," she said, checking her neck, her legs and her arms, making sure they were all still in working order. "He just knocked me down."

"I don't know how that idiot could have missed seeing you," the man exclaimed. "You expect this sort of thing to happen in Seattle, of course -- it happens there all the time -- but who would have thought it could happen in a quiet little place like this?"

"Quiet little places like this can be deceiving," Lily told him.

"Well, if you're sure you're all right," he said. "Because otherwise, my car's right across the street, and I'd be more than happy to drive you to a hospital."

"That's very kind of you," she said, "but my office is just down the block. I think I'll go on over there and clean myself up."

"Well, I don't know if it will help any," the elderly man said, "but if you want to file a complaint, I'm pretty sure the truck that hit you was a red Chevy Silverado, and the three letters on the license were AJN. I'm sorry, I didn't get the numbers."

Lily looked at him in surprise. "Thank you," she said. "Whether it helps or not, thank you."

"And you're sure you're okay?" he persisted. "Because I don't want to leave you here if there's even a chance that you're not."

"I think so," she told him. "I'll go to my office and rest for a while, and then see how I feel."

She already knew how she would feel -- furious. And by the time she got through the front door of the Victorian, she had a pretty good start on it.

"My God, what happened to you?" Wanda exclaimed when she saw a wet, dirty, and disheveled Lily.

"This is getting out of control, and I've about had enough of it," Lily snapped, launching into as detailed a description as she could of what had taken place.

"It was deliberate?" Wanda gasped.

"As deliberate as it gets," Lily fumed. "So suppose we get the police up off their collective asses once again.

There can't be too many red Chevrolet Silverados in this county, with the letters AJN on the license plate, whose driver has it in for someone who's just trying to do her damn job. Port Hancock's finest surely ought to be able to track it down."

It was only then, as she turned toward the stairway, that she realized she had an audience, that it wasn't only Wanda, who had heard every word.

"This gentleman has been waiting to see you," the receptionist murmured.

Lily took a deep breath and did her best to compose herself. "I'm so sorry you had to wait," she said. "What can I do for you, Mr. -- ?"

"Dancer, Ma'am," he said. "You can call me Dancer."

"All right, Mr. Dancer, how can I help you?"

"Just Dancer, Ma'am," he said. "And I'm here doing a favor for a friend. This friend thought maybe you could use a little backup, of the unofficial kind, and from what I just heard, and what I see, I'd say this friend was right on."

Lily frowned at the stranger. "Friend?" she echoed. "Backup? I'm sorry, but I don't know what you're talking about."

He pulled his identification out of his back pocket and handed it to her. It and the badge he presented confirmed that he was a US Marshal from Spokane, a city all the way on the other side of the state.

"I've got a pretty reliable 4-Runner parked out front that can take you anywhere you might need to go," he told her. "I have an excellent driving record. I'm on leave from my department for as long as necessary. And as far as I'm concerned, what you do, or don't do, and who you do it for, is nobody else's business but your own."

Lily was stunned. She knew there was only one person in Port Hancock who had the kind of reach this maneuver had required.

"Thank you," she said as politely as she could, "but I don't need a bodyguard."

"It sure didn't sound that way to me just now," Dancer said easily. "To me, it sounded like you could use all the help you can get. What you just got there was a warning, Ma'am. Next time, on some other road, on some other day -- or night, that truck might not bother to miss. So maybe you ought to reconsider."

"I don't mean to be rude, Mr. Dancer," Lily responded, perhaps a bit more bravely than she felt at the moment. "But I was born and raised here. This is my town. I know these people. I've known them all my life. And while it's true that sometimes they like to blow off steam, when it comes right down to it, they're basically good people, and they do the right thing. I really don't need to be protected from them."

Dancer shrugged. He took a card from his wallet and dropped it on Wanda's desk. "I'll be around for a couple of days. Let me know if you change your mind." Then, with a polite nod, he departed.

"Are you sure you shouldn't have taken him up on his offer?" Wanda inquired, picking up the card and making a point of tucking it away in her desk drawer.

"No, I'm not sure," Lily had to admit. "And once I think about it, I'll probably regret that I didn't."

It took less than a week. Lily was returning to town after a routine visit with Jason Lightfoot when a red Chevrolet Silverado ran her green Toyota Camry off the back road and into a ditch. Before she could even react, someone was throwing a hood over her head, yanking her out of the car, and dragging her into the bushes.

"The damn Injun killed a cop," a man's voice close to her ear said -- the words and the voice ringing eerily familiar. "A good cop. A cop with lots of friends." His breath was heavy with liquor. "The bastard ain't nothin' but pond scum, and he deserves to hang. You wanna stay healthy, you see to it he gets what he deserves." She felt his hands on her body, touching her in places he had no right to touch her. She heard him snicker. "Sorry," he murmured in her ear. "Much as it would be fun, you don't do a thing for me, bitch." And then he was gone. She heard the truck start up, and tear off down the road. She pulled off the hood. She was alone.

"I know who it was," she told Joe and Megan and Wanda after she had to wait for the owner of the local garage to come help get her car out of the ditch, and then had to explain why she was so late getting back to the office.

"Who?" Joe asked.

"One of the guards over at the jail," Lily said with certainty. "I didn't see him, but I recognized his voice."

"Was it the same guy who sideswiped you the other day?"

"No. Same truck. Different voice."

"Find that red Chevrolet, and you'll have him, and whoever his buddy is," Wanda suggested.

"That would be too easy," Joe said.

"You're looking for a red Chevy Silverado, with AJN on the license plate," Lily told Arnie Stiversen and Paul Cady when they showed up, in response to Joe's call, two hours later. "But I'm pretty sure you're going to find it burned beyond recognition in some field somewhere, or at the bottom of the Strait, or reported stolen maybe a week ago."

The two police officers exchanged glances.

"Two out of three," Cady murmured.

"We already found it," Stiversen said. "It was burning a big hole in the ground over at Maxwell Flats. The owner claimed it went missing about ten days ago."

"How'd you know?" Cady asked.

Lily shrugged. "Two incidents. Same vehicle. Too risky to keep."

"Same guy?"

"No," Lily said.

"What else?" Stiversen asked.

"That's all," Lily said.

The police officer's eyes narrowed. "You know at least one of them, don't you?"

Lily shrugged again. "This is a small town," she replied.

"You sure you don't want to file a complaint?" he pressed.

"I'm sure."

Lily sat alone in her office after Stiversen and Cady were gone, more shaken than she was willing to admit. The guard and his buddy, whoever he was, were a pair of jerks, and she would have liked nothing better than to take them down, but she sill had the Indian's trial to get through, and pressing charges would not only be a major distraction for her personally, it would be a public relations nightmare. She could see the headlines already: COP KILLER'S LAWYER CRIES FOUL. She sighed, knowing, whatever the outcome, it would likely do more harm than good.

But that didn't mean she had no options. It just meant it was time to be sensible. First being sideswiped and then being run off the road and inappropriately manhandled were clear indications that this whole thing was escalating out of control, and she had no way of knowing how much further it would go. Nor did she care to find out.

Lily swallowed her pride, retrieved John Dancer's card from Wanda's drawer, and called the number on it.

• • •

"To be honest, I really didn't expect you'd still be here," she told him.

"I had a feeling you'd be calling," he said.

They sat in her office barely an hour after Stiversen and Cady had left.

"Thank you," she said.

There was an easiness about John Dancer, about his tone, about his manner. She noted that right away. He seemed totally comfortable, not only in his clothes, but in his skin as well. "I've been on the job for going on twenty years now," he told her. "A while back, I got involved in a high speed car chase when I should have known better. Landed in the hospital with more busted bones than I thought I had whole to begin with. As you can imagine, I was awhile healing. And then, just when the doctors said I was ready to get off my butt and back into gear, I get this phone call."

Lily nodded, as it all began to make sense. "From the Honorable Grace Pelletier, I presume."

He smiled. "Yes, Ma'am, that would be the lady," he said. "She and my mother go way back. Anyhow, when she explained what the situation was over here, I figured I could do a lot worse than spend a few months riding shotgun for a lawyer who was just trying to do her job. And I guess my captain felt the same way, because he didn't argue too much. Not after the judge talked to him, anyway. So here I am, on loan, so to speak, to see to it that you get from here to October in good health, so you can try your case in a court of law, and not in the court of public opinion."

Lily contemplated him for a long minute. "Why do I think there's more to this story?" she inquired finally. "Something you've left out."

"The judge said you were sharp," Dancer said with a grin. "It's like I told you, she and my mother go way back -- my mother being from the only Native American family in an otherwise very white neighborhood. Grace lived across the street. She was an equal rights advocate even in grade school -- always defending my mother, always standing up to the bullies. She was the one who introduced my mother to my father. And she was the one who prosecuted the man that shot and killed my father just because he refused to take my mother out of a public restaurant where they went to celebrate their wedding anniversary. And she won the case, too."

And now all the pieces fit. Lily nodded slowly. "And you believe that Jason Lightfoot deserves a fair trial."

"Yes, Ma'am, I do," the US Marshal said. "Guilty or innocent."

"I keep a pretty hectic schedule," she warned him.

"That's all right, I've already got myself a room over at Miss Polly's," he said. "As soon as I explained to her why I was here, she said never mind the schedule she keeps to -- I could have a key to the front door, and she would be happy to fix me my meals whenever I wanted them. So all you have to do is tell me when to be where, and I'll take it from there."

"What about your family?"

"I've got a wife and three kids back in Spokane," he said.

"And how do they feel about this?"

"They're behind me, one hundred percent."

"Well, we'll have to work out some time -- you know, when you can go home and be with them," Lily told him.

"That would be much appreciated," he said. "But we don't have to worry about that right now."

"Then I guess it's settled."

"Yes, Ma'am."

Lily couldn't believe it. She had actually agreed to put her life in the hands of another person. It meant, of course, admitting that she feared for her safety. It was not a position she had ever thought she would be in -- not in her town, not in her life. Nevertheless, she felt an almost overwhelming sense of relief.

• • •

"There's someone I'd like you to meet," she told her father that evening.

"And who might that be?" he asked.

She smiled. "Oh, just a guardian angel," she said.

The on-loan US Marshal had followed her home to Morgan Hill, and stood in the driveway, watching, as she locked the Camry in the garage.

"You can take it out again in November," he assured her with a grin.

"Not so fast," she retorted. "You haven't passed the final test yet."

"Oh, and what would that be?" he asked.

"My father."

It would be fair to say that Carson Burns liked John Dancer right from the start. The man from Spokane was as low-key as it got, easy-going, soft-spoken and intelligent. He would fit right into the community without arousing much concern -- the kind of man who could take care of himself and, Carson decided, who would be able to take care of his daughter, too.

"You'll stay to dinner, young fellow," the former Jackson County Prosecutor declared, after no more than fifteen minutes, and it was more a directive than an invitation.

Lily smiled broadly at the man from Spokane. "I guess that means you passed the test," she told him.

John Dancer smiled in return. It had been a long time since anyone had called him young.

• • •

Sunset was coming later and later to the Pacific Northwest, as spring went scurrying into summer. It meant that the sky was still blue at nine o'clock that evening when John Dancer pulled to the side of a road to check the name on a mailbox that sat at the end of a dirt drive leading to a small bungalow. Satisfied with what he saw, he left the 4-Runner where it was, and walked up to the house.

"Evening, Ma'am," he said pleasantly through the screen door to the nondescript woman who responded to his knock. "I apologize for the lateness of the hour, but I wonder if I might have a word or two with your husband."

With a shrug, the woman disappeared inside the house and, a few moments later, was replaced by a balding, heavyset man wearing a T-shirt and jeans, his stomach bulging over his waistband, a bottle of beer in his hand.

"Yeah, you wanted to see me?" the man asked, the slight slur to his words an indication that this was likely not his first beer of the evening.

"Yes, sir, I surely did," Dancer replied politely enough, resting his hands casually on his hips, which pushed back just enough of his jacket so that the guard could see he was carrying both a badge and a weapon. "The name is Dancer, and I wanted you to be one of the first to know that I'm here in town to make sure that Lily Burns gets to represent her client, Jason Lightfoot -- in a court of law, not a court of public opinion, just like she's supposed to, just like every citizen deserves -- without any further interference."

"Yeah, so what's it to me?" the man retorted, but not before Dancer noted a dark flush creep up his neck and across his face.

"Maybe something, maybe nothing," Lily's new protector conceded. "But like I said, I just wanted you to know that, as of now, the fun and games are over. I'll be watching her back, and should there be any other, let's just say, misguided encounters, the person or persons involved -- whoever he or they may be -- will be answering to me."

"Don't have the faintest idea what you're talking about," Buzz Crandall, the guard from the Jackson County Jail, declared.

"Well, it's good that we had this little chat then," Dancer said, "before anything else happens -- and the fox ends up in the henhouse."

Crandall visibly paled at that, but stood his ground and said nothing.

"And now that we understand each other," the marshal concluded, "I'll wish you a pleasant evening." With a little nod, he turned and sauntered back down the drive to his car, acutely aware that he was being watched every step of the way.

• • •

By the end of June, the soft-spoken man from Spokane had blended neatly into the fabric of Port Hancock society. After all, what was one more Indian to the whites, and another brother to the tribes? He was unassuming, minded his own business, and wasn't out looking for trouble.

Word got around quickly, and people learned who he was and why he was there. But it didn't matter. Many may not have liked that Lily was representing Lightfoot, but most of them liked Lily, and after they'd heard about the threats and the incidents with the red Silverado, they were glad she had protection and wished her no harm.

When he wasn't shadowing Lily around, Dancer was making the acquaintance of all kinds of people in the community, not just those in Old Town, and even New town, but those around the county, as well.

"Just sizing up the enemy," he told Lily. "How many. How diverse. How determined."

"When do you sleep?" she inquired.

He laughed at that. "Learned a long time ago that four hours of good sleep a night is a lot better than eight hours of tossing and turning," he told her.

Grace Pelletier put out the word that anyone messing with Dancer would answer to her, and he assured the local police that he was not there to step on any toes, or do anyone's job for him. He was, he said, here for the sole purpose of seeing to it that Lily Burns made it to trial. To that end, he took her to and from work each day, escorted her wherever else she had to go, and kept his eyes and ears open in between. Once or twice a week, he dined with Lily and her father at their Morgan Hill home. The rest of the time, he partook of Miss Polly's fare, which was quite good, and was included in the price of his room.

It didn't take him long to realize that there really were two separate cities in Port Hancock, but they had little to do with geography. There was the one that waited impatiently for the Indian to have his day in court and be executed for his crime, and there was the one that believed Jason Lightfoot was being railroaded, and hoped against hope that truth would prevail.

Some of the latter hung out at The Last Call Bar & Grill down at the lower end of Broad Street. And there, John Dancer was a favorite.

Four

The school year ended the week after Memorial Day, as it always did, and now it was coming up on Father's Day. As had become a tradition over the years, Lily's sisters and their families, the Cahills from Portland and the Ingrams from Denver, had descended on the Morgan Hill house for the weekend, taking over the entire third floor.

Knowing that she would be spending most of her time at home for the next several days, Lily had given her bodyguard the weekend off.

"You have a bodyguard?" her eldest sister Janet Cahill inquired, when she overheard her father telling Diana that Dancer had gone home to Spokane and would, therefore, not be joining them for dinner on Sunday.

"Don't even go there," Lily told her.

"Did you just say Lily has a bodyguard?" her middle sister, Karen Ingram, questioned.

"What's a body god?" seven-year-old Carly Ingram asked.

"It's someone who guards you and keeps you safe," her twelve-year-old brother Cody explained.

"But why would you have to have your body guarded, Aunt Lily?" nine-year-old Jack Cahill wanted to know.

"Your body has a god?" exclaimed Jimmy, his wide-eyed six-year-old brother.

"See what you started?" Lily said, making a face at Janet.

"It's nothing, kids," Janet told them. "Your aunt's gotten herself involved in a difficult case at work right now, and she just needs someone to help her out for a while."

That seemed to satisfy everyone but the twelve-year-old. "If you need protecting, Aunt Lily," Cody whispered, "I can take care of you."

Lily gave him a hug. "I have a client who isn't very well liked in town," she explained, "and that sort of thing can sometimes rub off on the people who are trying to help him."

The boy nodded. "I stuck up for a kid in my class last year because some of the other kids didn't like him," he told her. "So they started to tease me."

"What did you do?" Lily asked.

"I told them only sissies needed to tease other kids," Cody confided. "Then I hung diapers on their lockers."

Lily gave him a hug. "Cody," she told him, "when you grow up, if you want to come live here in Port Hancock, I promise I'll make you my Number One Bodyguard."

"You better watch out, Aunt Lily," the boy said, grinning broadly. "I just might do that."

• • •

Dinner around the big mahogany table in the grand dining room was the same happy, noisy affair it had been when Lily was a child growing up in this house. She watched her father, smiling and laughing and chatting with his children and grandchildren, and realized, to her surprise, that she was also enjoying the moment. And the surprise was not just in realizing how much Carson Burns missed having his family around, but how much she did, too.

Becoming a lawyer had always been first and foremost on her mind, from the time she was a lot younger even than Cody. It wasn't that she didn't intend to marry and have a family one day -- it was that establishing her career had been the more pressing matter at hand. But now that college and law school were behind her, and her practice was firmly established, and in the fun-filled presence of her sisters and their husbands and their kids, Lily wondered if she had waited too long.

There had been boys in high school that she had liked more than just as friends – Jeff Nordlund, for one, who had been her date for the senior prom, and with whom, on one particularly beautiful spring night, she had lost her virginity. And there had been men in college and law school, and a few even since then, that she had been attracted to. But nothing had ever really gone beyond the dates and the proms and the beautiful spring nights. Somehow, none of it had managed to advance from courting to commitment.

Lily told herself it was better not to have found the one and only, only to have it end in divorce, as it had ended for Amanda after just two years. When she married, Lily wanted it be for the rest of her life, just as it had been for her parents and as it looked like it was going to be for her sisters.

As if reading her mind, Janet looked at her questioningly. "So, anyone interesting in your busy life these days?" she asked.

"You mean other than cop killers?" Lily replied.

"Yes," her sister said.

"Not at the moment," Lily told her lightly. "But I hear there's going to be a new suit in the prosecutor's office, so you never know." It was a put-off, of course, but there actually had been talk about a new deputy prosecutor coming on board.

Whatever her intention, the exchange now had everyone's full attention.

"Tell us more," Karen said. "Is he cute? Is he single?"

"Stop," Lily protested, as she felt herself blushing. "I don't know a single thing about him. It's just the word that's been going around."

"You be sure to keep us posted," Janet said, a twinkle in her eye.

It was a special weekend, and Lily had to admit she was sorry when it was over, and time for her sisters to leave.

They sat around the dining room table on Monday morning, wolfing down Diana's delicious pancake breakfast, and chattering on about absolutely nothing important. Then Lily helped them pack up their belongings, drag the suitcases down from the third floor, and load their respective vans.

She got right in the middle of all the hugs and kisses and tearful goodbyes, and then she stood in the driveway, beside her father, as they waved the Ingrams off to Denver and the Cahills on their way back to Portland.

"Makes you wish they lived closer, doesn't it?" Carson said with a sigh, knowing they wouldn't be back again until Thanksgiving.

Lily leaned down and hugged him. It was exactly what she was thinking.

. . .

The walls were closing in on Jason Lightfoot. From where he sat on his metal bunk, he could see a bit of blue sky in the morning and a star or two at night, if he were lucky, but even though the jail was quite close to the foothills, he couldn't see a mountain or a tree. If he stood up on the bed and grasped the steel bars that covered the slit of window above his head, he could pull himself up just far enough to catch a quick glimpse of a bird flying by. It was agony.

The headaches were agony, too. And the feeling like he was coming right out of his skin. The fellow the lady lawyer had sent, Greg Parker, explained it to him. He had been poisoning his body for years, and now he was going through a forced withholding of that poison. His whole being, both physical and mental, was screaming for alcohol in every way it knew how. And, as Parker had told him, if he didn't deal with it, it would kill him.

Jason wondered which was worse -- sitting in a cell for years, waiting to die at the end of a rope, or dying quick from alcohol poisoning. He had visions of rum bottles lined up in front of him, and of him drinking until he dropped dead. At least, he reasoned, he would be going out on his own terms.

Still, he had to admit, it wasn't as awful as it had been in the beginning -- the first few weeks, when the shakes were so bad he couldn't stop his teeth from chattering, and the nightmares had him literally screaming. In that respect, he had to concede, Parker had really helped.

Much to Buzz Crandall's dismay, Lily was able to make special arrangements for her client. She got permission for Jason to have a cell phone, so he could call Parker when things got really bad, and that helped. Parker would talk him down, if he could, and if he couldn't, he would get over to the jail as soon as possible. Lily made arrangements for that, too.

"Which would you prefer," she asked the warden, "that he kill himself on your watch, or that he lives to stand trial, and you're the one who saw to it that he got there?"

It may have been unorthodox, but the warden wasn't stupid. He put out the word that Jason Lightfoot was to get the treatment he required.

And so far, it seemed to be working. After four months, the nightmares were fewer and farther between.

The shakes had mostly subsided, and Jason was no longer snapping at everyone. The only thing that hadn't improved was his memory. Stuff was still all muddled up in his brain, and hard as he tried, he couldn't remember anything meaningful about the night of the murder.

His uncle came to see him once a month, his older sister came in March and May, and his younger sister came in April and again in June. They sat there facing him, one after the other, with a Plexiglas partition between them, and talked over a telephone. Determined to avoid discussing what was uppermost in their minds to discuss, because they understood that every word they uttered was being recorded, and could be used as evidence against him, they had little to say. His uncle was still eking out a living on the farm. His older sister lived in Anacortes, and had two children who attended university. His younger sister worked as a nurse's aide in a hospital in Longview. Her three children were going to white schools there.

That was it. His mother never visited. She had lost her license to drive years ago, and no one volunteered to bring her. Jason didn't want her to see him like this, anyway. Besides, according to his uncle, she was pretty much in a drunken stupor all the time now.

His only other visitors were the lady lawyer and her bodyguard. But they weren't really visitors. Lily

Burns was just doing her job, coming by once a week or so, to see how he was, and to ask if he needed anything. Needed anything? He needed to get out of this place! Sometimes, she brought him books and magazines, and when there weren't any legal issues to discuss, she did her best to make polite conversation.

To say that Jason was surprised the first time the bodyguard appeared on the scene would be an understatement. The only thing he knew about anything was what that guard Crandall had told him, sneering through the bars of Jason's cell, suggesting that his lawyer had better quit his case, if she knew what was good for her. But, when he asked her about it, she just brushed it aside, telling him it was nothing, and assuring him that she had no intention of quitting his case. It was funny, and he'd never admit it, not to her, not to anyone, but hearing her say that actually made him feel better.

And then the bodyguard started showing up.

Jason liked John Dancer. Not because he was part Indian -- well, okay, not only because he was part Indian. He liked him because he stood in the background, watching, maybe even listening, but never intruding. Not that there was much to intrude on. And he never tried to make polite conversation.

"Do you like games?" Lily asked him one day, after the legal matters had been gone over, and his health issues had been discussed, and the polite conversation had run out, but the hour hadn't.

"Games?" he replied. "What do you mean games?"

"Oh, I don't know – gin rummy, checkers, Monopoly, Scrabble?"

"Rummy's okay, I guess," he said. Years ago, Barney Cosgrove had taught him to play.

Lily remembered. The next time she showed up, with Dancer in tow, she brought a deck of cards with her, and they played gin rummy for half an hour. She was pretty poor at it, he was pretty good. Jason suspected that Dancer was very good at it, but the bodyguard said nothing when Jason let Lily win some of the time. Yes, it would be fair to say that Jason liked John Dancer. He liked John Dancer a lot.

He supposed that Lily Burns was all right, too, but he could tell that, except for setting him up with Parker, she was pretty much just doing whatever it was she had to do, just going through the motions, and that, as far as the mess he was in was concerned, she had already written him off.

The rest of the time he spent alone with his fears and his doubts. He had killed a man, and he didn't know why. He couldn't understand what had festered so deep inside of him that it would have erupted in such a violent manner. Jason devoutly believed in living his own life and letting others live theirs. He harbored no ill will toward anyone, not even the mean-spirited cop who had rousted him all those times and was now dead, presumably because of it.

Over and over again, he asked himself the same question -- what had happened that night? Every time that Scott had rousted him, the situation, whatever it was, had been resolved in the cop's favor, generally because Jason was unwilling to argue with a man with a gun. In fact, Jason was generally unwilling to argue with anyone. So what had been different that night? And why couldn't he remember?

● ● ●

Lily stretched out in the lounge chair in the back yard of Amanda Jansen's weekend cottage. It was Sunday, the end of the three-day July 4th holiday. She and Dancer had taken her dad over to Whidbey Island to spend some time with his sister, and then she had sent Dancer on to Spokane for what would likely be his last break before his job in Port Hancock was done.

She had to admit she had gotten used to having him around. Over the past couple of months, although the hate mail had kept up a fairly steady pace, there had been no further incidents involving red trucks and errant drivers. She had become, if not exactly complacent, at least a bit less concerned about her physical safety.

It was a glorious spring that had turned into summer -- filled with blue skies and warm days. And the fact that she had just prevailed in a rather thorny lawsuit didn't exactly hurt, either.

Lily couldn't remember the last time it had rained, but it was long enough ago that sprinklers were at work everywhere, and meteorologists were starting to talk about the prospect of forest fires, especially near the foothills. Although, admittedly, there were probably few people around that were paying very much attention. The old saying was true -- summer in the Pacific Northwest was what made the long dreary rest of the year bearable.

The cottage, which had been left to Amanda by her grandparents, was the perfect place to just hang out. It sat on one side of a small lake, up in the foothills, surrounded by trees and shrubbery and just a couple of distant neighbors. The two women could sleep in, go skinny-dipping, blast the stereo, or have an orgy, if they wanted to, and probably no one would notice. Except maybe the squirrels and birds that kept them company. Or the deer and raccoons and coyotes that ventured by, but rarely came that close. Or the occasional private plane that flew out of the small regional airport west of town that was little more than a blip and a buzz above the mountains.

During the week, Amanda lived in a lovely New Town condo and worked as a child psychologist. Her biggest client was the Jackson County School District and, on more than one occasion over the years, she had provided valuable expertise for Lily in court. But by mutual agreement, "work talk" was off-limits at the cottage. The cottage was for getting away from all that, if only for a while. So it came as no small surprise when, from her stomach on the chair beside her, Lily heard Amanda say, "So, are you getting all geared up for the Lightfoot trial?"

Jason Lightfoot's attorney opened her mouth to reply, and then closed it again. It wasn't that she was unwilling to discuss the matter -- it was that she had nothing to say. Aside from her duty visits to the jail, she hadn't really thought much about the case in the past couple of months.

She gave the usual reasons. Other clients required her attention, which was true, the prosecution was slow in turning over evidence, which was also true, and it was barely summer, and the trial wasn't scheduled to begin until autumn, which meant there was still plenty of time.

But she had to acknowledge that she could feel the winds starting to shift. Media coverage, which had dropped off after the initial flurry, was beginning to rev up again in anticipation of the trial due to start in

October. At least once a week now, editorial perspectives were being published in the *Port Hancock Herald*, call-in commentaries were being aired on the area's popular talk radio station, and previews were popping up all over the local cable television channel. And by a margin of four to one, the good citizens calling in, making appearances, and sending letters to the editor had hanged her client before he had even stepped foot inside the courtroom.

The truth was, Lily didn't like to lose, and like just about everyone else around town, she had identified this case as a loser. As proof, she needed only to remember that the Indian had been indicted in less than ten minutes. And from what she knew of the case, there was little evidence she would be able to challenge and few defense witnesses she would have to prep to testify. Which didn't mean she wouldn't give it all she had. But realistically, she knew that the best she would be able to do was argue mitigation and hope she could get someone on the jury to listen.

Lily had always imagined that her first death case would be a fight for right, where she would hoist the banner of justice and do battle to the end for her client. Because of course, her client would be innocent -- not some pathetic homeless drunk Indian who couldn't even remember what he had done. And it made no difference that she had a reasonable argument to make -- that Jason

Lightfoot was too drunk to know what he was doing, and therefore, it was not a matter of murder one, but at best, manslaughter -- when her client didn't even care.

She resented Jason Lightfoot for ruining her dream, and if it bothered her that she wasn't exactly doing due diligence at this point, she had only to remember that he had as good as told her not to bother. She had shot the best wad she had in getting John Henry to consider taking the death penalty off the table, and in return, her client had essentially shot her right out of the water.

"Well, let's just say," she told Amanda, "that it's not what I would have chosen for my first death case."

"All the more reason to give it everything you've got then, I guess," her friend, the psychologist, responded.

Lily sighed. It was pretty much the same thing her father always told her.

"Absolutely," she murmured, effectively putting an end to the conversation. She hiked up her bathing suit, adjusted the towel on the chair beneath her, and prepared to turn over onto her stomach to let the sun get at her back.

It was just as she was starting to turn over that she caught a glimpse, from the corner of her eye, of something that was not quite as it should have been, and even before she fully realized what it was, she stopped in mid-turn.

A small, single-engine plane, no more than a blip in the sky, that had been flying high above them, had made an abrupt turn, gone into a sudden dive, and was now swooping down toward the ground, traveling so fast and dropping so low that it appeared to be in real danger of colliding with the trees.

It was so close that Lily could clearly hear the noise made by the engine, and plainly see there were black stripes running the length of the gold body. It looked for certain like the plane was out of control and going to crash. And then, at the very last minute, before it surely would have crashed, she saw it pull sharply out of the dive and veer away, heading back up toward the mountains, but not before she also saw something come hurtling out of it.

At first, Lily assumed the plane was in distress, and the thing falling from it was a parachute. But she realized the plane had fallen too low for any kind of safe jump, and the pilot surely had to know that. Then she thought perhaps it was a piece of the plane that had broken off.

Whatever it was, it fell swiftly toward the ground, and before she had any chance to react, it hit the chimney on the roof of the cottage, not more than thirty feet from where she and Amanda lay, and exploded, shattering the peaceful summer silence and sending shards of glass, and chunks of wood and pieces of stone and shingle flying everywhere.

The last thing she remembered was hearing her best friend scream.

· · ·

It was by pure chance that Joe Gideon was walking out of the Port Hancock Medical Center when the ambulances carrying Lily Burns and Amanda Jansen came screeching in. And he couldn't believe what he was told. There had been an explosion at Amanda's cottage that had injured them both? What kind of explosion was the first question he asked, but the paramedics had no information.

Amanda's injuries were confirmed to be fairly manageable, he was then advised, but Lily was another matter. Her injuries were extensive, and couldn't be fully determined until after surgery.

Joe was dumbstruck. But he knew where he was going.

He found Arnie Stiversen and Paul Cady at the Jansen property. With them were Detectives Roy Flynn and Teri Coello, who were conferring with Ben Dawson and Andy Cooper, the police department's two crime scene investigators. Also on the scene was a significant part of the Port Hancock Fire Department that was engaged in putting out the fire that had burned the cottage to the ground.

"We've got the right team working on this," Stiversen assured Joe. "And you have my apology. I know now that Paul and I should have taken this thing about Lily a whole lot more seriously than we did."

"What do you mean?" Joe asked. "What have you got?"

"Looks like it was a pipe bomb," nineteen-year veteran Roy Flynn confirmed.

"A pipe bomb?" Joe was incredulous, having figured it was probably something like the furnace blowing. "How? Where?"

"We don't know yet," Andy Cooper said. "All we have are pieces."

"It must have been a pretty big explosion though," Stiversen added. "The neighbor who called it in lives clear on the other side of the lake. Said he thought at first it was fireworks, but when he came outside, he saw the fire."

"Was that all he saw?" Joe asked.

"So far as we know," Cady replied.

"We're going to need to talk to the two women," Teri Coello said. "We're hoping they can tell us something."

"That could be a while," Joe told her. "They were taking them into surgery as I was heading over here."

Coello shrugged. "Well, there's really not a whole lot more I can do around here," she said. "So, if it's okay with you, can I hitch a ride?"

• • •

John Dancer couldn't remember the last time he was this angry.

He and Lily had driven Carson to his sister's Whidbey Island home on Thursday evening, after which he had dropped Lily back at the ferry. Amanda was going to pick her up on the other side for a weekend at the cottage. Then, as planned, he had taken off for Spokane.

On schedule, he had returned to pick Carson back up on Sunday afternoon, and they were already off the ferry and on their way over to collect Lily when they learned that something had blown the cottage to smithereens, and injured Lily and Amanda -- he didn't yet know how badly -- in the process.

It was Joe who called the Carson home and told Diana Hightower what had happened. It was Diana who gave Joe the number for Carson's cell phone. And it was Joe who then had to call Carson.

Dancer swore only half under his breath when he and Carson met up with Joe at the hospital. "I thought it was okay to leave," he said. "I thought she'd be safe."

"Don't blame yourself," Joe told him. "Even if you'd been here, what could you have done?"

"I don't know," Dancer refused to concede. "But I'd damn well have done something."

Joe wasn't buying it. "More than likely," he said, "you'd have ended up getting blown to smithereens, too, and how would that have helped?"

• • •

It was a somber group that assembled in the second floor waiting room of the Port Hancock Medical Center, waiting for whatever the word would be -- Joe, Dancer, Carson, and soon after that, Diana, Wanda, Megan, and then Amanda's parents, with Maynard Purcell making regular trips to the dayroom to report on what was happening.

Carson called Lily's sisters, promising to keep them updated, and assuring them he would let them know if, Heaven forbid, it was going to be necessary for them to journey back to Port Hancock, barely three weeks after they had left.

But Janet Cahill was having none of it. After making certain that her husband John would be able to take care of the house and the children, she threw some things into an overnight bag, and, within an hour, was in her car and on the road, speeding up the highway from Portland to Port Hancock.

"What's going on around here?" Amanda's mother asked Teri Coello, who waited with the rest of them. "This used to be a peaceful town."

"I wish I had a good answer for you," the detective replied. "I guess there are just some people around here who don't like the idea of cop killers getting all the benefits of ordinary folk."

"Crap," Carson told her. "This isn't about regular folk, and you know it. It's about a small group of racists who don't care much for our system of justice -- unless, of course, it's one of them who's caught up in it."

"Wait a minute," Amanda's father exclaimed. "What are you saying? That this wasn't the boiler exploding or something? Are you saying someone deliberately blew up the cottage?"

"Right now," Coello conceded, "that's the way it's looking."

"We think whoever it was, was after Lily," Joe added. "Trying to get her off the Lightfoot case. But this goes way over the top." He looked meaningfully at the detective. "And I'm sure the Port Hancock Police Department won't rest until the perpetrator is apprehended."

"You have my word on it," Teri Coello assured them all.

• • •

It was eleven o'clock, eight hours after surgery had begun, three hours after Janet had arrived from Portland, and two hours after Carson had insisted that Wanda and Megan go home, when Maynard Purcell finally appeared with the news they had been waiting for.

"I don't mind telling you, they were damn lucky."

"Are they out of surgery?" Carson asked, as a collective sigh of relief spread through the group.

The exhausted physician nodded.

"Tell us," Amanda's father said.

"Well, the way it looks, the girls were out in the back yard, probably sunning themselves, maybe thirty feet or so away from impact -- which is very likely what saved their lives," Purcell began. "We think Amanda was lying on her stomach, because she had a fair amount of shrapnel on the back side of her, but most of it was shallow. Her left leg was fractured, though, so she'll have a cast on for a while. She did have one small glass fragment lodge in the back of her skull, but the surgeon doesn't think it did any serious damage. She probably suffered a mild concussion, which means she'll have a pretty good headache for a few days, but I think she should be just fine."

"Oh, thank God," her mother murmured.

"We think that, intentionally or not, Lily may have saved Amanda from far worse injury," Purcell said.

"How do you mean?" Carson asked.

"Well, from the extent and location of her injuries, we believe that Lily was closest to the explosion, and that she was either sitting upright, or partially upright, but enough to shield Amanda to some extent, and take the brunt of the blast."

"How can you tell where they were?" Janet wondered.

"Can't tell for sure," Purcell replied. "And we won't know until they can tell us. But if they'd been inside the cottage, or even a few feet closer than they were, we would be having a very different conversation right now."

"Tell us," Carson said.

"Okay, without the varnish," Purcell continued. "Lily sustained what we think is a mild to moderate traumatic brain injury, causing swelling that will result in, hopefully, just a temporary level of functional disability. There were shards of glass and a fair amount of shrapnel that penetrated her face, chest, abdomen and thighs. She also suffered several fractured ribs that lacerated her liver and collapsed her right lung, and her right arm was almost completely severed. She's lost a good deal of blood. The fact that the paramedics reached the scene as quickly as they did quite likely saved her life. The surgeon was able to remove the glass shards and some of the shrapnel. The rest of it will have to wait until she's stabilized. She's currently on a ventilator, she's got chest tubes to drain the blood and air, and her arm is in a cast."

Carson couldn't believe what he was hearing. His daughter was lying in a hospital, severely injured, because some idiot didn't want her to do her job?

"Do you think she knew what was coming?" Diana asked.

"Hard to say," Purcell replied. "And we may never know."

"Can we see her?" Janet asked.

"Can we see Amanda?" the Jansens asked.

"Not yet," Purcell told them. "They're both in recovery. You should be able to see Amanda in a couple of hours. As for Lily, she'll be on the ventilator for twenty-four to forty-eight hours and heavily sedated."

"Heavily sedated?" Carson echoed.

"That's to keep her out of it until we can take her off the ventilator."

The group looked from one to the other. It was going to be a long night.

In fact, it was after one o'clock before Amanda Jansen was awake and talking. Her parents hovered by her side, while Detective Coello stood at the foot of the bed, pen and pad in hand.

"I wish I could tell you something," Amanda said. "But I don't have any idea what happened. One minute, Lily and I were in the back yard, taking in the sun, and the next, I think I heard some kind of big blast, and that's all I remember."

Amanda had suffered multiple contusions and lacerations across her back, buttocks, and legs from shrapnel, and several shards of glass had punctured her head and shoulders. But thankfully, they were small and shallow, and the doctors had been able to remove them without incident. Her concussion was determined to be mild, meaning she would indeed have a headache for a few days, but there would be no lasting damage.

"So, you didn't see anything before the explosion, someone making a delivery, or maybe just hanging around the cottage?" Coello persisted.

"No," Amanda said. "It was just us. It's pretty remote up there. If there'd been anyone else around, I think I'd have known it. To be honest, I thought the explosion was from some fireworks gone awry."

"The doctor says we should be able to take you home tomorrow," her mother said. "And you'll be going home with us, until you're fully healed."

"What about Lily?" Amanda asked.

"I'm afraid she's going to be staying here for a while," her father replied.

• • •

When she opened her eyes, all Lily could see was white -- white ceiling, white walls, white curtains. She felt groggy and everything was fuzzy. She had no idea where she was, or what time it was, or even what day it was. She tried to turn her head, but it felt unbearably heavy and it hurt. She tried to raise her arm, but she couldn't. In fact, she realized, she was hardly able to move at all. A wave of panic washed over her as she tried to open her mouth, only to find she couldn't do that very well, either.

Barely a whimper escaped her lips, but it was enough to catch the attention of the ICU nurse hovering nearby.

"Don't try to talk," the nurse said, moving quickly to Lily's side. "You're in the hospital. You were involved in a pretty bad accident. But you were lucky, and you're going to be just fine."

Most of what Lily could see of the woman was a blur, and she had no idea what she was doing in a hospital. What hospital? Where? What accident? What was the woman talking about? And why couldn't she move her arms?

"Move?" she managed to murmur, forcing the word out of her mouth, only to realize that her throat was horribly sore.

"I imagine you want to know why you can't move very much," the nurse interpreted with a gentle smile. "Well, it's because you've been in surgery, and you're still being sedated, and we have your arms restrained. You have a mess of tubes and needles going in and out of you that are helping you get better, and we want to make sure you don't inadvertently pull any of them out. The reason you can't open your mouth very far is because you sustained some pretty bad cuts to your face that had to be sutured. And in case you're wondering, the reason your throat is feeling so sore is because we had you on a ventilator until just a little while ago."

"Day?" she breathed.

"Today is Tuesday," the nurse told her. "Five minutes past one o'clock Tuesday afternoon to be exact."

Tuesday? It was Tuesday? She tried to think, but Tuesday didn't mean a thing to her. What day should it be? Where should she be on Tuesday? What should she be doing on Tuesday? What was Tuesday?

The blur that was the nurse was still there. "Now that you're awake," she said, "can you tell me your name?"

Her name? Now Lily was even more confused. Why was this woman asking her name? Didn't they know her name? She was in their hospital, they were supposed to be treating her for something, and they didn't even know who she was? She opened her mouth as wide as she could, preparing to reply, but only air came out.

"That's all right," the nurse said soothingly. "Don't worry about talking just now. You let that sore throat rest a bit. The doctor will be along after a while, and he'll tell you everything you need to know. Meanwhile, just relax."

Relax? She was in a hospital -- she didn't know why. She had been in some kind of an accident -- she didn't know what. She was so groggy and everything was so fuzzy, she couldn't move. And she couldn't even say her name. How was she supposed to relax?

• • •

The next time Lily opened her eyes, a man in a white coat was standing by her bedside, and although her head still ached and her vision was still blurry, she was relieved that she could at least see something of him.

"Hello, Lily," Dr. Jeffrey Nordlund said. "I'm glad to see you're awake. I don't mind telling you, you gave us quite a scare."

Lily blinked. Who was he? A doctor, she assumed, but he had called her by name. Did he know her? Did she know him? He looked familiar, but she just couldn't remember.

"Know-you?" she breathed.

"You used to," he said with a smile. "Back in high school."

High school? She had known him in high school? Why couldn't she remember?

"Name?" she mumbled.

"My name?" he replied. "I'm Jeff Nordlund." There was a twinkle in his eye. "As a matter of fact, I was your date for the senior prom."

"Date?" They had dated in high school, and she couldn't remember who he was?

"Yes," he said. "I know you don't remember that right now. You probably don't remember a lot of things. But don't worry, that's pretty normal for what you've been through. You were in an accident and you have an injury to your head that's kind of jumbled things up in your brain a bit. It's just going to take some time for you to sort it all out again. So, what do you say we get going on that, okay? We'll start with the basics -- can you tell me your name?"

It took a moment, a frantic moment, when she had it and then lost it and then had it again, and was finally able to get it out.

"Li-ly."

"Nice to meet you again, Lily," he said.

"Day?" she murmured.

"Today?" he replied. "Let's see, it's Wednesday morning, about nine o'clock. You've been here since Sunday afternoon."

Sunday afternoon? It was Wednesday, and she had been in the hospital since Sunday afternoon? She was completely bewildered.

"What -- happed?"

"Well, we're not exactly sure," Nordlund told her. "We're hoping that you'll be able to tell us in a few days, when you're feeling better. All we know right now is there was some kind of an explosion, and you and Amanda got caught in it."

"Who?"

"You and Amanda."

Lily tried to think. An explosion? She and Amanda were caught in some kind of an explosion? But nothing registered.

"Man-da?" she repeated.

"She was with you at the time," Nordlund said. "You were at her cottage. And yes, she was hurt, too, but not as badly as you were."

Lily closed her eyes, but there was nothing, nothing she could see, nothing she could remember, nothing she could put together that made any sense to her. Her head was throbbing, her throat was sore, and she ached all over. "Pain," she breathed.

"Well, that's something we can take care of," was the last thing she heard Nordlund say.

• • •

Carson wasn't really prepared for what he saw when Diana wheeled him into Lily's corner of the ICU and planted him beside the bed. His daughter was lying there, bruised and bandaged from head to foot, tubes and needles running in and out of her, and her right arm buried inside a cast.

It was just past four o'clock on Wednesday afternoon, and he had been at the hospital since Sunday, refusing to go home, even when the doctors told him it could be days before Lily was fully awake. He and Janet had been allowed to see her through the doors to the ICU on Monday, when she was under very heavy sedation, and again early on Tuesday, when she was still sedated, before they had taken her back into surgery to remove the rest of the shrapnel and to check her brain and her lung and her lacerated liver.

Even after Amanda had been discharged, and a reluctant Janet went back to Portland, and he had sent Joe home, and convinced Dancer to go get some sleep, he had refused to budge from the dayroom until he had seen his daughter up close, until he knew for himself that she was going to be okay.

He had tried to send Diana home, too, but she was having none of it.

"If you're staying, I'm staying," she said firmly. "Besides, who else is going to get you to the bathroom when you need to go, and make sure you get something proper to eat?"

Maynard Purcell had pretty much told him what to expect, and Jeff Nordlund had filled him in on more of the specifics, but he still couldn't believe his eyes. She looked so small and so pale lying there, the skin that wasn't bruised was almost as white as the bandages that covered the rest of her, and there were more tubes and needles attached to her than he could count. He had to lean close to see for sure that she was actually breathing.

She had had her share of accidents growing up, of course, a couple that were even serious enough to have landed her in the hospital -- like the time she had broken her left leg in three places, falling from the jungle gym when she was five, and the time she had dislocated her right shoulder falling off her bike when she was eight. And she had had a tonsillectomy when she was ten, and then she had had her appendix removed when she was sixteen. But none of that had resulted in her looking the way she looked now.

"So what did you go and do to yourself this time?" he asked, mustering up a humor he certainly didn't feel.

Lily's eyes fluttered open, her glance roaming around the fuzzy white space before landing on the man in the wheelchair beside her bed, and then she stared at him for a full minute before she spoke.

"Dad?" she breathed finally.

"Who else would it be," he said gruffly, blinking away the tears that had welled up in his eyes.

Traumatic brain injury, oxygen deprivation and blood loss, Purcell and Nordlund had said, all leading to blurry vision, dizziness, difficulty speaking, headaches, and memory failure. Whether all her memory would return, or only parts of it, was currently unknown. The blunt force trauma alone, they said, could result in permanent memory loss. She had also sustained a hemo-pneumothorax when the fractured ribs had damaged her liver and punctured her lung. But at least he now knew it wasn't going to be total memory loss, and she was going to survive, and he felt an almost overwhelming sense of relief.

"Why is she still in the ICU?" he had asked.

"We want to monitor the TBI," he was told, "and then there's the air and the blood in the chest that has to be expelled. We'll keep her under constant observation for at least forty-eight hours, to make sure there are no complications -- no infection, no bleeding, no embolism, no stroke. We're lucky there was no skull fracture."

"Why-you-here?" Lily asked, through her still stiff and swollen lip.

"You were in an accident, and you got hurt," Carson replied. "So where else would I be?"

"Don't-mem-ber," she said. "Why-don't-mem-ber?"

"Don't worry about that now," he told her. "Just worry about feeling better. The rest, well, it'll take care of itself."

• • •

On Thursday afternoon, Lily was moved out of the ICU and into a private room. Although she was still heavily bandaged, and had the arm cast, the chest tubes, and the excruciating pain from the fractured ribs, she was no longer restrained. She had discovered that, in addition to the injuries she thought she knew about, there were others she apparently didn't.

"Tell me," she said. Her voice was a little stronger now, her throat a little less sore, and she had figured out how to form fairly comprehensible words around the stiff, swollen lip.

Maynard Purcell filled her in on the details, after her father had called him in, and after she thought that just maybe she recognized him.

"It's a miracle you survived," the family physician said, after he had accounted for every stitch, every bandage, every needle, and every tube.

"What happened?" she asked.

He shook his head. "We don't know. All Amanda could tell us was that it was some kind of explosion."

Carson wheeled his chair a little closer to her bed. "Lily?" he said tentatively.

"Yes, Dad?"

"What do you remember?"

"Nothing," she said, after a moment. "Everything's kind of fuzzy."

"Well, let me ask you a different question," Purcell interjected. "Where do you live?"

Lily blinked. "With Dad don't I?" she replied hesitantly, and then something in her mind suddenly clicked into place. "Right next door to you."

"That's good, that's very good," Purcell said with a chuckle. "And what do you do for a living?"

This time, Lily did not hesitate. "I followed my father into the law," she said. "I work for him."

Both Carson and Purcell frowned at that. "Lily, do you know what year this is?" the doctor asked gently.

She started to respond, and then stopped. "Wait a minute," she said. "I forgot. I don't work for Dad anymore. He retired. I jumped ship. I opened my own law practice."

Purcell nodded. Carson sighed with relief.

"Good for you," the doctor said.

"What does it mean?" Carson asked.

"It means the TBI didn't cause total memory loss, and she could make a full recovery," Purcell told him.

"One more question, Lily, and then I'll leave you alone -- what case are you working on now?"

"I think I think I just won the Wicker case, didn't I?"

"Yes, you did, Sweetheart," her father said gently. "And now tell us, what's your next case? The one that's set for trial in October."

This time, it was quite a while before she responded, as her mind appeared to chase itself around in seemingly endless circles. "Let me see," she said finally. "I guess I guess it must be the Indian case Is that right?"

Carson looked at Purcell and smiled. "Yes, that's right, Sweetheart," he said. "That's absolutely right!"

After that, it was as though her brain were a machine that wouldn't stop running, as it constantly, painfully, arranged and then rearranged pieces of her life, like a jigsaw puzzle, trying to fit them into a picture she could recognize. Little pieces at first, starting around the edges, like the house on Morgan Hill where she had grown up, like Diana who took care of her father, like her sister, Janet, who came up from Portland to see her, like the Victorian on Broad Street where she had her office, and like the hospital, the nurses, the technicians, and the doctors who had been swirling around her for what seemed like weeks, but was really only days.

From somewhere in the recesses of her mind, even if she couldn't put it all together yet, she knew what the Indian case was. She knew that someone named Jason Lightfoot had committed a murder, and that she was going to be defending him in court, but she had no clear memory of the details of the case, or of who Jason Lightfoot was accused of murdering, or even of who Jason Lightfoot actually was.

She vaguely remembered Wanda and Megan and Joe, and she finally remembered Amanda -- her best friend since childhood. Amanda had been in the hospital, too, she was told. She wondered why. She thought it quite odd that they would both be in the hospital at the same time. Was it a coincidence, or had they been together when they were hurt?

Ever so slowly, in fits and starts, the pieces of the puzzle began to come together. And the next time that Jeff Nordlund came to see her, Lily actually blushed.

"I remember you now," she said.

The surgeon chuckled. "In that case," he said, "I think it's time we got you up and out of that bed."

• • •

It was over her parents' objections that Amanda Jansen returned to the hospital she had left just five days earlier, and made her way, with cast and crutches, to the private room on the second floor. She had been told about the amnesia, so it was with great relief that she saw Lily smile when she entered.

"I was so worried about you," she said, sitting down ever so cautiously in the chair next to the bed before carefully laying her crutches down on the floor beside her.

"Do you know what happened?" Lily asked, eyeing her friend's cast.

"All I remember is we were out in the back yard, minding our own business, grabbing some sun," Amanda said. "And then I think there was an explosion."

"The back yard?"

"At the cottage."

"We were at the cottage?"

"Yes."

"I don't understand why I can't remember," Lily said. "I know, the doctors told me, I was hit in the head and it affected my memory. But not to be able to remember is driving me nuts."

"The doctors said you got the worst of it," Amanda told her. "So give yourself a break. Whatever needs to come back will come back. It'll just take some time."

"I'm glad you're okay," Lily said.

"Wish I could say the same for the cottage," Amanda said ruefully. "My parents tell me all that's left is a pile of burned-out rubble."

"We were at the cottage," Lily said, perhaps more to herself than to her friend. "We were in the back yard at the cottage."

"We were," Amanda confirmed.

"And it's gone?"

"Blown to smithereens."

"What were we doing at the cottage?" Lily asked.

"You mean, when all hell broke loose?"

"Yes."

"Well, let's see," Amanda said, wanting to get it straight, even in her own mind. "It was warm. We were being lazy. We were enjoying the July 4th weekend. We were out on the lounge chairs. I was lying on my stomach. I think you were on your back."

"We were in the back yard," Lily repeated slowly, trying to remember. "We were on lounge chairs. We were talking about something -- about what? I can't remember."

"I don't think it matters," Amanda said. "I can't remember, either."

"And then there was an explosion?"

"Yes."

"I heard you scream."

"You could have."

"No, I remember that," Lily said, growing excited. "I remember hearing you scream!"

"Good," Amanda exclaimed. "Do you know what the explosion was? The police asked, but I didn't know."

"No," Lily admitted. "I just remember being there -- at least, I'm pretty sure I remember being there -- and I know I heard you scream."

"Well, that's a start."

"I can't believe the cottage is gone." Lily couldn't really remember what it looked like, but she was fairly certain that it had been a wonderful place. "We loved going there, didn't we?"

"Yes, we did," Amanda told her. "But all is not lost. My parents say they'll rebuild it. It might not have the same charm, but it'll still be a place we can go when we want to get away from it all."

Get away from it all. Was that what they were doing at the cottage when all hell broke loose, Lily wondered -- getting away from it all?

• • •

Getting Lily up and out of the bed was the next challenge. The process consisted first of leg, toe, and finger flexing, three times a day -- to maintain muscular dexterity, she was told. She was encouraged to sit up and dangle her legs off the side of the bed. Once she could do that without dizziness, she was told it was time to stand up and move around the room, with assistance in the beginning, and then, as she got steadier, on her own. And finally, she was allowed to go to the bathroom all by herself.

Then came the real test -- where she was walked repeatedly up and down the length of the corridor, and then up and down a flight of stairs, in an effort to help her strengthen her muscles, and reinforce her balance.

By the time she had been in the hospital for ten days, she was itching to go home. The bandages had come off, most of the stitches had been removed, x-rays, lab tests, and a CT scan showed there was no further liver damage, that her lung had re-expanded, and that there was no bleeding in her brain. With the help of medication, the ferocity of her headaches had diminished, and the pain from her fractured ribs was almost bearable.

"All right, I'll let you go home -- on one condition," Jeff Nordlund told her. "A therapist will come to your house every day to work with you for as long as it's necessary. Agreed?"

Lily agreed. What choice did she have?

Dancer came to collect her. He walked beside her as a nurse wheeled her outside, and then he helped her into his 4-Runner. It had been almost a week before she remembered who he was and why he was in Port Hancock. And with that piece of the puzzle came the realization that, although the details were still sketchy, what had happened at Amanda's cottage might not have been an accident.

• • •

Life on Morgan Hill was certainly not the way it had been. Lily could not come and go as she pleased. She was confined to the house and the grounds. A physical therapist made daily home visits to help her with muscle, balance, and stamina issues. And Amanda stopped by often to help her with memory, concentration, and mounting frustration matters.

The regimen was tedious, but necessary, Lily was told, and she had to admit it was helping. The better she felt physically, the more she and Amanda were able to focus on the mental side of her recovery -- and she knew the sooner she was able to recover all the pieces of her memory, the sooner she would be able to go back to work.

And there was one more change that was made to the way things had been -- and it involved Dancer. With Carson's blessing, and Diana's hearty approval, the U.S. Marshal gave up his room at Miss Polly's, and moved into the Morgan Hill house, to a room just down the hall from Lily's.

"This time, I'm not going to let your daughter out of my sight for more than a bathroom call," he assured her father. "At least, not until after the Lightfoot trial is over."

"Look, I don't want you blaming yourself for what happened to Lily," Carson told him. "But I expect it'll make us all feel a lot safer, having you here."

• • •

A week after Lily's return home, she was grudgingly getting used to the routine, thanks mostly to the results, although they were slower coming than she would have liked. But the saving grace was the afternoon hour she got to spend on the back patio, sharing the peace and quiet and glass of wine with her father and Dancer, relaxing, soaking up the summer weather, and talking about absolutely nothing that was of any importance.

On this particular day, the temperature was a comfortable 75 degrees. Dressed in shorts and a tank top, she wasn't dwelling on the scabs and the scars that covered much of her body, or the cast on her arm, or the ribs that still ached, preferring instead to lie back and enjoy a gentle breeze, and watch the puffy white clouds, high above, as they slid slowly across an endless expanse of blue sky.

And then something caught her eye -- something small and metallic that swooped in and out of the clouds, just a blip, really, rising and falling in a rhythm of its own. It wasn't a bird, she was sure. And she was fairly certain it was flying way too high to be a kite. And then she knew

-- she knew exactly what it was. And she sat bolt upright, spilling her wine all over herself.

"What's the matter?" Carson asked in alarm.

"A plane!" she exclaimed.

"Yes," her father said. He, too, had seen the blip.

"No, a plane!" she insisted. "It was a plane!"

"What was a plane, Lily?" Dancer asked.

"At the cottage," she cried. "The explosion -- it happened right after something fell out of a plane!"

Carson and Dancer both stared at her.

"Lily, are you sure?" Dancer asked.

"I'm sure," she said. "I was just starting to turn over, and I saw it -- it was a plane. It was diving and I thought it was in trouble and going to crash, and then just as it flew over us, it started to climb back up, and I saw something fall out of it, and that's what hit the cottage!"

Dancer pulled his cell phone out of his pocket.

"Who are you calling?" Carson asked.

"I'm calling Joe," the US Marshal said. "He'll know just what buttons to push to get action on this."

Five

Joe Gideon made his way through the front door of police headquarters. It was three-thirty on Thursday afternoon, and he had hung up on his conversation with John Dancer exactly three minutes ago. Then he had raced all the way from the Broad Street Victorian.

"Hi, Sarge," Manny Santiago greeted him.

"Hey, Manny, how're things?" Joe said.

"Can't complain," the police officer replied. "What can I do for you?"

"Is the chief in?"

"I think so," Santiago said. "Want me to go check?"

"I'd appreciate it," Joe said, and then paced the reception area until the duty officer returned.

"You're in luck," Santiago told him. "Go on up."

Kent McAllister was stretched out in his chair behind a huge oak desk in his second-floor office, his hands folded behind his head, when the private investigator entered. The Port Hancock Chief of Police was tall and muscular, with a handlebar moustache reminiscent of another century.

"Good to see you, Joe," he said amiably.

"You, too, Chief," the private investigator said.

"What can I do for you?"

Joe could hardly contain himself. "I wanted to let you know -- it was a plane."

"Beg pardon?" McAllister responded.

"It was a plane," Joe repeated. "The pipe bomb at the Jansen cottage -- it was tossed out of a plane."

McAllister sat straight up. "How do you know that?" he asked.

"Lily remembered."

"Well, I'll be damned," the chief murmured, almost to himself. "Of all the things we thought of, I got to admit, we never thought of that."

"Shouldn't be hard to track down," Joe said. "Can't have been that many planes in the air that day."

"Even if there were," McAllister said, "at least it gives us a starting point." He stood up and extended his hand. "Thanks for coming in, Joe. Flynn and Coello are out on another call, but I'll fill them in as soon as they get back. You be sure to tell Lily we're on it. And tell her we all hope she's back on the job soon."

· · ·

The Port Hancock Regional Airport was a private recreational facility some twenty miles west of town. It existed for the benefit of local flight enthusiasts with enough time and money to own and operate their own planes. As it turned out, there were a surprisingly large number in the county. With paved runways, clean hangars, and a well-trained staff of mechanics, almost a hundred small planes called the site home.

Joe didn't intend to wait for Flynn and Coello. He pulled up in front of the airport office at just after four o'clock.

"Long time no see, Joe," Rick Hanlon, the airport owner, said, his hand outstretched.

"How've you been, Rick?" Joe responded, grasping the hand for a hearty shake. He and Hanlon went all the way back to high school.

"Can't complain. So, what brings you out this way?"

"Need a favor," the private investigator said.

"Name it," Hanlon told him. Their friendship wasn't just about high school. Fifteen years earlier, the airport owner's son had gotten caught up in a sting operation involving drugs. The boy was mentally slow, and had been duped by two classmates to make the drop. While scooping up all those involved, Joe had managed to extricate Hanlon's son from the mess, and his father had never forgotten.

"I need a list of all the planes that were up on Sunday, July 6th."

"I can get that for you. Mind telling me why?"

"It has to do with the explosion up at the Jansen cottage," Joe explained.

"I heard about that," Hanlon said. "How's Lily doing?"

"She's getting better every day, thanks," Joe told him. "And she's beginning to remember things. That's how come I'm here. The pipe bomb that blew up the place -- she says it was tossed from a plane."

Hanlon's eyes widened. "And you think it was from one of mine?"

"Well, you're the only small craft facility within a hundred miles. So I figured this was as good a place to start as any."

"You'll have that list in ten," the airport owner declared.

Hanlon was as good as his word. "Turns out, it was a busy day," he said exactly ten minutes later, as he handed over two typewritten pages. "We had thirty-five planes up on Sunday."

The list contained not only names, but recorded flight plans as well. Hanlon ran a tight ship, and took his responsibilities seriously. Both takeoff and landing times were also documented.

"Roy Flynn and Teri Coello will probably be coming along, asking for the same thing," Joe told him. "If you don't mind, I'd prefer if you didn't tell them I was here first."

"For you, anything," Hanlon assured him. "It was a damn shame what happened to Lily. And I hope you find the son-of-a-bitch -- even if he *is* one of mine."

Joe pored over the list well into the night, checking names, flight plans, and times. He knew that anyone with a specific destination in mind, such as a bomb drop, would not be likely to post his actual flight plan, but there was nothing that person could do about masking takeoff and landing times, which were monitored by airport personnel.

Of the thirty-five planes that had filed flight plans for that Sunday, there were twenty-two that were recorded as having been in the air within the timeframe of the bombing.

With that list in front of him, Joe hit the computer, beginning with background checks, looking for anything he could find that would cut the list down further. He found no criminal records associated with the any of the plane owners, no felony convictions, not even any misdemeanors.

Next, he checked out the families of the owners. Again, no local felony convictions recorded, but there were a surprising number of misdemeanors -- mostly teenage stuff associated with vandalism and drug possession, a few drunk driving citations, a couple of attempted break-ins, and there was one case of assault that was later dropped.

Joe frowned thoughtfully. There was something in the back of his mind about that assault case, and he tried to remember what it was. It had happened about twenty years ago -- a couple of teenaged boys were involved in beating up another teenaged boy.

He couldn't recall all the details, but something was telling him he needed to go back and take another look at that case. Of course, he no longer had access to the file, but it just so happened that he knew someone he could ask who did.

• • •

Roy Flynn and Teri Coello were doing something else Joe Gideon could no longer do. As Port Hancock police detectives, they were officially interviewing the owners of all thirty-five private airplanes that were listed as having had their planes in the air on July 6th. They had received the same information from Matt Hanlon that Joe had gotten, and first thing Friday morning, they had begun the process of knocking on doors.

Joe, on the other hand, was back at police headquarters first thing Friday morning, looking for his pal Arnie Stiversen.

"Can you help me out?" he asked. "I need to take a look at an old case file."

"Sure," Stiversen said. "Which one?"

"I'm not sure," Joe told him. "It was an assault case, about twenty years ago, a couple of kids beat up another kid pretty bad. It was dropped when the victim suddenly declined to identify his assailants."

Stiversen led the way down to the file room, which took up most of the basement. Cabinet after cabinet, and boxes upon boxes, representing decades of cases, were lined up against walls and stacked on metal shelving. "We're computerizing everything now, you know," he said, "but it'll be years before we get through all this old stuff."

Together, the two men searched the cabinets, until finally the police officer pulled a folder out of the back of one of the cabinet drawers. "I think this is it," he said.

Joe opened the file eagerly. There wasn't much there, just a couple of typed reports, two statements that had been hand-written and signed, a medical report from the emergency room at the Port Hancock Medical Center, documenting a horrific series of injuries, several x-rays, half a dozen photos, and two names. But it was enough.

Joe read through it, studied the x-rays and the photographs for a few moments, and then stared at the names of the two suspects.

"Do me a favor, Arnie," he said softly. "Lose this file for me, will you? Put it somewhere where no one can find it. Just for a while."

"Okay, what's going on?" Stiversen wanted to know.

"I can't tell you yet," Joe said. "But I will as soon as I can, and I promise you won't get in any trouble."

The police officer eyed his former colleague for a long moment. Joe Gideon was the best cop he had ever known or worked with -- smart, thorough, persistent, and most of all, honest. And, too, he was his mentor and his friend. Stiversen took the file.

Joe's next stop was at the residence of one Michael White Horse. The thirty-six-year-old was a computer programmer who worked from his cozy little cottage on the outskirts of town, partly because he could do everything he needed to do from home, but mostly because he was confined to a wheelchair.

"I remember you," White Horse said, when he opened his front door and saw the former police officer standing there.

"Can we talk?" Joe asked.

"Am I in trouble?"

"No," Joe assured him. "Actually, I need your help."

White Horse shrugged. "I suppose it can't do any harm at this point."

"That's true," Joe agreed. "And it just might do some good."

With Joe following, White Horse wheeled his way into a small living room, filled with piles of technical books on shelves and numerous computers on tables, but not much in the way of comfortable furniture, and gestured Joe to a lone chair in one corner.

"What can I do for you, Sergeant Gideon?"

"Not anymore," the former police officer corrected him. "I retired from the force several years ago. Now, I do a little private work on the side. So, its not Sergeant, it's just Joe."

"I seem to remember hearing about that," White Horse said. "And it's too bad. As I recall, you were pretty good at what you did."

"Well, let's hope I'm still pretty good at it," the investigator said.

"So, how can I help you with your private work -- Joe?"

"If you don't mind, I'd like you to tell me something that you wouldn't tell me twenty years ago," the former police officer said. "I'd like you to tell me why you recanted your identification of the two boys who assaulted you."

White Horse looked at him for a full minute. "I'm afraid I can't do that," he said finally.

"What you mean is, you can't tell me because you signed a confidentiality agreement, right?"

The computer programmer sighed. "I guess you already know then, don't you?"

"I didn't, until just now," Joe admitted. "Not for sure, anyway. But as I said, I'm not a cop anymore. And I'm not trying to reopen any old cases. What we say here stays here. I just need to know what kind of deal you agreed to."

"Does what I did have something to do with another case?"

"Yes, it does," Joe said. "A case involving an attorney I work with who was almost killed, very likely because of a case she was working on."

White Horse nodded slowly. "Lily Burns," he said. "I heard about that, too, and I felt real bad."

"Bad enough to help me help her?"

"You really think that what happened to me is connected to what happened to her?" the Indian asked. "It was twenty years ago."

Joe shrugged. "I don't know, but I think it's possible."

White Horse thought about that for a long moment. "All right, I'll tell you what you want to know," he said, "on the understanding that it can't leave this room."

"You have my word," Joe assured him.

"In that case, yes, I signed an agreement, one that guaranteed me lifetime medical care, a full college education, and a home of my own. And for recanting my statement, and declaring that I really couldn't identify the two boys who beat me half to death -- I've gotten all three."

Joe nodded. "That's pretty much what I thought," he said. "And now for the most important part -- the assault -- do you know why it happened?"

"Let's just say that, back then, there were some people who didn't take too kindly to some other people going to their high school," the Indian said. "Especially if those other people happened to be more intelligent than they were, got better grades than they did, and played better football."

"What you really mean is -- Native Americans who were more intelligent, got better grades, and played better football, don't you?" the private investigator suggested.

"That might have had something to do with it," White Horse conceded.

"Thanks," Joe said. "You've given me exactly what I needed." He got up to leave, but then paused for a moment. "There are likely going to be a couple of detectives coming to call in the next few days," he told the Indian. "I was never here, and you and I never had this conversation. So you can tell them whatever you like."

• • •

The call that came from Arnie Stiversen didn't surprise Joe nearly as much as he realized it should have.

"What the hell are you getting me into?" his former protégé inquired.

"What do you mean?" Joe responded.

"You show up, you don't tell me anything, you just ask me to do you a favor and hide a file, and not even two hours after that, two suits from Seattle show up, looking for that same file."

"What did you do?" Joe asked, because two suits from Seattle meant only one thing -- high-level attorneys.

"Played dumb, of course, like you wanted me to," Stiversen said. "But I got to tell you, I'm not anxious to get my neck stuck in a noose here."

"That's not going to happen, Arnie," Joe promised. "You have my word on it."

"Yeah, well, I hope so," the police officer said, relieved because he knew Joe Gideon was as good as his word.

"Meet me tonight, around six, at The Last Call," Joe added, because he now knew more than he had before. "And I'll tell you what's going on."

The location of the meet told the police officer two things -- that the file he had buried was somehow connected to the Lightfoot case, which he had already assumed, and that Joe Gideon wanted to tell him something he didn't want anyone else on the force to know about -- something Arnie Stiversen wasn't sure he wanted to know about, either.

"Okay," he said with a sigh.

At the same time that Arnie Stiversen was getting ready to meet with Joe Gideon, Roy Flynn and Teri Coello were sitting in Kent McAllister's office, reporting on the interviews that had taken up the better part of their Friday.

"If that bomb came out of one of those planes, it sure was a surprise to everyone we talked to," Flynn said.

"Is that a surprise to you?" McAllister asked.

"No, of course not," Coello said. "We're just trying to tell you we basically drew a blank. Let's face it, no one's going to jump up and admit they just happened to drop a pipe bomb on two unsuspecting women."

"Do you think it could be unrelated, someone out of another airport, another county, maybe just a holiday prank?" the chief inquired.

"Anything's possible," Flynn said. "But my money's on a local."

"Mine, too," Coello said. "I don't think this was any freak prank."

"Based on what?"

"Gut instinct, I guess," Flynn said, and Coello nodded. "I think this was personal. I think it was intentional. People around here know Lily is defending Lightfoot. No one out of county gives a damn what goes on here. All that hate mail she got, those other run-ins she had. The idea that someone else just happened to fly into Jackson County, and just happened to drop a pipe bomb on a remote cottage in the foothills where she just happened to be spending the weekend? No, I'm pretty sure this was about Lightfoot, and it was personal."

"I agree," Coello declared.

"Well, that may be," McAllister conceded, "but what can we do about it? You say you talked to everyone, and you got nowhere. And you've got no real evidence on anyone."

"We'd like to maybe take a look at some of the old cases," Flynn told him. "Cases that might have involved Lily or the Jansens, or maybe had to do with some kind of racial issues."

"Why would you want to do that?" McAllister asked sharply.

"To see what's there," Flynn replied. "To see if there are any dots we can maybe connect. This just doesn't come across like an isolated incident to us."

"Sounds like a big waste of time to me," the chief said.

"Would you rather that we dropped it?" Coello asked.

"On the chance that it's slipped your mind, we're a detective down and we've got a few other cases to work," McAllister reminded her. "I'd rather you put your time into something that might get us some results." He paused for a moment, and then added: "Do we have anything else we can look at on this, any other direction we can go in, other than the past?"

"Well, we have the bomb," Flynn said. "The lab boys have been taking a look at it. Maybe they can come up with something -- a signature maybe, that might tell us who made it."

"Okay, I suppose you can follow up on that," the chief said, rising, signaling that the discussion was at an end. "But keep me in the loop."

"Did that just strike you as a little weird?" Teri Coello asked her partner as they left McAllister's office and headed downstairs.

"What -- that the chief wasn't all that interested in our spending a lot more time on this case?"

"When you put it that way," she said, "yeah." They had worked as a team long enough that the two detectives tended to see things in a pretty similar way.

"Well, you got to remember that he's political, and we're not," Flynn told her. "And maybe sometimes, that means he has to look at things from a different perspective."

• • •

The Last Call Bar and Grill was enjoying what was a pretty normal Friday evening for the summer boating season -- the place was crowded and boisterous. As Arnie Stiversen made his way in, he met up with the owner, Billy Fugate.

"Evening, Officer," the barkeeper said. "Your friend's over there, waiting for you."

He pointed to a small table near the far wall, where the private investigator was indeed seated.

"Thanks," the Stiversen said.

"I really appreciate your coming," Joe said, pulling out the chair beside him.

"Like I had a choice," Stiversen said.

Joe had a pitcher of beer and two glasses in front of him. "Want some?" he asked.

"What kind?" Stiversen countered.

Joe shrugged. "I don't know," he said. "It's whatever's on tap."

"Sure," Stiversen said, and watched as his friend poured for both of them.

"Before I get into anything," the private investigator began, "I need you to tell me something -- something that stays just between you and me -- is there anyone in the department you wouldn't trust with your life?"

Stiversen stared at him. "You kidding?" he said. "How could I do the work I do, if I didn't trust the other people working with me? You worked there for twenty-five years, for Pete's sake -- what did you think? Did you think there was anyone you couldn't trust?"

"Well, let me put it another way," Joe countered. "Why do you think two suits from Seattle just happened to show up, looking for that particular file, at this particular time?"

Stiversen hesitated because it was pretty much the same question he had been asking himself. "You tell me," he said finally. "You got me into this, and now I need to decide what to do."

"All right, let me lay out a chronology for you," Joe said, taking a long swig of beer, and leaning forward in his chair. "Jason Lightfoot, a Native American, is arrested for killing Dale Scott. Lily is assigned as his attorney. As the news gets around, hate mail starts showing up at Lily's office. Her car gets keyed. Her tires get slashed. A rotten tomato is thrown at her. She gets sideswiped as she's walking across the street. She gets run off the road driving back from the jail. She almost gets killed by a pipe bomb thrown from a plane while she's spending a weekend at a cottage without her bodyguard."

"A plane?" Stiversen echoed. "It came from a plane? How do you know that?"

"Lily remembered. She saw it."

"Wow," the police officer breathed.

"Now add this," Joe continued. "The son of the owner of one of the twenty-two planes that were in the air at the time of the bombing was a suspect in an assault case twenty years ago, a case in which the victim, who was beaten half to death, just happened to be a Native American. And, as luck would have it, the best friend of this son who, by the way, was also a suspect in that assault case twenty years ago, just happens to have had a red Chevy Silverado that was conveniently reported missing around the same time that a red Chevy Silverado was reported being involved in two attacks on Lily -- the same kind of pickup, by the way, that then conveniently turned up burning a big hole in a field."

"You're kidding me," Stiversen said.

"Oh yes, and the son of that plane owner," Joe added, "turns out, he's not only a licensed pilot, he also happens to have been the one who filed the flight plan for his father's plane on Sunday, July 6th."

Stiversen let out a low whistle.

"There's more," Joe told him. "Another little story about this airplane owner's son and his good friend. Four years after the White Horse incident, while the two of them were enrolled at Washington State University, there was a girl at the school -- a freshman, who was there on a full scholastic scholarship. A bright, beautiful Native American girl from Omak who, it turns out, was pledging the very same sorority that the girlfriend of the airplane owner's son was pledging. And as the story goes, this Native American girl turned up missing exactly one day after the sorority accepted her -- but rejected the girlfriend. Her body was recovered ten days later, beaten almost beyond recognition."

"And you found this out how?"

"Once I was pointed in the right direction, all it took was a little digging," Joe explained. "Old newspaper accounts. Old police reports. And a good guy with a long memory."

"And you think?" Stiversen was almost afraid to ask.

"I don't think anything," Joe said. "What I know is that the minute the police over in Pullman started asking questions, two suits from Seattle swooped down and yanked those two boys right out of the university. The case went cold. No one's ever been charged. Now, tell me, how hard can it be to put together a Michael White Horse, a Native American girl from Omak, and a defense attorney, who's currently representing Jason Lightfoot -- coincidentally, another Native American?"

Stiversen drank his beer in one swallow. "And the minute someone was about to connect planes flying on July 6th to a specific pilot and an old assault case, the whole house of cards was in danger of collapsing. No wonder the suits showed up. Someone wanted that file to disappear."

"My question," Joe said softly, "is why would two suits from Seattle think they could walk right into the police department here in Port Hancock and just make a file disappear? Who would let them do that?"

Stiversen scowled into his empty beer glass. "I'm not sure I like where this is going," he said.

"I don't blame you," Joe agreed. "Look Arnie, you're here with me right now for one reason, and one reason only -- because I trust you. And I always have. I'd trust you with my life."

"Right back atcha, man," Stiversen said, and meant it.

"Okay then -- so tell me, who else in the department can you say that about?"

"Well, up to a few minutes ago, I would have had a simple answer to that question," Stiversen told him. "But now, I guess I might not be so sure. The thing is, the only two people who could have authorized handing over a file just like that would be the chief or the deputy chief. No one else could've done it. But you already knew that, didn't you?"

"How many in the department are up on the details of Lily's case?" Joe inquired.

"There's only six of us who've been working it steady," Stiversen said. "Me and Paul from the beginning -- the hate mail, her car, the Silverado, and all that. And then Roy Flynn and Teri Coello since the bombing, and of course Ben Dawson and Andy Cooper. I know Paul's young and can be a hothead sometimes, but he's a good cop. Besides, he doesn't know any more than I did before you filled me in. And I haven't said a word to him about it."

"And the others?"

"Ben and Andy, they're just about gathering evidence. As for Roy and Teri, I'd go to the wall for them," Stiversen declared. "If you're wanting to bring someone else in on this, they'd be my pick."

Joe nodded. "Kinda the way I saw it, too," he said.

"So what do we do now?"

"We invite Roy and Teri for a drink."

• • •

Lily picked up half of her chicken salad sandwich and took a bite. Along with her father and Dancer, she was having lunch on the patio, and she was pretty proud of how adept she was becoming at using her left hand.

"If I can do it, you can do it," Carson had told her. "And look on the bright side -- at least it's only a temporary inconvenience for you."

"Yes, but I'm getting so good at it, maybe I should never go back to being right-handed," she declared with a chuckle.

Carson chuckled in return. "I'll believe that the next time you need to sign your name on something official," he said.

"Well, maybe I'll be ambextrous then," she amended.

"What's that?"

"Ambex -- ambibex," she tried to say, but the word she wanted got lost somewhere and wouldn't come out.

"I think you mean am-bi-dex-trous." Carson said gently.

"Yes, that's what I meant," she said. "Am-bi-dex-truss. After all, I shouldn't let all this retraining go to waste."

"Never let it be said that you let anything go to waste," her father chided.

"From what I can see, she's letting a perfectly good fruit plate go to waste," Dancer observed.

"No, I'm not," she retorted. "I just haven't gotten to it yet."

As if to emphasize the point, she picked up her fork, poked it awkwardly into a big piece of melon, and proceeded to shove it into her mouth. "See?" she said, but both the word and the melon got caught in her throat, and she started to choke.

"Watch it there," Carson said, and Dancer reached over and slapped her a couple of times on the back.

She managed to spit out the errant piece of fruit, but she was still choking. Dancer reached for the water pitcher that sat in the middle of the table. The sky was cloudless, and as he raised the pitcher, sunlight glinted off it and, for an instant, the water seemed almost to glow.

Lily froze in mid-choke. "Gold," she croaked.

"What?" Carson asked.

"Gold," she repeated. "Metallic gold. The plane -- it was painted metallic gold, and there were two black stripes running along the side."

• • •

They met at The Last Call, at a back table only slightly larger than the one Joe and Stiversen had sat at the evening before. It was Saturday afternoon, the day and time having been chosen specifically because none of the three police officers was on duty.

The surrounding tables were empty, and only a few people sat at the bar, probably because it was still early -- barely past three o'clock, which suited Joe just fine. He didn't need any unauthorized ears around. He was the first to arrive, Stiversen following right behind, and the two detectives showing up ten minutes later.

"As you know, I've been working with Lily on the Lightfoot case," Joe began, once the obligatory pitcher of beer and glasses had been placed on the table, and they were more or less alone. "But when that bomb got dropped on the Jansen cottage, I guess you could say, my attention got a bit diverted."

"No one could blame you for that," Flynn said.

"At all," Coello added.

"Well, while my attention was diverted, I happened upon some rather interesting information," Joe continued. "Information that I think could be key to making the case. But the thing is, it doesn't do any good for me to have it, since I can't do much with it -- officially, I mean. And, too, Lily is recovering, and pretty soon she's going to be getting back to work. And since we're pretty much done with July, and the Lightfoot case is going to trial in a little over two months, that's going to have to be my priority."

"It was my idea for Joe to bring you in," Stiversen told the two detectives. "Obviously, because it's your case, but more important, because we trust you to do what's right."

At that, both Flynn and Coello hunched forward in their chairs.

"Well, you sure have our attention," Coello said.

"What I'd like to do," Joe said, "is to turn over what I've got to someone who can legitimately pursue it." He looked at the two detectives. "As Arnie says, it's your case, so the question is -- do you want what I've got?"

The two detectives looked at each other. "Lay it on us," Flynn invited, "and we'll see if we think we can do something with it."

Joe proceeded to do just that -- lay out for the detectives pretty much everything he had shared with Stiversen the day before.

"Wow," Coello said, when the private investigator was finished. "We weren't anywhere close to making that connection."

"Neither one of you was here when the assault went down," Joe told her. "You would have had no way of knowing. And when the victim recanted, the case was essentially closed. The fact that I remembered it helped me narrow the playing field, and then putting the rest together turned out to be pretty easy."

"When the victim recanted," Coello inquired, "did you believe him?"

Joe shrugged. "Didn't matter, had no choice at the time," he said. "But I suspected then, and I still do now, that there may have been coercion involved."

"I'd like to take this on," Flynn said. "The chief was trying to tell us, just yesterday, in fact, that we'd hit a blank wall, and it was time to move along, but I think maybe he'll have a change of perspective once he hears some of this."

"There's just one small hitch," Stiversen said with a sigh. "The assault case file -- two suits came looking for it yesterday."

"What do you mean?" Coello asked.

"I mean that two lawyers from Seattle showed up at the station yesterday, trying to get their hands on it, probably intending to make it disappear."

"Are you kidding?" Flynn exclaimed.

Stiversen shook his head. "Wish I was."

"Did they get it?"

"No, they didn't," he was told. "They sure looked for it, but it seems it might've gotten misplaced. Anyway, they couldn't find it."

"What does that mean?" Coello asked.

"It means you're going to have to tread very carefully," Joe said. "Attorneys from Seattle don't just waltz into the Port Hancock Police Department, wanting a case file, and expecting to get it. They have to be invited. Or at least given permission."

"And that kind of permission would have to come from pretty high up, don't you think?" Stiversen added.

"Who else knows about this?" Flynn asked.

"You mean, the suits and the file?" Joe replied.

"No, the plane."

"Other than Arnie, I've told just one other person, and Arnie says he's told no one." Joe said. "But I didn't know about the suits at the time, just about the plane. And I didn't remember the file until later. I don't know who else knows about the suits or the file. Arnie and I were hoping you might."

"You told the chief about the plane, didn't you?" Coello said.

"Yes," Joe confirmed. "And I assume he told the two of you, which is how come you know about it."

"Yes," Flynn said.

"The problem is, we have no way of knowing who else he might have told," Joe added.

Flynn frowned thoughtfully. "This information has opened up a whole new road for us to go down," he said finally, "and I think that I speak for Teri as well as myself when I say that we're willing to take it as far as it goes."

"You do indeed speak for me," Coello agreed. "After the chief told us about the plane, we interviewed all the owners of planes that were up that day, which is probably what triggered the suits showing up."

"But we sure as hell didn't give anyone permission to take the file," Flynn added. "We didn't even know about the assault case."

"I didn't think you did," Joe said. "Frankly, if I had, we wouldn't be here now, having this conversation."

Flynn nodded. "Joe, we'll keep you and Arnie in the loop on this," he assured them. "But until we know for sure what's going on here, I think we're going to be very careful about what we say, and who we'll say it to."

"I'm definitely on board with that," Coello confirmed.

"We were hoping you'd see it that way," Stiversen declared. With that, he produced the White Horse file. "This is what the suits didn't get when they showed up yesterday. Now it's yours, to do with as you see fit."

• • •

Joe drove to Morgan Hill, pulling up to the Burns' house just after five-thirty. Dancer met him outside.

"How'd it go?" the US Marshal asked.

"Just as we'd hoped," Joe told him. "Flynn and Coello are on board, and we can trust them."

Dancer nodded. "Good," he said.

"You know none of this would've happened if you hadn't told me about that Pullman case," Joe said. "Two incidents can maybe be a coincidence, but sure as hell not three."

"Some cases you just don't forget," Dancer said. "I'd been with the service maybe two or three years at the time. It was my first recovery."

"You think we should tell Lily?" the private investigator inquired.

"I don't know why not," Dancer replied. "I think she can handle it. As a matter of fact, she has something to tell you, too."

"What?"

"She can describe the plane."

Joe's jaw dropped. "Lead me to her!"

"You think Wayne Pierson and Grady Holt are the ones who dropped the bomb?" Lily exclaimed. "I can't believe it." She knew them both well enough. They had been one year behind her in school.

"Right now, they're sure looking good for it," Joe said.

"And when you get your mind around that, there's another piece of the puzzle that slides into place," Dancer said. "Grady Holt's uncle is none other than our good friend Officer Buzz Crandall. And you remember *him*, don't you?"

Lily's eyes widened. "You mean, the guy in the pickup -- the first guy, the one who almost ran me over -- that was Grady?"

"It all fits," Joe said. "It was his Silverado that sideswiped you. And then Crandall was driving it when you got run off the road. A little too convenient to be just a coincidence, I'd say. But you'll know for sure as soon as Port Hancock's finest get you in to identify Holt's voice. You do remember his voice, don't you?"

Lily nodded. "I'll never forget it." And then she laughed. "Oh wow!" she said. "You have no idea how great it is to be able to say that about something again -- that I'll never forget it."

"In that case, keep up the good work," the private investigator told her with a grin, "and you'll be back to your old ornery self in no time."

• • •

Dancer left his 4-Runner in the Jackson County Jail parking lot, and made his way to the third floor visiting room. Ever since the bombing, he had been coming to visit Jason Lightfoot. Since Dancer was not an attorney, regulations required that they meet on either side of a Plexiglas window, at opposite ends of a telephone, instead of in the private room where they had spent so many hours playing gin rummy and discussing the case with Lily. But Jason didn't mind all that much. He and Dancer could fill up an hour talking about anything and nothing before either of them even realized it.

"How's the lady lawyer doin'?" he always got around to asking.

"She's getting better every day," Dancer told him, always mindful that, unlike conversations with an attorney, every word they spoke was being recorded. "She's starting to remember all sorts of things now. As a matter of fact, she told me to tell you that, if she can get her memory back, after everything she's been through, she expects that you can do the same. I think that means it won't be long now before she'll be back to work."

"Yeah, well, that's good, I guess," Jason replied. "'Cause October's gonna be comin' around pretty soon."

• • •

It was almost seven when Joe parked his car in his garage and let himself into his cozy rambler on the outskirts of Port Hancock. His wife of twenty-nine years was waiting for him in the living room.

"I think I liked it better when you were with the Police Department," Beth Gideon called out when she heard the door to the garage close. "At least, then I knew when your shift ended you'd be on your way home."

"Sorry, Sweetheart," Joe said, coming into the living room to give his wife a kiss. It was then that he realized she wasn't alone. His son and his daughter were there as well, and he stopped short. "Uh-oh, what did I forget?" he asked.

"Well, that all depends," his son replied.

"Happy Birthday, Dad," his daughter declared.

"Today?" Joe said. "Is today the 27th?"

"All day," Beth told him. "And dinner's waiting."

"Well, let's not let it wait any longer," her husband said, leading the way to the dining room.

"And what's keeping you so busy these days, Dad?" his son asked when they were seated around the table, and Beth was serving up roast beef, baked potatoes, and corn on the cob.

"A murder, a couple of silly attempts at murder, and a bombing that almost resulted in murder," his father replied.

Alex Gideon was twenty-six years old, unmarried, but in a dating relationship that was threatening to become something more serious. He lived in Bellingham, up toward the Canadian border, where he was employed as a high school math teacher. He didn't get back to Port Hancock very often.

"That's a lot of cases to be juggling, isn't it?" he observed.

"Actually, as it turns out, it's all just one case," Joe told him.

"Sounds ugly," Tracy Gideon exclaimed. "I hope you're not in any danger. Retirement was supposed to be about getting you away from all that risky stuff, remember?" The twenty-four-year-old, who was also unmarried, worked in the emergency room at Seattle's Harborview Hospital.

"I promise you, I keep my nose to the ground, and out of harm's way," Joe assured her. "Anyway, all I do is the footwork."

"That means he gathers the information, and someone else gets to follow up on it," Beth said. She had struggled through twenty-five years of worrying about him, day and night, and she had no desire to see his current career become a repeat of his last.

Alex raised his wine glass. "In that case, happy birthday, Dad," he said. "And here's to many more to come."

• • •

Lily had been home for almost two weeks before she finally got up enough courage to approach Diana. She found the housekeeper in the laundry room on Tuesday afternoon, humming softly to herself as she sorted whites from colors. It was, Lily acknowledged, both ironic and appropriate.

"Okay, tell me, am I a racist?" she asked without preamble.

If she had taken Diana by surprise, the housekeeper didn't show it. "No more than most around here, I guess," she said.

Lily was dumbfounded. "I had no idea."

Diana, who knew she was in no danger of losing her job, eyed the attorney for a moment. "There are those who know what they are, and live by it," she said. "And then there are the rest who don't really think about it much, unless for some reason they have to."

"Have I ever said anything or done anything to offend you?"

"No, you haven't," the housekeeper conceded. "But sometimes attitudes can speak louder than words or actions."

"But I'm outraged over how the community feels about Jason Lightfoot," Lily declared.

"No, you're outraged about how the community feels about *you* because you're defending him," Diana corrected her. "We all know you didn't choose Jason to be your client -- he was forced on you. And you resent that because you feel the same way most everyone else around here does -- that he's guilty and doesn't deserve defending."

Lily opened her mouth to respond, but the right words weren't there for her to say -- because Diana Hightower was right. Her resentment had little to do with her knowing Lauren Scott and wanting justice for the murder of her husband, and more to do with what her professional life in Port Hancock was going to look like after she defended the Indian, and whether people would hold it against her to the point of seeking legal assistance elsewhere.

• • •

It didn't take long, or even much effort, for Flynn and Coello to confirm both the White Horse story and the Pullman story. Nor, the detectives discovered, were they the only instances of violence against Native Americans that Wayne Pierson and his friend Grady Holt had been involved in. A little digging uncovered a trail of incidents, going back years, that had been given short shrift by police across the state, thanks to high-powered attorneys from Seattle and more than likely, Flynn and Coello suspected, a generous greasing of palms.

There was no actual proof of anything, of course. There was the White Horse matter, in which the victim had recanted his identification of his assailants, and an even thinner case in the Pullman murder, where the two men now in question had been listed only as persons of interest, but had not been officially questioned by authorities before being whisked out of town. As for the rest, it was only hearsay, distant memories of police officers about distant cases -- eighteen cases, to be exact, over the past twenty years, involving the same two gentlemen. But it was enough to get the detectives to the Jackson County Prosecutor.

"Do you two know who you're dealing with?" John Henry inquired in surprise. "Walter Pierson wears some pretty big boots around these parts."

In fact, Walter Pierson was even bigger than that, and the detectives were well aware of it. His family had settled in Port Hancock before there even *was* a Port Hancock. He owned the largest bank in town that owned some seventy percent of the mortgages across the county -- thanks in no small part to his oldest son's interest in the largest real estate company in town, and his middle son's stewardship of the biggest title company in town.

He was a generous donor to the political party of his choice, and in fact, there wasn't a conservative cause he wouldn't champion, in a district that had once been reliably conservative. He was wined and dined in Olympia, and his support was routinely sought by conservative hopefuls across the state and beyond.

"We're willing to take the heat, if you are," Flynn told the prosecutor flatly.

"Between you and me," John Henry, whose family had been in Jackson County every bit as long as Pierson's had, said, "I hope you can nail the kid. He's always been bad news. And it wouldn't hurt if the old man got taken down a peg or two, either. Let's just not be in any big rush to tell the mayor, okay?"

Flynn and Coello exchanged glances. The last piece to the puzzle, perhaps, about the White Horse file and the two suits from Seattle.

Arnie Stiversen didn't ask how, but bright and early on Wednesday morning, warrants were issued to search the private plane of one Walter Pierson, and to search the homes of Walter Pierson's youngest son, Wayne Pierson, and his longtime friend, Grady Holt. The Presiding Judge of Jackson County, Grace Pelletier, signed the warrants herself.

"What do you think you're doing?" Kent McAllister barked when Flynn and Coello declared their intent to execute the warrants.

"Our job," Flynn told him.

"Then why didn't you run this through me, first?" the police chief snapped. "I thought you were to going to keep me in the loop on this."

"And that's exactly what we're doing," Flynn said.

"I mean, before you went after the warrants."

"I'm sorry, but you weren't available when we made the decision," Coello said, which was true. McAllister had been in a closed-door meeting with the mayor. "So we took it to the prosecutor ourselves. It was routine. John Henry didn't seem to have a problem with it. Neither did Judge Pelletier. I'm not sure I understand why you do."

"I assume you've got something that looks like probable cause here?" the chief said, ignoring the implication.

"We do," Flynn assured him. "And it would be best if we got to serve these warrants without someone tipping off the Piersons first."

McAllister glared at him. "I don't think I like the sound of that," he snapped.

"And we didn't like the idea of two suits from Seattle showing up last week, trying to interfere with our investigation."

Roy Flynn had been with the Port Hancock Police Department for nineteen years, and Teri Coello, going on twelve. Kent McAllister had had his job for nine.

"I wasn't aware that anyone was interfering in your investigation," the chief said sharply.

"Good," Flynn said. "We were a little concerned about politics getting in the way of police work."

McAllister bridled at that. "Go serve your warrants," he said. "And when you come up empty, I'll expect apologies all around. And I can assure you the Piersons will, too."

"Do you think he'll warn the mayor?" Coello asked as they were leaving the station.

"Not if he knows what's good for him," Flynn replied. "We gave him cover -- he didn't know about it until it was done. If he's as smart as I think he is, he'll hide behind it."

They met up with Stiversen and Cady in the parking lot. And shortly after that, they were joined by Ben Dawson and Andy Cooper.

"What's going on?" Dawson asked.

"We're going to do a little investigating," Coello said. "We're looking for anything to do with a bomb."

"A bomb?" Cooper echoed.

"Yes, a bomb," Coello confirmed. "As in the bomb that demolished the Jansen cottage."

"Arnie, you and Andy ride with Teri," Flynn directed. "Paul and Ben, you two come with me. We'll serve the home warrants first." He nodded to Coello. "You take the Holt place," he said "And we'll do Pierson."

If there was going to be trouble, he knew it would come from Pierson, and he didn't want his partner taking the heat.

"Why not do the airport first?" Stiversen asked. "We know what we're looking for there."

"Just in case the chief has a change of heart," the detective said for the officer's ear only. "I doubt they built the bomb in the plane, anyway, which makes getting to the homes as soon as possible more important."

"What the hell's going on?" Cady wanted to know as soon as he, Cooper and Flynn were in Flynn's police car and on their way to Wayne Pierson's home.

"The less you know, the better," Flynn told him. "As far as you're concerned, you're simply serving a search warrant that was issued in connection with the bombing at the Jansen cottage."

Cady whistled softly.

• • •

Wayne Pierson lived alone in a tidy, three-bedroom home at the south end of his father's hundred-acre property just west of the Port Hancock city limits. The thirty-four-year-old was divorced, with a ten-year-old son who lived most of the time with his ex-wife. He was worked as the assistant manager at his father's bank.

He was not at home when the police arrived, so Detective Flynn and Officer Cady went up to the main house, an exquisite Edwardian mansion, at least five thousand square feet in size, and rang the bell. The woman who answered the door identified herself as the housekeeper when Flynn produced his badge.

"Mr. Pierson hasn't come downstairs yet this morning," she said. "You can leave a card, if you like, and he can get back to you."

"We don't need him to get back to us," Flynn replied. "We're here to serve a search warrant on the home of his son, Wayne Pierson. Since there is no one at home there at the moment, we have two choices. We can get a key from someone here, or we can break down the door."

The housekeeper blinked. "I really don't think Mr. Pierson would appreciate your breaking into his son's home," she said.

"Then it would probably be a good idea if someone provided us with a key," Flynn suggested.

"Wait just a moment, please," the housekeeper said, and hurried up a grand staircase.

Five minutes later, man in his seventies, wearing pajamas and a robe, came stomping down the same flight of stairs, with the aid of a cane.

"Who the hell do you think you are?" he demanded, eyeing the man in plain clothes and the man in uniform. "Coming to my house at this hour of the morning, and telling my housekeeper you're going to break my son's door down?"

"Actually, I'm the same detective who interviewed you about your private plane on Friday afternoon, Mr. Pierson," Flynn reminded him. "And this officer and I have with us a warrant that gives us permission to search your son's home."

"A search warrant?" the man bellowed. "Who let you get a search warrant?"

"The Jackson County Prosecutor and the Presiding Judge," the detective replied.

"You saying Kent McAllister approved this?"

"I'm afraid the chief of police wasn't available when we decided to get the warrant."

"You have one hell of a nerve," Pierson declared, brandishing his cane, "and I'll have your badges over this."

"You're free to do whatever you think you need to do, sir, but we have work to do, and very little time to waste," Flynn said mildly, even as he took a small step back and, behind him, Cady quietly slid his hand over his holstered service weapon. "We gave you the courtesy of coming up here, and asking politely before we acted. So, the only question is -- do you want to give us the key to your son's home, or do you want us to enter by force?"

The old man stared malevolently at the detective for a full minute before he realized that Flynn was not going to back down. "Harriet, go get the key to the boy's place," he snapped at the housekeeper over his shoulder. "My son is at work, and I'll expect you to leave his home in exactly the same condition as you find it."

Thank you, sir," Flynn said. "I assure you we'll be as quick and as careful as possible."

The hour-long search didn't turn up anything suspicious, no unregistered weapons, no radical literature, no bomb-making materials, and they were about to give it up when Paul Cady called out from the master bedroom. He had happened upon a small safe, hidden away at the back of the closet, and he had pulled it out and unceremoniously broken it open. Inside, he found a thick file and a laptop computer.

"Hey, Roy, you're not going to believe this," he told the detective. Inside the file were dozens of old clippings, from various newspapers around the state, going back almost two decades, detailing incident after incident of racially motivated violence, from physical abuse to property damage -- all unresolved.

"Guess he just couldn't help himself," Flynn observed, peering over Cady's shoulder and shaking his head in disgust. "I bet he has a real bad habit -- pulls this out any time he needs a high, and gets himself off reliving his past accomplishments."

"There's got to be more than a dozen cases in here," Cady declared.

"Well, they might prove he's a racist," Flynn said, "but unfortunately, it's not going to prove he had anything to do with the bombing."

"No, but this might," Ben Dawson said. He had followed Flynn into the bedroom and turned on the computer, only to find it was password protected. "Who lives alone and still protects a computer that's kept in a closet unless it's got something to hide?" he wondered aloud.

"Can you get into it?" Flynn asked.

Dawson shook his head. "Not my specialty, I'm afraid," he said. "But get hold of someone who can, and I'd be willing to bet you'll find what you're looking for."

"Okay, it goes with us," Flynn told him. "Now let's pack it up, and get out of here -- before we overstay our welcome."

At that moment, his cell phone rang.

"I think you might want to get over here," Coello said.

• • •

Grady Holt's mother was at home when the police rang the doorbell of a classic bungalow at the edge of Old Town.

"You can't just come barging in here like this," she cried. "I've got rights."

"Yes, Ma'am, I'm afraid we can," Coello told her, showing her the warrant.

"Well, my son isn't here. Can you wait while I call him?"

"You're certainly free to call him," Coello said, "but we aren't going to wait."

Splitting up, it took them about an hour to declare the house clean, and then another five minutes to find the locked room at the back of the separate garage. When Holt's mother claimed she didn't know where the key was, they broke the lock, after which it took less than ten seconds to find what they were looking for -- a counter, running the length of the back wall, that was littered with pieces of pipe, two inches in diameter, Teflon tape, zip-lock freezer bags, wooden matches, firecrackers, tiny nails, small ball bearings, and a significant amount of gunpowder.

"Wow," Cooper breathed. "There's a lot of stuff here. Too much, as a matter of fact. You think maybe they're not done yet, that they've got some other targets in mind?"

"What I think is that we need to photograph every square inch of this place before we start processing," Coello told him. "And then we need to call in reinforcements."

• • •

Joe was still at the office when the news he had been waiting for came in.

"We got everything we needed from the Holt place -- bombs in the making, fingerprints, DNA, the works," Flynn told him.

"That's just great," Joe said.

"I'm sure we'll get a match to Holt, and I think the chances are pretty good we'll get a match to Pierson, as well," the detective continued. "And something else you can tell Lily. Of all the planes at the airfield, there was only one we had a warrant to search -- and it just happened to be one that was painted metallic gold with a double black stripe."

"That's real good work, Roy," Joe said. "I'll tell her."

"We got hold of Pierson's computer, too," Flynn concluded. "And as soon as we find someone who can get inside it, I'm thinking we'll be able to throw the book at both of them."

"Computer?" Joe echoed. "You found a computer at Pierson's place?"

"Yep. It was in the closet in Wayne's bedroom."

Joe thought about the ironies of life, and about a man who, after twenty years, might finally have the opportunity to even the score. "I think I just may know the person who'd be able to help you out there," the private investigator informed the detective.

Michael White Horse was only too happy to oblige when Joe came knocking on his door again and explained the situation. And with the private investigator's assistance, he was at police headquarters less than an hour later.

"There might be a little poetic justice in this," Joe told the man in the wheelchair.

White Horse laughed. "Even after all this time," he said, "I have to tell you -- nothing would please me more."

Flynn wheeled him into one of the interview rooms, where Stiversen, Dawson and Cooper were waiting. "To preserve chain of custody," he explained, and then a twinkle appeared in his eye, "and to maybe teach Ben and Andy here a thing or two."

It took the computer programmer less than ten minutes to get into Wayne Pierson's laptop. "Not all that sophisticated," he said.

"Anything that can help us?" Dawson asked anxiously, after White Horse had been poking around for about half an hour.

"Well, how about half a dozen different searches for how to build a pipe bomb?" White Horse replied. "Will that help?"

"You got to be kidding!" Stiversen gasped, and he dashed out to find Flynn.

"It's all right here, plain as day," the computer programmer told the detective as soon as he came in. "He didn't encrypt anything. He didn't even try to erase anything -- although I could probably still have found it, even if he had. He's an amateur."

Flynn grinned broadly. "Well now, then, there," he said, "let's see his father try to get him out of this one."

Six

It was the middle of August before Lily felt confident enough to return to the office, and get back to work.

Her memory was still spotty -- and things she remembered one minute she discovered she could just as easily forget the next. Sometimes, she found that she had difficulty speaking -- that words didn't come out of her mouth the way she intended them to. Or she would hear herself repeating things for no reason. And more often than she liked, she had difficulty concentrating, and then she would get frustrated with her inability to keep things straight.

She spoke to Amanda about it. "How can I get up in a courtroom and represent a client if I can't even trust that the words that are going to come out of my mouth are going to come out right, or that I won't throw a tantrum in front of a jury?"

"If it becomes a problem, we'll deal with it," her friend assured her.

In fact, Amanda had already spoken with someone -- a therapist who was having significant success working with veterans from Iraq and Afghanistan, and with professional athletes who had suffered traumatic brain injuries.

According to the doctors, the swelling in Lily's brain had receded, her lung was working properly again, and her ribs had pretty much healed themselves. She still had the cast on her arm, but that was scheduled to come off in a just few more weeks. What would be left were the scars from the shrapnel and the glass. They might fade with time, but she knew she would always be able to see them, even if they were just in her mind.

She knew how lucky she had been, how close she had come. And she knew she had put her best friend in unspeakable jeopardy. More than anything, it made her angry -- angrier than she could ever remember being. But that anger was not directed only at the two men who had tried their best to blow her to smithereens.

Before she returned to work, Lily knew she had to take a good long look in the mirror. While she had never thought of herself as prejudiced, Diana had hit a nerve. It was true that she had not gone out of her way to befriend Native Americans or accept them as clients, and had maybe, without being consciously aware of it, even seen them as somehow lesser. It was true that she had, from the beginning, seen not just the Lightfoot case, but Jason Lightfoot, himself, as losers. And it was true that she treated John Dancer, who had come all the way across the state just to protect her, more as an employee than as an associate. And it was also true that she had had no intention of wasting any more of her time and energy on this trial than was absolutely necessary.

Now the realization that the behavior of a few stupid men -- who had simply acted on impulses that she, herself, harbored -- had become more than just an eye-opener. And she was not only angry, she was ashamed. And that shame fueled a transition she welcomed, but had never expected.

Before the bombing, she had resigned herself to losing the Lightfoot case -- to be honest, maybe even looked forward to it. Now, she was determined to fight the good fight. She might well lose, she understood, but at least Jackson County would know there had been a battle.

It helped that Wayne Pierson and Grady Holt had been arrested. And that Buzz Crandall had been suspended without pay from the Jackson County Jail pending the outcome of assault charges against him. Lily had given a full statement to John Henry regarding both incidents with the Silverado, as well as the plane that had dropped the bomb. But she knew it wasn't enough. She knew the rest would have to come from her.

"Broad Street," she announced to Dancer as soon as breakfast had been eaten, and she had gathered her things together.

"Yes, Ma'am!" the bodyguard replied with a broad smile.

When she marched into the Broad Street Victorian, she was loaded for bear, hugging Wanda and pouncing on Megan. "All right, we're eight weeks from trial," she told her paralegal. "Bring on the Lightfoot case!"

There wasn't much. Crime scene photos that showed Dale Scott lying in a pool of his own blood, a bullet hole in his head. And there was the ballistics test that had matched the bullet to the detective's own gun -- the gun that was found in the possession of Jason Lightfoot. And gunshot residue, DNA tests, and fingerprints that proved the Indian had indeed fired the weapon.

In addition, there were a number of injuries to the victim's face and body, including those not unlike the ones Jason had suffered at the hands of Paul Cady, clearly indicating that there had been a physical interaction of some sort prior to his death. And blood alcohol tests, performed approximately twelve hours after the crime, suggested that Lightfoot had no alcohol in his system.

She picked up the police file on the Indian. It wasn't thin. It went back almost twenty years. There were fourteen separate times that Scott had cited him for drunk and disorderly conduct. But there was no record of violence on the part of Lightfoot associated with any of the charges, at least nothing that was serious enough that it earned him more than a night in jail and a minor fine. There was one instance of him urinating on a fire hydrant, another of him doing some kind of chant at the top of his lungs at three o'clock in the morning, and an accusation of petty theft that was eventually dismissed when the clerk at the fast food shop was unable to pick him out of a lineup.

What had happened this time to make it so different, she wondered. What had gone down -- that had not gone down so many times before -- that had incited a fight that had escalated into murder? And, whether her client wanted her to or not, what could she possibly find in these few pages that might help mitigate the crime, at least so far as to remove the death penalty from consideration?

"What about self-defense?" Megan, the brown-haired, brown-eyed paralegal, suggested. "If there was a fight, maybe Jason feared for his life."

Lily frowned. "If Dale was attempting to arrest Jason, and Jason resisted, and a fight started that ended with Dale's death, that's not going to get us to self-defense," she said. "Resisting arrest is a crime in itself." She flipped back and forth through the file. "If we can't find something else, we're going to be stuck with with "

She stopped in mid-sentence, shaking her head back and forth, as if to clear it, searching for the words that had been on the tip of her tongue just a few seconds ago.

"With diminished capacity?" Megan asked gently.

"Right -- dim-in-ished cap-a-city," Lily repeated, frustrated with herself. "Which means we have to be able to prove he was not just drunk -- he was drunk out of his mind."

. . .

"Hey, how ya' doin', Lady Lawyer?" Jason Lightfoot said when he was ushered into the visiting room. "Long time no see."

"I'm doing okay, Jason," Lily replied. "Sorry it's been so long since I've been here."

"That's okay," he said. "Your bodyguard kept me company." He looked her up and down. "Guess you had a few other things on your mind."

She smiled. "If you think I look bad now, you should have seen me a month ago."

"You don't look so bad," he assured her. "It's the two who did that to you that are gonna look bad once I get done with them. From what Dancer here says, I figure we're all gonna end up in the same place."

"Never mind that," she said. She looked him over carefully. "How are *you* doing, Jason?"

"I been better, I guess," he replied. "But I ain't doin' so bad. Your friend Parker -- now he's been a real help."

"I'm glad to hear it," she said. "Any chance you've remembered anything that could help us?"

He shrugged his shoulders. "Not yet, at least not anythin' you'd be interested in knowin' about," he replied. "The memory -- it just keeps comin' and goin'."

"Well, I wish I could say I didn't," she told him with a dry chuckle, "but I know exactly what you mean."

• • •

"I must be missing something," Lily said over dinner at the Morgan Hill house.

Carson Burns looked up from his carefully cut up braised pork chop. "Are you being critical of Diana's cooking?" he asked.

"Very funny," she said, making a face at him. It was Friday evening, she had been mulling over the Lightfoot case all week, and she was plainly frustrated. "The Lightfoot case -- I can't figure it out."

"What can't you figure out?" Dancer asked.

"Why this time was different," she said. "The guy has a record going back years. But it was all small stuff, and there was never any violence."

"You mean, on Jason's part," Carson reminded her.

"That's right," she said. "He's got over a dozen D&Ds on his record, and each time, they haul him in without resistance, he pays a fine, he sleeps it off, and that's it."

"But Dale was the one who used to beat up on him, wasn't he?"

"Yes, I know, I know Dale was a bully, and he liked to take his frustration out on people like Jason," she conceded. "But my point is -- there's no evidence, anywhere in the record, that Jason ever resisted. And there's nothing to explain why, this time, he goes off the deep end, gets into a fight with Dale, and then winds up putting a bullet in his head. If I'm going to argue diminished capacity, I'm going to have to explain to a jury what was different this time -- unlike all those other times they had run-ins -- that caused him to do what he ended up doing. And the problem is, I can't even explain it to myself."

"Did you ask your client?" Carson inquired.

"I did -- he doesn't remember a thing."

"Everyone has his breaking point," Dancer suggested. "Maybe he reached his. Maybe it had nothing to do with Dale Scott. Maybe it was about something else entirely, and Scott just happened to be in the wrong place at the wrong time."

"Now that's a thought," Lily was willing to concede. "But if my client doesn't have a clue what it was, how am I supposed to figure it out?"

"Maybe what you ought to do is take a totally different approach," her father suggested.

"A different approach?" she echoed. "What do you mean?"

"You're trying to figure out why your client killed a police officer. Maybe the best way to do that is to start from the other direction."

"What other direction?"

"Well, I assume you're going on the assumption that Lightfoot is guilty, right?"

"Of course."

"So, instead of assuming he's guilty, why not, just for the sake of argument, assume that he's innocent?"

"But he isn't," she reminded him. "Remember -- he fired the gun."

"Maybe he is and maybe he isn't," her father conceded. "But, tell me -- how do you defend a guilty client?"

Lily sighed because she knew the answer to that question better almost than she knew her own name -- even her muddled up brain couldn't forget it. "By working twice as hard as I would for an innocent one," she recited.

"Exactly," Carson declared.

"So if I give the case the same scrutiny I would give it if I believed Jason Lightfoot was innocent," she said slowly, almost to herself, "I might just find out what put him over the top that night."

• • •

Lily mulled over her father's suggestion all weekend, and on Monday morning she went looking for Joe Gideon.

"Just the man I want to see," she said brightly when she found him in the kitchen, making himself a cup of coffee from the community Keurig. "I'm in need of your expertise."

"For you, anything," he replied. "What's up?"

"The Lightfoot case."

"Of course, what could I possibly have been thinking?" the private investigator said with a chuckle. "What about it?"

"I want to take a whole different look at it," she told him. "Starting with everything."

"Everything?" he repeated.

"Everything," she said. "If I'm going to beat the grim reaper, I have to find something I haven't found yet."

"But isn't your client the one who says he'd rather die than spend the rest of his life in prison?" the private investigator inquired.

"He's the one," Lily confirmed. "But I can't care about that right now. Whatever he may say he wants, my job is to defend him, and in order to do that, I need to know everything about what went on in that alley. So, make this whole scene come to life for me, my friend. And while you're at it, dig hard around the edges of Jason, too -- dig real hard. I want to know everything there is to know about him. I want to know what it was -- good or bad -- that pushed him over the edge that night."

Joe whistled appreciatively. "Well now, you've got the blood boiling this morning, haven't you?" he teased.

"You'll have a copy of everything I've got in an hour," Lily declared.

"Yes, Ma'am!"

"Good morning, Wanda, it's a whole new day," she said, as she marched out of the kitchen and greeted the receptionist. "Make a copy of the Lightfoot file for Joe, will you, please? Absolutely everything we have. Don't skip a page." It was a joke, of course. The whole file didn't add up to fifty pages.

"And good morning to you, too," Wanda said. "I'm on it."

Lily put Megan to work, too. "Haunt the prosecutor's office," she instructed. "Make a list of every bit of information we should have, and then make sure we have it. And if we don't have it, do whatever you have to do to get it."

Megan grinned. "And who put a bee in your bonnet this morning?" she asked.

"My father," Lily acknowledged.

This might not have been the case she would have chosen, but it was the case she had. And the redemption she needed. And like it or not, Jason Lightfoot was going to get the best legal representation of his life.

• • •

Charles Graywolf was sixty-eight years old. He pulled on his jeans and his work boots, tied his long white hair back at the neck, and farmed every day of his life. His family was grown and gone, but there was still his wife and himself to provide for, and of course his sister, who was doing her best to drink herself to death. Except for that part, he didn't mind doing what he did at his age. It gave him a reason to get out of bed in the morning.

"Jason's a good boy," he told the private investigator who knocked on his door. "Responsible. Honest. Worked hard. Never complained about anything. And never asked for nothin' in his life he wasn't entitled to."

"Did he ever mention the police officer he killed?" Joe asked. "Did he ever say anything about there being any bad blood, or any kind of issue, between them, or that he held a grudge against him of any kind?"

"You talkin' about that Scott fella?" Graywolf shook his head. "Jason never held no grudge against no one -- never even heard the name before what happened," he replied. "From then on, of course, that's all there was to read about in the papers and hear about on the news -- all about some big long feud between them two that I can tell you never was."

"How often did you see your nephew?"

"After he got hurt bad that time on the boat, and before all this stuff happened and he got himself arrested, I saw him just about every Sunday. He'd hitch a ride out here from town. And if he couldn't hitch, he'd walk. Ten miles. Bad for his leg, but he did it anyway. Spent the afternoons with his mother, though she didn't know it half the time, poor woman. Then he'd come and have supper with me and the wife. After that, I'd drive him back to town, over to that bar where he was workin'."

"And he never talked about Dale Scott?"

Graywolf shook his head. "He never once mentioned the cop, or that he was havin' trouble with anyone. He never had a mean word to say about nobody, not even the folks that stiffed him for work he did. He always said they probably had it tougher than he did."

"And that Sunday?"

"As far as I remember, that Sunday wasn't no different than any other," Graywolf said. "He came. He spent time with his mother. He ate his dinner. He left."

"What time was that, exactly?" Joe asked.

"Same as always," the Indian said. "I had him over to the bar by nine o'clock." He shook his head. "I gotta tell you, Mister, I don't know what happened after I left him off. He was perfectly fine when he got out of the truck, and he was thinkin' perfectly clear, as far as I could tell. So he had to have been provoked real bad to do anything like what it is they're sayin' he did."

• • •

Miss Polly Peterson ran the Bayview Avenue Boarding House, and had been running it for more than forty years. A round, comfortable spinster woman in her late seventies, she had seen them all come and go in her time -- from the misplaced and the displaced, to the proud and the pitiful, to those on their way up and those on their way down, to those who were simply passing through.

"And which of those categories would you say Jason Lightfoot falls into?" Joe inquired from an overstuffed chair in the parlor of the scrupulously tidy Victorian, as he politely tried to balance a cup of coffee and a plate with fresh blueberry muffins on his knees.

"Jason?" Miss Polly replied with a bright smile. "Oh, he doesn't fit into any of them. He's a lovely boy."

Joe's eyebrows shot up. It was certainly not a term that he would have used to describe the Indian. "How so?" he asked.

"He's sweet-tempered, he's got a good heart, and he wouldn't hurt a soul," she told the investigator. "I don't care what others may be saying. They don't know him the way some of us do. And not one of us who really knows that boy can even begin to understand what all this nonsense is about."

"He killed a policeman," Joe reminded her.

"If he did, and mind you, I'm not saying that I believe he did any such thing, then he must have had a real good reason," Miss Polly declared. "The Jason I know would go a mile out of his way not to so much as step on a spider. And he's had a lot of opportunities, too. All those people he's done for over the years who never paid him, just took advantage of his good work and his good nature. Believe me, he's had plenty of reason and plenty of opportunities. And he never did anything to any of them."

"I take that to mean you like him?"

Miss Polly nodded. "I most certainly do," she said without the slightest hesitation. "I know he has his problems with his mother -- her going into such a funk over losing his dad, and turning to the bottle and all. And I know he has trouble with the bottle, himself. But he's a good boy. I tried for years to get him to come stay with me, instead of living in that box of his. Told him -- breakfast, lunch, dinner, laundry, and a clean room. It wouldn't cost him a penny. Told him he could fix things up around the place for his rent, and I wouldn't take advantage of him. But he always just smiled and said he'd do for me anytime I wanted, but he liked living in that box. Although I'm sure I don't know why."

"You think it was something about him wanting to be his own man, maybe?" Joe asked.

"Maybe," Miss Polly conceded. "But then again -- if he'd done what I told him he should do, well maybe he wouldn't be in the situation he's in now, would he?"

• • •

Joe sat at the bar, nursing a beer, as he waited.

The Last Call Bar & Grill -- a bit dark, a bit seedy, with well-worn wooden floors, good beer on tap, and the irresistible smell of hearty cooking -- was, for the most part, frequented by what the locals called boat people. Billy Fugate had worked the docks in his youth and had learned, firsthand, just how much dockhands and fishermen liked their liquor. He had bought the place from the previous owner's widow some thirty years ago.

"Hear tell you wanna talk to me?" he said.

"Sure do, if you've got a few minutes," Joe replied.

"I been waitin' six months for someone to come talk to me," the barkeeper said, leaning thick arms on the polished mahogany bar that had already seen over a century of use. "But nobody ever did. And now you come along, and hell, you ain't even a cop no more."

"You mean, the police never interviewed you?" Joe said, surprised.

"Nope," Billy declared. "Don't know how many times I told Dancer, it ain't right -- they want to convict a man for murder, they should at least talk to the people who know him."

Joe smiled at that. "I take that to mean Dancer's a regular here."

"As a matter of fact, he is," Billy conceded. "We were real happy when he showed up to watch out for Miss Lily. And even though he thinks different, and still beats himself up over it, it wasn't his fault -- what happened to her."

"Well then, you were probably wondering why we didn't show up to talk to you, either."

"Not really," the barkeeper said. "Dancer told me you'd get around to it, sooner or later, and looks like he was right. So now you're here, and seein' as you're on Jason's side, I'll be happy to help you any which way I can."

"You like him, do you?" Joe asked.

"Jason? Known him since he was sixteen," Billy replied. "It's not just that he's a good kid, there are lots of good kids in the world, it's that there ain't a mean bone in that whole body."

"You know him that well?"

"Know him well enough to know that whatever he may have done that night, if he actually done it, he done it for a good reason."

"All right, talk to me," Joe invited.

"The cop was a bully," Billy said flatly.

"How do you mean?"

"He used to patrol around here, back before he got promoted," the barkeeper replied. "And he'd hang around late, you know, on purpose, just lookin' to cause trouble, and then dishin' out more than was necessary. Like he wasn't gettin' enough of somethin' at home, you know what I mean? So what if a guy has a little too much to drink? Don't mean he belongs in jail -- just means he belongs in bed."

"Was he hanging around that night?" Joe asked.

Billy shook his head. "No, that's the thing, you see," he said. "Not since he got promoted to detective.

After then, it wasn't his job no more -- hasslin' us kind of folk like he used to. Only time we seen him since then was when he come in as a customer, maybe once a month. It was kinda weird, too -- he'd show up just before closin', order a beer he never paid for, then leave half of it. And I don't mind tellin' you, we didn't take too kindly to it. A lot of folks who come in here are people who maybe had reason to know him -- he'd show up, and sure enough, ten minutes later, the place would be pretty much cleared out."

"Did you see him that night -- the night he was killed?"

The barkeeper shook his head. "Nope. Don't mean he wasn't at some other place around town, but he wasn't here."

The private investigator sighed. "Was Jason drunk that night?"

"Jason is drunk pretty much every night," Billy replied. "I wish it wasn't so, but I ain't his keeper, and that's the way he chooses to live his life."

"How drunk is drunk?" Joe probed.

"He takes his rum neat," the barkeeper said. "Six, seven shots a night wouldn't be unusual for him. He eats, he works, and he drinks his rum. Then he goes out back, to his box, and goes to bed."

"Did he have six or seven shots of rum that night?"

"Matter of fact, he had seven," Billy confirmed. "Poured 'em out for him myself, like I did every night. Said he was gonna be workin' on a new boat the next mornin' and he needed to get a good night's sleep."

"And after drinking seven shots of rum, how would you describe his demeanor?"

Billy thought about that for a moment. "That night wasn't no different from any other night," he said finally. "He wasn't no different. And he went out under his own steam."

"What time would you say he left?"

"Sunday nights, we close up at eleven. So it was maybe half an hour, forty-five minutes after that."

Joe looked around. "Do people use the back door much to come and go?" he asked, hoping, although no one had yet come forward, that there might have been a witness to what had happened in the alley that night.

Billy frowned at the question. "Nope," he replied. "Other than me, sometimes, Jason's the only one who's got cause to go out back."

"Okay then," Joe pressed, "when he left here that night, did he look like he maybe had a chip on his shoulder about something, or was looking to start something with someone?"

"If you're askin' whether he said anythin' about havin' it in for anyone, or if he was havin' trouble with anyone, the answer is, Jason don't share much about himself. But if you're askin' how he was that night, I can tell you this -- when he left here, he wasn't lookin' to get into anythin' but his own bed. Whatever happened after that, if you want my opinion," the barkeeper said, "that cop probably got exactly what he deserved."

"Thanks for your time," Joe said, dropping a bill on the bar for the beer, but Billy shook his head and pushed it right back.

"Just help Jason," he said.

With the barkeeper's permission, Joe let himself out the back door and stood in the middle of the alley, halfway between the bar and the stone wall where Jason's box had been wedged, looking first up toward the business district, and then down at the docks that were practically within hailing distance. He wondered what had happened that night when Jason Lightfoot had come out of the bar and met up with Dale Scott. What had started the fight? Why had it escalated into a shooting? All the questions he had once asked himself as a police officer working a crime he was asking again, but now from the other side of the fence.

The private investigator scratched thoughtfully at his busted left ear because one more question had just occurred to him that had little, if anything, to do with Jason Lightfoot. If Dale Scott no longer laid in wait for

Billy Fugate's customers, as the barkeeper claimed, and Joe had good reason to believe since he knew that patrolling for drunks wasn't part of a detective's job description, and if he hadn't been a customer at The Last Call -- then what had he been doing in the back alley on that Sunday night in February?

It was a little after six o'clock, and there were at least half a dozen other bars at this end of Broad Street. Joe pulled out his cell phone and called Beth.

• • •

"Over here," Arnie Stiversen shouted over the crowd noise as he caught sight of Joe coming through the front door of The Hangout.

"Thanks for meeting me," Joe replied, dropping onto the barstool beside his former colleague.

"Any time," Stiversen said with a smile. "Still working the long hours, I see."

"Yup," Joe confirmed.

"Okay, you called me," the police officer declared, as soon as a bottle of beer had been placed on the bar in front of his friend. "So, what can I do for you that I can do for you without jeopardizing my job any more than I already have?"

Joe chuckled before he frowned. "I guess what I want to know is how come Dale was where he was on the night he was killed?"

It was past nine, and Joe had been to every bar on both sides of lower Broad Street and then to every other bar within a reasonable distance of the place in the back alley where Scott's body had been found.

"What do you mean?"

"I mean, was there an operation going down that night that he was involved in? Was there a raid that had been planned? Was he meeting a contact? I guess what I'm getting at, what I'm trying to figure out is -- what was he doing in the back alley that night?"

Stiversen looked blank. "I don't know as I've got an answer for you," he said. "Nobody ever said anything about what he was doing there. I'm not even sure the question ever came up. We just assumed he was out on his own and something in the alley caught his attention. Maybe the chief would know more."

"I guess I'll have to ask him," Joe said.

"Go ahead," Stiversen said, gesturing with his head. "He's down at the other end."

Sure enough, when he looked past his friend, Joe could see the police chief seated at the far end of the bar, engaged in an animated conversation with Port Hancock's mayor.

"To tell you the truth, I haven't a clue," Kent McAllister said, when Joe made his way over. "Dale and Randy worked the docks as part of their drug detail, but there was no operation on for that night -- at least, not one I was aware of. In fact, best as I recall, neither one of them was even on the schedule for that night. But you might double-check with Randy about that."

· · ·

"I don't know what Dale was doing down on Broad Street that night," Randy Hitchens, the clean-cut, boyish, earnest former partner of the deceased detective declared when Joe and Stiversen caught up with him on the second floor of the police station the next morning. "We weren't on duty. In fact, I was home all night with a head cold."

"And you didn't see him, at any time that night?"

"No," Hitchens confirmed. "Like I said, I was in with a cold -- just me and a box of Kleenex. Real romantic, huh?"

Stiversen wasn't participating in the conversation, but he was listening. He looked from Joe to Hitchens and then back to Joe again, but added nothing.

"Did you talk to him that night?" Joe persisted.

"Yeah, I did talk to him," Hitchens said. "It was sometime around eleven, I think, but he was calling from home and he didn't say anything about going out." The detective's pale blue eyes now reflected concern and remorse, and his voice was beginning to crack. "I wish to hell I had. Head cold or not, I'd have had his back."

Joe nodded. "Well, thanks, anyway."

"He should have taken the deal, you know," Hitchens said.

"What are you talking about?" Joe asked. "What deal?"

"The thirty-to-life -- he should've taken it."

"You know about that?"

"Sure," Hitchens confirmed. "Everyone knows about it."

"Didn't realize it was common knowledge," Joe murmured.

"Don't know how common the knowledge was, but as far as I'm concerned, it was better than he deserved," the detective declared. "Glad he turned it down, though. This way, I'll get to see him hang."

Joe nodded thoughtfully, thanked the detective again, and then let Stiversen walk him down the stairs.

"Did you know, too, Arnie?" he asked.

"About the deal?" Stiversen replied. "Yeah, I knew. And I can't say as I really blame Randy for feeling like he does. If it had been my partner, I might be feeling the same way."

"Yeah, well I guess it doesn't much matter how I might feel," Joe said. "I still have a job to do."

"I get that," the police officer said. "And as long as you get that I got to do my job, too, I'll be happy to help you out any way I can. As for Dale, I figure he probably just decided to go out on his own that night -- and ended up in the wrong place at the wrong time."

"Could be," Joe conceded. But it didn't make any sense, and he knew it. And he had a gut feeling that Stiversen knew it, too.

• • •

Lauren Scott opened the door to her gracious Carey Meadows home on the east side of Port Hancock. The pleasant residential neighborhood may not have been on the same scale as Morgan Hill, but it was certainly several steps up from the kind of community that a police officer could rightfully have afforded to live in. It was generally assumed that Maynard Purcell had had a significant hand in its purchase.

"Come on in, Joe," Lauren invited, her smile genuine.

The private investigator followed her across the foyer, through a large sunken living room, out a pair of French doors, and onto a slate patio. A pot of fresh coffee and a plate of cookies sat on a glass-topped table.

"I don't get many visitors now," Lauren said, sitting in one of the chairs that surrounded the table, and pouring out two cups of coffee. "Oh, my parents come over every couple of days, of course, and friends visit, but it's not like it was, well, right after Dale died."

"That must be a big relief," Joe said. "Having to put on a smiling face and keep it up when all you're doing is crying inside can't be a lot of fun."

"Oh, I didn't really mind it so much," Lauren confided. "It kept me from having to think. I could just stay in a state of perpetual numbness and not have to do anything or decide anything or plan anything, and everyone understood, you know what I mean?"

Joe nodded. "Yeah, I guess I do."

"Dale used to be in charge of everything," she said. "And then, for a while, others were. But now I've got a household to run, two kids to take care of, and decisions to make, all by myself. And I don't mind telling you, it's a bit overwhelming." She gestured him to a chair. "So, what brings you here today?"

"First off, I need to tell you that I'm working with Lily on the Lightfoot case," he said, sitting.

"Oh dear," Lauren said. "I remember I jumped all over her at the cemetery for that. But I wasn't myself. I know she was just doing her job. I felt terrible about it afterwards, but I just didn't know how to tell her."

"I'm sure she understood," Joe said.

Lauren looked at him with troubled brown eyes. "I know I should have called her long before now, to apologize, to tell her that I wasn't myself. I just never got up the courage. You tell her for me, Joe, will you?"

"Sure."

"And tell her how happy I am that she wasn't killed in that dreadful explosion, too. Can you believe it -- that Wayne and Grady would do such a thing? I always thought they were such nice boys."

"I'll tell her," Joe said.

The smile returned. "Randy says I don't have to talk to you, you know, but I don't see why I shouldn't," she told him. "As long as you understand that I have no interest in helping the man who killed my husband, I'll tell you whatever I can."

"Randy said that?" Joe asked. "You keep in touch, do you?"

"Of course," she said. "He's been very good to us ever since Dale died. I mean, he was always good to us, a real friend, right from the beginning when he and Dale first partnered up, and it was such a relief to learn that he was still willing to be here for the girls and me, whenever we needed him. I guess, in the past few months, I've really come to rely on him. You know, like a brother. I never had a brother, but having Randy around -- well, that's pretty much exactly what I think it would be like."

Joe nodded sympathetically. "It's important to have someone like that, at a time like this."

"Yes, it is," she agreed. "So now, what was it you wanted to ask me?"

"I was just wondering if you knew what Dale was doing down on Broad Street the night he died?"

Lauren's face went blank. "No," she replied. "I really have no idea. Dale didn't talk much about his work. He always said his job could be ugly, and he didn't want to bring any of that into our home."

"Do you by any chance remember what time it was that he left the house that night?" the cop-turned-private-investigator asked.

"Well, let me see, it must have been around eleven," she said. "We'd finished dinner, the dishes were in the dishwasher, the girls had already gone to bed, and the late news had just come on, so, yes, it had to have been around eleven."

"Was that normal -- for him to go out so late on a Sunday night?"

"I don't think it was abnormal," she told him. "He worked all kinds of odd hours, on any given day. Why, is it important?"

"Well, the thing is, according to Randy, Dale wasn't scheduled to work that night."

Lauren frowned. "Randy said that?"

"Yes," Joe confirmed. "He told me they weren't on duty, and he was home with a head cold."

"Well then, I don't have the faintest idea where Dale was going," she said with a shrug. "I guess I just assumed he was going to work. I mean, that's where he said he was going when he left, and I had no reason to doubt it."

· · ·

"I know I'm supposed to be concentrating on Lightfoot," Joe reported back to Lily, "but I've been taking this where it's been leading me, and I've found out something that could be important."

"Let's have it," the attorney prompted, giving him her full attention.

"Dale wasn't on the job that night."

"What do you mean?"

"The night he was killed," Joe told her, "he was apparently out on his own."

"Really?"

"Yep. Got it from his partner. Lauren told me he said he was going to work when he went out, but Randy said they weren't on duty, and he was home sick, and there wasn't anything going on he knew about. And McAllister confirmed that."

"But that doesn't make any sense," Lily murmured. "On a Sunday night, if he wasn't on duty, then what was he doing on lower Broad Street. More specifically -- what was he doing in the alley?"

"Not clear," Joe said. "I talked to Billy Fugate over at The Last Call. He told me it had been years since Dale had made his hassling rounds. And the owners of the other bars I went to all told me the same thing. So, I don't know what he was doing in the alley, but I'm thinking, whatever it was, it didn't have anything to do with keeping the neighborhood safe from Jason Lightfoot."

Lily frowned. "I know this seems a silly question to ask -- but do detectives even go on that kind of patrol these days?"

"No, they sure don't," Joe told her. "That particularly pleasant duty is reserved for lowly patrolmen. Which means there was no reason for him to be in the alley, unless, of course, there was some kind of operation going down."

"Which Randy and McAllister both said there wasn't, right?" Lily wanted to clarify.

"Right," Joe confirmed.

"So, strange as it may seem, is it possible he just went out on his own to have a drink or something?"

Joe shook his head. "Well, if he did, he wasn't at The Last Call," he said. "And no one else could remember seeing him that night."

"Okay, so, if it wasn't about booze -- what *was* it about?" she mused.

"Well, of course, there's always the old standby. He might have had someone on the side. It would fit the timing -- late at night, and it would also fit the fact that he told Lauren he was going to work."

"I guess that could explain what he was doing out on his own at that hour," Lily said, but she didn't seem convinced.

Joe thought about it. "But the thing is, Dale never struck me as the pro type."

"And what exactly is the pro type?"

"Well, I mean, look at the wife he had. Unless she was cold as stone, and she sure doesn't come across as being that way, why would he have needed to step out on her?"

"Sometimes, you just don't know what goes on in other people's marriages," Lily reminded him. "But let's suppose that he *was* there to pick up a prostitute -- why the alley? That's so last century. These days, there are at least two motels on lower Broad Street that rent rooms by the hour. No one needs to do someone up against a back alley wall anymore, especially in the middle of winter."

"Oh, and what exactly do you know about rooms by the hour, and walls in back alleys?" Joe inquired.

Lily laughed. "Oh, you'd be amazed at how extensive my knowledge is," she said, "And be sure to note that I said knowledge -- not experience."

"Of course," Joe conceded. "I wouldn't have thought anything else."

"Now, don't get me wrong," she said. "I'm not saying he didn't have a woman on the side, but knowing Dale, if he did, she would have had her own place, and it all would have been neat and discreet."

"Well, if he wasn't there for another woman," Joe wondered, "what the hell was he there for?"

"We've been assuming that we're talking about something legal here," Lily said slowly. "But what if we should be talking about something that maybe wasn't so legal?"

"What are you thinking?"

"Well, don't forget," she reminded him, "he wasn't on duty that night, but he had his service weapon with him, didn't he?"

A light suddenly went on in Joe's head. "Wait a minute," he said. "Randy and the chief both said there was no operation on for that night that they knew about. But that doesn't mean Dale couldn't have been working something on his own -- something that maybe he hadn't filled them in on yet. He was on the drug detail, wasn't he? And the drugs come in off the docks, don't they? He could have been there for some kind of a meet, maybe it was a new snitch that he wasn't too sure about yet. And if that was the case, then it would have been perfectly reasonable for him to have his gun with him for protection."

"If you're right," Lily said, "then we may have ourselves a witness."

"A reluctant witness," Joe corrected her. "No one's come forward yet. So, what kind of person witnesses a crime and doesn't come forward?"

"The kind who doesn't want to get involved. The kind who doesn't want anyone to know he was there when the killing went down."

"Exactly."

"And who would that be?"

Joe shrugged. "Well, if we eliminate the other woman, what does that leave us with? It had to be a source that Dale was trying to develop. A potential snitch, maybe. And the time and the location tell me we're probably talking about drugs."

"Which makes our chances of finding him slim to none."

"Probably," Joe agreed. "But I think I'll nose around a bit."

If either of them realized that their investigation of Jason Lightfoot in connection with the murder of Dale Scott had just turned a very sharp corner, neither mentioned it.

• • •

Not unlike the city itself, the Port of Port Hancock was actually two ports in one -- the one that promoted an exclusive marina that catered to private yachts, charter boats, and tourists, and the one that catered to commerce. And there were two kinds of commerce -- the one that was carried on openly and officially, and the one that avoided regulation, required no manifest, and wasn't very official.

The Port Hancock Police had for years tried to shut down the illegal traffic, with only limited success, and drugs, alcohol, cigarettes, and other contraband continued to find their way onto the peninsula with very little interruption.

Old Eddie wasn't hard to find, if you knew where to look. Joe didn't know him by any other name, and doubted anyone else did, either. He had always been Old Eddie, from as far back as when Joe was a kid with a fascination for the sea.

He knew the old man must now be at least eighty years old. He was tall and gaunt and bent, with a long sweep of white hair he tied back in a ponytail, a scraggly beard, and slanting brown eyes above high cheekbones. Reported to be half white and half native, he had never really been comfortable in either camp. The docks had been his home, his family, and his livelihood for more than sixty years, and would be his legacy long after he was gone. After all this time, there probably wasn't much about the docks that Old Eddie didn't know.

"Hello there, Joe," he greeted the private investigator, talking around the worn-down stem of a hand-carved pipe that was always wedged in the corner of his mouth.

"How's it going, Eddie?" Joe asked, plunking himself down on the bulwark beside the ancient mariner.

"Got no complaints, no complaints at all," Old Eddie replied. "How about you?"

"Too many to name," Joe told him with a chuckle.

"Hear tell you're doing some work on the right side of the Lightfoot case."

"That I am," the former police officer confirmed.

"Nice boy, that Jason," Old Eddie said. "It was a loss for the docks when he got himself hurt like he did. And it'll be a loss for the whole community if they end up hangin' him like folks think they'll do."

"True enough," Joe told him. "Only it isn't Lightfoot I've come to talk about."

Old Eddie peered at him. "My mistake then," he said. "What -- you workin' another case concernin' the docks?"

"No," Joe said. "Same case. Different angle."

The old Indian's eyes narrowed. "Ah, I get it. You've come nosin' around about the dead cop, ain'tcha?"

"Yeah."

"Took you long enough."

"Well, you know how it is," Joe told him. "Sometimes things crank around slower than they should."

Old Eddie nodded. "That they do," he said. "That they do. And what do you think I can tell you about him?"

Joe shrugged. "I don't know, Eddie. That's what I'm here to find out. We're looking for a reason he was in the alley the night he got killed, and we think he might have had a meet set up with maybe a potential snitch he was trying to recruit."

"Potential snitch?" Old Eddie echoed.

"Yeah," Joe said. "And because he was killed in the area, like right up the alley, we thought this potential snitch he could have been meeting up with might be connected to the docks. Which means that this potential snitch could have been a witness to the murder. In which case, I sure would like to talk to him -- unofficially, of course."

Old Eddie nodded slowly. "The detective and his partner worked the docks some," he said. "I kept telling them it was a losin' battle, that for every illegal shipment they caught, three more would get through right behind it, but they kept at it. The partner liked to say, every little dent they made mattered, and besides, they were gettin' paid by the good citizens of Port Hancock to keep the community as safe as they could. Real idealist, that one, still has stardust in his eyes."

"And the other one?"

"The other one," Old Eddie said, "he wasn't so idealistic."

"How do you mean?"

"Seems to me, the longer he was a cop, the less conscientious he got, if you get my drift."

"Really?" Joe said, not sure where Old Eddie's drift might be headed.

At that, the man who had lived most of his life on the docks began to cackle. "You really don't know, do you?"

"Know what?" Joe parried, because he didn't have a clue what Old Eddie was talking about.

"This ain't comin' at you first-hand, you understand, which means I wouldn't be any too interested tellin' this to anyone but you," the ancient mariner cautioned. "But the word floatin' around was that maybe this particular cop got a little too close what he was doin'."

There wasn't much that surprised Joe Gideon anymore, but this certainly did. "Too close, as in you mean he was playing both sides?" he wanted to clarify.

"Let's just say, the way I heard it, he was literally enjoyin' the benefits of both," Old Eddie confirmed.

• • •

Lily's eyes widened. "Old Eddie told you Dale was on the take?" she gasped.

"I don't know that it's true," Joe told her. "I'm just telling you what the talk around the dock was. And according to Old Eddie, it wasn't money Dale was taking."

Lily couldn't believe it. "But he was such an upstanding public servant," she said. "At least, I always thought he was."

"You and me, and probably everyone else in town."

"So, instead of a snitch," she added, following the thought, "he may have been meeting with his supplier that night. Oh my, that certainly shakes things up a bit, now doesn't it?"

"Yeah, it does -- if it's true," Joe agreed. "In which case, we're not looking for a witness -- at least, not a witness we're ever likely to get to come forward."

"I suspect you're right."

"The coroner set the time of Dale's death at sometime around midnight. So the timing would have been about right."

Lily nodded. "Are you thinking what I'm thinking?"

"Well, according to Billy Fugate, it was around that time that Jason left The Last Call. Could be he walked right into the meet."

"And that could have posed quite a problem for our friend Dale."

"It certainly could have," Joe said. "At the very least, it would have compromised his position. He knew Jason. And drunk or sober, Jason certainly knew him. If there was even the slightest possibility of exposure, I'd say Dale wouldn't have hesitated."

Lily found herself actually getting excited. "You know what this means, don't you?" she exclaimed. "It means that Jason might not have killed an upstanding police officer -- he might have killed a dirty cop."

"And the chances are he might have done so because he didn't have a choice," Joe added. "But thinking it and being able to prove it may turn out to be two very different things."

Lily knew that, but it didn't matter. For the first time since she had been handed this case, she had something she could grab onto. "If that's how it went down," she said, "then we may just have ourselves more than a mitigating circumstance."

• • •

Rocky Tabalione was a street punk in every sense of the word. Out on his own since the age of fourteen, he had clawed his way through his youth doing whatever he had to do, legal or illegal, to survive. He had done a two-year stint in juvenile detention for drug possession when he was fifteen, and a couple of years later, survived a three-year hitch for possession with intent to sell -- both of which turned out to be nothing less than a badge of honor in his circle.

He was a good-looking kid, with black hair and bright blue eyes and a small gold ring through his lower lip. He wasn't terribly bright, but he was street smart, and could be a real charmer when he wanted to. By the age of twenty-four, he had made himself into Port Hancock's busiest go-between.

"Found a niche I figured I could fill," he always said.

He knew everyone who was anyone in the underbelly of Jackson County, and he had a real knack for putting people who wanted something and could pay for it together with people who had something they wanted to be paid for -- legal or otherwise. It didn't make any difference to him. And as the middleman, he got his cut from both sides.

He agreed to meet with Joe Gideon, but only if the meeting took place at a bar out on the highway east of town, far enough, he hoped, from prying eyes.

"You want me to tell you if there was a cop playin' both sides of the street?" he asked.

"Was there?" Joe prodded.

"And if I tell you -- what's in it for me?"

"You tell me what I want to know, and I keep your name totally out of it," the private investigator said. "But you even try to play me and I spread the word that you're a snitch across four counties."

Tabalione laughed. "Always liked doin' business with you, Sergeant Gideon" he said. "So, okay, yeah, there used to be a cop playin' both sides. But I hear he ain't doing it anymore."

"Yeah, and why not?"

Tabalione smirked. "Because nowadays I hear that this cop that used to be playin' both sides -- I hear he's six feet under," the kid said. "And while I have no firsthand knowledge, you understand, I'm told it's pretty hard to operate from down there."

"You got a name that goes on that headstone?" Joe asked, his heart beginning to race.

"How many dead cops you heard about lately?" Rocky replied.

"I need a name, kid," Joe said softly.

Tabalione shrugged. It was no skin off his nose. "Scott," he said.

"And how do you know that Scott played both sides?"

"Cause that's a big part of my job, man -- knowin' who's doin' what -- to who and with who."

"And what was Scott doing?"

"From what I hear, he wasn't dirty just for the sake of bein' dirty, if you know what I'm sayin'. He was dirty because he was usin', and his habit had outgrown his means. So, in exchange for certain favors, particularly of the cocaine variety, he was protectin' his supplier. Quid pro quo, like they say."

Joe wasn't as shocked as he knew he should have been, but he was sick to his stomach. Still, he wasn't about to give this punk kid the benefit of knowing it.

"Give me the name, Rocky," he said.

Even way out where they were, and the place being all but empty in the early afternoon, Tabalione looked around carefully before he spoke. "The Van Aiken brothers would probably be a good place to start," he murmured.

Joe nodded slowly. He had gotten more than he had come for. Sadly, much more. He dropped a hundred-dollar bill on the table, patted the kid on the shoulder, and left.

• • •

"You'd better have more than Old Eddie and Rocky Tabalione," Carson told his daughter after she had spent the better part of the dinner hour telling him what Joe had uncovered. "Grace is a tough cookie. She's not going to let you tarnish the good name of a Port Hancock police officer without some hard evidence."

"That's why I'd like to search his house," Lily said. "Only I've got no probable cause."

The former prosecutor shrugged. "Lauren could always give you her permission."

"Sure," his daughter said with a laugh, "about the same time that pigs start flying."

"Have you asked her?"

"Do you really think I should?"

"What do you have to lose? She might just surprise you and say yes. Look at it this way -- either she knows something or she doesn't. If she does, and she says no, it could be she's trying to hide whatever it is. If she doesn't, she wouldn't care. Six months after the fact, though, I don't know what you'd find."

Lily mulled that over for a moment. "I guess what I'm looking for -- what I'm hoping to find -- is probably going to be something she wouldn't know is there."

• • •

"I don't know what you think you're going to find," Lauren said three days later when she let Lily and Joe into her home. To Lily's surprise, when she had called, her former friend and neighbor had agreed to having her house searched without the slightest hesitation.

"I don't know, either," Lily conceded. "But we don't know why Dale was down on Broad Street that night, and we're hoping to find something that will tell us, which in turn might tell us why he's dead."

Lauren stiffened. "You think my husband was involved in something that was criminal?" she asked sharply.

"No, of course not," Joe assured her calmly. "We're just trying to figure out what it was that put him and the defendant in the same place at the same time that night. Or to be more specific -- we know what Lightfoot was doing there, and we think it might be important to know what Dale was doing there, too."

The widow sighed. "All right, go ahead," she said. "I have nothing to hide." She looked at Lily. "I'm really only letting you do this, you know, because I still feel bad about what happened at the funeral. You were only doing your job then, and I suppose you're only doing your job now, too -- whether it matters or not. So look to your heart's content. I'm sure you're not going to find anything. At least, you're not going to find anything that would make my husband look bad."

"I don't expect we will," Lily said gently.

They started in the study, going through the drawers of Dale's desk for any papers, any notes, any clues about that night. Clues the detective might have left behind. Clues that could tell them what he had been doing down by the dock at that late hour. But there was nothing -- literally nothing. The desk was essentially empty.

Then they worked their way around the living room, the kitchen, and the family room before heading upstairs. Carson had been right. Six months after the fact, there wasn't much of Dale Scott left in the house. His gun collection had been sent to his father, his fishing gear had been given to the Boy Scouts, and his books and magazines had been donated to the public library.

In the master bedroom, one side of the huge walk-in closet was vacant, devoid even of hangers, his clothes having gone to the local thrift shop. The top of the armoire was bare, and its drawers all empty. The nightstand that sat to the left of the king-size bed had nothing either on it or in it. All his personal effects had simply disappeared.

"It's kind of creepy," Lily murmured. "It's almost as if he never even lived here."

"Or as if someone didn't particularly want to remember that he had," Joe murmured back as he moved toward the bathroom.

"Whatever it is you're looking for," Lauren said, "you aren't going to find it. I mean, whatever Dale was doing in that alley, it couldn't have been illegal. Being a policeman meant everything to him. He would never have jeopardized that."

"I'm sure you're right," Lily said. "I don't think Dale would have been involved in anything illegal."

"We just want to know why he was where he was that night," Joe added. But he wasn't an ex-cop for nothing. He opened the bathroom door. Like the rest of the house, the room was pristine, without a trace of the man who had once lived there. Only one set of towels hung on the rack. Half of the shelves in the medicine cabinet were empty. It was as if someone had come through and scrubbed away every last speck of Dale Scott's existence.

Still, there was one last place to look, and it was a place that, unless someone knew what to look for, the scrub brush wouldn't reach. Joe pulled the cover off the toilet tank, pried the lever out of the inflow pipe, and reached a finger as far down as it would go. And there it was, about two inches down, taped to the side of the pipe.

"What are you doing?" Lauren asked.

"There's something in here," Joe told her, carefully sliding his finger out, already knowing what it was. "Is it okay with you if I have a try at getting it out?"

"What is it?" the widow asked.

"I won't know until I see it," he replied.

She hesitated for a moment, biting nervously at her lower lip, before finally nodding. "Go ahead. It's probably nothing but some toilet tissue."

Joe plucked a long thin pair of tweezers from a kit he carried in his jacket pocket, and began to work at the tape until it came loose, and then, slowly, carefully, he pulled a small plastic packet from the pipe.

"What is it?" Lauren demanded, peering over his shoulder. "Oh my god, what is that?"

What Joe had found was a sealed waterproof bag containing two smaller bags, each of which was about the size of a commercial sugar packet. He carefully opened the outer bag, and pulled out one of the inner bags. Inside it was what looked, to the former police officer's eye anyway, to be about a gram of cocaine. To make sure, Joe dipped a finger into the powder and licked it. Then he sighed. He had found Dale Scott's rainy day stash.

"I'm not sure," he told the widow. "Will you let me take it and have it tested?"

"I don't care what you do with it," Lauren cried. "Just get it out of here! Get it out of my sight!"

• • •

The Van Aiken brothers, Neil and Karl, had started life in Los Gatos, California, the youngest sons in a blue-collar family of ten. Recruited by dealers when they were still in high school, they moved out on their own after graduating, but came up short of expectations in San Jose, had no luck in San Francisco or Portland, got rebuffed in Seattle, and so made their way out to Port

Hancock, arriving in the late seventies to find an almost virgin territory. The drug boom of the decade had barely touched Jackson County. The brothers could hardly believe their good fortune. They staked their claim, set up shop, and never looked back.

The shop they set up was a real estate office in the heart of town. The market had been moving in the right direction, making it a perfect front. What the two young men lacked in real estate acumen, they more than made up for in other ways. They quietly let it be known around the county that they were a pair who would be happy to fill whatever need anyone might happen to have.

With their old Los Gatos connections and ready supply route -- by way of a chartered boat that made routine late-night trips from California and Mexico to the Port Hancock docks, they found it easy to build a network. There were always enough folks looking for a quick way to make a quicker buck. And it wasn't just high school dropouts and dead-enders, either, it was respectable people, too -- underpaid teachers, unemployed professionals, struggling laborers, and bored housewives who were more than willing to help -- for appropriate consideration, of course.

They began with marijuana, slowly, in no hurry, hooking anyone and everyone, from eighty-year-old tribal elders to twelve-year-old school kids. By the end of the eighties, goods were moving in and out of the back of the real estate office at a prodigious rate.

By the late nineties, they had stepped up to oxy and meth and cocaine, where the real payoff was. The Indians, who by that time were making more money from their casinos than they had ever dreamed they could make, went wild for it. And the Van Aiken brothers were only too happy to accommodate them.

It was the turn of the century before serious competition began to make inroads on their territory. A few scuffles ensued, but as soon as it became clear that there was enough business to go around, the brothers declared a truce, and boundaries were set. By being careful, they always managed to keep the boundaries firm and stay one step ahead of the law. It was rumored that they had someone on the inside, but no one had ever been able to prove it.

When Joe walked into the posh Parkland Street offices of Van Aiken Real Estate at just after three o'clock in the afternoon, at least half a dozen eager young men, with lists of prime homes for sale sitting on their desks, looked up expectantly.

"I'd like to speak to Mr. Van Aiken," Joe told the receptionist.

"Which one?" the buxom brunette asked with a plastic smile.

"It doesn't matter," the private investigator replied.

She didn't seem to know quite how to respond to that. "Just a minute, please," she said and disappeared from sight, only to reappear a moment later. "I'm sorry, but may I have your name?"

Joe gave his name, and she vanished a second time. A moment later, a beefy man with a shock of gray hair and a neatly trimmed beard, wearing an expensive, if ill-fitting, suit came into view.

"Sergeant Gideon, to what do I owe the honor?" he asked pleasantly.

"I'm on the other side now, Neil," the ex-cop replied with a smile.

"So I hear, so I hear, and quite successfully, too, I'm told," Neil Van Aiken said. "So, what brings you to my humble establishment, Joe? Interested in some real estate?"

"Perhaps."

"Buying or selling?"

"Well, why don't we go talk about it," Joe suggested.

Van Aiken took the hint. He led Joe past the eager staffers and into his private office and closed the door behind them. The room was big and airy and looked more like a living room than an office, filled as it was with a selection of comfortable sofas and armchairs and side tables.

"What can I help you with, Joe?" the businessman asked, lowering himself into one of the chairs and gesturing Joe to another.

"Dale Scott," the private investigator replied.

"The police detective who got himself killed last winter?"

"That's the one."

"What about him?"

"I'm investigating a link between the detective and the drugs, and I figure, if I want to know about the drug part, I should start at the top."

Van Aiken laughed. "I heard you were working for the Indian."

"Actually, I'm working for his attorney," Joe corrected him. "And I'm trying to find a reason for Scott being where he was on the night he was killed. If he was into drugs, and I can confirm it, it'll go a long way toward establishing mitigating circumstances. And just so we're clear, I'm not looking to cause any trouble. Anything we say here -- stays here."

"And what if I say I don't know what you're talking about?" Van Aiken ventured.

"I don't have time, Neil," Joe said smoothly. "Trial starts in a few weeks. I know you had someone on the inside. I think it was Scott. All I'm looking for is confirmation."

"And if I give it to you, then what?"

"I'm not on the job anymore. You tell me what I want to know, I get up and walk out of here, and it's like we never had this conversation."

"And if I don't?"

Joe shrugged. "Then I get up and walk out of here, and it's like we never had this conversation."

Van Aiken chuckled. "All right, Joe, I'll tell you," he said. "Because I think you'll keep your word, and because it doesn't really matter if you don't. Yeah, Scott was our inside man."

"For how long?"

"For four, maybe five years," Van Aiken allowed.

"Why?"

"Simple. He got hooked on coke. And just like any other junkie, he had to feed his habit."

"How did it work?"

"It was no big deal. He got himself and his partner assigned to the drug detail." The drug dealer laughed. "It was kind of funny, actually -- watching the fox guarding the henhouse. All we had to do was supply him. Then, if there was a raid or something scheduled to go down, we got prior notice, and the raid came up empty. And if one of our people got careless, and it would have blown his cover to do nothing, well then, he'd figure out a way to make it go away as quietly and painlessly as possible."

"And his partner?"

Van Aiken shook his head. "Scott always put on a great act. I don't think the partner had a clue."

"So who was meeting up with Scott the night he died?"

Van Aiken shook his head again. "Sorry to disappoint you," he said. "Sure, we kept him happy in exchange for his cooperation, but after a while, he got too expensive for us -- in more ways than one."

"What do you mean?" Joe asked.

"About two years ago, he stopped being a social user, and went hard-core. It made him even meaner than he had been before, and worse, it made him reckless. We finally had to cut him loose."

"When was that?"

"Maybe three or four months before he was killed."

"Weren't you worried?"

"Hardly," Van Aiken said. "We had as much on him as he had on us."

"Do you know where he would have gone?"

The drug dealer shrugged. "I can give you a couple of names, but that's all it would be -- just a couple of names. I couldn't tell you which one. You want to know, you ask your police buddies. You ask 'em -- during those few months, which dealer was suddenly at home, watching TV with the wife and kiddies, when the raids went down."

He scribbled some names on a piece of paper and handed it to Joe.

"I appreciate it."

"I wish you luck," Van Aiken said. "I really do. I hope this isn't just a lot of busy work for you. And I hope that things work out for the Indian. Scott was a pig, and speaking personally, I have no big problem with him being dead."

"Thanks," the private investigator said, starting to wonder if maybe Jason Lightfoot hadn't done a lot of people a big favor.

"And just so you know, we don't do kids anymore. Not even high school. Now, it's all about coke and meth and adults only -- responsible, consenting adults. Oh yes, and believe it or not, it's also about real estate," Van Aiken added with a smile. "I guess, after thirty-five years, we had to learn something. And now that this recession is more or less over, and the economy's coming back, we're actually getting pretty good at it -- if you're ever in the market."

"After all these years," Joe acknowledged with a dry chuckle, "it's nice to know you're finally providing a civic service."

• • •

There were three names on the list Van Aiken had given him. Joe recognized all of them. But, when he met up with Arnie Stiversen at The Hangout that evening, he had no idea which one it was.

"So tell me," he asked his former protégé, "Did McAllister know?"

"Did McAllister know what?" Stiversen replied.

"That Dale was dirty?"

The police officer's eyes popped. "What are you talking about?" he exclaimed.

"Oh come on, Arnie," Joe chided, "don't play dumb with me."

"I'm not," Stiversen protested "Honest-to-god, I don't know what you're talking about."

"You mean, you never wondered, not once, not even a tiny little bit, what was going down when all the drug raids on a particular party kept coming up empty on Dale's watch?"

"In case it's slipped your mind, I wasn't assigned to the drug detail," Stiversen declared. "And no, I never wondered what was going down, because I didn't know anything about it. And anyway, what exactly are you trying to say?"

"I'm not trying," Joe declared, "I'm saying it -- whatever happened to basic police investigation? You railroaded the Indian without a second thought. You should have investigated."

"He was there," Stiversen argued. "He had the murder weapon, his fingerprints were all over it, he was covered in GSR, and he had history with the victim. What did you expect us to do?"

"Your job," Joe declared with a heavy sigh. "I expected you to do your job."

Stiversen scowled hard at the private investigator for a long moment. "It wasn't our call," he said finally.

"What do you mean?"

"I mean, it was Randy's call, from right before we even took the Indian in. McAllister put him in charge. Until you showed up, Paul and I, we just did what we were told to do."

Joe thought about that for a moment. "McAllister put Randy in charge of his own partner's murder case?" he asked finally.

"Yeah," Stiversen told him.

"What about Roy and Teri?"

"No, they were never involved in Dale's case," the police officer assured him. "They came on for the bombing."

Joe couldn't believe it. "I don't get it," he murmured. A policeman was never put in charge of his own partner's death investigation.

Stiversen shrugged. "It was Randy, right from the get-go," he said. "I thought it was a little weird, myself, but then again, Randy has always seemed to be on an inside track -- hell, he made detective after just six years, didn't he?"

"I'm sorry about that, Arnie," Joe said, and he meant it.

The police officer shrugged. "I got past it."

Joe sighed. "In that case, I need you to do one more thing for me," he said dropping his voice, although the football game that was blaring from the big screen television set on the wall at the end of the bar had everyone else's rapt attention.

"What?" Stiversen said warily.

"I need you to check something. I need you to go back maybe three or four months before Dale was killed. I need you to check on any drug raids he may have been involved in, or more importantly, the results of any drug raids he may have been involved in."

Stiversen frowned. "What do you know?"

"I don't know anything for sure yet," Joe said, "but I'm thinking the Indian may not be the killer you all are trying to make him out to be."

"What do you mean?"

"I mean, what if he stumbled into a meet of some kind -- something he wasn't supposed to see? And what if he saw a cop doing something he wasn't supposed to do? What do you think that cop would have done?"

"Are you thinking Lightfoot could have been defending himself?"

"I'm thinking he could have been," Joe told him. "I'm thinking he could have walked into the middle of something he wasn't going to walk out of so easy. And much as I can't believe I'm saying this, I'm thinking we better to do right by him."

"All right," Stiversen said, because now he had more questions than answers. "Let me see what I can find out."

• • •

There was a hearing in September, held in the Presiding Judge's chambers, informal, off the record, and out of sight of cameras and reporters.

The suits from Seattle reviewed the evidence connected with the bombing of Amanda Jansen's cottage. They listened to testimony from Lily Burns about the two traffic incidents with the red Chevrolet Silverado, and about the gold plane with the black stripes that had dropped the bomb.

They heard from Jeffrey Nordlund who had treated Lily's injuries. They heard from Andy Cooper who had found pieces of the bomb at the scene, and had identified identical bomb-making materials in Grady

Holt's garage -- with the fingerprints and DNA of both Holt and Wayne Pierson on them. And they heard from Ben Dawson who had found the computer in Wayne Pierson's home.

When it was over, they recommended that Pierson and Holt not go to trial.

"We've bailed you out of more trouble over the past twenty years than we care to remember," one of the attorneys told the two men. "You're not children anymore. When are you going to stop behaving like you are?"

Walter Pierson fussed and fumed, but he knew that, short of buying off a judge and a jury, there was nothing more he could do for his youngest son. He gave the boy and his friend a piece of his mind, and then he gave the go-ahead to the attorneys, who arranged a meeting with the prosecutor to hammer out a deal.

"As you already know," John Henry told Lily after the meeting had concluded, "Washington State has an eighty-five percent law. Which guarantees they're going to do most of their time."

"What did you offer?" Lily asked, flexing her right arm that, after eight long weeks, had finally come out of its cast.

"Well, I started at forty," he said with a shrug, "which is less than I would have asked for at trial, but I was able to get them to agree to thirty, which is more than I expected. It means they'll do at least twenty-five, and they'll do it all at the Jackson County State Prison. But I told them there was no agreement unless you signed off."

Lily thought about it. What Pierson and Holt had done was reprehensible, but had they not done it, perhaps she would not have found her own salvation and the resolve to fight for Jason Lightfoot. Spending twenty-five years in prison for the crime the two men had admitted they committed might not have seemed long enough to her, but she knew that hanging for a crime her client may not have committed would be forever.

"As part of the deal, I want Walter Pierson to pay for rebuilding the Jansen cottage," she said.

"I think I can arrange that," John Henry said with a little smile.

"What about Crandall?"

"He didn't want to go to trial, either," the prosecutor told her. "He's already agreed to forty-five months, and he'll do all of it."

"Okay," Lily declared. "It's time for this to be settled.

• • •

There was a party at the Carson home that night. Dancer was there. Joe and Beth came. Amanda showed up, along with her parents. Wanda came, too. Megan found a babysitter so that she could come. Maynard and Helen Purcell dropped by. And Grace Pelletier made an appearance. Carson wheeled his chair into the middle of the group and raised his glass of wine.

"To justice," he said. "May it always keep us honest.

Seven

Port Hancock lay in the shadow of the Olympic Mountains, protected from the harshest of the Pacific Northwest weather.

In other areas of the state, pelting rain could fall nonstop for weeks, while in Port Hancock it was more a matter of days. The worst winters were usually followed by the best summers -- long lazy days of clear blue skies and warm sunshine that hung on well into September and only reluctantly let go in October.

This year was different. This year, summer ended abruptly the first week of September and autumn arrived, bringing with it abnormally cold temperatures. Literally overnight, an arctic wind blew in and the thermometer dropped by thirty degrees. And to everyone's surprise, it wasn't a one-day fluke.

"Hell, this can't be fall, it feels too much like winter," the locals cried.

Nevertheless, leaves on the trees turned gold, then brown, and then fell -- all in little more than a week. The ground froze, the skies turned steely gray, and heavy marine air greeted morning risers. Meteorologists were at a loss.

"It's downright November," the locals complained. "What the devil is going on?"

And then, as though it had all been just a bad joke, blue skies returned to usher in October, the sun shone brightly once again, and daytime temperatures soared into the eighties. It was that rarity of rarities in the Pacific Northwest -- Indian Summer.

"The question is," Lily said, as she was preparing to go to trial, "is it a good omen or a bad omen?"

• • •

The main courtroom on the second floor of the Jackson County Courthouse was as opulent as the rest of the building. The floors were polished marble, the walls were paneled in mahogany, the bench and the podium were hand-carved rosewood, and the church-like spectator seats were of sturdy oak. Windows ran the length of the room on the left, high and arched. One mahogany railing separated the court from the gallery, while another set off the jury box on the right. Two large rectangular rosewood tables sat between the bar and the bench. The table that was closer to the jury would serve the prosecution, while the table that was closer to the windows would serve the defense.

On the first Tuesday in October, as the Honorable Grace Pelletier was preparing to enter the courtroom, John Henry Morgan was hovering around the prosecution table, chatting with someone Lily had never seen before, while Lily, Megan, and Jason Lightfoot were going over their notes at the defense table. Behind them, the gallery was filled with one hundred and fifty people from around the county who had been summoned for jury duty.

Without warning, the prosecutor crossed over to stand in front of the defense table. "Want you to meet my new second in command," John Henry said. "Tom Lickliter, meet Lily Burns."

She had heard about the new suit on staff -- a transplant from Seattle, so the scuttlebutt went. Some suit, Lily thought. Tom Lickliter looked to be in his mid forties, around six feet tall, with blue eyes, a ready smile, and dark hair with just a hint of gray at the temples.

In other words, he was exactly what you would want a prosecutor to look like -- that was, if you were on the state's side. Lily couldn't help it, she almost laughed out loud. For all his posturing and self-assurance, John Henry wasn't going to take any chances with his first capital case.

"It's very nice to meet you," she said with a polite smile.

"It's nice to meet you, too," Tom Lickliter replied graciously. "I have to say, your reputation precedes you, as does your father's."

Lily's eyebrows shot up. He had done his homework. Perhaps he wasn't just a suit, after all. Perhaps John Henry had gone for Hollywood but had landed Harvard instead, and there was some acumen lurking beneath the summer-weight pinstripe suit.

The clerk brought the court to order before she could respond, the prosecutors hurried back to their table, and everyone rose.

Judge Pelletier entered the courtroom and took her seat on the bench. She made note of the fact that the state, the defense, and the defendant were represented, and then nodded to the clerk who proceeded to call off twelve numbers. In turn, twelve nervous people jumped out of the wooden pews where they had been seated, and took their places in the comfortable leather chairs of the jury box.

It was a totally random group in many ways -- race, gender, age, education, profession, economic means, and it represented, to a great extent, the kind of mix that had, over the past thirty years, become Jackson County.

John Henry began the juror questioning. In his blunt, but folksy way, he was trying to determine which twelve of the hundred and fifty assembled would likely favor the prosecution's position in the matter of the State of Washington versus Jason Lightfoot.

"Good morning, Ma'am," he greeted Potential Juror Number 28, a seventy-seven-year-old retired schoolteacher, as he stood at the podium. "Have you ever served on a jury before?"

"As a matter of fact, I have," Julia Estabrook replied proudly. "Three times, if I'm not mistaken."

"You've done your civic duty three times," John Henry marveled, "and now we're calling on you again."

"No, wait," she amended. "It was four times. I forgot that arson case five years ago."

"Four times, then," John Henry said with a smile. "Excellent. In that case, I certainly don't have to tell you how all of this works, so we can move right along." The woman smiled in return, and he decided he had her. "Have you ever had any personal interaction with the police?" he asked, plunging right in.

"I most certainly have," Julia Estabrook declared. "Two years ago, my house was broken into while I was up in Bellingham, visiting with my sister. I called the police as soon as I came back, and they came right out. The officers were very nice, but they told me there wasn't much chance of my getting any of my things back." She sighed. "Sadly, they were right. The thief was never caught."

"Do you believe that policemen, because of the very nature of their jobs, are more vulnerable than others in our community and deserve our respect and appreciation?"

"I most certainly do," the prospective juror replied. "They put themselves in harm's way every day to protect us."

"In that case, would you have any trouble sentencing someone who killed a policeman to the maximum penalty -- to death?"

The woman blinked several times at that. "Well, I must say I don't generally believe in an eye for an eye," she said, "but when you put it that way -- I suppose I could."

"Thank you," the prosecutor said.

When it was her turn, Lily didn't stand at the podium. Instead, she stood directly in front of the woman.

"Would you assume, just because the victim of a crime was a policeman, that the person who was accused of killing him was guilty?" she inquired.

"My dear," Julia Estabrook declared, "I don't care what people around here are saying. I wouldn't assume that anyone was guilty of anything unless it could be proven to me beyond a reasonable doubt."

In Lily's head, a question mark turned into an exclamation point.

• • •

"Tell me, sir, do you drink alcohol?" Lily asked Potential Juror Number 9, a fifty-six year old employee at the Port Hancock Paper Mill.

"Can't rightly say that I don't," Hector Aquino replied.

"Well then, have you ever been drunk?" Lily pressed. "I mean, really, seriously drunk?"

Aquino laughed. "Sure have," he said. "Probably more times than I can remember."

"And can you remember what you did on those specific occasions?"

"What do you mean – did I get up and do a dance on the bar? Did I punch out someone I didn't even know? Did I walk down the middle of Broad Street without any clothes on? Or did I crash my car through a plate glass window -- is that what you mean?" the mill hand inquired.

"Yes," Lily said with a smile, "did you ever do anything like that."

"Well, if I did, I sure don't recollect, which is probably a good thing," he declared with a chuckle.

"When I drink like that, sometimes, I don't even remember how I get home."

"So, if you'd had, say, a fight with someone while you had been drinking -- would you be able to say, with any certainty, how the fight came about, or what actually happened?"

"Don't recall if I ever got into it with anyone like you're talkin' about, and to be honest, don't really know if I could recall it," he told her. "When I drink like that, everything tends to be a bit of a blur, which is of course pretty much why I drink in the first place."

At that, a little giggle rippled through the prospective jurors seated in the spectator section.

"Let's say you did do something while you were drunk, something that was criminal, even if you couldn't remember what it was," John Henry countered. "If it could be proven to you that you really did do it -- do you think you should take responsibility for it?"

"I guess, if I did somethin' that was really criminal, I should take what's comin' to me," Hector Aquino said with a shrug. "After all, no one's makin' me drink except maybe the wife."

• • •

"Good Morning," John Henry addressed Potential Juror Number 73, a fifty-year-old Native American who worked for the State Forest Service.

"Mornin'," Rocker Greenwood said in return.

"This case has had pretty wide coverage in the media," the prosecutor began. "Have you heard much about it?"

"Sure have," Greenwood replied. "Can't hardly get away from it."

"I see, and what would you say would be your main source of information -- the newspaper, the radio, the television?"

"The local bar," the potential juror said.

Another little ripple of laughter rolled across the courtroom.

"The local bar," John Henry repeated. "Do you go there often?"

"Pretty much every night, after I get off work," Greenwood told him.

"And a lot of people have been talking about this case at this bar you go to?"

"You bet," Greenwood replied.

"So, tell me," John Henry zeroed in, "after all the talk at this local bar that you go to pretty much every night, have you formed an opinion about this case?"

The potential juror nodded. "I guess you could say that."

"And will you share with us what that opinion would be?"

"If you want my opinion," Rocker Greenwood declared, "that dead cop was nothin' but a pig, and the kid, if he really done it, he oughta get a medal for it."

"I have nothing further," John Henry said.

• • •

"Have you heard much about this case?" Lily asked Potential Juror Number 64, a forty-five-year-old woman who looked like she was dressed for a luncheon at the country club rather than a grueling question-and-answer session in an eight-five degree courtroom.

"I've heard a great deal about it," Martha Heidt replied. "I read the newspaper, I listen to the radio, and I watch the television."

"And have you discussed what you've read and heard with others?"

"Indeed I have," she confirmed. "Every Wednesday at the club, where we all meet for lunch. It's much more interesting than a lot of other stuff we talk about."

Lily nodded. "And have you and your luncheon companions, reached any conclusions about the case?"

"Of course, we have," Martha Heidt declared. "And pretty much all of us agree that your client over there should hang from the neck until he's very, very dead."

• • •

"Are you related to any member of the Port Hancock Police Force?" John Henry asked Prospective Juror Number 82, a young woman with flaming red hair.

"No, I'm not," Evelyn Wolcott said. "I don't even know any member of the police force yet." The twenty-four-year-old had moved to Jackson County for a job in a beauty salon five months earlier.

"Have you heard much about the case we're dealing with here?" the prosecutor inquired.

"I've heard some," Evelyn replied. "The customers talk about it."

"And has what you've heard led you to form an opinion as to the guilt or innocence of the defendant?"

"Well, I haven't been in Port Hancock for very long, you understand," she said, "but the general opinion around town certainly seems to be that he's guilty."

"Despite what you may have heard at your beauty salon, or what the general opinion around town may be," Lily inquired, when it was her turn, "if you were chosen for this jury, do you believe you could set all that aside, listen to all the evidence as it's presented, and then render an impartial verdict in this case?"

"Well, I think I could," Evelyn Wolcott replied. "After all, I don't see as anyone really knows all the facts yet."

• • •

"What do I know about the case?" Prospective Juror Number 31, a forty-eight year old insurance salesman, rephrased John Henry's question. "I know a Port Hancock police detective was shot and killed, and that the man sitting over there has been accused of the crime."

"And have you formed any opinion as to his guilt or innocence?"

John Boyle shrugged. "If I say yes -- do I get to go home?" he asked.

A number of prospective jurors in the gallery suddenly leaned forward, eagerly awaiting the prosecutor's response.

"I'm afraid it doesn't work that way," John Henry said with a smile, and the gallery let out a collective sigh.

"Then I guess I'd have to say I haven't really been following the case closely enough to have an opinion yet," Prospective Juror Number 31 said.

• • •

"I've been on the other side of the country for the past six months," Prospective Juror Number 16 said, when asked about her familiarity with the case. "Before I left, I'd heard about the murder, but I'm afraid I wasn't paying very close attention."

"Where were you for those six months?" Lily inquired.

"I was in Connecticut, seeing to my daughter and her family," fifty-six-year-old Anne Hagen replied. "She was having a very difficult time with her third pregnancy, and the doctors told her she had to stay in bed until she gave birth. But she has a husband and two other children, and someone had to look after them."

"Obviously, you had more important things on your mind than what was going on around here," Lily said. "Is your daughter all right?"

"Thank God, yes," the prospective juror said, beaming. "And I have a beautiful new grandson, too."

"Congratulations!"

"So, if you're looking for someone who knows what this case is all about," Anne Hagen added, "I'm afraid I'm not your person."

• • •

And on and on and on it went, for the rest of the day, and then the day after that, and then the day after that, until a week had passed, and finally seven women, five men, and two female alternates were found to be satisfactory to both the prosecution and the defense, and were sworn in as the jury that would decide the fate of Jason Lightfoot.

• • •

Jason had been in the courtroom for the whole jury selection process, wearing a pair of pants, a shirt, and a sport coat his uncle had gotten for him at the local thrift store. He couldn't remember the last time he had worn a real suit. But it looked like he would be wearing one from now on. The lady lawyer had picked it out for him, and it really wasn't his style. Still, she said she wanted him to look good in court, so he kept his mouth shut and put it on, along with the white shirt and the striped tie and the shoes and the socks that went with it. By the time the barber came in, he was resigned to the idea that her intent wasn't as much to make him look good, as it was to make him over in the image of a white man. And he probably wouldn't have minded even that so much, had the benefits of being white gone along with the suit and the haircut.

The truth was, he was willing to let them do just about anything if it meant he could get out of his cage and see the sky and feel the sun on his face again -- even if it was only during the twenty-minute drive from the Jackson County Jail to the Jackson County Courthouse and back again.

"Well now, you look quite handsome," Lily said when she saw him.

"You mean I look more like you," he said, but he was smiling.

"I didn't think there was that much difference," she responded. "Do you?"

He laughed. "What're you sayin' -- that I been hearin' it wrong my whole life?"

Lily thought about that for a moment. "I think we hear what we want to hear," she told him.

He shrugged. "Okay, you try bein' a minority and see how it feels."

Her eyebrows shot up in real surprise. "You think I'm not?" she said. "I'll tell you what -- you spend one day walking around in a profession that somebody has decreed should be only for women, and then you can tell me that I don't know anything about being a minority."

He looked her up and down. She was wearing a crisp gray linen suit with the jacket unbuttoned at the neck and high-heeled shoes. He'd never thought about lawyering being a man's business. Actually, he'd never thought much about lawyering at all. He wondered if she felt any more comfortable in her fancy getup than he did in his.

"What -- am I supposed to feel sorry for you?" he asked.

She grinned at him. "No sorrier than I'm supposed to feel for you."

As far as he was concerned, the courtroom they kept taking him to, the one that was supposed to be the biggest and most impressive in the building, was nothing more than old and dark. The walls were dark, the floors were dark, and the furniture was dark. The row of windows that ran along his side of the room was the only reprieve, but it didn't do a lot to lighten the place up. And, too, there was the smell, the musty smell of age that was sunk deep into everything.

He was put in the chair closest to the windows. Being able to see out was probably the only thing that made being in that room day after day, hour after hour, tolerable. The windows were tall and wide, and looking through them was like catching little glimpses of heaven. He could see blue sky, fluffy clouds, treetops, rooftops, and even the occasional seagull flying by.

Old, dark and musty though the courtroom was, it was still a world apart from the cage where he had spent the last eight months.

A guard removed his handcuffs, but the shackles around his legs and waist stayed on. They jangled softly every time he shifted his position, and he wondered if the people in the jury box could hear. He decided it would be best not to move any more than was absolutely necessary.

He studied the jurors that had made the cut, while trying to pretend that he wasn't. Although he had been there for every day of the selection process, he hadn't concentrated on them individually. Now he did, and they looked to him like pretty ordinary people. He thought that the oldest was a spry little woman with neatly coifed white hair, and that the youngest was a girl with flowing red hair and a skirt to match. There were eight whites on the jury, two Hispanics, one African American, and one Asian. The alternates were both white. There wasn't a single Native American.

"How come?" he asked.

"There were only three in the jury pool," Lily explained. "And I'm afraid they were all dismissed for cause."

"Is that fair?" he wanted to know. She had told him he was going to be judged by a jury of his peers.

"No," she said with a sigh. "But it's legal."

• • •

At nine o'clock in the morning on Monday, October 13th, the trial of the State of Washington versus Jason Lightfoot began.

The date would be remembered for many years in the Port Hancock area, not just because it marked the start of the trial, but for the record high temperatures that were set that day and every day thereafter for the rest of the month.

The courtroom was stifling. Packed to the rafters as it was with onlookers who wanted nothing less than the opportunity to second-guess the jurors, the air-conditioning was all but useless. For members of the jury and spectators alike, summer suits, sundresses, shorts, and tank tops had been pulled from the depths of closets and the bottoms of drawers where they had been stowed only a scant few weeks earlier. Nylon hose were abandoned, high heels gave way to sandals, and the smell of sweat mixed with perfume and aftershave would linger long after the proceedings ended each day.

Still, there was an unmistakable buzz of anticipation in the room. It was the biggest trial the city had seen in as long as anyone could remember. Reporters, not just from the *Port Hancock Herald*, but from newspapers all around the region were in attendance. And it would be the first trial in the history of Jackson County to be televised, if only by the local cable station.

It was impossible not to feel the electricity in the air. Even Dancer, who sat where he would sit every day that court was in session -- in the pew just behind Lily -- could feel it.

John Henry Morgan stood for his opening statement and faced the jury. He may have looked a bit pompous in his three-piece suit and starched shirt, especially considering the temperature that hovered close to ninety, but his status as the Jackson County Prosecutor spoke for itself.

"Good morning, Ladies and Gentlemen of the jury," he began with a benevolent smile and a folksy tone, and then waited for the half-smiles and murmurs that came in response. "Now, I'm not going to waste your time introducing myself, or even introducing this case. You all know who I am, and you all know why we're here. We're here to right a wrong. It's as simple as that. A veteran police officer has been murdered. That's right -- a dedicated man who put his life on the line, day in and day out, for fourteen years, to protect all of us from harm -- was gunned down in a back alley, and it's going to be up to you to hold his killer accountable."

He paused to take a sip of water, and to let his words sink in.

"Through evidence and witness testimony, the people will prove that the man who murdered Detective Dale Scott is sitting right over there," he continued, swinging his arm out in a dramatic arc to point directly at Jason without deigning to look at him. "And after we prove it, it's going to be up to you to tell the world that this isn't some backwoods hick place, inhabited by barbarians, but a lawful society that punishes those who break our laws."

He waited for a moment, to make sure he had every single juror's attention, and then he launched into a lengthy recounting of the facts of the case, as he had decided they should be understood, and then he detailed how he intended to prove those facts.

"Of course, the defense over there is going to try to convince you that the defendant was drunk," he told them as he was coming to the conclusion of his multiple-hour statement. "They're going to tell you that he was so drunk that night that he didn't know what he was doing. And the truth is, he *is* a drunk -- which is how come he and Detective Scott knew each other so well. But whatever they say, we will show you that on February 10th, he wasn't so drunk that he couldn't point a gun at Detective Scott's head and pull the trigger."

John Henry pursed his lips and then proceeded to pace the length of the jury box and back again, ending up somewhere in the middle.

"This is a simple case," he concluded. "One man is dead by the hand of another. There's no argument about that. We will prove that Jason Lightfoot harbored resentment towards Detective Scott. We will prove that the two met in an alley where there was a confrontation -- we don't know why, and we aren't required to tell you why, but it's possible the defendant was resisting arrest. And we will prove that, at some point in that confrontation, the defendant gained possession of the detective's gun, and executed him with a bullet to the head. Now in my book, Ladies and Gentlemen -- that's murder. And I expect, by the time we have presented our case, it will be murder in your book, as well."

The jurors shifted in their respective upholstered seats. John Henry Morgan sat down.

• • •

Lily stood up, her linen suit now more wilted than crisp. The lunch recess was over, court was back in session, and this was it.

She had practiced endlessly in front of the full-length mirror in her bedroom, forcing herself to remember every sentence, every word, knowing that not only was Jason's fate in her hands, but perhaps her own, as well.

She had been working for hours with the therapist Amanda had recommended. She knew how bad it would look if she stumbled, if she lost her way, if she couldn't communicate what was in her mind and her heart to these twelve people. She took a deep breath.

"I don't mind introducing myself to you again," she began with a friendly smile. "My name is Lily Burns, and I represent the defendant in this case. His name is Jason Lightfoot. And I think I should tell you that, in the beginning, I didn't want to represent Jason Lightfoot. I knew Dale Scott, you see. I grew up right next door to his wife. I was a bridesmaid at their wedding." She paused to look over at Helen and Maynard Purcell, who were seated in the second row, behind the prosecution. "And I felt just like I expect a lot of others felt, perhaps like some of you probably felt -- I wanted to see the man who killed him punished, not exonerated, for what he did. But then I started to learn some things about the case, things that suggested that maybe it wasn't quite as open-and-shut a matter as the prosecutor would like you to believe -- or as simple. And the truth is -- this case is anything but simple. And you won't have to look very hard to figure out why."

She paused again, this time, taking the opportunity to look each juror straight in the eye. "We all know that there are two sides to every story," she told them. "And there are certainly two sides to this one -- two totally different sides. So listen carefully as the prosecution presents its side, as they tell you what they want you to believe, and when they're done, I won't just tell you the other side -- I'll show you exactly how easy it is to turn their whole story on its head."

Lily sat down, breathing a huge sigh of relief that she had gotten through it without a stumble. The jury let out its collective breath, too, without even realizing it had been holding it, while over at the prosecution table, John Henry Morgan clenched his teeth, and Tom Lickliter, the new suit in the Jackson County Courthouse, smiled a little smile of appreciation.

The battle had been joined.

• • •

The prosecution began its case the next day by calling Martin Grigsby to the witness stand.

"Good morning," John Henry said, once the witness had been sworn in, taken his seat, and spelled his last name for the record.

"Good morning," the witness, nervous to have so many eyes focused on him, said in return.

"Will you please tell the jury what the company is where you are employed and what the duties of your job consist of?"

"I work for the Port Hancock Disposal Company," Grigsby replied. "I collect the garbage."

"And how long have you worked for the company?"

"Going on fifteen years."

"Now, will you tell the jury where you were at approximately ten minutes past six on the morning of Monday, February 10th, of this year?"

"My driver and I were in our truck, and we were picking up garbage, same as always."

"Was there anything different that occurred on that morning?"

"There sure was," Grigsby attested. "We were heading down the Broad Street alley, like always on Monday mornings, and we were almost at The Last Call, getting ready to make our regular pick-up, when we spotted something in the middle of the alley up ahead of us."

"And what did you do?" John Henry wanted the jury to know.

"Well, we didn't know what it was at first," the witness said. "But whatever it was, we didn't want to run over it, so we stopped the truck and got out to have a look. It was still dark, and it was foggy, too, but the headlights on the truck were good enough for us to see. And what it was, lying there, was a body -- the body of a guy, and he was dead."

"Did you touch the body?"

"No way," Grigsby declared. "But we got close enough to tell he wasn't going anywhere."

"How did you determine that?"

"He was lying on his side, but he was like sort of stiff, you know, not relaxed like someone is who's just sleeping it off, and his eyes were open, and he was staring straight ahead into nowhere, and he wasn't blinking, and he wasn't breathing."

"What did you do then?"

"Called the cops, of course. And then hightailed it right out of there."

Members of the jury couldn't help but smile at the witness's candor, and some of the less restrained spectators in the gallery giggled.

"Thank you, Mr. Grigsby," John Henry said, hiding his own smile as best he could. "I have no further questions."

"Does the defense wish to cross-examine the witness?" Judge Pelletier inquired.

Lily didn't try to hide her smile. "No, Your Honor," she said. "I think Mr. Grigsby has told us all he can."

• • •

Paul Cady was next to testify. The five-year veteran of the Port Hancock Police Department looked nervous, which may have been understandable given it was the first time he had been called on to testify in a homicide case.

"Officer Cady," John Henry began, "will you tell the jury something about yourself?"

"Yes, sir," Cady said, turning to face the jury. "I come from the Tri-Cities area. My parents still live there. I have three brothers and two sisters. They still live there, too. I'm twenty-five years old. I'm not married. I have a certificate in criminal justice and law enforcement. I've been with the Department for five years. This is my first job. I never wanted to be anything but a police officer."

He stopped, looking at the prosecutor, as if to ask whether he had said enough. The jurors smiled.

"Thank you, Officer Cady," John Henry said. "I think that gives us all a pretty good idea of who you are. Now, can you tell us, please, what your duties as a police officer entail?"

"I'm a patrolman," Cady replied. "I have a partner. When we're on duty, it's our job to patrol around the city, making sure that folks are safe and don't need any help, and we're also looking for any suspicious activity."

"What exactly do you mean by 'suspicious' activity?"

"We usually look for evidence of crimes, like break-ins, vandalism -- that sort of thing," Cady explained. "And we take note of people who maybe aren't where they should be, or who are maybe doing things they shouldn't be doing."

"According to police records, you and your partner were on the midnight to eight shift on February 10th of this year," John Henry continued. "Is that correct?"

"Yes, it is."

"And where exactly were you and your partner at approximately six-twenty-five that morning?"

"My partner and I were responding to a call from lower Broad Street, near the docks."

"Who had placed the call?"

"I believe it came from an employee with the local garbage company."

"And what was the call about?"

"We were told it was about a body that had been found in the alley behind Broad Street, not too far from the dock, and right across from the back entrance to The Last Call Bar and Grill."

"And what happened when you responded to that call, and went into that alley?"

"We found Detective Scott there," the police officer replied. "That is -- we found his body. He was deceased."

"Will you please describe for the jury the condition that the body was in when you found it?" John Henry prompted.

"Well, he was lying, kind of on his side, with his knees bent, in the middle of the alley, in a puddle of blood. We could see he'd been shot in the head. We could tell he was dead, because his body was stiff -- and it was cold and it was a little damp, too."

"What did you do?"

"We called headquarters and told them we needed the M.E. -- I mean, the medical examiner -- to come quick," Cady replied, "and we asked for the crime scene investigators, too."

"And then?"

"And then, we started looking for anyone who could help us."

"Help you?"

"We went looking for someone who might have been a witness, who could maybe tell us what had happened."

"And what did you find?"

"We found the defendant."

"Will you tell the jury what the circumstances were of your finding the defendant?"

"Well, it never occurred to us that someone who had just killed a police officer would hang around the scene of the crime, so when we found the Indian asleep in his box, we were hoping that maybe he had seen something. We didn't realize he would turn out to be the killer."

"Objection, Your Honor," Lily said mildly. "The witness is offering an opinion."

"Sustained," the judge said.

"Without stating your opinion on the guilt or innocence of the defendant, Officer Cady," John Henry continued smoothly, "would you please tell the jury what happened when you encountered the defendant, Mr. Lightfoot, asleep in a box at the scene of the murder."

"Well, we woke him up, and asked him to come out of his box so we could talk to him and -- "

"His box?" the prosecutor interrupted.

"Yes, sir," Cady replied. "He sleeps in a box out in the alley behind the bar. Detective Scott's body wasn't more than fifteen, twenty feet from where he was, so we thought maybe he might have seen or heard something."

"I see, thank you," John Henry said. "Go on."

"Well, we asked him to come out of the box, and just as he was coming out, we saw the gun."

"The gun?"

"Yes, sir, the gun. It just sort of skittered out from under him. And then it turned out it was Dale's gun -- I mean, Detective Scott's gun. And that's when we knew he was more than just a potential witness. And then, when we told him we were going to take him in for questioning, he tried to take off."

"Take off?"

"Yes, sir -- he tried to run. Consciousness of guilt, is what we call it. So we stopped him and then we arrested him."

Lily thought about objecting again, but decided not to.

"Thank you, Officer Cady," John Henry said, and turned to Lily. "Your witness."

• • •

"Let me see if I have this straight," Lily began her cross-examination. "You thought he might be a witness until you saw the gun, and then you thought he might be guilty. He tried to run, and you decided he was definitely guilty. Is that about it?"

"That's about it," Cady agreed.

"And what else did you do, Officer Cady?"

"What do you mean, Ma'am?"

"I mean, you tried to take him in, he ran, you caught him -- and then what did you do?"

Cady shrugged. "I guess I hit him a couple of times," he said. "I had to subdue him."

"A couple of times?"

"Well, maybe a few times. But he tried to run."

"A few times, you say." Lily nodded to Megan, who jumped up from the defense table to operate the projector that had been placed on the podium. "Your Honor, at this time, I would like to enter Defense Exhibits 1 through 14 into evidence."

"Any objections, Mr. Morgan?" the judge inquired.

John Henry wanted to shout yes, but he knew it was just a formality, and that the exhibits were going to come in.

"No objection, Your Honor," he said.

"The evidence is so entered."

"Will Your Honor please have the lights adjusted?" Lily requested.

The lights in the courtroom were dimmed, and Megan proceeded to operate the projector. Being displayed on a big screen in the corner of the room behind the bench, in plain view of the entire courtroom, were the photographs of Jason Lightfoot that Lily had ordered taken on her first meeting with him. One after another, they showed the injuries the Indian had suffered at the hands of the police officer who had arrested him -- the crusty abrasions, the bloody lacerations, the deep purple bruises.

"These photographs were taken four days after the injuries depicted here had been inflicted, Officer Cady," she said. "Are these the injuries my client incurred from a few hits?"

Cady bristled a bit at that. "A good friend of mine had just been killed, and okay, I guess I got a little carried away."

"Let's see, earlier you suggested that Jason Lightfoot's attempt to run could be interpreted as consciousness of guilt," the defense attorney continued. "So, what would you say this action on your part could be interpreted as -- police brutality?"

"Objection," John Henry said.

"Withdrawn," Lily responded smoothly, knowing she had made her point. "Officer Cady, I believe you said earlier that you went looking for a witness after finding Detective Scott's body -- because it never occurred to you that someone who had just killed a cop would hang around the scene of the crime, is that so?"

"Yes, Ma'am, I think I said that," Cady conceded.

"And has that been your experience as a police officer these past five years -- that those guilty of committing crimes don't tend to stay around the scene of the crime?"

Cady saw the trap, but it was too late. He had already put his foot in it. "Sometimes," he was forced to admit. "But obviously, not always."

"And on those occasions, when someone you believed had indeed committed a crime was still at the scene when you arrived -- what was the reason they gave for being there?"

"Mostly, they thought they could talk their way out of it," he replied. "Like claim they were too drunk or too high to know what they were doing. And I've known one or two who thought they could claim they were just in the wrong place at the wrong time."

"And it never turned out to be true -- that they really were too drunk or high to know what they were doing, or that they actually were just in the wrong place at the wrong time?"

The witness was clearly uncomfortable with this line of questioning. "It may have -- once or twice."

"Officer Cady," Lily said, knowing again that she had made her point and abruptly changing the subject, "prior to the morning of February 10th, did you know Jason Lightfoot?"

"No, Ma'am, not really, I mean, not personally," he said. "I knew he hung around one of the local bars, and I'd heard the name because he had a sheet. But we never had any cause to interact."

"A sheet?"

"Yes, Ma'am, he had a pretty long history of arrests."

"Arrests? Arrests for what?"

"Drunk and disorderly, disturbing the peace, public nuisance, that kind of stuff."

"Was he ever convicted for any of these numerous crimes?" Lily inquired.

"No, Ma'am. He was not."

"Why not?"

"I guess they were considered minor offences -- you know, pay a fine, spend the night, go on home."

"Was there anything in that long history of arrests that involved drugs?"

"No, I don't recall seeing anything about drugs."

"How about assault?"

"No, not as I recall."

"How about battery?"

"No, Ma'am."

"How about murder?"

"No, of course not."

"How about anything recent -- anything at all?"

"No, Ma'am," Cady conceded. "We checked. There was nothing on his sheet for the past five years."

"So, for five years, as far as you knew, Jason Lightfoot was living his life peacefully, he was minding his own business, and he was staying out of trouble, is that right?"

"As far as we knew."

The jurors had been given pads and pens to take notes, if they wished. Several of them were now writing furiously on their pads.

"About that long sheet he had, listing all those arrests for minor offences -- who was the arresting officer involved?"

"Mostly, it was Detective Scott -- well, I guess he was Officer Scott back then. It was before he got promoted."

"I see," Lily said. "So would it be fair to say, then, that Jason Lightfoot knew Detective Scott -- in fact, knew him quite well?"

"I guess you could say that," the police officer confirmed. "I guess you could also say he harbored some serious resentment toward him."

"Serious resentment?" Lily echoed. "How would you know that?"

Cady shrugged carelessly. "Well, he killed him, didn't he?"

"Did he?" the defense attorney said in surprise. "I'm sorry, did I miss something here? I didn't realize the charges had already been proven, and he had already been convicted by the fine members of this jury."

"Well, I meant -- "

"Yes, I think we all know what you meant, Officer Cady," Lily declared.

"Look, it was a good collar," Cady retorted. "He had the weapon, he had the motive, and he had the opportunity."

"So you say," Lily said. "But if it's all the same to you, I'd prefer to present all the evidence to this jury, and then wait and hear what they say."

"Well, of course," Cady murmured.

"Now, when the defendant came out of his box, at your request, how did he appear to you?"

"I'm not sure I know what you mean, Ma'am?"

"I mean -- was he acting normally?" Lily specified. "Did he appear to be impaired in any way? Did you notice anything about him that would have indicated if he was under the influence of alcohol or on medication, perhaps?"

"He seemed pretty normal to me."

"You mean, he was acting perfectly normally -- his eyes were clear, he wasn't stumbling, he wasn't slurring his words?"

Cady glanced over at the prosecutor, as if hoping for guidance, but there was none forthcoming. He sighed deeply. "He may have been stumbling a bit," he said. "And he may have been slurring his words some. But then, we had just woke him up. I stumble around and slur my words sometimes when I get woke up."

"And his clothes, Officer Cady," Lily pressed. "Did you detect any particular smell from the clothes he was wearing?"

"Yes," the officer was compelled to reply. "They reeked of dirt and sweat and alcohol."

"I see -- they reeked of dirt and sweat and alcohol," the defense attorney repeated thoughtfully. "What about his breath? What did that reek of?"

"It was awful," Cady said.

"Awful, as in -- ?"

"Okay, yes, his breath smelled of alcohol, too," Cady allowed. "But that just meant he'd been drinking, not that he was drunk, if that's where you're going. The breathalyzer said his alcohol level was zero."

"And when was that, Officer Cady?" Lily inquired. "How long after the time of Dale Scott's death did you get around to testing the defendant's alcohol level?"

At the prosecution table, John Henry cringed.

"It was maybe about twelve hours later," Cady conceded.

"Twelve hours?" Lily echoed. "And just how reliable have you found that test to be -- twelve hours after the fact?"

"I wouldn't know," the officer had to admit.

"No, I don't suppose you would," she murmured. "Just one more thing then -- when you tried to take the defendant into custody, you said he attempted to run?"

"That's right, he did," Cady confirmed.

"But you caught him?"

"Yes, we did."

"And after you caught him -- did he put up a fight?"

"No, Ma'am."

"He didn't assault you?"

"No, Ma'am."

"He didn't try to get your gun away from you?"

"No, Ma'am," Cady said with a slight snicker. "He sure didn't."

"So you hit him behind his knees with your baton, he crumpled to the ground, and then you stood over him and beat him almost senseless, while he did nothing but try to protect himself. Is that about right, Officer Cady?"

The police officer grit his teeth. "Okay, maybe I shouldn't have done that. But you have to understand, he killed a cop -- one of my brothers, and then he tried to run. I had to subdue him."

"Yes, of course," Lily conceded. "And while you were subduing him, did he make any attempt to fight back?"

"No, he didn't do anything but curl up and try to cover himself."

"He never fought back -- not in any way?"

"No, he didn't," Cady said. "But he would have been stupid to. He could see that we were police officers. And that we had guns. He knew he wouldn't have stood a chance."

"Yes, that's right, isn't it?" Lily said with a sudden smile. "He may not have known you personally, as he did Dale Scott, but he knew you were police officers. And you had guns. And he knew he wouldn't have stood a chance against you. Thank you, Officer Cady. I have no further questions."

A few of the jurors were still scribbling in their notebooks.

• • •

"How did the defendant know you were a police officer?" John Henry inquired on redirect.

"I was wearing my uniform," Cady replied.

"And your partner," the prosecutor asked, because he knew there was nowhere else to go, "was he also wearing his uniform?"

"Yes, he was."

"Thank you, Officer."

Cady was dismissed. He scowled as he left the witness stand and strode up the aisle, out of the courtroom, and out of the courthouse.

It wasn't the redirect that bothered him -- it was the cross-examination. He didn't know what he had said to make the defense attorney so happy. He was still agitating over it when he stormed across the plaza and pushed his way through the front door of the police station.

"What did I say that was so wrong?" he exclaimed, almost stomping his foot.

"Who said you said anything wrong?" Arnie Stiversen asked.

"You weren't there," Cady replied. "You didn't see. She smiled when she was done with me. She smiled! Something I said made her happy. It was like I had made her whole case for her or something."

"Maybe it was a lawyer's trick -- you know, like she was just trying to rattle your cage, and then see what you would do about it," his partner suggested.

"Why would she want to do that?" he snapped. "My testimony was over. She was done with me."

"Well, don't make any more out of it than you should," Stiversen advised. "I'm sure she didn't do it on purpose."

Cady punched one fist into the other. I screwed up," he said. "I must have said something I shouldn't have -- something that helped her damn client."

· · ·

"It was around six-thirty in the morning, and let's just say that Jason was sober by the time Cady and Stiversen got to him."

Lily was back at the office for the lunch break, discussing the morning's events with Joe. In the background, Dancer, her shadow, watched and waited.

"So?" Joe wondered.

"So, he still didn't fight back."

"Maybe because he knew Cady was a cop."

"Exactly," Lily declared. "In his whole history, he never fought back, drunk or sober. And this time, he didn't fight back, either. Why not?"

"It's not in his nature," Dancer put in.

"What do you mean?" Lily asked.

"His nature," the man from Spokane explained -- it's not assertive, it's subservient. It's pretty obvious -- he was raised to respect authority, not to defy it."

"Well, if that's so," Lily reasoned, "and Jason recognized Dale in the alley, as the prosecution contends, why would that night have been any different than every other time?"

"It's hard to say," Dancer responded.

"I suppose enough alcohol could make an otherwise rational person do stupid things under certain circumstances," Joe offered.

"But why this time?" Lily persisted. "What was different? Jason didn't just know Dale was a cop -- he knew Dale. How many times had they been to the dance together? And each time, Jason got knocked around some, but never fought back. So what made this time different?"

"Okay, I don't know," Joe conceded. "But I can see you're dying to tell us -- so have at it."

"I think Old Eddie may have been onto something," she said. "I think there really is no other plausible explanation."

"For what?" Dancer inquired.

"Well, if all Dale was doing was trying to arrest Jason yet again, there wouldn't have been any argument," she told him. "Just as there had never been any argument all those times before."

"So?" Joe pressed.

"So, I'm starting to believe that Dale really was there to meet his supplier, and he wasn't about to leave any witnesses -- at least not any live ones. I don't know what the injuries all over him were about, and there's no telling which injuries that Jason had could have come from a fight with Dale before Cady took after him, but I think I'm now willing to bet even money that it really was self-defense."

"It's a pretty good theory," Joe conceded.

"And it would go a long way toward explaining things," Dancer said.

She sighed. "Yes," she said. "Now all we have to do is prove it."

• • •

A ballistics expert from the State Patrol Crime Lab took the stand after lunch, to confirm, in somewhat laborious detail, but with compelling photographs to illustrate what he was talking about, that the bullet that had killed Dale Scott had in fact been fired from the detective's own police issue Sig Sauer P250.

"No two guns fire exactly alike," Edward Padilla explained to the jury. The dark-haired, heavy-set man with thick glasses knew his job thoroughly. He had been doing it for more than twenty years. "Based on manufacturing and usage, the barrel of a gun gets what we call a rifling impression pattern, which is a pattern of striations and scratches that transfers from the barrel to the bullet and can be identified as unique to that gun."

"And the bullet in question here?" John Henry asked.

"The bullet that killed Dale Scott was a forty caliber Smith and Wesson, which matched the rest of the bullets that were found in the detective's gun at the time," the expert explained. "When I test-fired the weapon, the striations on the bullets matched exactly the ones on the bullet recovered by the crime scene investigator at the scene of the shooting."

"So your testimony here today is that the bullet that killed Dale Scott was fired from his own gun?" John Henry concluded.

"Yes," the expert said.

There was nothing to cross-examine the analyst on. The bullet was the bullet. And Lily couldn't do very much about the gun, either. She knew she couldn't dispute the fact that a bullet, fired from his own gun, had killed Dale, or that Jason had fired it. All she would be able to argue to the jury was why, and a scenario was already beginning to take shape in her mind.

• • •

The last witness of the day was the lab technician who had tested Jason's blood alcohol level.

"It was at zero," the technician confirmed.

"And what does that mean?" the prosecutor asked.

"Zero means that, when I performed the test, there was no detectable alcohol in his system."

"So he wasn't drunk?" John Henry pressed.

"No, at least not at the time of the test," the technician replied.

• • •

"And when exactly did you perform this test?" Lily inquired on cross-examination.

The technician checked his notes. "I performed the test at twelve-thirty-five in the afternoon on February 10th," he replied.

"And that was what -- at least twelve hours after the estimated time of death?"

"Well, I didn't know that at the time," the witness confirmed. "But, apparently, yes, it was."

"Let's assume -- hypothetically, of course," Lily pressed, "that Jason Lightfoot had consumed, let's say, seven shots of alcohol between eleven and eleven-thirty that night. What would you expect his blood alcohol level to have been at twelve-thirty-five the following day?"

"It most likely would have been zero," the technician said.

"And can you explain for the jury how you would reach that conclusion?"

"Well, the body expels roughly an ounce of alcohol an hour," the technician explained. "A shot of liquor is generally assumed to be around an ounce and a half. Which means that seven shots would add up to roughly ten-and-a-half ounces. So, twelve hours after someone had drunk seven shots of alcohol, his blood alcohol level would pretty much test out at zero."

"So, someone who had perhaps been functionally drunk at midnight, could have tested totally sober twelve hours later?"

"Sure."

• • •

"Is it possible," John Henry inquired on re-direct, "that the defendant's blood alcohol level could have been the same twelve hours earlier as it was when you tested it?"

"Of course," the technician replied.

"Under what circumstances would that have been the case?"

The technician shrugged. "If he hadn't been drinking."

• • •

"So, how do you think things are going?" Carson asked his daughter, when Dancer was finally able to get her out of the office and drive her home for a very late dinner.

"Not too bad, I guess," Lily said.

"From what I saw and heard," her father said, "you held your own."

He had, of course, been watching the proceedings on the local cable channel. And, in fact, if the trial weren't being broadcast, he would have managed, somehow, to be in the courtroom.

"Well, there's nothing like a compliment from the master," Lily said with a chuckle. "I think I might just have boxed in the police officer who found the body and then beat Jason to a pulp when he tried to run," she added. "And I think I also may have put a little bug in the jury's ear about the blood alcohol test being something less than reliable. But we still have a long way to go."

"Do you have a plan?" her father inquired.

Lily smiled. "Of course," she said. "Don't you always tell me that, no matter which side of the aisle I'm on, I have to have a plan?"

• • •

On Wednesday, Dr. Stanley Bellerman, the fulltime pathologist at the Port Hancock Medical Center, and Jackson County's part-time medical examiner, took the witness stand. A thirty-year veteran, the steel-haired doctor detailed for the jury the condition of Dale Scott's body as he had found it on the morning of the murder. With the benefit of slides, he described the bruises and abrasions he had noted on the deceased, as well as the bullet wound. He had a fatherly demeanor, he spoke slowly, clearly, and without affect, and he answered every question the prosecutor asked in layman's terms. The jury loved him.

"Were you able to determine a time of death?" John Henry asked.

"Yes," he replied. "I was able to put the time of death at between midnight and one o'clock on the morning of February 10th."

"And that determination was based on. . . ?"

"It was based on the condition of the body, as I found it, on the liver temperature, and on the extent of rigor mortis," Bellerman said. "I also took into account the weather conditions at the time."

"And what did you determine about the weather conditions?"

"According to the information I was provided, it had been clear during the night," Bellerman reported. "Then around five o'clock in the morning, heavy marine air had moved in, and it was still around when I got to the scene, which was, I believe, just after seven-thirty. In addition, I was able to confirm that the temperature during the night and into the morning hours had been above freezing, and ranged between thirty-five and forty degrees."

"And can you tell the jury what the condition of the body was when you first saw it?"

"It was damp, but not soaked through," the medical examiner replied. "The blood on the ground was not completely dried. I noted a number of bruises and abrasions on the victim's face and torso that I judged to be about seven to seven-and-a-half hours old. The cause of death was a bullet that had been fired into the left side of his head."

"From how far a distance would you say the bullet was fired?"

"Judging from the amount of stippling that remained -- I mean, the gunpowder residue that remained on the skin -- I would say that the bullet was fired from no more than two or three inches from the point of entry."

"Could you determine Detective Scott's position when he was shot?"

The medical examiner provided a demonstration to answer this particular question. Using an articulated dummy provided by the prosecution, he showed the jury what the angle of the bullet had been when it entered Dale Scott's head, and the position he believed the victim had been in when the bullet was fired.

"My conclusion was that the victim was kneeling when he was shot, in what I call an upright fetal position, which was most likely in response to the serious bruising to his abdomen -- and the shooter was standing to his left."

"Is it possible that this shot was fired by accident?" John Henry inquired. "As in 'I was too drunk to know what I was doing, and the gun was in my hand, and it just happened to go off' before I could stop myself'?"

"From the angle of the bullet's entry," the medical examiner replied, "which entered just above the ear, directly into the brain, in a downward trajectory, that would seem unlikely. In my opinion, the shot was aimed, it was not accidental."

"Thank you, Dr. Bellerman," John Henry said. "I have nothing further."

• • •

"It would seem unlikely that the shot to Detective Scott's head -- the shot that killed him -- was accidental, is that your testimony, Dr. Bellerman?" Lily inquired on cross-examination.

"Yes, it is," the medical examiner replied.

The defense attorney frowned. "Is that something a medical examiner usually determines?"

Well, no, it isn't," Bellerman conceded with a shrug. "My job is to determine the cause of death and the manner of death. But I was asked by the prosecutor to speculate on what the context of the death might be, and so I did."

"I see," Lily said. "So, according to you, we can rule out an accidental shooting."

"Yes, I would say so."

"How?"

"Mostly because of the wound itself," he replied. "It appeared to have been aimed."

"Okay, so, let's say we rule out an accidental shooting. I take it there was no evidence suggesting that Dale Scott shot himself, was there?"

"No, there wasn't," the medical examiner confirmed. "First, there was no gunshot residue on his hands, second, he was right-handed and the bullet was fired into the left side of his head, and third, the gun wasn't found anywhere near the body. All of which led to my conclusion that the manner of death in this case was incompatible with suicide."

"All right, so if we rule out an accidental shooting, and we rule out suicide," Lily said thoughtfully, "what's left?"

Bellerman looked perplexed. "I beg your pardon?"

"Well, you seem to be suggesting that the only other option is intentional murder, isn't that true?"

"Well, yes, I suppose what I said did imply intentional murder, and it could have been that."

"Only could have been? But if not intentional, what else?"

Bellerman frowned. "I'm not sure I understand your question."

"Well, you said that the victim had sustained injuries to his face and torso, didn't you? Doesn't that suggest there had likely been a physical confrontation of some kind that occurred prior to his death?"

"I can't say for sure what it was," the medical examiner replied. "There was certainly evidence of some sort of physical encounter, because the victim had sustained multiple bruises and abrasions, but there was no way for me to determine if the two events were actually related."

"But you did confirm that this physical encounter took place at around the same time as death occurred, didn't you?"

"Yes, I did say that," Bellerman conceded, "and I believe that the two encounters did occur at around the same time, but there was no way for me to determine, at least, not with any medical assurance that I would feel comfortable testifying to, whether they were separate or connected events."

"Fair enough," Lily said. "Then, just for the sake of argument, let's say -- hypothetically, of course -- that Detective Scott pulled his gun on his assailant for reasons we may or may not know at this point. Let's further say there was some sort of a struggle, and in the course of that struggle, the assailant got hold of the gun. Was there anything in your autopsy that would eliminate the possibility that the shot that killed Dale Scott was fired in self-defense?"

The medical examiner looked a bit startled. "Self-defense?" he echoed, and then he shook his head. "No, there was nothing in my findings that would eliminate that as a possibility."

"Thank you, Dr. Bellerman," Lily said. "I have nothing further."

• • •

"Where the hell did that self-defense crap come from?" John Henry demanded, when he and Tom Lickliter caught up with Lily in the corridor after court had recessed for the day. "You never said anything about self-defense. Besides, resisting arrest doesn't get you to self-defense, in case you've forgotten. Anyway, I thought you were going to claim he was drunk. I thought you were going to argue diminished capacity?"

"Did I say that?" Lily said.

"Yes, you did," he reminded her. "You said he was drunk. You said he was so drunk he didn't know what he was doing. You said you could argue diminished capacity."

"And I suppose I could," she conceded. "But then again, I just might have a better option."

"What do you think you have?"

"Did I say I had anything?"

"This is all just a load of crap you're trying to fill the jury's head with, and you know it," he exclaimed.

John Henry was a by-the-book, follow-the-rules, put-one-step-in-front-of-the-other kind of prosecutor, and more than anything else, he hated being thrown a curve.

"Maybe so," she agreed, "but I'll tell you what let's do -- let's let you try your case, and let's let me try mine."

John Henry sputtered. Lily shrugged. There was a faint smile on Tom Lickliter's face as he took it all in.

• • •

Ben Dawson was the first witness to take the stand on Thursday. The Port Hancock Police Department's senior crime scene investigator testified in general about his experience, and then what his specific responsibilities were in connection with the Scott crime scene, and he confirmed that he and his partner had arrived in the alley just after seven o'clock on the morning of the murder.

"The M.E. wasn't on scene yet, so we didn't touch the body except to confirm that he was dead," the witness said. "As soon as we determined that, we began to collect evidence. We wanted to get as much stuff identified and photographed as we could before Doc Bellerman showed up and started rearranging things. The shot that killed Detective Scott was a through-and-through, and we found the bullet about ten feet from the body, up against the stone wall that runs down the alley, in pretty good condition, all things considered."

"Through-and-through?" the prosecutor repeated for the jury.

"Yes," Dawson confirmed. "Through-and-through means the bullet went into his head, but it didn't stay there. Instead, it went through his brain, and then exited out the other side of his skull."

"All right, what else?" John Henry asked, noting jurors taking notes.

"We took samples of the blood in the area. We took Detective Scott's gun into custody. We took trace evidence from the victim and we took the defendant's fingerprints and DNA, and tested him for GSR. Because of the weather, we weren't able to get much good quality trace or DNA from the actual place of death, but we did the best we could. And, of course, we took a lot of photographs."

"And when you were done, what did you do with the evidence you had collected?"

"Everything we collected was sealed and signed to preserve the chain of custody, and taken directly to the State Crime Lab.

• • •

"Were there any usable footprints or shoe prints belonging to the defendant at the scene of the crime?" Lily inquired of the witness.

"No," Dawson replied. "In fact, there were no usable footprints or shoe prints belonging to anyone at the immediate scene."

"Was there any DNA belonging to the defendant found at the scene or on the victim?"

"No," the investigator admitted, "we were unable to find any definitive samples of the defendant's DNA either at the immediate scene or on the victim."

"Was any blood associated with the defendant found at the scene?"

Again, the investigator had to concede there was not. "The only blood we were able to recover belonged to the deceased."

Lily frowned. "So, you were unable to find any actual evidence that the defendant was anywhere near Dale Scott when he was killed, is that what you're testifying to?"

"Other than the fact that he fired the gun," the witness said, "no."

"Did you find any other DNA at the scene," Lily inquired. "DNA that didn't belong either to Detective Scott or to my client?"

Dawson shifted a bit in the witness box. "Well, yes, as a matter of fact, we did collect some other DNA samples, from Detective Scott's clothing," he replied. "But there was no saying when they were left, or under what circumstances."

"Male DNA or female DNA?"

"Both," the witness said.

"So, we have none of the defendant's DNA found anywhere near or on the victim, but there was DNA from two other people found on the victim," Lily said thoughtfully. "Thank you, Officer Dawson."

• • •

John Henry jumped up immediately. "Officer Dawson, will you again tell the jury whose DNA was found on the gun that killed Detective Scott?" he asked on redirect.

"There were two donors in the samples of DNA found on the gun," Dawson replied. "The victim's and the defendant's."

• • •

"Am I having a dysfunctional brain moment here, or does this whole thing not make a lot of sense?" Lily wondered when court was in recess.

"What do you mean?" Megan asked.

"There was none of Jason's DNA found on Dale's body, or even at the scene," Lily explained. "And yet he fired the gun. Do any of you think that someone else got into a fight with Dale and then just left him there, and Jason came along and decided to take his gun and shoot him?"

"Contrary to popular opinion, you don't always leave usable DNA behind, you know," Joe reminded her. "And don't forget -- it was damp."

"But it wasn't too damp for DNA from two other people to stick to Dale's clothing."

"Which might indicate that it was left at some other time," Megan suggested. "When it wasn't damp."

"And the female DNA could well have been Lauren's, which would make sense," Joe said.

"Maybe," Lily said. "And maybe there's an explanation we haven't thought of yet."

• • •

An analyst from the Washington State Patrol Crime Lab took the witness stand on Friday, and confirmed for the jury that Jason Lightfoot had indeed been the one who had fired Dale Scott's gun on the night of the murder.

"He tested positive for gunshot residue on both his hands and his clothing," Fletcher Thurman reported. "In addition, there were fingerprints and skin cells matching the defendant's DNA that were found on the murder weapon."

"Were you able to determine how many bullets had been fired from the gun?"

"Yes," the analyst replied. "The Sig Sauer P250 is an automatic loader, and we believe Detective Scott was carrying a full clip, as most officers do. The clip holds twelve bullets, and there were eleven bullets remaining, meaning that one bullet had been fired."

"So, we aren't talking about some wild drunken shooting spree here, are we?" the prosecutor inquired. "We're talking about one bullet, fired with precision, into the brain of the deceased?"

"That's how it looked to me," Thurman concurred. "And that's also how it looked to the medical examiner when I spoke with him. In any case, my understanding was that the defendant's blood alcohol level was zero."

"In other words -- the defendant wasn't drunk?"

"No, not as far as the test results I saw showed."

"If you had to describe what took place that night, based on your analysis of the evidence, what would you say occurred?"

"It appears the victim was down on his knees at the time he was shot, and he was shot in the head at close range."

"Do you mean execution style?" John Henry inquired.

The analyst nodded. "It could have been."

• • •

"Mr. Thurman, will you please tell the jury what the conditions were in the alley behind the Last Call Bar and Grill at the time of Dale Scott's death?" Lily began her cross-examination.

"I don't know what the conditions were firsthand," Thurman replied. "I relied on the weather service data, the report of the investigating officers, and the photographs."

"You mean you weren't there?" Lily wanted the jury to know. "You didn't do any actual on-site gathering or evaluating of the evidence?"

"No."

"Is that normal?"

"Yes, it is," Thurman said. "Most small cities like Port Hancock have crime scene investigators, but they can't afford to have a crime scene analyst on staff. There's generally not enough major crime to warrant the expense."

"So, what do small cities like Port Hancock do?"

"Their investigators gather all the evidence they can, according to guidelines we set out, and then, on anything more important than fingerprints or routine DNA testing, they forward what they collect to us for analysis."

"In that case, what were you told about conditions at the time of death?"

"I was told by the medical examiner that the death had occurred around midnight and I learned from weather data that conditions were clear until about five o'clock that morning," Thurman replied.

"Were you told where the death had occurred?" Lily inquired.

"Yes. It happened in a back alley."

"Were there any streetlights in the alley?"

"In the alley?" Thurman shook his head. "No one said anything about streetlights."

"Where you told if there was a moon shining at the time of the murder? Were there stars in the sky? Was there anything that could have provided enough light for someone to actually see by?"

"As far as I know, it was clear around midnight," the analyst replied. "There were stars, but the moon was a crescent, with only three percent illumination."

"So then, would it be fair to say that the alley would have been pretty dark that night?"

"Yes, I think it would be fair to say that."

"Dark enough, so that if you were walking back there, and you saw someone perhaps fifteen or twenty feet away -- even if you knew that person, you might not be able to recognize him?"

"Objection, Your Honor," John Henry cried. "Calls for speculation. The witness has already testified he wasn't there."

"I'm perfectly willing to recreate the scene in the alley and have the jurors decide for themselves, Your Honor," Lily responded innocently. "I just thought the expert witness put up by the prosecution could save us the time and expense."

Grace Pelletier hid a smile. "Objection overruled, but rephrase the question, Miss Burns."

"All right, based on your expertise in crime scene analysis, Mr. Thurman," Lily rephrased, "what would you say the probability would be that you could recognize someone in an unlit alley, under a crescent moon, from, say, fifteen feet away?"

"Under the conditions I understand were present at the time, probably not very good," the analyst replied.

"One last point on this, then," Lily pursued. "To your knowledge, was Dale Scott wearing a uniform that night, or a badge, or anything at all that would have identified him in the dark as a police officer?"

"No, I don't believe so," Fletcher Thurman replied. "As shown in the photographs, Detective Scott was wearing street clothes -- brown slacks, tan sport shirt, brown leather jacket."

"Street clothes," Lily echoed. "No uniform, no badge, nothing that would readily identify him in an alley in the middle of the night?"

"No. But I don't think that's unusual. It's my understanding that detectives don't wear uniforms."

"If that's the case, is it conceivable then that the defendant might not have realized that the man he encountered in the alley that night -- the man that he would ultimately be held responsible for killing -- was a police officer, and not just some sinister stranger wielding a gun?"

"Yes, I guess it's conceivable," the witness allowed.

"In the middle of the night, without any light, Dale Scott could have been anybody, couldn't he?" Lily pressed the analyst. "He could have been an innocent person stepping outside for a smoke, or a homeless person looking to find shelter, or even someone who had chosen that location specifically because it was dark and it was usually deserted, and he was up to no good -- isn't that possible?"

The witness nodded. "Yes, it's possible."

"Thank you," Lily said. "All right, now, I'm particularly interested in your theory of the shooting. You said that, based on your reconstruction of the crime scene, Dale Scott was down on his knees at the time he was shot."

"That's correct."

"How did you reach that conclusion?"

"I reached that conclusion based on the position that the body was in," the analyst said. "It fell sideways as a result of the force of the shot, and it was bent in a manner that indicated that the victim had been kneeling at the time the shot was fired."

"And you were able to discern this from looking at the crime scene photographs?"

"Yes," Thurman confirmed.

"Were you able to tell if the body had been moved?"

"Based on the information I was given by the investigators, and on my analysis of the photographs taken, I concluded that the body had not been moved."

"How can you be so sure?"

"The blood pool was consistent with the body having been in the position where it was found and photographed."

"You concurred with the prosecutor's opinion that this could have been an execution-style shooting, did you not?"

"I did."

"Would you be good enough to describe such a scenario for the jury?"

Thurman turned to the jury. "When we say an execution-style shooting, what we usually mean is a head shot where the victim is on his knees or has his back to his assailant, and the shooter is standing either behind him or beside him. In this case, it was beside him."

"Beside him?" Lily repeated. "The shooter was standing beside him, not kneeling beside him?"

"No, from the angle of the shot," the analyst said. "I would say he was standing beside him."

"How tall was Dale Scott?"

Thurman checked his notes. "He was five-feet-ten inches tall."

"And what did he weigh?"

"My notes say that Detective Scott weighed two hundred and sixteen pounds."

"And will you tell the jury how tall the defendant is, and how much he weighs?"

The analyst looked blank. "I have no idea," he replied. "I was never asked to measure him or weigh him."

"You weren't asked to measure or weigh him?" Lily echoed. "Well, when you analyzed the trajectory of the bullet, what did the angle of the shot tell you about the height of the shooter?"

Thurman glanced over at John Henry and then back at Lily. "I was never asked to perform a trajectory analysis," he said.

"A capital crime, involving the murder of a police detective, and you were never asked to do a trajectory analysis?"

"No."

"Why do you suppose that was?"

Thurman shrugged. "This is a county that doesn't waste taxpayer money on unnecessary tests," he replied. "I was told it was an open and shut case, and all I was required to do was confirm who had fired the gun."

"I see." Lily shot a withering glance in the direction of John Henry, who shifted uncomfortably in his seat. "Well then, I guess we'll just have to do a little analyzing right here, won't we?" She turned to the defendant. "Jason, will you stand up for the jury, please?"

Jason Lightfoot did as he was told, pushing back from the table and uncoiling his long body from the chair. The chain around his waist that was attached to his leg irons was hidden beneath his suit coat, but the jury could hear the jangling as he rose.

"Unless the prosecutor is unwilling to take my word for it, Your Honor," Lily addressed the bench, "I would like it noted for the record that Jason Lightfoot is six feet four inches tall, and at the time of Dale Scott's death, weighed one hundred and seventy-two pounds."

"So noted," Grace Pelletier said.

Lily turned to the witness. "How tall are you, Mr. Thurman?"

"I'm five-foot-eleven."

"Close enough," she said. "Your Honor, may I ask that the witness be allowed to step down and stand in front of the jury, and that the defendant be allowed to approach?"

"Objection!" John Henry cried, jumping to his feet. "For what possible purpose does defense counsel seek to divert the jury's attention by engaging in some kind of courtroom theatrics?"

"Miss Burns?" the judge inquired.

"If the police and the prosecutor's office had done their jobs properly, Your Honor," Lily replied, "there would have been a trajectory analysis performed, and no need for me to have to demonstrate what I now feel I have to demonstrate for the jury."

"I object to that, too," John Henry declared. "It's not up to opposing counsel to tell us what our jobs are or how we're supposed to do them."

"The first objection is overruled, the second is sustained," the judge ordered. "The witness may step down and the defendant may approach."

The prosecuting attorney quietly fumed. The deputy prosecuting attorney frowned. The defense attorney swallowed a smile. The crime scene analyst stepped down from the witness box.

"Now, sir," Lily directed, "will you be kind enough to face the jury and assume the position you have testified that Detective Scott was in at the time he was shot."

Fletcher Thurman went down on his knees, wrapped his arms around his midsection, and hunched over. "Judging from the way he fell, and from the position of his arms and legs," he explained, "I concluded that the victim was in this position when he was shot."

"Like you are now?" Lily asked.

"Yes," Thurman confirmed. "He had abrasions on his face, and deep bruises on his chest and abdomen, meaning he was likely in some pain from the beating he sustained, and was likely trying to protect himself in what the medical examiner calls an upright fetal position."

"All right," Lily said, having first-hand knowledge of precisely what the analyst was talking about. She walked over to the evidence table and picked up Dale Scott's Sig Sauer P250. Even unloaded, the weapon was heavy. She turned to her client. "Jason, I'd like you to come over here and stand to the left side of Mr. Thurman."

His chains clanking, Jason stepped out from behind the defense table and shuffled awkwardly across the room.

"That's good," Lily said when he reached the appropriate spot. She reached out and handed him the gun, noticing as she did so that several members of the jury instinctively shrank back. "Now, will you please point the gun at Mr. Thurman's head, as though you intended to shoot him just above the left ear."

The Indian raised the gun slowly, awkwardly, clearly uncomfortable to be holding the weapon, almost to the point of being unsure how to hold it, which was also noted by some of the jurors. As he pointed the dead policeman's weapon at the analyst's head, it became clear, not just to the jurors, but to just about everyone in the courtroom that, had he fired the fatal bullet from a standing position, as the prosecutor claimed he had, it would not have entered Dale Scott's brain at all -- it would have gone almost straight down through Dale Scott's jaw.

"All right, Jason, now hunch over a bit, and try again," Lily instructed.

Although the position was quite painful to his bad leg, Jason hunched over as best he could, and then grit his teeth and forced himself to go down even further, but nothing he tried fit the angle that the witness had described.

"I'm sorry, Jason, but I'm going to have to ask you to kneel beside the witness."

"I can't" the defendant said. "I got a bum leg. Can't bend it much more'n it already is. It already hurts like hell. Can't put much weight on it, either."

Lily frowned for the jury. "You're physically unable to fully kneel?"

"On both knees -- yeah."

"Objection!" John Henry cried. "Your Honor, the defendant is testifying!"

Lily turned to the judge. "If necessary," she said, "I can have a doctor come into court and testify that

Jason Lightfoot's right leg was smashed in an accident ten years ago, and put back together with steel rods and pins. He can bend it only slightly, he can't tolerate much weight on it, and I defy anyone to assume a kneeling position where one leg doesn't have to bend very much or carry any weight."

"Your Honor, now *she's* testifying!" John Henry protested.

Grace Pelletier banged her gavel. The clock on the wall above her head read: 11:40. "It's almost time for lunch," she declared. "Court will be in recess until two o'clock. I admonish the jury not to discuss this case amongst yourselves or with anyone else." She glared at the attorneys. "In my chambers!" she ordered.

• • •

"Your Honor, the defense is attempting to prejudice the jury," John Henry complained, the moment he and Lily had been ushered into the judge's chambers that were located just behind the courtroom, and the judge had shut the door.

"On the contrary, Your Honor," Lily argued. "The prosecution has now presented two witnesses that claim to know exactly how the murder took place. I'm simply trying to demonstrate to the jury that the defendant couldn't possibly have done it the way Mr. Morgan chooses to believe he did."

"I want a mistrial," the prosecutor declared angrily.

"You're not getting any mistrial, Mr. Morgan," the judge informed him. "Miss Burns, I assume you can, in fact, produce a witness that will testify to the defendant's infirmity?"

"I can, Your Honor," Lily said. The orthopedic surgeon who had performed Jason's surgery was not on her witness list, but had indicated that, if necessary, he would be more than willing to appear on the defendant's behalf.

"Then we shall proceed," Grace said. "Mr. Morgan, the defense will provide you with the name of this witness, and you will be free to interview him or her, as you choose."

• • •

Lily and Megan spent the lunch recess tracking down the surgeon, and confirming his willingness to testify. When court resumed, the judge addressed the jury.

"You are instructed to disregard the statements made by the defendant and his attorney," she said. "They were not part of any testimony given under oath." Then she turned to Lily. "You may proceed."

With that, Fletcher Thurman was called back to the witness stand.

"Now, to continue, Mr. Thurman," the defense attorney said as soon as he was seated and reminded by the judge that he was still under oath, "if I were to ask you how a six-foot-four-inch tall man could hold a gun to the head of a five-foot-ten-inch man who was kneeling in what, I believe, you called an upright fetal position, and shoot him just above his left ear, at hardly any downward angle -- what would you say?"

"I analyzed the entry wound," Thurman replied, at a loss to explain what had been made clear to him. "The photos showed there was gunshot residue indicating a close-range shot, and an angle that would indicate that the perpetrator was standing just to the left side of the victim. But my analysis did not take into consideration a perpetrator as tall as the defendant. So I guess I could have been wrong."

"In what way?" Lily prompted.

"It's contrary to my analysis," Thurman said, "but it would appear that either both had to be kneeling, or both had to be standing."

"Shall we try again?" Lily offered. "Shall we have the defendant step out and see if the angle is accurate while you're both standing?"

"Your Honor," John Henry warned.

"Never mind, Miss Burns, you've made your point," the judge admonished. "Move along."

"Yes, thank you, Your Honor," Lily acknowledged. "Mr. Thurman, you testified earlier that your own analysis, along with that of the medical examiner, led you to believe that Dale Scott had been shot execution-style, is that correct?"

"That's what I said."

"Well then, assuming that the victim was indeed kneeling on the ground in the upright fetal position you've described when he was shot, how many execution-style shootings have you analyzed, or read about, or even heard about, for that matter, where both the perpetrator and the victim were kneeling at the time?"

"None."

"So then, would it be fair to say that your description of this event as an 'execution-style' shooting could have been inaccurate?"

"Given the demonstration you were able to put on earlier," Thurman was forced to admit, "I think it would be fair to say that my conclusion may have been inaccurate."

"In that case," Lily pressed, "was there anything in your analysis that would preclude a fight over the gun that resulted in the defendant having shot Dale Scott, let's say -- in self-defense?"

Thurman shook his head. "At this point, I couldn't rule that out."

"Thank you." Lily began to turn away and then abruptly turned back again. "Oh, one more thing," she said. "I believe you testified that the toxicology screen on the defendant had come back with a blood alcohol reading of zero, is that correct?"

"It is."

"And what about the victim? What did his toxicology screen indicate?"

The analyst looked blank. "We didn't do a toxicology screen on the victim," he said.

"You didn't? Why not?"

"Because we weren't asked to. According to the medical examiner, the the cause of death was obvious."

"That's right, I forgot," Lily said. "You said the county doesn't waste taxpayer money on unnecessary tests, didn't you?"

"Yes, I did say that," Thurman replied. "And no, it doesn't."

Over at the prosecution table, John Henry could only sit in his seat and seethe inwardly. He knew he should be objecting to something -- he could see it on the faces of the jurors -- he just didn't know to what.

"So the victim's body could have been full of any number of substances that might have been relevant to his death," Lily suggested. "He could have had a boatload of, let's say -- cocaine -- in his system, and it wouldn't have any bearing on this case simply because no one bothered to order a toxicology screen?"

Fletcher Thurman had no axe to grind. He wasn't beholden to either the prosecution or the defense. He was paid to do a job, no matter what the results turned out to be.

"I'm afraid so," he said.

"How convenient is that?" Lily said in disgust.

John Henry finally found an opening. "Objection," he complained.

"Withdrawn," Lily declared because, again, she had made her point. "I have no further questions."

"Redirect, Mr. Morgan?" the judge inquired.

John Henry remained where he was for a moment, stone-faced, trying to decide whether it would be better just to let this witness go, or to try to rehabilitate him. Lily Burns had dealt his first-degree murder case a potentially serious blow.

Beside him, Tom Lickliter leaned his elbow on the arm of his chair and rubbed his chin. She was good, he thought. Every bit as good as he had heard. She was deft at putting little ideas into the jurors' heads, not belaboring them, just slipping them in there, and managing, ever so gently, to shift the jury's focus.

In one cross-examination, she had been able to suggest police incompetence, a rush to judgment, and prosecutorial disregard. He wondered what else those involved in the investigation of Dale Scott's death had overlooked or discarded as irrelevant. He wondered what else Lily Burns had up her sleeve.

The prosecutor stood, knowing he couldn't let Lily's cross-examination stand.

"Mr. Thurman," he asked, "what killed Dale Scott?"

"A bullet to the head, fired from his own gun."

"And who fired that gun?"

"All the evidence we have strongly suggests that the defendant did."

"Whether he was standing, kneeling, or lying flat on his face?"

"Yes."

"Thank you," the prosecutor said. It was the best he could do, under the circumstances. "I have nothing further for this witness."

• • •

"Where the hell can she be going with this?" John Henry asked irritably after court had adjourned for the day, and he and Tom were heading upstairs to their offices.

"Can't say as I have a clue yet," Tom replied. "But it sure sounds like she really intends to open the door to self-defense. Have you ruled that out as a possibility?"

"There was no evidence of it."

"No injuries to the defendant?"

John Henry sighed. "The thing is, he was covered in them. But the officers who brought him in had to subdue him when he resisted arrest, so we couldn't tell what injuries came from what encounter."

The deputy prosecutor shook his head. "You could have a real problem here," he said. "Have you considered a deal?"

John Henry bristled. He had removed his suit jacket to counter the ineffective air-conditioning, but it wasn't sufficient. He was sweating profusely, causing Tom to wonder if it was only because of the heat.

"A deal?" John Henry snapped. "Now, why would I want to think about that?"

If there was one thing he had learned from his years in public office, it was that defense attorneys came groveling for deals -- not prosecutors. Besides, he had already offered to take the death penalty off the table, and the Indian had turned it down cold.

"Well, for one thing," Tom said mildly, "I've been watching the jury, and it looks like you're starting to lose them. That's always a bad sign, especially when it happens in the middle of the state's case. For another, if Lily Burns can get them to seriously consider self-defense, the defendant walks."

The Jackson County Prosecutor smiled stiffly, because he had no intention of losing this case. "You're new here, Tom," he said, "and so far, I like what I see -- I like it a lot. But you don't know this county or even this city very well yet. You don't know the people -- you haven't developed a feel for them. I have. As a matter of fact, I've known them all my life, and I can guarantee you that what the overwhelming majority of them want is to see this guy hang."

"Maybe so," Tom conceded, because he had been listening to the radio and reading the *Port Hancock Herald*, and he knew what people were thinking and how they were feeling. "But have you taken a good look at the jury lately? They're seeing some pretty slipshod investigating. I know, I am. Now, you're certainly right when you say that I don't know much about the people over here yet, but I've found that people are pretty much the same wherever they are, and over in Seattle, I can tell you, this case would be starting to look a lot like reasonable doubt."

John Henry had looked. He knew exactly what Tom was talking about. Most of the jurors were now hanging on every word Lily Burns uttered, but that didn't tell him whether they were buying her story. "You know as well as I do that you have to try the case you've got," he said. "So, let me ask -- do you think it was self-defense?"

"What I think is that opposing counsel is doing the best she can to turn that pie-in-the-sky theory into a real possibility."

"But do you believe it?" the prosecutor pressed. "Do you believe it was really dark enough in that alley and Lightfoot was drunk enough that he didn't know it was a cop that he fought with and then shot in the head?"

"Given what I've seen and heard so far, if I were an ordinary citizen, I might be persuaded," the deputy prosecuting attorney had to reply.

John Henry scowled. "If the jury buys it, the Indian walks, and I didn't bring this case to trial to see him walk."

"No, I don't think you did," Tom said. "I think you went with what you thought was solid."

"The son-of-a-bitch killed a cop," the prosecutor declared. "A cop with almost fourteen years on the force. However it went down, if we can't convict him for it -- what credibility do we have? What kind of message does that send?"

Tom Lickliter was nothing if not a pragmatist. "That's precisely why I'd rather walk away with something I could hand the public than end up with nothing."

"We're not done with our case yet," John Henry said, because he was too proud, or too stubborn, to contemplate defeat at this point, especially not at the hands of a lawyer who had once worked for him. "We still have some pretty powerful testimony to go. Besides, you don't know Lily Burns. If we were to go to her now, she'd smell that we're scared, and believe me, she wouldn't deal -- she'd take us all the way to verdict just to see us squirm."

At least one part of John Henry's comment was accurate, the Jackson County Deputy Prosecutor thought to himself -- he didn't know Lily Burns. . .yet.

Eight

Tom Lickliter was a true Seattle native. Born and raised on Queen Anne Hill, in the heart of the city, and educated at the University of Washington, he could honestly say he had never lived anywhere else. Married to his high school sweetheart at the age of twenty-six, and then abruptly widowed at the age of forty-three, he had, on pure impulse, accepted an offer of employment from a remote little place on the other side of Puget Sound, pulled up stakes, and moved to Port Hancock.

Leaving Seattle was hard. It didn't just mean uprooting his two sons from the only home they had ever known. It also meant getting used to a new job, trying to make a home in a new house, finding his way around a new town, and maybe one day, even beginning a new relationship.

Those who knew Tom called him a workaholic, and there was truth to that. So much so that he blamed himself for not having spent more time with his wife, for not realizing how sick she was until it was too late, for not being able to save her. It was her ruddy complexion that deceived him -- deceived everyone. After all, how could anyone who looked so healthy and been so cheerful have been so sick?

Lily Burns was nothing like his late wife, nothing at all. Where Jean had been short in stature, Lily was rather tall. Where Jean had been a bit on the plump side, Lily was trim. Where Jean had been dark-haired and dark-eyed, Lily was fair. And where Jean had been content to putter around the garden or in the kitchen, or work behind the scenes for worthy causes, Tom suspected that Lily more often than not put herself right out front, championing her causes, challenging the system. No, she was nothing at all like his wife. But there was something about her that, in spite of himself, he was starting to find very appealing.

• • •

For the first time since being summoned to Grace Pelletier's chambers back in February, Lily was beginning to think she might actually have a chance to win this case. "Self-defense is looking better and better every day," she told Megan with a satisfied smile. "And if you want to know the truth, I could very easily be convinced that's exactly what it was."

"You mean you could have argued it, even if you didn't believe it?" Megan asked.

"Legally, you can argue almost anything," Lily replied. "It just makes it more convincing when you believe what you're arguing."

"You seem pleased," Megan observed. "You didn't used to be, you know -- you used to want this case to go away and you wanted Dale Scott's killer brought to justice. Even if he was you own client. Now you don't seem so sure."

Lily shrugged. "The justice system is supposed to be about the search for truth, about holding the state to the highest standard, but it's really all about winning," she told her paralegal. "This time, though, in little old backwater Jackson County, the system may just end up working the way it's intended to work."

Megan smiled. "It's not only about the search for truth," she said. "Or even that you hate to lose, which I'm in a unique position to know you do. No, if I'm not completely misreading the signs, I'd say it isn't just your case that's looking better every day, it's your client, too."

"I do have to admit," Lily conceded, "I'm learning a few things that do make him seem a lot more credible."

And it was true -- Lily was indeed thinking better of Jason Lightfoot. She liked the way he handled himself in court. He was quiet and he was respectful, and other than an occasional murmured question indicating he was paying at least partial attention to the proceedings, he didn't interfere, or make any demands. He just let her do her job.

And, too, she had just about persuaded herself that he could have killed Dale Scott in self-defense, and that made a huge difference. Not to mention how relieved she was that he had refused to take the deal that would likely have put him in jail for the rest of his life. He was slowly earning her respect and, in return, she was growing more and more willing to go to the wall for him. In other words, she was finally prepared to admit how wise Grace Pelletier had been eight months ago.

• • •

Carson Burns was indeed following every single word of the trial on the local cable television channel. Half an hour before court was called into morning session, he made Diana help him up out of his wheelchair and into his favorite recliner in the library, with a sizeable mug of coffee and a plate piled with biscuits that he largely ignored on the small table by his side, and then, as soon as she left, he would turn on the television. Each time the proceedings broke for lunch, or some other reason, she would make him take a break, too, to eat something, or go to the bathroom, or take a nap, or do whatever she could get him to do. In turn, when court reconvened, he insisted on being taken right back to the library.

Grace Pelletier had made the controversial ruling to allow cameras in the courtroom after the local cable channel petitioned on the basis of educational value as well as the people's right to know, and neither the prosecution nor the defense voiced any serious objection. As a result, two cameras, one in the rear of the courtroom and the other along the side, covered the proceedings. It was a first for the county, and it afforded Carson a unique opportunity to watch his daughter at work.

"All the theatrics are fine, and you're making some good points," he told her over dinner on Friday evening. "But none of it will matter if you can't get around the fact that your client fired the gun. That's what John Henry is going to drum into the jurors' heads at every opportunity. And I worry that, even if you can prove that Dale was up to his eyeballs in cocaine and dirty policing, the best you might get out of a self-defense argument is a hung jury, which means you'll have to start all over again."

Lily sighed, because she knew he was right. "I have the weekend," she said. "Let's see what else I can come up with."

• • •

Jason's cell was stifling -- air-conditioning not being a high priority in the penal budget. His orange jumpsuit was soaked with sweat. He pulled the bedding off his bunk, stripped down to his shorts, and stretched out on the bare metal, hoping for some relief, but it made little difference. With nowhere to go, the hot air just hung in the small space.

He tried not to think about the trial. He had nothing in the world to do except think, but he didn't want to think about the trial. He just couldn't help it. As hard as he wanted to push his mind in other directions, it kept coming back to that big, dark, smelly room where the rest of his life was being decided by a bunch of people who didn't even know him. He wondered how it was possible that these people who didn't know the first thing about him could hold his life in their hands, and he wanted to jump up and shout at them that they had no right. But of course he didn't.

He appreciated what the lady lawyer was trying to do -- make a case for self-defense, or maybe it was something to do with him being drunk -- but he didn't see as it was really doing him any good.

Every day, he watched the jurors. They never looked at him. They didn't want to know him, or anything about him. They wanted someone to pay for what happened to the cop, and he was all they had. So they wanted him to pay. He could tell. Even though they were listening to what the lady lawyer said, he could see it in their eyes, in their body language. A cop was dead. That was what reached out and touched them, and made them feel vulnerable -- not some poor homeless excuse for a man. They didn't care about mitigating circumstances -- whatever that was. They didn't care about him.

And what if the lawyer did convince them that it wasn't his fault he killed the cop? What difference would it make? They would still make him pay for it. And, truth be told, it would be a relief. Jason wasn't anxious to die, but there was no way he could live, caged up like this, much longer.

If he hadn't known that before, he certainly knew it now. In just the past eight months, his skin had developed a grayish tinge from lack of sunlight, and he had lost close to thirty pounds -- thirty pounds he didn't have to spare. The clothes the lady lawyer bought for him to wear to court were two sizes smaller than he used to wear. His orange jumpsuit hung on him.

It was the food, of course -- greasy, overcooked, inedible stuff that turned his stomach sour, and more often than not was left untouched. He couldn't remember the last time he'd had a decent cup of coffee. He longed for one of his uncle's ham steaks. And, despite all the good that Greg Parker may have done for him, he ached for a shot of rum.

But more than anything, he yearned for the sweet smell of the mountains, the gentle touch of a highland breeze, the peaceful sound of a wandering stream or a bird chirping, and the indescribable feel of high-ground dirt beneath his bare feet.

• • •

The call came at 11:30 on Sunday morning.

"Sorry to have to bother you at home, Counselor, but we have a problem," the warden at the Jackson County Jail declared without preamble. "Your client broke out of here about an hour ago."

Lily was dumbfounded. "What happened?"

"Well, he was having his hour out in the yard, just like always, and because we've never had a problem with him, the guard turned his back for just a minute or two," the warden told her. "He was over the fence and gone before anyone could do anything about it." Jailbreaks at the county jail were almost unheard of and, as a result, the barbed wire that topped the cement fence surrounding the facility, while meticulously maintained, had never been electrified. "I've notified the Port Hancock police, of course, and the county sheriff, and the state patrol. I wouldn't have thought he could get over the wall with that bum leg of his, but you just never know about these Indians -- here one minute, gone the next. And real quick and efficient about it, too."

The facility backed onto the foothills that led directly into the mountains where, Lily knew, there was an ample supply of fresh water and food, and endless places where a knowledgeable person could hide. The reservation where Jason Lightfoot had been born and raised was well within hiking distance.

"I'll be happy to do whatever I can to help," she told the warden. "But I don't hold out much hope of anyone finding him up there."

"Maybe not, Ma'am," the warden said, "but we sure as hell got to try."

True to his word, state patrol helicopters were soon buzzing Port Hancock on their way up to the mountains, police units from all over the county hit the foothills and fanned out in all directions, and canine teams were brought in to try to track the Indian's route from the jail.

"What the hell happened?" Joe exclaimed when Lily called him.

"I guess he didn't want to die, after all," she said. "Maybe the further we got into trial, the more inevitable it looked to him."

"And here I thought you were doing such a damn good job of defending him."

Lily sighed over the phone. "I guess he must not have thought it was good enough."

Word spread quickly around town.

"He must have had help," someone suggested.

"An inside job, maybe," someone else said.

"Or an outside one."

People congregated outside after church. A cold-blooded killer had broken out of jail and was on the loose. "How can we protect our families?" they asked their priests and their pastors.

Worried women met at the supermarket. "If he could kill a policeman, he could kill anyone, couldn't he?"

Men gathered at the auto supply shop. "Sure would like to know how he got away so clean," they said, perhaps a bit wistfully.

It was the lead story on the evening news, the main topic of conversation on talk radio, and the headline in morning newspapers all across the state. How could a man with a bad leg scale a ten-foot cement fence topped with barbed wire, in less than a minute, and get away clean, people wanted to know.

As it turned out, however, it wasn't in less than a minute. The yard guard had been on his cell phone, having a heated conversation with his new wife about his ex-girlfriend, with his back to the prisoner for at least ten minutes.

"He'd never tried anything before," the guard complained. "He was out there an hour every day, and all he'd ever done was volunteer to wash the wall down. Said he needed the exercise."

"What's your preference?" Joe asked Lily. "That they find him, or that they don't?"

"I think I'm going to hold my cards close on that for now," Lily said. "Meanwhile, I guess, it's still our case."

• • •

It took Jason several hours to reach the mountains he knew so well, and then a few more to climb his way up to the specific spot, in the shadow of two peaks, that he had dreamed about seeing again for so long.

He had been forced to take a rather roundabout route, in and out of myriad rivers and streams, to make sure he would leave no scent behind for search dogs to pick up and track.

His leg hurt so much it that was all he could do to keep himself from screaming at the top of his lungs. But when he finally entered the small clearing he had been heading for, and saw the spring-fed mountain pool close to the small cave he remembered so well, he knew that all the pain had been worth it.

His first task was to build a fire that no white man would ever see. His second was to fashion a crude spear from a piece of dead tree limb, honing the tip of the branch on a big rock until it was sharp enough. Then he took aim at a small fish in the pool, quite pleased with himself when he needed only three tries to snag it. He plucked some of the edible mountain plants, made a nest for his fish, rested it carefully over his fire, and cooked the first decent food he would eat in months.

All around him, the sky was glowing as the last rays of sunshine dipped below the mountaintops, and he leaned against the big rock and watched as the world went from day to dark, and first one and then another and then another blink of star peeked through the pale blue, dark blue, and finally black sky. He was sure there were at least a trillion of them out there, and they were so bright and so close that he knew he could just reach up and touch one of them if he wanted to.

After a while, he gathered up a load of leaves and made a bed on the floor of the cave. But, try as he could, he just couldn't get himself to sleep. It was the exhilaration of being free, of course. Although exhausted from his journey, he dragged himself back out of the cave, sat down against the rock, and watched the stars dancing across the sky all night.

• • •

At nine o'clock on Monday morning, Grace Pelletier called her court to order, issued a bench warrant for Jason Lightfoot, and then declared that the trial was on hold.

"I apologize to the members of the jury, but we're going to be taking a little break in the proceedings," she said, wondering if it was going to be possible to keep the defendant's escape from jail a secret from them, and knowing, just from the looks on their faces, that it was not going to be possible -- that they already knew. "Should this delay exceed two weeks, I will declare a mistrial."

She then called the attorneys into chambers. "All right, what the hell is going on here?" she demanded, glowering at Lily.

"I'm afraid I don't know anything more about this than you do, Your Honor," the attorney assured her, embarrassed nonetheless. "I found out about it after the fact -- just like everyone else."

"No hint? No clue? Nothing in his behavior to indicate he might do something like this?"

"Nothing," Lily insisted. "On the contrary, he seemed to be dealing with the trial quite well."

"Mr. Morgan?" the judge inquired.

"We're not looking for sanctions, Your Honor," John Henry said. "We don't believe there was any collusion involved."

"Good, then we're agreed." She turned back to Lily. "Should your client contact you, however, Miss Burns -- "

"Yes, Your Honor," Lily said before the judge could finish her sentence. "I will urge him to surrender himself, and I will notify the court immediately."

• • •

"Damn it!" Lily exploded as soon as she was back in the safe confines of the Broad Street Victorian. "We hadn't even put on a single witness yet, and I was beginning to think maybe we wouldn't have to, our case was going so well." It was only a slight exaggeration.

"I agree," Megan said sympathetically. "You'd already gotten that crime scene analyst to pretty much admit that his whole theory about kneeling and standing and an execution-style shooting didn't make much sense."

"All we needed was some confirmation on the drug angle," Lily added, "and I just know we could have found at least one member of that jury to think reasonable doubt. Urrrgh, Jason!"

"You can't really blame him, though," Dancer said softly. "He didn't understand very much of what was going on. I was watching him, and I could tell. I think all he knew was that, if he didn't get to breathe in some fresh mountain air pretty soon, he was going to up and die. I know that's how I would have felt."

"Do you think that's where he went?" Lily asked him with a faint smile. "Into the mountains?"

"If I were him, that's where I'd be," the bodyguard said.

"But you know as well as I do that's the first place they're going to look for him."

"Maybe so," Dancer conceded. "But if I know Jason, unless he wants to be found, they'll never find him."

• • •

"If you're lookin' for my nephew," Charles Graywolf said, "I'll tell you what I told them others -- he ain't here, and I ain't heard from him."

"Relax," Joe said. "I'm not here to bust your chops. I'm just here to give you a message to give to him -- should you happen to hear from him."

"And what makes you think I'm gonna?" the Indian asked.

The private investigator shrugged. "Let's just say, gut instinct," he said. "So, when you do get to talk to him, tell him his lawyer's got a better case to make for self-defense than he realizes, and she wants him to come back and let her present it."

"Does she really think she'll get to finish this trial?"

"She's hoping to," Joe told him. "And she's hoping, when she does, that it'll all turn out right."

"And Jason's supposed to believe that?"

"I know the lawyer," Joe said. "And I believe her. Now, whether he believes it or not is up to him."

"If I hear from him, I'll be sure to tell him," the uncle said.

"That's all I can ask."

The conversation was over. Graywolf walked his visitor to his car. "They'll never find him up there, you know," he said. "He knows them mountains better than any white man ever will. If he wants to, he can stay lost in 'em forever."

Joe nodded. "I know," he said.

• • •

"Quite an interesting turn of events," Carson Burns observed that evening.

It was just the two of them, sitting in the library after dinner was done. Lily had sent Dancer down to the Last Call, and the other bars along lower Broad Street, and over to the casino at Cypress Ridge, and anywhere else he could think of to go, to nose around, to pick up any stray word that might be floating about, to see if anyone had any idea where Jason Lightfoot was hiding, and what he might be thinking.

"Tell me about it," she said

"Do you believe what you told Grace?"

"Actually, I do," Lily replied. "The trial was going pretty well. And even though I realize that Jason wasn't holding out much hope of getting an out-and-out acquittal, I'm reasonably sure he understood we at least had a good shot at a hung jury." She sighed.

"What?" her father asked.

"Well, I guess I agree with Dancer," she said. "Maybe he wasn't paying so much attention. Maybe what he was seeing out the window had a stronger pull on him."

"They won't find him, you know," Carson said.

Lily nodded. "I know," she said. "That's what Dancer says, too. And what Jason's uncle told Joe. And to tell you the truth, I'm not sure how to feel about it. On the one hand, I would have liked the chance to argue self-defense. I think we could have put up a strong case for it. On the other hand, who really knows if the jury would have bought it?"

"You think it's a hanging jury?" her father inquired, because the one thing that the television cameras were not allowed to show were the jurors. So he wasn't able to see their faces or their expressions or their body language, which was how he had always judged how a jury was leaning.

"I think there's a dead cop, and the feeling in the community is that someone's got to pay for that," Lily said. "What I was hoping for was that I could get first-degree down as far as maybe manslaughter. But at this point, I suspect nobody's thinking about reasonable doubt."

. . .

With the trial on hold, Joe Gideon and Arnie Stiversen met again at The Hangout.

"Why am I doing this?" the police officer asked. "The guy's gone. We can't find him. The State Patrol boys can't find him. No one's going to find him. Why am I putting my neck on the line for him?"

"Because Lily isn't ready to give up on him yet, so I can't," Joe told him. "And besides, the judge could always decide not to declare a mistrial and try the guy in absentia."

"Yeah, well, if anyone finds out what I'm doing here," his former colleague said, "it won't just be my badge, you know -- it'll be my pension."

"No one's going to hear a word about it from me, I can tell you that," Joe assured him. "As far as I'm concerned, and I'll get up in court and testify to it, if I have to, there's any number of ways I could have gotten this information."

"Yeah, well, if that's so, then I wish you'd gone one of those ways," Stiversen said wryly. "Not that I blame the guy for running," he added. "Self-defense was going to be a pretty steep climb, even for Lily. And from what I was hearing, the jury might have been intrigued by her courtroom drama, but they weren't necessarily buying into it."

"She never got to put on her case," Joe reminded him.

"Yeah, well, if we do catch him, it'll make it even worse for him, you know -- everyone will be assuming he ran because he was guilty, and then what've you got?"

"A bigger problem than we've got now, I guess," Joe replied.

"You might say," Stiversen said with a brief chuckle that was quickly followed by a thoughtful frown. "The thing is," he added, "if we do catch him, and he does go back to trial, I don't want to see him hang if all he tried to do that night was protect himself."

With that said, he slid a small folded piece of paper across the bar toward his friend.

Joe unfolded the paper. The name that was written on it was indeed one of the three that Neil Van Aiken had given him.

"Thanks," he said.

"I hope you get to use it."

"So do I."

Joe slipped the paper into his pocket, and took a big slug of beer. "Dale wasn't such a bad cop when I knew him -- maybe just a little rough around the edges," he said. "Any idea what happened?"

"Not really," Stiversen replied. "He always had a pretty hot temper, as you know. But over the past couple of years that changed. Then it was like he would be calm as can be one minute, and the next, he'd be flying off the handle for no reason at all."

"Did you know he was using?"

"No, I didn't," the police officer said. "But I guess it didn't come as such a big surprise to find out. Did you know he was suspended for a month last year? He put a shoplifter in the hospital with a ruptured spleen -- a homeless guy, who all he did was steal a turkey sandwich, for Christ sake. The chief had no choice, but he did his best to keep it in the house."

"Yeah, I think I heard something about that," Joe said. In fact, he didn't have a clue what Stiversen was talking about, but he wasn't going to let him know that. He simply filed the information away in his head, on the chance that it might become relevant down the road.

"Some of us started talking back then, you know, trying to figure out what was going on with him," his friend continued. "We knew there was something wrong. Not that we came up with drugs, mind you -- he was apparently very discreet about what he was doing in that department -- but there was something. We thought maybe he was having trouble at home, you know. I wish now we'd figured it out."

"Not your fault," Joe told him.

"All the same," Stiversen said, "I want you to know that I'm sorry about Lightfoot. I'm sorry I didn't do a better job."

"Like you said, it wasn't your call," Joe reminded him.

"Still, I jumped to a conclusion, when I should have been objective."

"Well, don't beat yourself up over it. I got to tell you, we pretty much all jumped to the same conclusion."

Stiversen looked around the bar, as if to check out who might be there, then hunched over close to Joe and lowered his voice. "I don't think we're going to find him," he said. "I'm hearing a lot of noise being made, but I think it's mostly for show. Maybe it's got something to do with the stuff about the investigation that Lily was starting to bring out in court. But between you and me, I don't see any big commitment being made, at least not by this department, when it comes to getting out there and searching for him."

"Between you and me," Joe said, "I doubt it would make any difference."

"You think he's long gone, don't you?"

"I think, wherever he is, he'll never be found -- at least, not by any of us."

"And you're still going through the motions?"

"It's Lily's call. And as long as she's committed, it's my job."

• • •

Charles Graywolf was in excellent physical condition for his age, but it had been decades since he had climbed the mountains. On this particular day, it was taking him far longer than it used to take to get where he was going, but it was not only because of his age, it was also because he assumed he was being tracked, and he had made a number of false turns and tricky detours to assure himself that there was no one behind him and no one above him who could determine his true destination.

Although he knew they didn't believe him, he hadn't deceived the police officers that came looking for his nephew, or misled the private investigator that came to talk about him. Jason had not come to his home and Graywolf had not heard from him. The part he didn't feel obliged to share was that he had a pretty good idea where his nephew would be. So he climbed.

It was after noon by the time he reached the flowing stream and followed it to the little clearing and the cave beside the pool where he and his nephew had camped at least a hundred times during the boy's youth. The fresh bed of leaves covering the cave floor told him that Jason had been there, but he wasn't there now. The old man was not concerned. He removed the heavy backpack he had been carrying and settled down to wait. He had told his wife not to expect him back until he found his nephew, and he meant it. But it felt good to sit, to rest. Graywolf decided it would be all right if he closed his eyes for a moment.

The shadows were long when he opened them again. A low fire crackled nearby. He sat up with a start to see his nephew hunkered over the flame, roasting a rabbit.

"Hello, Uncle," Jason said, almost as though he had been expecting him, and perhaps he had. "Are you hungry?"

Graywolf realized he wasn't just hungry -- he was ravenous. It was a long trek through the mountains, and he hadn't eaten since breakfast. He reached for his backpack and pulled out some of the provisions he had brought with him -- bread, corn, and beans that his wife had prepared, and beer. The two men settled down to feast. Graywolf popped the caps off two bottles of the warm beer and offered one to his nephew.

Jason looked at it for a long minute. Warm or not, he knew he could down it in one gulp, like a man whose thirst was so deep it could never be quenched. It may not have been rum, but it was better than nothing. He shut his eyes, took a deep breath, and shook his head.

"Thanks, you drink it for me," he said.

"You gotta be kiddin' me!" Graywolf exclaimed, truly surprised.

"My lawyer got me this guy," Jason explained. "Showed me what serious drinkin' could do to the body. I guess knowin' about all that and thinkin' about what it's done to my mother, well, it kinda opened my eyes. So, you drink it for me." He laughed, but it was a humorless laugh. "Sure never thought I would hear myself sayin' that."

His uncle shrugged and downed the beer, and then drank his nephew's, as well. It wasn't the alcohol so much as it was that he was also quite thirsty.

"Sorry," the old Indian said. "I guess, where you been, it could change a whole life around real quick."

"That's okay," Jason told him with a grin. "It only hurt for a minute."

Their meal was devoured, the fire was down to embers, and the two men were settling into the cave for the night. Graywolf had brought Jason a blanket, a change of clothes, a pair of moccasins, a towel, and some soap.

"So, tell me -- how'd you get out of that place?" he asked.

"I found some cracks goin' up the wall," Jason said. "I worked at 'em, every chance I got, till I got enough of 'em big enough, and then it was just a matter of waitin' until no one was watchin', and then puttin' one toe in and then another toe, and finally just heavin' myself over the top. Got a coupla cuts from the wire, and gave my leg a real poundin' when I landed, but nothin' was gonna slow me down."

"What's your plan?"

"To stay here for a while, see the sun come up in the mornin', watch the stars dancin' at night, breathe the fresh air, eat my fill of good food, and with a little luck, clear my brain."

"And after that?"

Jason took a deep breath. "After that, well, we'll just have to see."

• • •

"Is there any reason why what you found in the bathroom has to be made public?" Lauren Scott inquired, making a deliberate point of dropping over at Lily's house during Sunday dinner with her parents. "Can't you maybe just throw it away?"

"It could be evidence at trial," Lily reminded her.

"Evidence of what?" the widow argued. "So maybe my husband used drugs sometimes, but I can't see how it makes any difference now. He's dead. The Indian is gone. It's been a week. They aren't going to find him. There isn't going to be any more trial. And he'll never pay for what he did to Dale. Isn't the fact that he ran away proof enough of his guilt? Do you have to drag a good man's name -- a man who did a lot for this community -- through the mud for no reason at all?"

"People run for a lot of reasons, not always having to do with guilt," Lily said -- fear coming to mind. "But I promise you this, if a mistrial is declared, no one will ever hear about what we found, at least, not from me."

It wasn't exactly what the widow had come for, but it was what she was willing to leave with.

• • •

It was dark, with only a few stars lighting up the night, and he wondered why he could see the two men at all. But he could. And he could hear them, too, loud and clear. They were arguing about something, going back and forth at one another. He couldn't make out what the argument was about, but he knew that, whatever it was, it was serious. Suddenly, one of them just up and punched the other one in the face, and then it wasn't an argument anymore, and the fighting started for real.

He tried to decide whether or not he should interfere, considering it was pretty one-sided, and the guy who had gotten punched in the face was clearly getting the worst of it.

It reminded him of the fights he used to go to with his uncle, years ago, when he was a kid -- loud and raucous and rough, and the crowd cheering it on -- except that this was one fight that should have been called by the referee way before now, and he wondered why it hadn't been.

He thought maybe he should help the guy who was down on his knees -- or at least find the referee, but he didn't. He didn't do anything. He just stayed where he was, warm and secure, and let it go on.

Until it was time for it to stop so he could get to sleep. He needed to get a good night's sleep. But it didn't stop, it kept on going. They had come to his place and ruined his sleep, and he'd had enough. But he didn't know what to do about it. The shouting became grunting and then the grunting became screaming. And all of a sudden, he was right there at the ring, shouting over the screaming, grabbing hold of the metal railing, trying to hang on to it, trying to keep his balance. And then there was a noise -- so loud, so close, it made him jump.

Jason awoke with a start.

• • •

On Monday afternoon, a week and a day after Jason Lightfoot had jumped the fence at the Jackson County Jail and made his escape, a clearly perplexed warden called Lily at her Broad Street office.

"I don't know exactly how to say this," he said, "but your client is asking for you."

"My client?" Lily asked. "What are you talking about?" Now that Jason was gone, she had no clients at the jail.

"I'm talking about Lightfoot," the warden said. "He's sitting right here in front of me, and he's asking to see you."

"You caught him?" Lily sat bolt upright. "When? Where? Nobody notified me. I haven't heard a word about it."

"Well -- uh -- that's just it, you see, we didn't exactly catch him," the warden said, clearing his throat. "He -- uh -- he just turned himself in."

"He -- *what*?"

"Half an hour ago, he just walked right through the front gate and gave himself up."

Even as she was leaping out of her chair and reaching for her bag and calling for Dancer, Lily was dumbfounded.

"Why?" she couldn't help herself from asking.

The warden gave a half-chuckle. "Beats me," he said.

"I'm on my way," she declared. "And Warden, I'm holding you personally responsible -- there'd better not be a mark on him."

"Far as I can tell, he's clean as a whistle," the warden told her.

· · ·

Lily and Dancer covered the ten miles from Broad Street to the jail in little more than ten minutes.

"I think maybe this is a conversation that has to be just between Jason and me," the lawyer told the bodyguard.

He understood. He had dealt with attorney/client privilege before. He leaned back against his seat and closed his eyes. After the week he had had, chasing all over the county and back, he decided a little downtime would be welcome.

Perhaps because there had never been such an occurrence in his thirty-four years at the Jackson County Jail, the warden didn't insist that Jason be immediately returned to his cell. He gave Lily and her client the privacy of his own office.

"All right, talk to me," she exclaimed the moment the door closed. "Tell me what the hell is going on."

He looked as though he had been out for nothing more than a Sunday stroll. He was bathed, his jeans and T-shirt were clean, he had on a nice pair of moccasins, and the orange jumpsuit he had been wearing when he made his escape was folded in a neat, river-scrubbed bundle beside him.

Jason shrugged. "I needed to clear my head," he said. "I needed to breathe."

Lily couldn't believe it. "You needed to breathe?" she echoed.

"Look, Lady Lawyer," he said amiably, "I ain't sayin' that you're not good at your job, or anything like that, but I'm gonna die. I know that and you know that, and there's nothin' gonna happen to change that. And I just couldn't stand the idea that I'd never see another sunset or hear another bird singin' or catch another fish or swim in a mountain stream again. I just wanted to feel like a man and suck in some fresh air and sleep under the stars one more time before I got locked away for good and that noose got put around my neck. The wall was there and the guard wasn't, so I figured it was the right time to go."

She didn't get it. "I guess I can understand the going part," she said, "but what I can't understand is -- why did you come back? You'd made it. No one would ever have found you. You had to know that."

Now it was Jason's turn not to get it. "I killed a man, didn't I?" he reminded her. "One way or another, I gotta pay for that, don't I?" Then he grinned. "And besides, I felt real bad about leavin' you high and dry."

It was at that moment that Lily Burns really saw Jason Lightfoot for the first time -- not the drunk, not the killer, not the client, but the man. And any doubts that may still have been lingering disappeared.

"My clients rarely surprise me," she told him. "You are certainly an exception."

• • •

Lily wasn't the only one who was stunned by the return of Jason Lightfoot.

"He did what?" people asked.

"He came back on his own?" several asked in clear disbelief.

"You mean, the cops didn't catch him?" others wanted to know.

"Oh, come on, you've got to be kidding," some declared.

"Is he crazy?" a few wondered.

"I've never heard anything like it," one of the town barbers said.

"He was out of it, he was free," a gas station owner observed, shaking his head. "All he had to do was -- nothing."

"The guy must be certifiable," a local dairy farmer insisted.

"They don't understand," Charles Graywolf said. "It ain't in Jason to walk out on unfinished business."

"Even if it means he might die?" Joe asked.

"There are a lot of ways to die," the Indian told him. "And when all is said and done, the only way that counts is the honorable way."

And then there was the fellow who went to talk to his pastor.

"You know," the parishioner declared, "if he escaped from that jail, and he ran and got away with it, and there was no one who was going to find him, and then he came back, all on his own, for no reason -- well, maybe he's not as guilty as everyone around here thinks he is. I've been having some pretty angry thoughts about him all this time, when maybe I should have been more charitable."

• • •

Judge Pelletier was notified, and the trial was scheduled to resume on Wednesday. Jason would once again have to wear the suit that Lily had bought for him, but he would no longer have to be shackled at the waist and ankles.

"Why bother?" the warden had said with a hint of actual respect in his voice. "He walked right out of the place when he wanted to, and then he walked right back in again when he was ready to. That told us something -- that told us plenty. Putting the rig back on him now would only be for show."

"I guess that means they don't expect you to escape again," Lily said.

Jason grinned. "Don't really think I could get away with it twice."

She called Joe. "Vacation's over," she told him. "Get back to work."

• • •

Antonio Morales wasn't hard to find. Joe found the Mexican American and his Indian wife and children at their ranch on the edge of the Cypress Ridge Reservation, west of Port Hancock.

Untouchable on sovereign territory, he was known as the Indian drug czar, although more of his customers were Hispanics who sometimes lived miles away, even in other counties.

With good contacts in Mexico, he was able to move everything from meth to cocaine to heroin, in quantities that compared only to the Van Aiken brothers. With casino money flowing freely, it hadn't taken him long to find out what they already knew -- how easy it was to turn alcohol-addicted people into drug-addicted people, and a drug-addicted person was a contact, a courier, and a cohort. Most of the tribal police were in his pocket, some actually on his payroll, and as long as he lived on the reservation, the feds could do little about it.

He had made his peace with the Van Aikens, carving out an area west of Port Hancock that included his wife's tribe, which was the biggest in the area, and the bulk of the growing Hispanic community that wouldn't trust anyone but a brother, anyway. As the economy in the county began to recover and the population began to grow, he had little trouble convincing the competition that there was more than enough to go around.

It was just in the last year or so, after marijuana had been legalized in the state, that the county sheriff's office had started leaning on him -- picking up his wife on one pretext or another when she left the reservation, snatching his kids out of school on phony charges that they were selling drugs to their classmates. He knew they were sending him a message -- a message that said his reservation cover might protect him from the feds, but it wasn't gong to protect him from them.

"I'm a law-abiding citizen," he told the former policeman who came to call, two gold teeth gleaming through his broad smile.

"Yeah, and I'm the tooth fairy," Joe said. "But not to worry, I didn't come out here to bust your chops. I'm just looking for a little information."

"And what do I get in return?"

"Why, the satisfaction of knowing that you did the right thing."

Morales laughed. "You were a smart cop, Sergeant Gideon, I always said that. So what information do you think I can give you?"

"I know the deal that you had with Dale Scott," Joe said.

"The cop that got himself killed?" Morales asked. "And why would you think I had some kind of deal with him?"

"Because it was the same deal he had with the Van Aiken brothers, and they spelled it out for me."

Morales shrugged. "So, if you already know what you think you know, what do you want from me?"

"I need to know if he had a meet set up with you or any of your people the night he died," Joe said. "I need to know if that's what he was doing in the alley."

"You working for Lightfoot?"

The private investigator nodded. "Yes -- for his lawyer."

"Can't believe the fool came back," Morales said, shaking his head.

"Well, we're all fools in our own way," Joe suggested.

"And if I tell you what you want to know -- what do you do with this information?"

"I tell the lawyer, I don't tell the cops," the private investigator assured him.

"And what does the lawyer do with this information?"

"She doesn't call you to testify unless she absolutely has to, and only after she first gets you complete immunity for your court appearance, and you know she can do that. Besides, she already knows that you, being the law-abiding citizen that you are, will want to do your civic duty."

Morales laughed again. "My civic duty -- I like that," he said. "Yeah, I was supplyin' Scott in exchange for certain services he was providin', and yeah, there was a meet on for that night. But all I'm doin' is tellin' you this -- I'm not gonna get up on any witness stand. And if you push it, I'll deny everything."

"All right," the investigator conceded, "suppose you just tell me what happened."

"The meet was set up for midnight, but I was running late," Morales said. "By the time I got there, it was all over."

"Over?"

"Yeah. The cop was dead and just lyin' there on the ground."

"And ?"

"And nothin' -- I didn't hang around. Got myself the hell outta there. Later, when I heard what had happened, I remember thinkin' that the Indian had done me a favor."

"Why is that?"

"We'd only been workin' with him for a couple months, and he was already gettin' greedy," the drug dealer explained. "Greedy people tend to get sloppy. His habit was big, but his influence not so much, if you know what I mean."

"So, tell me, have you replaced him yet?" Joe asked lightly.

"Oh, come now, Sergeant Gideon," Morales said, his tone softly mocking, the gold teeth gleaming. "What kind of question is that to ask a law-abidin' citizen?"

• • •

John Henry sat glumly in his seat at the prosecution table as the trial of Jason Lightfoot resumed at nine o'clock on Wednesday morning. He felt at a distinct disadvantage. The tide of public opinion was inexorably turning, in the town and around the county, as many were beginning to see the defendant as some sort of hero.

"Why would a guilty man escape, and then return on his own?" they were asking.

The Indian actually had a fan club -- a group of about thirty people who now believed him to be completely innocent of all charges, and was having no problem being as vocal as possible about it -- on the radio, in the newspaper, even standing in front of the courthouse. And according to the reports John Henry was getting, the group was growing bigger by the minute. A number of them had even maneuvered their way into the spectator gallery, where they jumped up, smiled, and applauded when the Indian was brought into the courtroom.

Then there was the jury. They weren't being sequestered for this trial, which meant they were out there, surrounded by all the chatter. Despite the judge's admonitions, he had no doubt they were watching, listening, taking it all in. And in the midst of all this, the prosecutor had to prove, beyond a reasonable doubt, that Jason Lightfoot was nothing but a cold-blooded killer. It wasn't fair. Feeling a bit desperate, perhaps, he called Kent McAllister to the witness stand.

The Chief of Police was born and raised in Seattle. A high school and college football star, he had joined the Seattle police force when he was twenty-five years old, after an injury cut short his professional career.

He had come to Port Hancock at the age of thirty-six, lured by the newly-elected mayor of the quaint city, whom he had known since college, to become the youngest ever to fill the position as the city's highest law enforcement official.

He had maintained his quarterback physique, boasted a full head of hair, sported a sweeping moustache, and was about to begin his tenth year in office. He had a reputation for being tough, but fair. There were few in town, or in the county, for that matter, who were as respected as Chief McAllister.

"Can you tell us how long Dale Scott had been a member of the Port Hancock Police Department?" John Henry began, as soon as the witness had been sworn in.

"Fourteen years," McAllister replied. "He was already on the force when I took office."

"And for how many of those years was he a detective?"

"The last five."

"What kind of a police officer was he?"

"An excellent one," the chief affirmed. "And he had an office full of commendations to back that up. The record shows that he cleared ninety-four percent of his cases, and the conviction rate associated with his arrests was the highest in the department. He was very thorough in his investigations, and always on time with his paperwork. He set a very high standard, not only for those who were already here, but for all those who came after him."

"Do you know what he was doing in the seaward alley on the night of his death?"

McAllister sighed. "In addition to their normal duties, Detective Scott and his partner were assigned to a regional drug enforcement task force. They kept their own hours on that. Sometimes, I knew where they were and what they were doing, sometimes, I didn't. That night, I'm afraid I didn't."

"Can you think of any reason why Detective Scott might have been in that particular alley on that particular night?"

"Sure," McAllister said easily. "A lot of trafficking goes on down on the docks -- illegal trafficking in stuff like alcohol, cigarettes, drugs -- the sort of thing that port cities unfortunately have to deal with. The contraband comes in mostly at night. Detective Scott could have been doing reconnaissance, or meeting with a snitch, or scouting for a raid -- there were a lot of reasons he could have been in that alley."

"Did Detective Scott know the defendant?"

McAllister nodded. "Yes, he did," he declared. "As a matter of fact, he'd had a number of encounters with Mr. Lightfoot over the years. According to the record, Dale had brought him in at least a dozen times. They were all minor charges, though, mostly relating to the defendant being drunk and disorderly."

"Would you say there was some animosity between the two of them?"

"Certainly not on Dale's part," the chief replied. "Arresting someone, whether for a felony or a misdemeanor, isn't something a police officer enjoys doing. It isn't personal. It's part of the job."

"Thank you," John Henry said. "I have no further questions."

• • •

"Chief McAllister," Lily began, "I believe you said that Dale Scott was a good police officer, is that correct?" It was the one thing she regretted -- having to destroy the reputation of Lauren's husband, after all.

"It is, and he was -- one of the best, and as I said, he had the commendations to prove it," McAllister replied.

"And you trusted him?"

"Absolutely."

"Absolutely?" Lily questioned. "Are you saying that, in all the years that he was a member of your department, he never crossed the line? You never had occasion to discipline him?"

"Dale Scott was a good police officer," Kent McAllister affirmed. "Day in, day out, he put it all on the line to keep this community safe, and he lost his life because of it. This is not an easy job -- it's a hard one. Sometimes, it's a real balancing act, and we all make mistakes."

"I take that to mean that he did cross the line, and that he did make mistakes, and that you did indeed have occasion to discipline him?"

"I doubt there's a police officer anywhere who hasn't gotten a bit overzealous at least once in his career," the police chief said.

"Once you said?"

McAllister shifted in his seat. "Well, yes, I said at least once, but it could have been a couple of times."

"A couple of times?" Lily echoed sharply. "How about a dozen complaints of unnecessary roughness filed just in the past two years alone? Black eyes, broken noses, split lips, cracked ribs, a ruptured spleen -- is that what you mean by overzealous?"

"Look, I didn't come here to make excuses for Dale Scott," the witness declared. "He was who he was, and he did his best, just like everyone else. Sometimes the kind of people he had to deal with weren't the most cooperative. Sometimes they resisted. Sometimes they had to be subdued. It would be great if it were otherwise, if everyone respected that a police officer was just doing his job, and a heck of a tough job at that.   But unfortunately, that's not always the case."

"Was it really part of the job -- or was it simply part of Dale Scott?"

"What do you mean?"

"I mean, his record seems to suggest that perhaps he got off on hurting people. In fact, weren't you constantly making excuses for him?"

"No, that's not true," the police chief declared. "All this stuff you're dredging up, it was all minor -- there was nothing major."

"Putting a hungry, homeless man in the hospital with a ruptured spleen because he stole a turkey sandwich is minor?"

"Objection!" John Henry cried because he didn't know what she was talking about. "Are we really going to put the victim on trial here?"

"I'm just trying to get all the facts before the jury, Your Honor," Lily said. "If they're entitled to know everything relevant about Jason Lightfoot, aren't they equally entitled to know everything relevant about Dale Scott?"

"It's just plain character assassination," John Henry argued.

"Is the prosecutor really saying that showing the jury who and what Dale Scott was, as it relates to the matter of his death, is character assassination?" Lily inquired.

"Never mind, Miss Burns," the judge said. "The objection is overruled, but tread lightly."

"Yes, Your Honor," Lily said and turned back to the witness. "So, Chief McAllister," she repeated for emphasis, "do you seriously believe -- do you seriously want this jury to believe, that beating up a hungry, homeless man badly enough to rupture his spleen and put him in the hospital just because he stole a turkey sandwich was just some minor mistake?"

"That's not what I'm saying, but you have to understand," McAllister tried to explain, even as he was trying to figure out how in the hell she knew about that, because they had done their best to keep it quiet, even to the point of shipping the indigent off to an out-of-town hospital. "Being a law enforcement officer can be very stressful."

"No doubt," Lily was quick to agree. "So tell us, aside from beating up on helpless people, how did Detective Scott deal with his stress?"

McAllister frowned. "I don't know what you mean," he said.

"I mean, quite simply, what did he do to alleviate the terrible pressure that being a law enforcement officer put on him?"

"I still don't know what you mean."

"Well, let's see -- did he drink to excess?" Lily explored.

"No, he didn't. I don't think he drank to excess."

"How about drugs -- did he use drugs?"

"Not that I was aware of. No, of course not."

"Are you sure about that?"

McAllister stiffened. "I'm as sure as I have to be. I can't be expected to know what the man did every minute of every day he was on duty, or what he did when he wasn't on duty, for that matter, but I can certainly testify that he never went out to work a shift either drunk or stoned."

"Yet under direct examination, you said Detective Scott and his partner made their own hours," Lily said, "so how can you be so sure?"

"Well, I meant on those occasions when I saw him, of course," the chief amended.

"Of course."

McAllister was clearly not happy. "Look, Dale Scott was a police officer who did his job as best he could, and he paid for doing it with a bullet to the head. To save your client, you're trying to blacken his name, and frankly, I'm not going to help you do it."

A big part of being a good trial attorney was knowing when to stop. "I'm sure we all appreciate your loyalty," Lily said, and sat down.

• • •

"I do believe we've found what we needed," Joe announced when court had recessed for lunch, and Lily had returned to the Victorian to find him waiting. "Dale did have a meet set up for Sunday night."

Lily was elated. "I take that to mean you found his connection?"

"Yes, I found him, and he told me, with just a little arm-twisting, that he and Dale had a meet in the alley set for midnight."

"And ?"

"And according to him," Joe continued, "he was running late, and by the time he got there, it was all over. Dale was dead, and he has no idea who did it."

"Do you believe him?"

"You mean, do I think he could have killed Dale?"

"Is it possible?"

The private investigator thought about it for a moment. "It's possible, I guess," he said finally. "He wasn't particularly sad that Dale was dead. But I think, if he had killed him, he wouldn't have put himself at the scene, either before or after. I think he would just have said there was no meet scheduled and left it at that."

"Well, that doesn't get us the witness we were hoping for," Lily said, "but it does give us the drug angle, and with it, a motive for self-defense." She sighed. "He won't testify, will he?"

"Of course not," Joe said.

"Any way we can compel him?"

Joe shrugged. "I doubt it," he said. "No reason in the world why he should, and every reason why he shouldn't."

• • •

"The people call Detective Randy Hitchens to the stand," John Henry intoned when the lunch break was over and court had resumed.

The thirty-six-year-old detective strode into the courtroom and down the aisle to the witness box. He was not a particularly big man, standing about five foot nine inches tall and weighing around one hundred and seventy pounds, but he was in excellent physical condition.

Above his pale blue eyes was a shock of sandy hair not yet beginning to thin. There was a boyishness that seemed to cling to him, an air of innocence that might have been inconsistent with his position as an ex-Marine and a law enforcement officer, but it allowed people to feel comfortable with him and to trust him.

He had done six years in the Marines before concluding that a military career really wasn't the career he wanted. So he came back home to Renton, did a couple of years at a community college and then entered the police academy in Burien. After earning his certificate, he sent his resume off to a dozen different police departments in the area.

The new police chief of a small city in the northwestern part of the state that was enjoying a pretty decent economy and a corresponding growth in population, and was looking to expand his department, was the first to respond. For the past nine years, six as a patrolman and now almost three as a detective, it had been a good fit. At least, neither side had yet to voice any opinion to the contrary.

He was single. He had begun a two-year affair with a female officer soon after joining the department that ended when she relocated to New Mexico, and then he had enjoyed an on-again-off-again relationship with another officer who had moved to Idaho just six months ago. Now he spent his off-duty time pumping iron at the local gym, hanging out at the bars along upper Broad Street, and restoring a vintage red MG he had picked up at a police auction a while back.

"Detective Hitchens," John Henry began his direct examination, "Dale Scott was your partner, is that correct?"

The witness nodded. "Yes, sir, he was."

"For how long?"

"Almost three years."

"What kind of a police officer would you say he was?"

"Dedicated, hard-working, detail-oriented, a good closer." He rattled off the words as though they had been memorized from a script.

"After he was murdered, were you put in charge of the investigation into his death?"

"I was."

"Will you tell the jury how you conducted this investigation and how you arrived at the conclusion you did?"

"We started with the crime scene evidence and the medical examiner's findings," Hitchens began. And he then went on to recount, step by step, the investigative process he had used in following up on the processing of that evidence and those findings, of personally interviewing the defendant and securing what he and his superiors considered, if not an out-and-out confession, at least a recognition of guilt. His manner was confident and courteous, and the jurors clearly liked him.

"And in the course of your investigation," John Henry inquired, "did you find any evidence to suggest that anyone other than the defendant was responsible for the death of your partner?"

"No, I did not," the detective said firmly.

"What about self-defense?" the prosecutor pressed. "Did you, at any time, find any evidence that could have led you to the conclusion that the defendant acted in self-defense when he shot and killed Detective Scott?"

Hitchens hesitated for perhaps the length of two seconds before he replied. "No, I did not."

"I have nothing further," John Henry said, and sat down.

• • •

Lily rose from her seat. "Detective Hitchens, you've testified that you were in charge of the investigation into your partner's death," she began and then stopped. "Come to think of it, wasn't that a little unusual?"

"What do you mean by unusual, Ma'am?" the witness hedged.

"Well, that you would be put in charge of an investigation involving your partner's death," she said. "I would have thought that someone else might have been more suitable, someone perhaps more objective."

"I guess Chief McAllister didn't agree."

"Oh, I see -- it was his idea."

Hitchens shifted in his seat. "Well, I may have suggested that I could handle it," he said. "But it was his decision."

"Of course," Lily murmured. "All right, as the officer in charge of the investigation into your partner's death, you were responsible for the evidence that was collected at the crime scene, is that correct?"

"I was."

"And you never at any time during this investigation considered that my client may have acted in self-defense when he shot Dale Scott?"

"I considered it," he replied. "But there just wasn't any evidence to take me there."

"Are you familiar with the testimony of the medical examiner and the crime lab analyst, who both stated that Detective Scott had incurred physical injuries before he was shot?"

"With some of it, yes."

"Well then, in light of their testimony, would you now be willing to consider self-defense?"

"At this point, I suppose I could second-guess myself. But at the time, I simply had to go with my gut."

"And at the time your gut was telling you this wasn't self-defense -- did it tell you this was a case of intentional, premeditated murder?"

"Yes."

"Why?"

"Because Dale had been shot in the head, at very close range."

"Perhaps you can explain to the jury what the difference is between evidence that indicates premeditation, evidence that indicates murder without premeditation, and evidence that indicates self-defense."

Hitchens frowned. "I'm not sure I know what you're asking."

"Nothing terribly complicated," Lily assured him. "Just tell the jury, generally, what evidence you found during your investigation that you considered consistent with premeditated murder as compared to what evidence you would have considered consistent with unpremeditated murder or self-defense."

The detective took a breath and turned to the jury. "Self-defense is when the perpetrator fears for his life and acts to protect himself," he declared. "There was simply no evidence of that in this case. There was just a drunk Indian who beat the crap out of my partner and then put a bullet in his head."

"I see," Lily said. "All right, suppose we try this another way. What kind of evidence was it that convinced you that self-defense was not involved in this case?"

"Objection," John Henry interjected. "Asked and answered."

"Hardly, Your Honor," Lily retorted. "Either to my satisfaction or, I suspect, to the jury's."

"Overruled," Judge Pelletier said. "The witness will answer."

Hitchens threw up his hands in exasperation. "I don't know what evidence you expect me to conjure up here," he declared, "but my partner had injuries all over his body -- his face, his arms, his stomach -- indicating he was not the aggressor in the fight that preceded his death."

"Could any of the injuries on the victim qualify as offensive wounds?" Lily wondered. "Such as the bruised knuckles?"

"I suppose," Hitchens was forced to admit.

"Ah, so what you really meant to say was that the deceased had what could be considered both offensive and defensive wounds on his body, is that correct?"

The detective stared at the defense attorney for a moment, as though weighing something in his mind.

"That's correct," he said finally. "He may have had a few cuts and bruises on him that could have been classified as offensive wounds. But not enough, in my judgment, to indicate that there had been any kind of a fair fight."

"I see. And your judgment that there was no evidence of self-defense involved in your partner's death was made mostly on a personal basis, wasn't it?"

Hitchens shrugged. "He was my partner."

"Yes, he was," Lily said. "And you were close?"

"Yeah, we were," the detective responded. "Not so close that I wasn't seeing clear about the case, but I'd say we were pretty close."

"Then let me ask you this," the defense attorney pressed, "would it come as a big surprise to you if I were to suggest that your partner -- with whom you were close -- was a drug user?"

"Objection!" John Henry cried. "Foundation."

"It's a hypothetical question, Your Honor," Lily said. "The witness said he and his partner were close. I simply want to determine how close."

"Objection overruled, the witness may answer," the judge declared, arching an eyebrow at the defense attorney. "But be careful, Miss Burns."

"We had a pretty close working relationship," Hitchens said. "That doesn't mean we socialized off the job or knew each other intimately or anything like that. So yes, it would come as a big surprise to hear he did drugs, and no, it wouldn't come as a big surprise. Since I wasn't involved in his private life, I really wouldn't know one way or the other."

"Do you know what your partner was doing in the seaward alley on the night of his death?" Lily asked.

"No, Ma'am, I don't," Hitchens said. "I was home with a head cold that night. He called me from home around eleven, I think it was, but he didn't say anything about going out."

"So then, for all you know, he could have been in that alley for any reason -- to meet a snitch, or to pick up a prostitute, or even to make a drug buy -- couldn't he?"

"I suppose he could've," the detective replied stiffly.

"Thank you, Detective," Lily said. "I have nothing further at this time."

Seated at the prosecution table, Tom Lickliter's eyes narrowed just a bit. Seated beside Dancer on the defense side, Joe Gideon frowned.

• • •

"He lied," Joe couldn't wait to tell Lily as soon as court had adjourned for the day and they were headed back to Broad Street.

"Who lied?"

"Randy," Joe said. It was the first time he had been in court to watch the proceedings. And he knew, based on the testimony he had just heard, that it would probably be the last.

"Lied about what?"

"About his relationship with Dale," Joe replied. "When I talked to Lauren, she told me how close Randy had been with the family, ever since he and Dale had partnered up. Said they were still close. He was like a brother to her was how she put it. The first time I went over there, she said Randy had told her she didn't have to talk to me. Gave me the impression he was still very much involved with the family. She had no reason to make that up."

Lily shrugged. "It may not be anything. It may just be he didn't want to give up his partner." She looked at Joe. "But it means you're out of the courtroom," she told him, confirming what he already knew. "I might need you to testify -- I'm going to put you on the witness list."

• • •

"I doubt that Lily Burns is just making idle conversation by bringing up all this drug stuff," Tom told John Henry. "I have a strong suspicion she's going somewhere with it."

"Where can she go?"

"I don't know, but she doesn't strike me as the type to waste her time on fishing expeditions."

"I have no idea what she thinks she could have, but what difference does it make?"

"Not sure," Tom said. "I guess I just don't like surprises."

• • •

There was an odd expression on Wanda Posey's face when Lily, Joe, Megan and Dancer got back to the Victorian, an expression that combined genuine puzzlement with a measure of mischief.

"What?" Lily asked.

The receptionist suspended a plain white envelope between the tips of her thumb and index finger. "I don't know," she said. "This came in the mail today."

"So?"

"So, see for yourself."

She passed the envelope to her employer. It was hand-addressed to the attorney, in neat block letters, but 'Lily' was spelled with two 'l's. Inside was a single sheet of plain white paper. Lily extracted it. The only thing on the paper, done in the same neat block lettering as the envelope, was a name: Margaret Dean.

"What do you think it means?" Wanda wanted to know.

"I haven't a clue," Lily replied.

Joe peered over her shoulder. "What's the big mystery?"

Lily handed him the letter. "You tell me."

"It seems pretty cloak-and-daggery to me," Wanda said.

Joe examined the evidence. "Well, this was obviously sent by someone who doesn't know you, but is trying to tell you something," he concluded. "It was mailed yesterday, and the postmark is from Trent. So, I would say that this someone wants you to know something about a Margaret Dean in Trent."

"I get all that," Lily said. "What I don't get is what exactly would someone who lives all the way out there want me to know about somebody named Margaret Dean?" Trent was some seventy miles west of Port Hancock, practically out at the Pacific Ocean.

Joe shrugged. "I don't know, but it looks like I'm going to be taking a little drive out there to find out," he said.

Nine

Trent, Washington, was a small, rural community, with a year-round population of just over three thousand, sitting between almost a million acres of national park land and the rugged Pacific coast, in no particular hurry to be discovered. It bordered one of the world's last untouched rainforests, was close to fine fishing and a sprawling new industrial park, and was not very far from a small airport.

It hosted mining, timber, and tourist interests, supported half a dozen churches, and featured a well-equipped community hospital and a school system that matriculated an impressive seventy-seven percent of its students. For the most part, the people were friendly, employed, and God-fearing.

The first thing Joe did after driving his Jeep Cherokee into town was to park in one of the diagonal spaces on the main street and go looking for a telephone book. He found three Deans listed, but after three phone calls, none of them turned out to be Margaret.

That would have been too easy, he thought.

He decided to start at the pharmacy on the corner. Stepping through the door was like taking a giant step back over a hundred years, with all the accouterments of that time, including rough plank flooring and a nineteenth century vintage soda fountain, complete with cracked leather swivel seats. He strolled over to the counter. "Pardon me, but have any of you seen Margaret Dean today, by any chance?" he asked. It was clearly a friendly town, the kind of town where he was sure everyone pretty much knew everyone else.

"You mean Maggie Bream?" a customer inquired. "She's gone more'n a year now, rest her soul."

"No, not poor Maggie Bream," Joe said, assuming a folksy demeanor. "I'm looking for Margaret Dean." He shrugged, feigning embarrassment. "Met her in Tacoma a while back, and she told me, if I was ever passing through, to be sure and look her up. Only thing is -- I lost her number."

The customer, a grizzled old man, and the clerk, a plump middle-aged woman, exchanged puzzled glances. "Don't know of any Margaret Dean here in town," the customer said. "There's Lizzie Dean. And there's Eudora Dean. Are you sure you got the name right?"

"Are you sure you got the town right?" the clerk chimed in.

"Well, I thought I had," Joe said. He offered a sheepish grin. "Maybe she was just pulling my leg."

The clerk smiled. The customer let out a hoot. "Got you all the way out here on a wild goose chase, did she?"

"She might be summer people," another customer, who had been listening in, suggested. "Nowadays, we've got more and more of them coming out over July and August. Not a bad bunch, mostly, maybe just a bit pushy."

Joe nodded. "Sure do appreciate your help," he said, and made his way out.

City Hall was next, a squat brick building that sat almost unnoticed in the middle of the block. But there was no record of a Margaret Dean ever being born or married or given birth or dying in Trent, Washington. And the local school department had no record of a Margaret Dean ever having attended school there.

He didn't have much better luck at the police station.

"I'm born and raised here, went to school here, go to church here, and I've never known anyone named Margaret Dean," the duty officer said. "And in addition to the locals, I know most of the summer folk, too."

"The name doesn't appear on any report of any kind of crime or accident?" Joe queried. "You've got nothing there involving a Margaret Dean?"

The deputy checked the files on his computer. "Nope, nothing," he confirmed. "Nothing with that name, victim or perp. And I'm going back ten years now."

Joe thanked the deputy and returned to his Jeep, sitting in the driver's seat without turning on the ignition, trying to figure what his next move should be. The letter sent to Lily was mailed from Trent, and Joe was convinced that the postmark was a message. It was where the sender was directing him to look for Margaret Dean. But if she wasn't a local, and she wasn't a summer person, what was she, and why had the sender lured him here to find her? What was going on in this remote community, almost an hour and a half from Port Hancock, that was in some way connected to Jason Lightfoot's murder trial?

It was approaching noon and a sudden growling in his gut told him it was time to eat. Joe glanced around. Across the street he spotted a cute little cafe. He climbed out of the Jeep and headed for it. He always thought better on a full stomach anyway. The waitress smiled as he entered. He took a stool at the counter and ordered the daily special, which turned out to be grilled salmon, basted with a lemon-basil sauce. It was as delicious as it was elegant. Maybe Trent wasn't as behind the times as he thought.

"Be careful of the bones," the waitress warned. "Had a couple of tourists passing through yesterday, he nearly choked to death. Had to hurry him over to the hospital."

The hair on the back of Joe's neck suddenly began to tingle, and he beamed at the waitress. If Margaret Dean was not from Trent, she had to be someone who had passed through Trent, and in passing through, had left behind some kind of record that the person who sent the letter thought Lily needed to know about. And if it wasn't a police record, or a school record, or a community record, there was only one other record he could think of. He finished his lunch and left an extra large tip on the counter.

• • •

Given its rather remote location, the Trent Community Hospital had become a surprisingly efficient little facility, required, as it was -- because of its location, to treat everything from a hangnail to an automobile accident to a coronary bypass, if necessary. It was listed third on the Chamber of Commerce's "need to know about" list.

Joe parked the Jeep in the hospital parking lot, and made his way to the main entrance. The lobby was bright and cheerful, with murals that looked like a child's painting covering the walls.

Three women were seated behind the reception desk. He approached the youngest, a pretty brunette.

"How may I direct you?" she asked brightly. The name on the tag that was attached to her blouse read: Bonnie.

Joe summoned up a bashful smile. "I'm looking for someone, Bonnie," he said. He pulled out the badge he had kept from his days on the Port Hancock Police Force, and watched her eyes pop and her shoulders straighten as she looked at it.

"A criminal?" she asked.

"Nothing so exciting, I'm afraid," he assured her. "Just a witness to a matter I'm investigating."

"And you think maybe he's here, your witness?" Bonnie gasped. "In Trent? At our hospital?"

"I'm hoping so," the private investigator said. "But it's not a 'he' I'm looking for -- it's a 'she'."

"Is it like she's in the witness protection program or something?" the receptionist asked breathlessly.

"Again, nothing so exciting," Joe said with a rueful smile. "But she just may have some important information that I really need to have."

"I'll help you all I can," Bonnie said. "Who is it?"

"Her name is Margaret Dean."

Bonnie frowned. "Well, I can't say that I know anyone by that name. And I think I probably know all the people who work here."

"Do you think you could check for me anyway?" Joe asked, although it was purely an exercise. He already knew that Margaret Dean didn't work there.

"Sure." She turned toward her computer. "Margaret, you said?"

"Yes, Margaret Dean."

After a few minutes, she shook her head. "I've just checked the whole employment file, and there's no Margaret Dean listed."

"How odd," Joe said. "This is where I was told I'd find her."

Bonnie turned to her co-workers. "Any of you know anyone who works here named Margaret Dean?"

The two other women shook their heads. "Is she an employee or a patient?" one of them thought to ask.

"I just assumed she was an employee," Joe said. "It never occurred to me she might be a patient."

"Well, let's see," Bonnie said, turning back to her computer. And sure enough, a moment later, a big smile lit up her face. "Here it is, Margaret Dean. She's been a patient on and off for several years, but she's not here now, and according to this, we haven't seen her since last winter."

"Can you tell me what she was admitted for?" Joe asked.

Bonnie considered the request. "I'm not allowed to give out that information, even to you," she said. "Not without a warrant or something."

"I'm afraid I didn't think to come with one," Joe said easily. "But I'll settle for an address."

"That I can do," the receptionist said. But a second later, she was frowning. "That's odd," she murmured. "We should have an address for her here, but there's none listed. There's no telephone number, either. Just the name."

"There's nothing in the file except her name?" one of the other receptionists echoed.

"Nothing," Bonnie confirmed. "Just her name -- Margaret Dean."

A woman in scrubs was walking across the lobby, a middle-aged woman with gray-streaked hair. She passed the desk at the exact moment Bonnie was speaking, and her head snapped around. But she didn't stop. On the contrary, she quickened her step.

Joe missed nothing. Out of the corner of his eye, he watched the woman exit the hospital. "I thank you for your help, ladies," he said to the receptionists. "I guess I'll have to search somewhere else for my elusive witness." He was out the door in a flash, following the nurse until she was about to step into a dark blue Pontiac. "Please wait," he said, startling her.

"Don't come any closer," she said.

"No, no, don't worry," Joe assured her, pulling out the badge. "I mean you no harm. I'm just looking for Margaret Dean. You know her, don't you?"

The nurse looked away. "I don't want to get involved," she said.

"Please," he pressed. "It's very important. I have to find her. A man's life is at stake here."

The woman hesitated. "Ask Mary," she said finally.

"Mary?" he asked. "Where do I find her?" But the woman had already jumped into her car and was speeding out of the parking lot.

Joe stared after the Pontiac. Then he retraced his steps to the reception desk. "I'm back," he said.

Bonnie grinned. "Still in search of Margaret?"

"No, not Margaret," he told her. "This time, I'm looking for Mary."

"Mary who?"

"Well, I don't know her last name," Joe admitted. "But suppose we start with the employees again."

"You sure are fickle," Bonnie said with a chuckle. She checked the computer again. "It looks like we've got three Marys," she reported after a moment or two of searching. "A lab technician, a pediatrics aide, and an emergency room nurse."

"Who's here now?" he asked

"The lab tech is here, and the pediatric aide should be," Bonnie told him. "The emergency room nurse won't be in until her shift starts, and that's not until three."

Once again, Joe thanked her and then followed her directions down a hallway to the left. Then he took a right and then another left, until finally he reached a door with a sign that read: Laboratory.

"Excuse me," he said, sticking his head in the door. "Would you be Mary?"

"Yes, I would," an overweight blonde replied. "Can I help you?"

He flashed his badge again and waited for the eye-popping response.

"I'm looking for someone," he said. "A patient by the name of Margaret Dean. Would you by any chance know her?"

The woman frowned. "Not offhand," she replied. "I run a lot of tests, but to tell you the truth, I'm usually looking at the blood, not the patient." The private investigator saw no subterfuge in her response, so he thanked her and departed.

He got a similar reaction from the pediatric aide, a slender brunette. "I pretty much know all the kids, but not the grownups," she told Joe. "If she's not a kid, I don't think I'd be able to help you."

He had one Mary left, and she wasn't scheduled to come in until three. It was now a little after one.

• • •

It was coming up on three o'clock, and John Henry had called all the qualified witnesses who could vouch for Dale Scott's training and his dedication, and all the expert witnesses who could explain his injuries and detail the cause and manner of death that he felt it necessary to call. He decided that what the jurors needed now was a change of pace -- a couple of witnesses who would humanize the victim.

"The people call Lauren Scott to the stand," he announced.

There was a hush as everyone turned to watch Dale Scott's widow enter through the double doors at the back of the courtroom and walk down the center aisle to the witness stand. She was wearing a burgundy gabardine skirt and jacket with long sleeves and a high-necked blouse, which would have been perfectly appropriate for any October 24th but this one.

She placed her hand on the bible, and then, in a clear if subdued voice, she took the oath to tell the truth, the whole truth, and nothing but the truth, after which she stated her full name and then sat down in the witness box. She radiated courage, generated sympathy, and looked, at least in Lily's eyes, as though she were about to play the role of her life.

"Mrs. Scott, may I begin by expressing our deepest sympathy to you and your family for your terrible loss," John Henry said sincerely.

Lauren smiled at him. "Thank you," she said.

"I promise to be brief," he promised her. "I have only a few questions."

Lauren nodded graciously. "You're most kind," she said. And Lily, pen poised over paper, listened intently to every word.

The prosecutor wasted no time in getting down to brass tacks.

"Did your husband use drugs, Mrs. Scott?" he asked.

"Oh dear, I always thought that was a private matter, but well, yes, we did experiment a little, Dale and I," Lauren admitted, actually looking a bit sheepish. "Nothing big, mind you, just a little recreational stuff, when the kids were asleep, and there was just the two of us. Dale always used to say it was important to know your enemy, and what turned your enemy on. And he also said he wanted to know what different drugs did to you, in case either of our girls had an idea about trying them."

Good for John Henry, Lily thought. Cut right to the chase, and try to preempt the defense. And good for Lauren, too -- making up such a ridiculous story with such a straight face to try to save her husband's reputation. The acting profession had really missed out.

"I suspect a great many of us either have or should have done the same for our children," John Henry opined, and then hurried to inquire further before Lily could object. "Do you know what your husband was doing the night he was murdered?"

"I assumed he was going to work," Lauren replied.

"Did he often work on Sunday nights?"

"He worked all hours, on any given day, so I didn't think anything of his going out on a Sunday night, or his leaving so late," she replied. "But I thought his partner -- Detective Hitchens -- would be with him. I wouldn't have felt comfortable if I'd known Dale was going out there all by himself. He did some dangerous work, you know, in some unsavory parts of town, and it wasn't the kind of work he should have been doing alone, as we found out."

"Please, tell us a little about your husband," John Henry invited. "What kind of man he was, what kind of husband, what kind of father."

"He was a strong man," Lauren began without any hesitation. "Not just physically strong, and emotionally strong, but spiritually strong. He believed that the Lord's way was the right way, and he always tried his best to live by it. He was a good and faithful husband, and a devoted father."

"Did he share much about his work with you?"

"No, he didn't," she replied. "He used to say that most of it was too ugly to bring home. But he always said he was born to be a policeman."

"Did he say why?"

"He used to say there was no job more important in life than to keep a community safe."

"Thank you," John Henry said, beaming. "I have nothing further."

. . .

Joe shook himself awake. He had spent most of the past two hours walking along the sand and rock beach, taking in the bright sun and fresh ocean air, before winding up back in the Jeep Cherokee, where he then managed to doze off. He rubbed his eyes, stretched, and then glanced at his watch. It was five minutes to three, time for the shift to change, time for him to start watching for the illusive Mary.

He spotted her immediately. He didn't know why he knew it was her, he just did. He chalked it up to the instinct born of twenty-five years on the job.

She pulled into the lot in an old Dodge Ram, parking just across from him, climbed out, and started walking toward the hospital entrance. He was out of the Jeep in a flash.

"Excuse me," he said. "You're Mary, aren't you?"

The woman turned around. She had long brown hair and high cheekbones beneath slanted eyes, and she looked to be in her late thirties.

"Yes, I'm Mary," she said cautiously.

Joe pulled out the letter. "You sent this, didn't you?" he asked.

She didn't look at the letter. Instead, she looked around the parking lot, as though to see if anyone might be watching.

"This really isn't a good time," she murmured apprehensively.

"I've been trying to find you since ten o'clock this morning because you sent this letter. Maybe it was just an impulse, but you sent it, and I think it's because you want us to know something -- something that might help Jason Lightfoot -- am I right?"

She was clearly torn. "The shift is changing, there are too many people around," she whispered. "If anyone finds out, I could lose my job. "

"No one will find out from me," Joe assured her.

She took a deep breath. "Is that your Jeep?" she asked. He nodded. "Twenty minutes," she said. And then she turned and hurried away.

Joe got back into the Cherokee to wait. Twenty minutes passed, then twenty-five, then thirty, then thirty-five. He was seriously contemplating walking right into the emergency room and confronting her, when he caught sight of her in his rearview mirror. She came up beside him, and he could read the nametag on her uniform: Mary Pride. She was carrying something concealed in a towel.

"I'm sorry, we had an emergency," she said, pulling a manila folder out of the towel and thrusting it through the open window. "I shouldn't be doing this, it's probably illegal, it's certainly unethical, but I just couldn't stand by and do nothing. I'm only doing it to help Jason. We grew up together, and I know him to be a good person. But please don't come back. It would cost me my job." And then she was gone.

• • •

Just as Lily was rising to cross-examine her former next-door neighbor, her cell phone began to vibrate. She quickly glanced at the text message. "I beg the court's indulgence, Your Honor," she said, flying blind because the message just said to wait. "Something urgent has come up. May I have a short recess before my cross-examination of this witness?"

Grace Pelletier glanced up at the huge Ethan Allen clock that hung on the courtroom wall behind her. It read 4:10. She then looked over at the jury, and then at the prosecutor. "Any objection if we recess for the day, Mr. Morgan?" she inquired.

John Henry shrugged. "I have no objection, Your Honor," he said.

"All right then," she said, turning to the witness. "Mrs. Scott, please return in the morning, prepared to continue with your testimony." And then, as she did every day at close of court, the judge turned to the jury. "We will adjourn until tomorrow," she said. "I caution you not to discuss any part of this case, either among yourselves or with anyone else during that time." And then she banged her gavel. "Court will be in recess until nine o'clock tomorrow morning."

A rare tactical error on Lily's part, John Henry thought smugly. He was delighted to let the jury spend the night thinking over Lauren Scott's glowing tribute to her husband.

• • •

They sat around the table in the conference room of the Victorian late into the evening -- Lily, Joe, Megan, and Dancer -- saying little, staring at the file spread out in front of them.

It was the medical file of one Margaret Dean, smuggled out of the Trent Community Hospital by an emergency room nurse, and it was complete with charts, notes, x-rays, and photographs that told a three-year story of grim and escalating brutality.

"My God," Megan breathed finally, when every word had been read, and every x-ray and photo had been scrutinized. "How could this have been happening all that time, and nobody knew?"

"Because someone went to a lot of trouble to make sure nobody knew," Joe suggested.

"No, someone knew," Lily said in disgust. "Someone knew, and went to a lot of trouble to make sure nobody else found out."

"Sometimes, it's easier to pretend something isn't happening, than to do something about it," Dancer said.

"I have a question," Megan declared. "Why didn't the hospital do something about it? The law is clear, isn't it? This sort of thing has to be reported."

"Unfortunately, there are always ways to get around that," Lily said.

Wanda appeared in the doorway. "I ran the name and the number," she reported. "Margaret Dean was the maternal great-grandmother. It was her social security number they used. She lived in Minneapolis. Died in 1979."

Lily nodded. "It had to be something like that."

"But what does it have to do with our case?" Megan asked.

"Maybe nothing, maybe everything," Lily said with a deep sigh. "You think you know people, and then something like this comes along, and you realize you never really knew them at all."

Joe stood up. "It's this kind of thing that makes you understand why people can kill," he said.

Lily nodded. "It's late," she said. "Let's go home. We're going to have a tough day ahead of us tomorrow."

• • •

At nine o'clock the following morning, Lauren Scott returned to the witness stand, this time wearing a long-sleeved, high-necked teal green silk blouse, over a full, flowery skirt.

Lily was wearing a simple beige suit that, like several others in the sweltering courtroom, was lightweight and open-collared. She rose slowly from behind the defense table.

"Mrs. Scott, yesterday you described your husband as being strong physically, emotionally, and spiritually, is that correct?" she inquired.

"Yes," Lauren replied.

"When you say he was spiritually strong, do you mean he had a keen sense of right and wrong?"

"That was part of it."

"We've heard previous testimony that your husband had a bad temper and was often violent on the job -- is that the sense of right and wrong you had in mind?"

"I wouldn't know anything about that," Lauren said a bit stiffly.

"In fact, we heard that he beat up a homeless man so badly, he ended up in the hospital."

"Dale didn't discuss his work with me."

"Then on what do you base your rather glowing evaluation of him?" Lily inquired.

"On how he behaved at home," Lauren replied.

"I see. So what you're saying is that, at home, Dale knew right from wrong, and always acted accordingly, is that correct?"

In the witness chair, Lauren uncrossed and then re-crossed her legs. "Yes, that's what I said."

"He was never violent at home?"

"No, of course he wasn't."

"He never lost his temper and he never flew into a rage over anything at home?"

Lauren shifted uncomfortably in the witness chair. "Not that I can recall."

"He never took the stress of his job out on you or on your children?"

"Certainly not. He loved his children."

"And you?"

"Well, he loved me, too, of course."

"Of course," Lily murmured. "All right, you've testified that you and your husband occasionally used recreational drugs, is that correct?"

"Yes, we did."

"How many times would you say you did that?"

"I don't know."

"Well, would you say it was so many you've lost count -- or so few, you can't recall?" the defense attorney pressed.

"Maybe half a dozen times," the witness responded reluctantly.

"Only half a dozen times? In thirteen years of marriage?"

"Yes."

"And this recreational use you refer to -- was it at the beginning of your marriage, in the middle of your marriage, at the end of your marriage, or was it spread throughout your marriage?"

"I don't know -- towards the end, I guess." Even the jury could see that the widow was uncomfortable with this line of questioning.

"And what drugs did you use?"

Lauren blinked. "I didn't know what they were -- it was whatever Dale brought home to try."

"You didn't know what the drugs were, but you used them anyway?"

"I didn't ask. I didn't think I had to. I trusted my husband. Besides, we were just experimenting."

"Well, let's see if we can figure it out -- tell us, how did you use the drugs?"

"What do you mean?"

"I don't mean anything terribly sinister," Lily assured her. "I mean, did you smoke them, did you snort them, did you inject them, did you swallow them?"

Lauren was obviously flustered. "I don't know that I can remember all that clearly, it was such a long time ago," she declared.

"I'm sorry," Lily said smoothly. "I thought you said the drug use you and your husband engaged in was towards the end of your marriage."

"I think we smoked some, and maybe we snorted some, and we probably swallowed some -- so what? What possible difference could it make now? My husband's dead."

"Which one did you swallow?"

Lauren sighed. "I don't know what it was called."

"What did it look like?"

"Like a pill."

"What did it taste like?"

"I don't remember."

"How did it make you feel?"

"I don't remember."

"All right, which one did you smoke?"

"Your Honor," John Henry said, "I fail to see the relevance of Mrs. Scott having to identify which recreational drugs she and her husband might have enjoyed in the privacy of their own home, and when they enjoyed them."

"If the court will give me a bit of leeway, Your Honor," Lily responded, I believe I can show the relevance."

"You have some leeway, Miss Burns."

"Thank you, Your Honor," Lily said, and turned back to Lauren. "Which one did you smoke?"

"Marijuana," Lauren said without hesitation. "It looked like dried grass -- which I guess is why they call it weed."

"What did you do with it?"

"We rolled it up in cigarette paper and lit it and smoked it."

"And what did it taste like -- bitter, sweet, salty?"

"Bitter."

"And how did it make you feel?"

"Like I didn't have a care in the world," Lauren replied.

"Was that the first time you had smoked marijuana?" Lily asked. "When you smoked it with your husband?"

"No," Lauren admitted. "I tried it a couple of times when I was in high school. Actually, if I recall correctly, you and I tried it together."

"That's right, we did," Lily confirmed with a smile. "And it did make us feel like we didn't have a care in the world, didn't it?"

"Yes."

"And which drug did your husband bring home that you snorted?"

"I think it was some sort of powder."

"And how exactly did you snort the powder?"

"We just sprinkled a little of it out on the coffee table and sniffed it up through a straw."

"You sniffed it?"

"Yes. . .I think that's what we did."

"And how many times did you do this?"

"I don't remember. Just once, I think."

Lily walked over to the defense table and picked up the waterproof packet Joe had found in the Scotts' toilet tank. "Defense Exhibit 15," she informed the court clerk, who marked the item into evidence.

"Mrs. Scott, do you recognize this?"

"Yes," Lauren said reluctantly. "You found that in the toilet in our bathroom. But I have no idea what it was doing there."

"You didn't put it there?"

"No, certainly not."

"Does that mean your husband put it there?"

"I don't know how it got there."

"Well, does anybody else have access to your private bathroom?"

The widow hesitated for a long moment before she responded. "No."

"Then who else could have put it there?" Lily asked reasonably.

"I don't know -- nobody else, I guess. It must have been Dale. He went on drug raids all the time, as part of his job, and it was probably something he found during one of them, and maybe he put it there for safe-keeping, or something."

"Or something," Lily murmured. "Do you happen to know what's in this packet?"

"I suppose it's a drug."

"Yes, it's a drug," Lily confirmed. "Do you know which drug?"

Lauren shook her head. "No, not by name."

"Well, it's called cocaine," Lily told her. "And it's a drug that comes in powder form. Is that what you and your husband sniffed?"

"It could be," the witness said with a shrug. "I'm afraid I really wouldn't know cocaine powder from baby powder."

"So you and your husband put some kind of powder out on your coffee table and sniffed it through a straw?"

"I guess so -- isn't that how it's done?"

"Yes, that's how it's done," Lily confirmed. "And on how many different occasions did you do this?"

"I don't know -- once or twice, maybe."

"Once or twice, and that was it? After that, neither you nor Dale had any further interest?"

"No," Lauren asserted. "We just wanted to try it, that's all we wanted to do. It was just an experiment. We wanted to know what drugs were out there that our girls might be able to get hold of, and what they would do to them."

"Do you know how much cocaine there is in this little packet?"

"No, I have no idea."

"Well, there's at least a gram of cocaine here. In other words, enough for more than twenty sniffs, or almost two dozen 'experiments'. What did you intend to do with it?"

"Like I said," the widow replied, "I didn't know anything about it."

"Is that really true, Mrs. Scott? Did you honestly not know what your husband was doing with this much cocaine in the house?"

"No, I didn't."

"Well, let me tell you what this little packet is known as on the street -- it's known as a rainy day stash. It's what an addict squirrels away in case his supplier is unable to deliver. Your husband was a cocaine addict, wasn't he?"

"I object, Your Honor!" John Henry cried, jumping to his feet. "What possible relevance can all this have to Detective Scott's murder?"

Grace Pelletier knew exactly what the relevance was, and she knew that the prosecutor knew as well. "Sit down, Mr. Morgan," she directed. "Your objection is overruled."

"Your husband was a cocaine addict, wasn't he, Mrs. Scott?" Lily repeated.

"No, he wasn't!" Lauren cried. "How can you say that? He was a good man. He worked very hard. He did his best. Sometimes, it just all got too much for him, and he needed to unwind, that's all. Don't you ever need to unwind?"

"You never used any drugs with your husband, did you?" Lily asked gently. "That's just a story you made up because you wanted to protect his reputation, isn't it?"

"No. . .yes," Lauren whispered, as tears began slipping down her cheeks. "I'm sorry. I didn't mean to lie. I wanted him to be remembered for being a policeman, not for what he did at home. Am I going to get in trouble?"

"I don't think so," Lily reassured her. "But now we have to talk about something else. About what Dale was like when he was using drugs."

Lauren dabbed at her eyes with a handkerchief. "I'm not sure I know what you mean," she said.

"Well, let's take the homeless man -- the one your husband beat up so badly for no reason at all. The one who ended up at a community hospital all the way out in Trent. Did you know about that?"

"No, I didn't."

"Well, he did." Lily looked her former neighbor straight in the eye. "You're familiar with that hospital, aren't you?"

The color suddenly drained from Lauren's face. "Yes, I know there's a hospital in Trent," she said carefully.

"So then, let me ask you again, how would you characterize your husband's behavior when he was on drugs?"

"When he took the drugs, he was fine -- euphoric, even."

"And when the high wore off?"

Lauren sighed. "He could have mood swings really powerful mood swings and paranoia, too," she responded. "Sometimes, he would tell me the whole world was conspiring against him. And other times, he would say there was a colony of red ants crawling up his body."

"Was he verbally abusive?"

"He could be."

"And what about physically -- was he physically abusive?"

Lauren looked at Lily. "Do I have to?" she whispered.

"There's no need to be afraid," Lily told her gently. "He can't hurt you anymore."

"Yes," the widow said, "my husband could be physically abusive."

"So, would it be fair to say then that his mood swings from the cocaine could make him lash out at someone, for any reason, at any time? Even at someone he loved?"

" Yes."

"He lashed out at you, didn't he?"

Tears were flowing freely down Lauren's cheeks. "Yes," she said.

"In fact, isn't it true that the reason you wear clothing with long sleeves and high collars -- even on a day like this, when it's ninety degrees in here -- is to hide the scars?"

"I didn't want anyone to know," Lauren sobbed, even as she nodded. "I didn't want anyone to know what a failure I was as a wife."

"Is that what he told you?"

Lauren nodded. "Yes."

"And you believed him?"

"Not at first but then, after a while "

"After a while, you began to believe it, didn't you? You began to believe you were a terrible wife and a worse mother."

" Yes."

There was a sympathetic gasp from the spectator section. Members of the jury frantically scribbled on their notepads.

"Thank you," Lily said gently. "I have no further questions."

• • •

At the prosecution table, Tom Lickliter closed his eyes and sighed heavily. He had been waiting for something like this, knowing it was bound to come, and knowing that when it did come, it was going to be a bombshell, and Lily Burns hadn't disappointed.

John Henry, on the other hand, wasn't sure what had just happened. He thought he had the perfect witness to knock down any theory that Dale Scott was an abusive drug addict, and it had just blown up in his face.

He knew it wouldn't do him any good to berate her. His next witness would have to redeem the victim.

"Mrs. Scott," he asked, his voice carrying into every corner of the courtroom, "the night your husband was killed, when he left the house, where did he tell you he was going?"

"He told me that he was going to work," Lauren replied.

"Thank you," the prosecutor said. "I have nothing further for this witness."

The widow fled from the witness stand, and from the courthouse.

• • •

"The people call Raymond Scott to the stand," John Henry declared above the murmuring gallery.

Dale Scott's father was ushered into the courtroom. He lumbered down the aisle and into the witness box, took the oath, and sat down. He was not much taller than his son had been, but he was a lot heavier. He had tried to dress appropriately for the occasion, but his jacket was already soaked through with perspiration.

"Detective Dale Scott was your son, was he not?" John Henry asked.

"My only son," Raymond Scott replied.

"Was he a good son?"

"The best," Scott said, his voice choked with emotion. "From the day he was born."

"There has been some here testimony that your son was a drug addict, and that he was violent. Do you have any information that would either refute or corroborate this?"

"I say no to both. I brought my boy up to be a good man, and he was."

"Was he violent?"

"He had a temper, sure, but it never got out of control -- not even when he was dealing with the scum he had to deal with. He used to tell me some of the stuff he had to do, and when he had to get rough, he told me it bothered him. He did it because he had to, but it bothered him."

"Do you know if your son used drugs?"

"How do you mean -- used drugs as in did he have a habit?"

"Yes."

"No way," Scott declared. "No way anyone's going to say my boy had a drug habit. He may have done a little experimenting in his time, sure -- doesn't everyone do that when they're young and ignorant and need to learn?" He looked to the jurors for confirmation, and several of them smiled. "But he wasn't any addict, if that's what you're asking."

"That's what I'm asking."

"Well, the answer is no. I knew my son better than anyone, and I would've known. I would've known."

"Can you tell the jury why you're so sure your son was not doing drugs, sir?"

"I know because he lived through it all with me," Raymond Scott replied. "I got hurt on the job when Dale was just a boy. Crushed two vertebras in my back, and there was nothing I could do for the pain but take the drugs. I got so hooked on them that, for a while there, I didn't know up from down. Dale lived through that with me, and it wasn't pretty. Learned a good lesson, he did. He always said it was the best lesson I could've taught him."

"Thank you," John Henry said. "No more questions."

• • •

The last thing Lily wanted to do was beat up on the man. He had suffered enough, as they say. Moreover, the jury obviously empathized with him, and it was never smart to show a bunch of people doing their civic duty how misguided they could be. But she had to do something.

"You and your son were close, weren't you?" she asked gently.

"Sure were," Scott declared.

"And, as his father, you'd have done just about anything for him, wouldn't you?"

"Of course," the witness said. "That's what fathers do."

"And I'm sure you kept in touch, right?"

"We sure did."

"In the last, say, two or three years, how often would you estimate you saw your son?"

"Mother and I talked to him on the telephone at least once a week," Scott declared.

"Yes," Lily pressed ever so gently, "but how often did you actually see him?"

"Every chance we had."

"Do you remember when the last time was that you saw Dale, Mr. Scott?"

"Of course I do," the man said, "That would have been last Christmas. The whole family come over and spent the day with Mother and me."

"That would be roughly two months before he was killed?"

"Yes."

"And how about the time before that -- when was that?"

"Time before that would've been summer, probably around the Fourth of July."

"Thank you," Lily said. "I have nothing further."

The judge looked over at the prosecutor, who shook his head.

"You're excused, Mr. Scott," she said, and everyone watched him leave the courtroom. "You may proceed, Mr. Morgan."

"The people rest, Your Honor," John Henry responded.

Ten

Totem Point Park jutted out above the Strait of Juan de Fuca on the eastern edge of Port Hancock. Combining a series of indoor and outdoor museums, it honored the tribes of Jackson County, and exhibited the finest examples of native art to be found in the Northwest. Walking paths cut into the grass connected totem clusters with small structures designed to look like tepees that displayed paintings, weavings, pottery, and other artifacts that depicted an extraordinarily rich culture.

Native food was prepared and served at tiny kiosks along the paths. Benches dotted the point, from which one could see all the way across the Strait to the rugged, snow-capped Canadian Rockies soaring skyward over British Columbia. Educational in concept, and a natural tourist attraction, the park had initially been bankrolled by the federal government, but it had been created and was now sustained by the tribes in an amazing show of unity.

Carson Burns and his daughter had been coming to this place on this date for the past ten years.

Unlike any other in recent history, this particular Sunday was magnificent. The sky was bright, the temperature hovered around eighty degrees, the frantic tourist season was well in the past, and the view was unparalleled.

They chose their favorite spot near the end of the point, a small stone bench beneath a large tree. Lily positioned her father's wheelchair so that it faced the Rockies, and sat down beside him. And Dancer, ever present, retreated to a safe distance to give them some privacy.

"A day like this, a place like this, you can hardly believe there's a thing wrong with the world," Carson observed. It was the tenth anniversary of Althea Burns' death.

Lily took her father's left hand in hers and they sat in silence for a moment, he remembering his soul mate of forty years, she remembering the soft-spoken nurturer she resembled so much.

"It's all just an illusion," she murmured.

"What is?" he asked.

"Life," she said. "And the tricks it plays on us."

"No point in fretting over what's done," Carson advised. "Better to concentrate on what needs doing."

Lily sighed. "That's the problem," she told him. "I am."

"I thought things were going pretty well for Mr. Lightfoot," he said in some surprise.

"On whole, I think they are," she said. "But there's still a piece missing -- right in the middle of my puzzle, and I guess I'm just not going to be satisfied until I find it."

"You telling me you won't be happy with an acquittal?" Carson queried. "Thought that's what you've been aiming at all this time."

"It is, and I would be delighted with an acquittal," she assured him. "But that doesn't keep me from wondering."

"Wondering what?"

"Why that night was different. Even if Dale was in the alley to meet Morales, even if he did pull his gun and intended to shoot Jason so there'd be no witness, even if Jason fought with him over the gun -- self-defense is obvious here, and I believe we should get an acquittal on it. But the beating Dale took -- that's what still bothers me. I don't care how drunk Jason was, that's just not who he is, and I want to be able to tell the jury that. I want them to know, because it's important. But I don't know how to do that -- because there's still that piece missing."

"Do you think the jury cares?" Carson asked. "He's become almost a folk hero in all of this. Do you really think they'll care that the one time he was facing certain death, he acted out of character?"

"I don't know," Lily said. "Before, I think all they cared about was holding someone responsible for Dale's death. Now, I think they're beginning to see Jason as a person, not just as a defendant, and Dale as a scoundrel. But I'm still not sure that's enough."

"Don't you think you're being a little too hard on yourself?"

Lily shook her head. "You don't get it, and I'm not sure I do, either," she told him. "Here's a client who thinks he's going to hang as sure as we're sitting here, and what does he do? He breaks himself out of jail, gets clean away with it, and then, instead of getting lost somewhere and having a life, he comes back. Like it was all just a momentary impulse. And here I am, wanting to shake him, and tell him he should have kept on going."

"Are you feeling guilty?" Carson asked. "Do you think he came back so as not to disappoint you."

"That may part of it," Lily admitted. "I'm afraid he thinks I'm going to pull a miracle out of my bonnet to save him. And what if I can't?"

Carson gave her a crooked little smile. "There are no guarantees in this line of work, my girl, you know that. But it seems to me, you've already pulled a couple miracles out already -- Morales, Trent."

She chuckled dryly. "You mean, I've used up my quota?"

"I mean -- are you so sure there's not another little one left to find?"

"Well, if there is, it's sure well hidden. And I don't want to see Jason go down because I wasn't good enough to find it."

"You have your whole case to put on," her father said. "If I were you, I wouldn't be giving up just yet."

"Hello," a voice behind them interrupted.

Lily twisted around in her seat. Tom Lickliter was standing behind her. He had his arm around the shoulder of one boy who looked to be about twelve, and was holding the hand of another boy of perhaps ten.

"Hello," she said. "Did John Henry actually give you a day off?"

"Not exactly," he teased. "He told me I should keep an eye on you."

Lily chuckled. "Always knew he was a smart man." She remembered her father suddenly, and jumped up to turn his wheelchair. "Dad, this is Tom Lickliter, the new DP at the house."

Carson Burns eyed the attorney. "Nice to know there's some fresh blood over there," he said. "It's been lacking ever since my daughter moved over." He twisted the left side of his mouth into a grin and thrust out his left hand, which Tom took and shook firmly in both of his.

"It's an honor, sir," the fresh blood said. The legend that was Carson Burns stretched far beyond Jackson County. Tom gestured to his children. "These are my boys," he declared. "Ryan and Evan."

The boys were polite. They said hello, but they didn't smile at the strangers.

"Is this your first visit to Totem Point?" Lily asked them. The boys nodded. "What do you think of it?"

"It's neat," Ryan replied. "All this Indian stuff in one place."

"Yeah, neat," Evan echoed.

"We haven't had much time to explore our new community," Tom said. "Moved in, school started, the trial began, bam, bam, bam -- so we're making a day of it." He looked out across the Strait. "You sure do get an extraordinary perspective from here, don't you? A real understanding of the balance between man and nature, power and weakness."

"One of our favorite places," Lily murmured with a little twinkle in her eye, "for just that reason."

"Daughter, behave yourself," Carson admonished.

Tom laughed. "I'm sure she didn't mean that in an adversarial way."

"Of course she did," Carson declared.

"Of course she did," Lily echoed, playing with him now. "I'll take any advantage I can get."

"You've already got most of it, I'm afraid," Tom said. "What your client did was brilliant."

"Brilliant?"

"Absolutely. That little trick of his has turned the whole community around. He's a hero now. Right up there with Robin Hood. Do you think there's a jury in the world that would convict Robin Hood?"

Lily smiled. "Let's hope not," she said.

"Dad, can we go now?" the boys wanted to know.

"Where to?" he asked.

"Food," they replied, already leading him away by the hand, toward the kiosks from which tantalizing smells were intentionally wafting.

"See you tomorrow, then, I guess," he said over his shoulder.

"Wouldn't miss it," Lily said, watching them as they went.

Carson was watching, too. "Now that's an interesting young man," he observes. "Or haven't you noticed?"

"Never mind that. Do you think that's what it was all about?"

"That your client could be a lot smarter than you've given him credit for?"

"That he knew exactly what he was doing?"

"Of course I do. But do I think that means he predicted the reaction of the community? I don't know. Why don't you ask him?"

• • •

"I don't know what I was thinking when I left," Jason said in response to Lily's question. "I was just trying to get my head clear. I sure couldn't do that in this hole of a place."

It was an unplanned visit, on a Sunday afternoon. "But did you realize what a stir coming back would cause in the community?" Lily pressed. "What a difference it would make?"

Jason shrugged. "I guess I never thought that much about it," he replied. "Even if I did, I figured people would think I was even guiltier. And what's the difference between guilty and guiltier?"

Fifteen minutes later, Lily and Dancer were headed back to Morgan Hill.

"I get where you're trying to go," the man from Spokane said. "But I don't think he's going to give you the answer you're looking for."

"Because he can't -- or because he won't?" Lily asked, because she had come to respect the quiet man beside her a great deal.

"That's a good question," he replied.

• • •

Not counting the interruption, the Lightfoot trial was entering its third week, and tomorrow, Lily would begin the case for the defense.

Dinner was over, and Lily, Carson and Dancer were in the library -- the men watching a football game, and Lily ensconced behind her father's desk, poring over every detail of the prosecution's presentation, every word of testimony, every exhibit, every report, every piece of evidence.

"Planning on burning the midnight oil?" Carson asked, signaling that the football game was over.

"Just want to make sure I haven't missed anything," she said.

"Well, I think a good night's sleep will serve you better than staying up and fretting all night."

"I just want to make sure I'm not missing anything," she told him. "But don't worry. I'm heading for bed pretty soon."

"You've got all the momentum on your side, what with Lauren's testimony and the drug angle and, of course, Robin Hood. In my opinion, you've got a good case for diminished capacity, and certainly as good a case for self-defense as John Henry was able to put on for premeditated murder."

"Yes, but you know the saying about how a woman in a man's world has to be twice as good to be equal."

"And aren't you?"

She grinned at him. "Sure I'm equal, but right now, I'd settle for one last little miracle."

• • •

Too soon, it was morning, and Lily was suffering all the tweaks and lurches of a nervous stomach.

"Is the defense ready to proceed?" Judge Pelletier inquired.

Feeling almost as wilted as the blue seersucker suit she was wearing, Lily rose to her feet. "We are, Your Honor," she said.

"Call your first witness."

Lily took a deep breath and let it out as slowly as she could. She had begun this case looking for nothing more than to keep her client off death row. Now, every fiber of her being was concentrated on trying to convince five men and seven women that Jason Lightfoot was in nothing less than a fight for his life when he shot and killed Dale Scott.

"Defense calls Charles Graywolf to the stand," Lily said.

The defendant's uncle, his long white hair flowing freely down his back, glided soundlessly down the aisle to the witness stand. He was wizened, as tall as Jason, and almost as lean. His city clothes hung awkwardly on him.

"Mr. Graywolf, you are Jason Lightfoot's uncle, are you not?"

"I am," Graywolf confirmed. "Jason's mother is my youngest sister."

"On the Sunday just before Dale Scott was killed, did you spend time with your nephew?"

"I did," Graywolf replied. "He hitchhiked out, went to his mother's place, like he did almost every Sunday, and then he came to our house. We ate dinner, we talked some, we walked a bit, and then I drove him back to Port Hancock."

"How did he seem to you that day?"

"He was normal."

"And what was normal?"

"He's a quiet boy by nature, and he was quiet," Graywolf said. "He may have been a bit more upset about his mother than usual. But as I recall, he was happy about some work he was gonna be doin', startin' the next day."

"What work was that?"

"He said he was gonna start workin' on a boat that come into dry dock. He lives to work on boats, that boy.

That accident he had ten years back was the worst thing ever happened to him. Anyway, he was gonna work for someone he'd worked for in the past, he said, so he was lookin' forward to gettin' paid."

"He didn't always get paid for his work?"

"Nope," the old man said. "A lot of times, people promised to pay him but then, for one reason or another, never did."

"How did he feel about that?"

"He took it better than I would've," Graywolf asserted. "He used to say if they were so hard up they had to stiff a homeless man, then they probably needed it more'n he did."

"Do you think he meant it?"

The Indian nodded. "He meant it. He's a free spirit, my nephew, and he lives a simple life."

"So he was happy on Sunday because he was going to be working on a boat on Monday and he knew he was going to get paid?"

"Yep," Graywolf said. "He's never happier than when he's got a boat under his feet."

"And would you say he acted more or less the same that Sunday as on any other Sunday you saw him?"

"Yes, I would."

"You didn't detect any stress? And agitation? Any anger?"

"Nope," the Indian said.

"Did he ever mention Police Officer Dale Scott to you?"

Graywolf shook his head. "Never heard the name until Jason got arrested for his killin'. Years ago, he used to get himself in trouble for bein' disorderly, and I know now that Scott was the cop that used to beat up on him. But I never heard about it from Jason. I had to read about it in the newspaper to find out."

"So, as far as you know, Jason held no resentment toward the deceased?"

"As far as I know, Jason holds no resentment towards no one."

• • •

John Henry and Tom Lickliter exchanged whispers, weighing the impact of Graywolf's testimony on the jury, deciding what to do about it.

"Mr. Morgan?" Grace Pelletier prompted. "Do you wish to inquire?"

"Oh, I'm sorry, Your Honor," John Henry said, as though not realizing the court was waiting on him. "We have no questions for this witness."

Lily smiled to herself. It was something she would have done as a prosecutor -- let the jury think the state believed the witness's testimony to be so inconsequential as to not even merit cross-examination.

"You may call your next witness, Miss Burns," the judge said.

"Defense calls Billy Fugate to the stand," Lily said.

The owner of The Last Call Bar & Grill walked slowly down the center aisle, his ill-fitting suit coat fastened too tightly around his girth, looking neither right nor left as the attorney had suggested. He didn't have to look anyway. He knew everyone was watching him. He could feel their eyes on him. When he got to the witness stand, he raised his hand as the attorney had told him he would have to do, and swore to tell the truth. Then he climbed the two steps up to the witness chair and sat down. He was perspiring profusely.

"Mr. Fugate," Lily began.

"Billy," he corrected her.

"I beg your pardon?"

"It's Billy," he repeated. "Just Billy."

"All right then, Billy," Lily corrected herself, "it's quite warm in here. Would you like to take your jacket off?"

"Yes, Ma'am, I sure would," he said gratefully, and peeled off the soggy suit coat.

"More comfortable now?"

Billy nodded. "I guess as comfortable as anyone can figure on, bein' up in front of a real judge and jury," he said.

Some of the jurors smiled, more than a few in the gallery tittered, and Grace Pelletier barely managed to stop herself from laughing. Billy looked surprised. He hadn't realized he was being funny.

"Billy," Lily said, "please tell the jury how you know Jason Lightfoot."

"Known him from the docks since he was sixteen," the barkeeper replied. "Come to work for me after Barney Cosgrove blew himself and his boat to smithereens." Most of those in the courtroom remembered the Seaworthy and her explosive end and they nodded as Billy spoke. "Barney been like a father to him, so how could I be less? His real dad was gone, and his mother wasn't much use, and I figured the boy needed an anchor -- you know, someplace where he knew he could always come to be safe."

"And how would you describe Jason to someone who didn't know him?"

Billy thought about that for a moment. "Quiet, respectful, real good worker, and minds his own business," he said finally.

"How many times have you seen Jason drunk?"

"You'd be better askin' how many times I seen him sober," the barkeeper replied with a shake of his head. "He's been drinkin' himself to sleep every night since I know him."

"Do you know why?"

"I know what Jason says -- says it quiets his mind."

"Do you know what that means?"

"No, not really. Jason don't talk much about himself."

"Does he have a chip on his shoulder about anything?" Lily asked.

"Not that I ever saw."

"Does he blame anyone for his lot in life?"

Billy shook his head. "He don't blame nobody for nothin'. His life is the one he chose and he knows that, and he seems all right with it. He don't cuss, he don't argue, he don't fight. Folks that know him like him."

"The night of Detective Scott's death, can you tell the jury what you observed about Jason?"

"He come in to work a little after nine o'clock, just like always on Sundays. We had a little grease fire in the kitchen, and that took a bit of time to clean up. So it was almost ten-thirty before he had ate his supper and sat down at the bar. It was about ten past eleven by the time all the stragglers were gone, and then he mopped up, washed up, had a last drink, took out the garbage, and went home."

"Home?"

"Home to him," the barkeeper explained. "He had a box out back."

"Was the bar crowded that night?"

"We had an okay crowd." Billy said, allowing a little pride to creep into his voice. "And there are always the regulars -- guys who are tryin' to squeeze the last drop out of Sunday before they have to face up to Monday."

"How many drinks did Jason have that night?" Lily asked.

"Poured him seven shots of rum," Billy replied. "That's what he drinks -- rum, and he takes it neat."

"And what time did he leave the bar?"

"I'd say, by the time he was done cleanin' up everything, eatin' and drinkin', it was maybe ten, fifteen minutes before midnight."

"Would you say that Jason is reliable?"

"Like the sun comin' up in the mornin'."

"Would you say he's conscientious?"

"Never had no complaint."

"Even when he's been drinking?"

"He's a sneak-up drunk," Billy said.

"What does that mean?"

"It means you never know how it's affectin' him until all of a sudden, it just does. And that's when his day is done."

"Billy, did you know Detective Scott?" Lily asked.

"Sure did," the barkeeper declared.

"How did you know him?"

"He used to come around a lot before he was a detective, when he was on patrol. He'd come lookin' for someone he could roust."

"And how would he do that?"

"He'd hang around outside, waitin' for someone who'd had maybe a couple too many to leave, and then he'd jump all over 'em."

"Objection, Your Honor," John Henry said. "The man is dead. He can't defend himself against such hearsay."

"Sustained," Grace Pelletier said.

"All right, never mind what he did," Lily said smoothly. "Where would Officer Scott be on those nights he came looking for drunks?"

"Hangin' around out front, mostly," Billy replied.

"Out front? Not out back? Not in the alley?"

"No," Billy said. "Not unless he was specifically lookin' to bust Jason. Otherwise, no one else uses the alley. Everyone comes and goes through the front door."

"Including you?"

"Includin' me."

"Can you think of any reason for Detective Scott to have been in the alley that night?"

"Nope, 'specially considerin' that once he got hisself promoted, he wasn't even on the prowl for drunks no more."

"Did you see Detective Scott that night?'

"Nope. He used to come in maybe once a month or so, have a beer and leave, but not that night."

"That night," Lily inquired, "what time did you leave the bar?"

"I locked up right behind Jason, so it was probably a few minutes before midnight," Billy told her.

"And where did you go?"

"I went home."

"Did you go out the front door or the back?"

"The front. I keep my car in the lot across the street."

"Did you hear anything as you went across the street?"

"You mean, did I hear a ruckus comin' from out back? No, I didn't hear nothin'. That is, nothin' other than normal noise -- just people on their way home on a Sunday night."

"Thank you," Lily said.

• • •

"Would it be fair to say you like Jason Lightfoot?" Tom Lickliter asked on cross-examination.

"It sure would," Billy said.

"In fact, you sort of see him as a son, don't you?"

"I guess you could say that."

"Do you have a son, Mr. Fugate?"

"Yep. Got two."

"And if one of them was in trouble, real trouble, you'd do your best to help, wouldn't you?"

"I'd go to the ends of the earth for my boys," Billy assured him. "That's what fathers do."

"So, if you see the defendant as a son," the deputy prosecuting attorney pressed, "and he was in trouble, you'd do whatever you could to help him, wouldn't you?"

"You tryin' to say somethin', fella?" Billy asked. "Why don'tcha just say it out straight? You askin' if I would get up here and swear to tell the truth and then lie to all these people here?"

"Well, would you?"

"The answer is no," the barkeeper said. I don't gotta lie -- for sure not when the truth is what can help out Jason the most."

Tom Lickliter nodded. The man wasn't as dumb as some might have assumed. "Thank you." He said. "I have nothing further."

• • •

"How'd it go?" Joe asked, after court had recessed for lunch.

"I don't know," she told him. "Ask me again, after the verdict."

He smiled. "Cheer up," he said. "It'll all be over soon. You don't have that many witnesses to call."

She made a face at him. "Why don't you just go out and find me another miracle," she retorted.

It was at that exact moment that Charles Graywolf entered the Victorian.

"I'm sorry to bother you," he said, "but I need to see my nephew."

Lily looked at him. "What's the matter?" she asked.

"I need to tell him," the Indian said. "I need to tell him that his mother up and died."

• • •

"Your Honor, I hate to beg the court's indulgence again," Lily was saying half an hour later, in chambers, before court had reconvened. "I know this trial has been delayed far too much already. But my client's mother just passed away. He needs some time."

"And just how much time do you think he'll need, Miss Burns?" Grace Pelletier inquired, clearly unhappy.

"I'd like a couple of days, at least," Lily replied.

"Mr. Morgan, your thoughts on the matter?" the judge invited.

"Under the circumstances, I have no objection to a couple of days, Your Honor," he said.

"All right then," the judge declared, "we'll adjourn until Thursday morning."

• • •

"It's about your mom," Charles Graywolf told his nephew when they were face to face. "She died last night. Went peaceful, in her sleep."

Jason blinked hard several times, but he didn't say anything. What was there to say? He knew the day was going to come, sooner or later. It had just come sooner than he had anticipated.

"Your sister was there first thing this morning," his uncle said, "but she couldn't wake her. I think she was ready. She was smiling."

The truth was, Jason's mother had died during the night from a self-inflicted stab wound after consuming a whole bottle of bourbon. Her daughter had found her in the morning, on the floor in the kitchen, when it was too late to do anything. But the family decided, under the circumstances, Jason didn't need to know any of that.

"We're arranging a service, of course. For Wednesday, I think -- Wednesday afternoon." Graywolf looked at Lily. "Can he be there?"

Lily nodded. "I'll make arrangements," she said.

Jason thanked his uncle for coming, and then looked at his attorney. "Now what?" he asked.

"We've got a delay for a couple of days. It's not much, but it's something."

Jason nodded. He thought about the woman who had given birth to him, suckled him, raised him up as best she could until his father died, and then simply chucked it all and let the alcohol take over. He wondered why she had done that to herself, why she hadn't been stronger, why she hadn't let anyone help her. It never occurred to him, not even as the bleakness of life washed over him and his whole being cried out for a drink, that not too long ago he had been well on his way down the very same path.

"I don't suppose my box is still in the alley, is it?" Jason asked.

"I don't know," Lily replied. "Why?"

"There's a picture of my mother -- I kept it zipped inside my bed," he said. "I'd kinda like to have it now."

"I'll get right on it," she promised, reaching for her cell phone.

An hour later, Joe was back in the alley behind The Last Call. But Jason's box wasn't there, and Joe remembered it hadn't been there when he had been in the alley before. He looked at the space between the two sections of the wall and felt a stab of real regret that he wouldn't be able to retrieve the photograph for the Indian. He assumed the box had been confiscated as evidence, and then it occurred to him that, if the crime lab boys still had it, perhaps the photograph was still in the bed. He was about to head off to follow up on that, when Billy Fugate stopped him cold.

"The cops don't have Jason's box," he said. "I been lookin' out for it. They took some of his stuff the day of the killin', but as far as I can tell, what they left behind still belongs to him, until I know for sure he ain't comin' back for it. So I'm seein' to it that it stays safe and sound. I don't want nobody lootin' what little he has left in this world. I moved the box down to my storeroom. You're welcome to look, if you like."

"I'd appreciate it," the private investigator said.

The barkeeper led the way into the basement. Jason's box sat in a corner. Joe looked inside. The dog bed he had slept on was clean, as was the remnant of carpet tacked beneath it and the blanket that lay on top of it. There were a few clothes, some toiletries, and a pile of magazines, mostly about boats and boating.

"Are you looking for something in particular?" Billy asked. "Maybe I can help."

"Yes, a photograph of Jason's mother," Joe told him. "She died yesterday, and he asked to have it."

"Well, I'm right sorry to hear that," the barkeeper said, shaking his head. "The poor fellow had more'n his share of grief over that woman, I can tell you that. As for him havin' a photo of her, though, I don't know where it would be."

"That's okay, I do," Joe said. "He kept it zipped inside his bed."

The investigator ran his hand around the edge of the fleece-covered circle until he came to the zipper. Slowly, he worked it open and slid his hand inside the bed, feeling around the stuffing until his fingers touched something hard. He began pulling it out. It was a small silver rectangle, framing a faded photograph of a woman sitting on a porch. He was removing it from the bed when it suddenly snagged on something. He tugged softly and the frame came free, but curiosity got the better of him, and so he went back and ran his flashlight slowly over the bed. What he saw literally made the seasoned ex-policeman's eyes pop.

A small hole, perhaps three-eighths of an inch in diameter, with what looked like burn marks in the fabric, went clean through the fleece. The hole, Joe knew instantly, was exactly the size that a forty-caliber bullet would make. He backed out of the box and stood up.

"What is that?" Billy asked.

"Good question," Joe replied. "I'm going out to my car," he told the barkeeper. "Will you stay right here, and try not to touch anything. It's very important."

"I just turned to stone," Billy said.

Joe practically ran all the way to the Jeep, diving into the front seat and extracting his camera. Then he made a beeline back to the basement. True to his word, the barkeeper hadn't moved. The private investigator began to photograph the hole in the bed, just as he had found it. Then he carefully lifted the bed out of the box and shined his light over the piece of carpet. Sure enough, there was a corresponding hole in the carpet. He photographed that, too. He turned to Billy.

"Do you have a screwdriver or a hammer or something I can use to pull up this carpet?"

"Sure thing," Billy said, disappearing and returning a moment later with a box of tools.

Together, the two men pried the tacks out of the carpet, and right where Joe expected to find it was a small hole in the bottom of the box.

The private investigator photographed everything.

"Help me turn it," he said. "And let's hope when Jason built this thing, he built it right."

Together, they managed to tilt the box over on its side, and just as Joe had hoped, the bottom was reinforced with a heavy metal plate. There was a dent in the plate, but no exit hole. Joe took more photographs.

"Okay, let's get it right side up again," he said.

"What is it?" Billy asked, as they returned the box to its upright position. "What did you find?"

"Something that has no business being here," Joe told him.

He pulled out his pocketknife and began digging carefully around the hole, stopping at every step for more camera clicks. When enough of the wood had been scraped away, he took a pair of long-nosed pliers from Billy's toolbox and, reaching into the hole, extracted what he was sure was going to be a forty-caliber Smith and Wesson bullet.

The private investigator took a final photograph.

"Now what in the world was that doin' in there?" Billy asked, peering at the object over Joe's shoulder.

"Good question," Joe replied. "Very good question." He took one of the small plastic bags he habitually carried with him from his pocket and dropped the bullet into it.

"What are you going to do with that?" Billy asked.

"I'm going to give it to an expert," Joe told him.

"Will it help Jason?"

"It just might." Joe was ready to leave. Almost as an afterthought, he turned to the barkeeper. "By any chance did you ever see anybody else come looking for this box?"

"Matter of fact, that very night, after all the excitement was over and everybody was gone, a guy did come nosin' around," Billy told him. "Said he was investigatin' the crime scene. I told him the box was gone, and I didn't know anythin' about it."

"Which wasn't true."

Billy shrugged. "Nope. Told the guy a lie."

"This guy," Joe asked, "did you happen to know him?"

"Yeah," Billy said. "He's a cop."

• • •

"A second bullet?" Lily asked, when Joe finally caught up with her, just as she and her father were sitting down to dinner. "What do you mean there was a second bullet? Where did it come from?"

Knowing that Lily would be at home all evening, Dancer had begged off on dinner, wanting to make the rounds, wanting to hear whatever was being said about how she had done on day one of her case.

Joe dangled the plastic bag containing the bullet under her nose. "It came from your client's bed."

"His bed? You mean, in his box?"

"Yep."

"But how did it get there?"

"If you're asking me, I'd say it got there from Dale Scott's gun. Of course, that would just be a guess on my part. We'd have to have ballistics confirm."

"But it doesn't make any sense," Lily said. "How could there have been two shots fired when only one bullet was missing from the gun?"

"Exactly what I was wondering."

"Could it have been there for a while? I mean, is there any way to know when it was fired?"

"Not really," Joe told her. "Gunshot residue doesn't last very long, only a matter of hours usually, maybe days under the right conditions, but certainly not weeks or months or years. But we can at least find out if this little baby came from Dale's gun."

"Do it," Lily said. "I don't care if I have to pay for the test out of my own pocket, do it!"

• • •

"A second bullet?" Carson Burns contemplated after Joe was gone. "Well now, that could put a rather big crimp in somebody's case, couldn't it? The question is -- whose?"

"That's just it," Lily said. "I don't know. We don't even know yet if the bullet came from Dale's gun. And even if it did, we would have no way of knowing when it was fired."

"True," Carson conceded.

"But, just for the sake of argument," she wondered aloud, "let's say it did come from Dale's gun, and let's even say it was fired that same night -- what could it mean?"

"Well, it could mean the Indian shot Dale, and then, as he stumbled into his box, he accidentally discharged another round."

"But is that really something a sober person would do?"

"No," her father told her. "A sober person would have shot Dale, wiped his fingerprints off the gun, left it at the scene, and found some other place to spend the night."

• • •

"The lab just confirmed it -- the bullet from Lightfoot's bed was indeed fired from Dale's gun," Joe reported back the following afternoon. What he didn't tell her was how hard he had had to lean on Edward Padilla to rush the results.

"So, it *is* what we thought," Lily murmured. "But now the question is -- what does it do for our case?"

"I guess we'll know that as soon as we know when it was fired."

"No," Lily told him. "What we have to figure out is why was it fired."

• • •

"What do you mean -- another bullet?" John Henry demanded, glaring at the hapless police detective standing in front of him.

"Joe Gideon took another bullet over to the lab for testing," Randy Hitchens explained. "Ballistics confirmed it came from Dale's gun."

"So they tested another bullet," the prosecutor said irritably. "So what does that have to do with anything?"

"There was only one bullet missing from Scott's gun that morning," Tom Lickliter reminded him.

John Henry frowned. "So where did Gideon come up with this other bullet?"

"I don't know," Hitchens said.

"I think it's obvious that they'll want to claim it's part of the crime scene and we missed it," Tom said.

"Even if it is, what difference does it make?" John Henry asked. "I mean, so there's another bullet. How can it hurt us?"

"A second bullet when we're saying only one was fired?" Tom replied. "It could compromise the whole case, couldn't it?"

"Nonsense," John Henry declared. "There's got to be a logical explanation for another bullet. Where did they find it?"

"Gideon didn't say," Hitchens told him. "He just took it in and asked the lab to see if it came from Dale's gun."

"All right then, can anyone prove when it was fired?"

"No," the detective conceded. "I don't think the lab could say when it was fired."

"Then who cares?" John Henry concluded. "It has nothing to do with our case. It could have come from anywhere. They can argue a second bullet all they like, but the facts are the facts -- and the fact in this case is there was only one bullet missing from Scott's gun that morning, right?"

"Right," Hitchens said.

• • •

"Did you ever get that little itchy feeling at the back of your neck that tells you when you might be onto something?" Lily asked over dinner Tuesday evening.

"You mean regarding a case?" Carson replied between bites of one of Diana Hightower's specialties -- five-cheese lasagna.

"Yes," his daughter said.

"I seem to recall one or two such instances," he conceded. "Why?"

"Well, call me crazy, but I think I'm going to get an acquittal here."

"You mean, on self-defense?"

"You bet," she said. "It may have been a long shot before, but it isn't anymore."

Carson raised his left eyebrow. "The second bullet?"

"Yes, the second bullet. I've been going over it and over it, and it doesn't make any sense. Let's just say, for the sake of argument, that it went down like you said -- there was a fight, Jason shot Dale, then took the gun into his box, and inadvertently shot off another round."

"So?" her father queried.

"Well, that theory stands up in court only if John Henry claims that, after shooting off the second round, Jason gets out of his box, goes back to the body, finds another bullet, puts it into the magazine, and then goes and gets back into his box again. Now, why on earth would he do that?"

"Drunks can do a lot of things that don't make sense to the sober," Carson told her. "And you're forgetting something rather important -- John Henry could also claim that you can't prove when the second bullet was fired."

"That's not necessarily so, " Dancer said softly.

Two pairs of eyes were suddenly fixed on him. "What do you mean?" Lily asked.

"Your prosecutor can't argue that the second bullet could have been fired years ago."

"Why not?"

Dancer had been present in the gallery, seated in the first row, right behind Lily, throughout the trial. "Because the murder weapon is a Sig Sauer P250, which is a fairly new model," he replied. "Didn't come out until sometime last year, I think. I doubt your police department has been using them for very long."

The wheels, which had ground to a halt in Lily's head, began to turn again. "And there's nothing to indicate that there was any history between Dale and Jason in the past year -- or even the past five years. So that makes it just about certain that the second bullet was fired that night."

"Which I think takes you right back to the second shot being accidental," Carson reminded her. "And you can certainly use it to bolster your case for mitigating circumstances. If he was so drunk as to shoot off the second round in his box, how deliberate could the first shot have been? It probably won't get you as far as an outright acquittal, but it might get you down to manslaughter."

Lily shrugged. "Maybe," she said.

"What? You still want to go for self-defense?"

"I can't help it. In my gut, I think that's exactly what it was."

"I guess anything's possible," Carson conceded. "But I'm not sure I see how you're going to get there."

"The drug connection was how I was going to make Dale the aggressor, and Jason being a witness to something he shouldn't have been was how I was going to argue self-defense."

Carson shrugged. "Then you're going to have to figure out how to put Morales on the stand and make him tell the truth," he said. "Even with all the good press your client's getting with his escape gambit, the jury isn't going to buy self-defense unless they can actually see how it went down."

Lily sighed. "I can have Joe talk to Morales again, but I'm not sure it will do us any good. He said there was a meet on for that night, and he had no reason to lie about it. But if he won't testify, how do I put Dale in that alley?"

"You've got him on drugs, and you've got him on domestic abuse. If it were me, I'd be wondering what else would fall out of Dale Scott's tree if I really shook it. If it were me, I'd get Joe on it right away."

• • •

Joe was already on it. "I've had a funny feeling about this whole thing for a while now," he told her. "Ever since Trent."

Lily smiled. "Is that like an itchy feeling at the back of your neck?" she inquired.

"Yeah, something like that," the private investigator said.

"But my father says we have to be right and we have to make it bulletproof -- pardon the pun."

"Your father's right," Joe said. "So let's go back to the beginning -- again."

"The beginning?"

"Yeah, the beginning," he told her. "And let's start with you and me having a little chat with the client."

• • •

In the sweltering interview room at the Jackson County Jail, Jason Lightfoot looked from Lily to Joe and back again. It was two hours after the service for his mother had ended. "What do you mean, there may have been a reason for the cop to go after me?" he asked.

"Well, don't get your hopes up too high," Lily advised him, "because we're nowhere near being able to prove it yet, but if we're right, we may have a good case for self-defense."

The shell of the man he had been eight months earlier smiled, and it was an ironic smile. "After all this time of thinking I was some kind of cold-blooded killer," he said, "you're tellin' me you maybe don't think I am anymore?"

"It's why we're here, Jason," Lily said. "We don't know. So we need to go over every single thing you remember from that night, and maybe a few things you don't realize you remember."

"Ask me," the Indian said in return. "I'll tell you whatever I can. It was a Sunday. Around noon, I hitched a ride out to my mother's place, like I did almost every Sunday. She was so drunk when I got there, I don't know if she even knew who I was. I fixed her something to eat, but she didn't eat it. Then I read to her for a bit, but I don't know if she heard me. Around five o'clock, I went over to my uncle's, just like he said. We sat around talkin' for a while, we went out for a walk, we had dinner, and then he drove me back to town. I got to The Last Call about nine. There was a grease fire, so I cleaned up the kitchen first. Then I ate. Then I sat down at the bar. After the bar closed, I cleaned up, and then I had one more drink."

"Is this what you actually remember, Jason, or what you remember your uncle and Billy saying in court?" Lily needed to know.

"I think I remember," he said.

"How many drinks did you have that night?" Joe asked.

"Just like Billy told you, I had seven shots of rum."

"Do you, yourself, remember drinking seven shots of rum that specific night?"

"I don't remember," Jason had to admit. "I don't remember much about any night."

Lily sighed. "Okay, then what?"

"Then like I always did, I took out the garbage and went to my box."

"Straight to your box?" Lily pressed him. "I mean, you're not just repeating what someone else said you did, or what you always did?"

Jason thought about it for a moment. "No, I remember."

"Okay, then, when you came out of the bar, do you remember seeing anyone in the alley?" Joe asked. "Anyone at all?"

"No," the Indian said. "I don't remember seein' anyone."

"All right," Lily said with a sigh, thinking he hadn't been much help. And then she remembered. "Before I forget," she murmured, pulling a slim package out of her briefcase and handing it to the Indian.

Jason's eyes grew large as he unwrapped it. It was the photograph of his mother. "You found it!"

"Sure did," Joe said. "It was right where you said it would be."

Jason nodded. "Thanks," he said, fingering the frame. "This was taken a couple of years before my father died -- when she still had reason to smile."

"Joe found something else in your bed, too," Lily said.

The Indian looked up, and it was clear he was confused. "What do you mean?" he asked.

"When I was getting the photograph of your mother," the investigator explained, "I found a bullet in your bed."

"A bullet in my bed?" Jason was clearly stunned. "I slept on that bed every night for years. I never knew there was a bullet in it. What was it doin' there?"

"Well we're assuming it was fired it into the bed at some time," Joe replied. "Do you remember any incident, going back as far as necessary, where Detective Scott might have shot at you or at your box for some reason?"

Jason shook his head emphatically. "I don't remember nothin' like that, nothin' at all. Sure, he used to rough me up, but that was years ago, and he never pulled his gun. I never gave him reason to. Is someone sayin' I did?"

"No, no one is saying that at all," Lily assured him. "We just had to ask. What else do you remember?"

"I remember puttin' the garbage in the dumpster," he said slowly. "I don't really remember gettin' into my box, but I guess I did, 'cause that's what I always did, and that's where the cops found me." He looked at Lily and Joe. "Then I must've gone to sleep 'cause I remember I had a dream."

Lily sighed, but Joe leaned forward. "Do you remember what you dreamed about?" he asked.

"I remembered it real good when I woke up," he said. "You know, all the details and everything. But now, well, now it's all a little hazy. What I remember is -- I dreamed I was at the fights."

Lily looked up sharply. "What?" she said.

"You dreamed you were at the fights?" Joe pressed.

"Yeah," Jason said. "Pretty ironic, don't you think?"

"I don't remember you saying anything about having a dream about being at a fight," his attorney said.

"Maybe because you never asked."

"Okay, well, we're asking now."

Jason shrugged. "I dreamed I was at the fights. Front row seat, too. Which may be why it stuck in my mind at the time -- I never sat front row at anything in my life. It was great. I could see and hear everything."

"And what did you see and hear?"

"What do you think I saw?" he said." I saw two fighters and they were fightin'."

"What did they look like?"

"They looked like two fighters who were fightin'."

"Think, Jason," Joe prodded. "It's very important. Tell us exactly what you saw."

The Indian blinked a few times, and then closed his eyes. "I was at the fights," he repeated. "I was sittin' in the front row. There were two guys in the ring and they were really goin' at each other. Well, not exactly."

"What do you mean -- not exactly?"

"Well, if I remember right, it was pretty uneven -- one of the fighters really outclassed the other. And I remember thinkin' the referee shoulda called it, but it didn't happen."

"What did you hear?"

"I don't know. I guess I heard gruntin'."

"Think, Jason," Lily pushed. "You guess -- or you did?"

"Okay, yeah. I heard shoutin' first, then I heard gruntin', and then I heard screamin'. And then I heard the bell ring -- real loud."

"What else do you remember?"

"Nothin' else. That's it. That's all."

"Jason, are you sure?"

"Yeah, I'm sure," he said. "After that, the next thing I remember is those two cops kickin' me."

Fifteen minutes later, Lily and Joe were on their way back to town. "Do you think it's enough?" she asked.

"Maybe no, and maybe yes," he declared.

• • •

One of the traits that had made Joe Gideon a first-rate police officer and now made him an exceptional private investigator was his laser-like focus -- his ability to zero in on something that didn't quite add up and go after it until it did. And there were a lot of things that were no longer adding up in the Jason Lightfoot case, and that meant a lot of alarm bells going off in his head at the same time. The first thing was Paul Cady's testimony. Not so much about what Cady said as about what he didn't say. Then there was the crime scene analyst. And again, it wasn't what he said but what he didn't say. And now there was this second bullet that had been fired into Jason's bed. Joe had no choice, he had to go back to his friend.

"You're really going to get me fired, you know that, don't you?" Arnie Stiversen said, when Joe rang his doorbell that evening.

"I'm sorry, but this is important, or I wouldn't bother you," Joe said.

He led Joe into the living room, filled with antique furniture from his wife Maura's New Town shop and, without asking, filled two glasses with ice and whiskey.

"You following the trial?" Joe began.

"Yeah, sure, when I can," Stiversen said. "Off and on, the whole department's following the trial. The prosecution finished its case, and now Lily's getting her turn, right?"

"She is indeed," Joe confirmed. "Which is why I'm here."

"What do you want from me this time?"

"Think back, Arnie. The morning you found Dale and rousted Lightfoot -- what did Lightfoot look like?"

"What do you mean, what did he look like?"

"I mean, when you first saw him, when he came out of the box, before Paul did a number on him, did he have any cuts or bruises on him?"

"Come on, it was six-thirty in the morning, it was still dark. And I don't think I really got that good a look at him."

"Arnie, this is important," Joe pressed. "If it was that dark, you'd have used your flashlight."

Stiversen sighed heavily. "Okay," he said, "I guess I gotta tell you, because it's been weighing on me, especially after the crime scene guy testified. I don't remember seeing any cuts or bruises on him. At least, not until after Paul was done with him."

"Lily had a lot of photos taken of Lightfoot four days after the fact," Joe said. "All the injuries I could see when I looked at them were defensive ones, on his arms and his shoulders and his back. If he had been in the kind of fight with Dale that the crime scene guy claimed he was, he would at least have had a few offensive injuries, like on his knuckles -- wouldn't he?"

"Yeah, I'd say he would have."

"So, where were they?"

"I don't know, they weren't there. I didn't see them."

"And you never said anything?"

"No one ever asked."

Joe nodded. There was an unspoken rule in the police department -- answer truthfully if you're asked, keep your mouth shut if you're not, and whatever else, cover the department's ass. "I don't think this went down like everyone's saying," he said softly.

"What are you talking about?"

"I'm going to confide in you, Arnie, because I know you to be a good man and an honest cop," Joe said. "But it's looking more and more like the Indian is being set up somehow."

"What do you mean set up? What are you talking about?"

"Some new evidence has come to light."

"What kind of evidence?" Stiversen asked.

"Evidence that might just tell an entirely different story."

"You think we set him up -- is that why you're here?"

"No, of course not," Joe assured him. "And that's not why I'm here. But what would you say if, the morning that you arrested Lightfoot, you'd found a bullet in the Indian's bed?"

"A bullet in his bed?"

"That's right. I found a bullet in his bed. And it was fired from Dale's gun. And if I said I believe it was fired that night -- what would you say about that?"

The police officer stared at his friend for a minute and then took a long swig from his drink, the ice chattering in the silence. "There was only one bullet missing from Dale's gun that morning," he said finally. "I know that for a fact, and I'm not going to change my mind about it."

"That's right," Joe said. "So, if there's a second bullet that suddenly shows up, then maybe we have to look at this case from a whole different perspective."

"I guess if there was another bullet, and no one can confirm it was fired at some other time," Stiversen said thoughtfully, "I'd have to be looking for some other way the shooting went down."

"And that's exactly what I'm doing," Joe told him.

"Could the Indian have fired it by accident when he got in his box?"

"Could he have deliberately aimed a shot into Dale's head to kill him and then carelessly put a bullet into his own bed?" Joe said. "You mean, was he sober when he shot Dale and drunk when he went to sleep?"

"I guess that doesn't make a whole lot of sense, does it?"

"No, not to me -- at least, not anymore."

"You think Randy knew and just sat on it?"

"Don't know what reason he'd have had," Joe replied. "After all, it was his partner who got killed. In the rush to pin it on the Indian, I think he just missed it. Except for a weird turn of events, I'd have missed it, too, same as everyone else."

Stiversen stared into his glass. "You know, I never could figure those two together," he said. "Couldn't have been more different. Dale was always right out there, whatever the situation, while Randy, he just sort of melts into the background."

It was true, Joe thought. Randy Hitchens was an unassuming kind of guy, who did his job as well as anyone, was polite to everyone, and kept his private life private. He was the perfect counter for the bombastic Dale Scott, learning from the senior officer what he could, and quietly, without seeming to do so, steering him in a gentler direction when necessary. In his nine years on the force, he had earned the respect of everyone in the department.

"It just might have been a better fit than anyone realized," Joe said. "When you stop and think about it, it might have been Randy who kept Dale from going over the edge long before he did."

"You think he knew -- about Dale and the drugs?"

"I think he'd have had to. Partners just know that sort of stuff about each other, don't they?"

Stiversen nodded. "Maybe he couldn't stop him, but he had his back all the way."

"At least, until he came down with a head cold," Joe said. "And I bet he's been beating himself up over it ever since."

Stiversen looked up, opened his mouth to say something, and then, apparently changing his mind, he closed it again. He and Paul Cady didn't have the kind of relationship that Joe had just attributed to Randy and Dale, but he still knew what Joe meant.

He drained the remaining whiskey from his glass in one last gulp.

• • •

"Looks like you've got three choices," Joe said, just before court reconvened. "Mitigating circumstances, as in Jason was too drunk to know what he was doing. Or self-defense, as in someone was shooting at Jason and he was somehow able to defend himself."

"You said three choices," Lily reminded him.

"Yeah, I did," Joe said with a little smile. "Call me crazy, but I think there may be room here for arguing just plain not guilty."

• • •

"Defense calls Joseph Gideon to the stand," Lily said. She might not have known everything yet, but she did know that it was now a whole new ball game, and all bets were off. She faced her witness. "Mr. Gideon, what is your occupation?" Lily began.

"I'm a private investigator," Joe replied.

"And will you tell the jury what your occupation was prior to your becoming a private investigator?"

"I was a member of the Port Hancock Police Department, retiring after twenty-five years of service." It was doubtful there were a handful of people in the courtroom, including members of the jury, that didn't already know that, Lily realized, but it didn't hurt to remind everyone.

"Will you tell the jury what connection you have to this particular case?"

"In my capacity as a private investigator, I am assisting the defense," he said.

"We've heard testimony that Dale Scott was shot and killed by a bullet from his own gun, and that there was only one bullet fired from that gun that night. Has your independent investigation confirmed that?"

"I can confirm that Dale Scott was shot by a bullet from his own gun," Joe testified. "However, I cannot confirm that only one bullet from that gun was fired that night."

The jurors were suddenly sitting up a bit straighter in their seats. Tom Lickliter shifted a bit in his. John Henry Morgan slumped against his.

"Why are you unable to confirm that only one bullet was fired that night?" Lily inquired.

"Because, in the course of my investigation, I discovered a second bullet that had been fired in close proximity to the actual scene of the crime," Joe replied.

The jurors blinked. Those in the gallery gasped.

"Objection," John Henry said, getting to his feet. "Is there any foundation for this line of questioning?"

"I was just getting to that, Your Honor," Lily said, as she headed for the defense table.

"Assuming you do, Miss Burns," the judge said with a meaningful glance, "the objection is overruled."

Lily picked up the plastic bag containing the second bullet, and passed it to the court clerk. Defense 16," she said. The clerk marked the bullet into evidence, and returned it to Lily, who in turn held it up, first for the prosecutors to see and then for the jury to see, before handing it to Joe.

"What are we looking at, Mr. Gideon?" she inquired.

"We're looking at a bullet I retrieved yesterday morning from the bed of the defendant, Jason Lightfoot."

A murmur ran through the gallery, and members of the jury sat up even straighter. They knew this was important, they just didn't know exactly why yet.

"Did you just say you found this bullet in the defendant's bed?" Lily repeated for effect.

"That's right."

"Under what circumstances?"

"The defendant slept on a large round dog bed in a wooden box. On Monday, I was asked to retrieve a photograph that he kept zipped inside that bed, and in the course of retrieving that photograph, I came across the bullet."

"Where was this box?"

"At the time of Detective Scott's death, it was wedged between two sections of the stone wall that runs along the seaward alley."

Lily picked up a handful of photographs and passed them to the clerk. "Defense 17 through 28," she said. The clerk marked the photographs into evidence and Lily again ran them by the prosecutors before handing them to the witness. "Will you tell us what these photographs show?"

"The first five photos show a bullet hole going through the bed in a downward trajectory, and then through the carpet beneath the bed," Joe described. "The next photo shows a dent in the metal plate that was fastened to the bottom of the box. The next three photos show the process I followed to dig out the bullet, and the final three photos show the bullet itself."

Lily collected the photographs and passed them to the jury, and waited as they were handed from member to member, each one studying them carefully before sending them on.

"And what can you tell us about this second bullet?" she asked, turning her focus back to the witness.

"It's a forty caliber Smith and Wesson -- the same kind of bullet used by Detective Scott."

"Was anyone with you when you discovered this bullet?"

"Yes," Joe replied. "Billy Fugate, the owner of The Last Call Bar & Grill was with me."

"Thank you," Lily said with a nod. "I have no further questions."

• • •

Tom Lickliter stood. "Can you tell the jury, with any assurance, when this so-called second bullet was fired?" he asked.

"No, I can't," Joe said.

"Thank you. I have no further questions."

• • •

"Defense recalls Edward Padilla," Lily said. The ballistics expert from the State Patrol Crime Lab returned to the courtroom. "Mr. Padilla, as you have previously testified, you performed the ballistics test on the bullet that killed Dale Scott, did you not?"

"I did," Padilla confirmed.

"And you determined that the bullet was a forty caliber Smith and Wesson, and that it was fired by the Sig Sauer P250 that had been issued to Detective Scott, is that correct?"

"It is."

"Did you also perform a ballistics test on a second bullet that was brought to you yesterday morning?"

"I did."

"And what did you determine from that test?"

"I determined that the second bullet had been fired from the same gun as the bullet that killed Detective Scott," Padilla confirmed.

"Thank you."

• • •

"Mr. Padilla," Tom inquired, "can you tell the jury when this second bullet was fired from Detective Scott's gun?"

"No, I can't," the ballistics expert responded. "The bullet was consistent with the other rounds that were found in the magazine of Detective Scott's gun at the time of his death, but there was no way for my analysis to determine when that particular bullet was fired."

"So, it could have been there for a month or even a year?"

"Yes, it could have."

"Thank you," Tom said. "Nothing further."

• • •

"Redirect, Your Honor," Lily said immediately. "Mr. Padilla, you've just testified that there is no way to prove that the second bullet was fired the night of Dale Scott's death, is that right?"

"Yes, that's right."

"Then isn't it just as correct to say that there is no way to prove that it wasn't fired that night?"

"I guess so," the neutral Padilla said. "There's nothing to prove, with any concrete accuracy, when it was or wasn't fired."

"Thank you, I have no further questions," Lily said. "Defense recalls Kent McAllister to the stand."

The Chief of Police was scowling as he returned to the witness box. The integrity of his department was on the line here, and he wasn't about to let one son-of-a-bitch loose cannon sink his ship. Whatever the defense lawyer wanted to know, he would tell her, and it would be the truth.

"Chief McAllister," Lily began, "since your first appearance here, we've heard testimony from a private detective that there was a second bullet found at the scene of Detective Scott's murder. And we've also heard testimony from a ballistics expert that he cannot confirm when that bullet may have been fired."

"I'm aware of that," McAllister said.

"Will you tell the members of the jury what your department's firearms protocol is?"

"All department episodes involving the firing of a firearm are required to be documented," McAllister replied.

"If that's the case, and since you have already testified that Detective Scott was very good at keeping up with his paperwork, will you tell the jury when he reported firing this particular bullet into Jason Lightfoot's bed?"

Lily held her breath, because she knew that her whole case might hinge on the response he was about to give.

"Detective Scott filed no such report," McAllister said. "The minute I heard about this second bullet, I ordered a thorough search. There was nothing in the records."

"What does that indicate to you?"

"Knowing Dale, as well as I did, it indicates that there was no episode that involved firing the bullet under discussion prior to the night he died."

"Anything else?"

The chief of police's career was potentially at stake here, and he was no fool. "It also indicates that we might not have done a very thorough job of investigating this crime."

Lily let out her breath, as much in surprise as in relief. "Thank you," she said. "Thank you very much. I have nothing further."

• • •

"Mr. Morgan?" the judge inquired.

John Henry Morgan and Tom Lickliter looked at each other. Both men knew it might be next to impossible to rehabilitate this witness, but John Henry knew he had to try. There was no way he could let this testimony stand without challenge.

"Chief McAllister, is it possible that this firearm episode went unreported because Detective Scott chose not to report it?"

"Yes, I suppose that's possible," the chief of police conceded. "Of course it is. Anything's possible."

"Thank you," the prosecutor said.

• • •

"Chief, does your department have any backup procedure in place for reporting firearms incidents?" Lily asked on redirect.

"We count bullets," McAllister replied, glaring at John Henry. "At the end of every shift, every officer is required to turn his firearm over to the duty sergeant for a bullet count. We also require the duty sergeant to check to see if the weapon has been discharged."

"And these checks of guns and bullets are all duly recorded somewhere, are they?"

"Yes, they are."

"When did this procedure go into effect?"

"Three years ago," McAllister stated. "We had an unfortunate series of incidents, involving an illegal use of a firearm and an officer who is no longer with the department, and, as a group, we devised this procedure to make sure it would never happen again."

"Is there a way to cheat the procedure?"

"I suppose there could be, but I wouldn't know how."

"And did Detective Scott's service weapon ever come up short in this examination?"

"No, it did not."

"Chief McAllister, if I were to present to you a case where one bullet was missing from a murder weapon, and yet another bullet fired from that same weapon was found very near that same crime scene, what would you, as a seasoned law enforcement official, think had happened?"

The chief of police was clearly uncomfortable. "I'd first think it had been fired at a previous time," he said. "However, if there was no record to confirm that, then I'd have to say it would be reasonable to conclude it was fired at or around the same time."

"Now, you've testified that this procedure of counting bullets went into effect three years ago," Lily continued. "Is it possible that the bullet found in the defendant's bed was fired prior to that?"

"No, it's not."

"Oh? And why is that so?"

The police chief shrugged. "We didn't start using the Sig Sauers until last January."

• • •

Carson Burns was seated in front of the television set in the library. He had been listening to every word of the testimony, weighing, evaluating, putting himself in Lily's place -- although he had never been in private practice -- and trying to figure out what it was that had been bothering him. And then he had it, and he smacked his left fist down on his recliner with such vehemence that it knocked the chair over, sent him sprawling, started him howling, and brought Diana Hightower running. But he wasn't howling because he was hurt. He was howling because it was so obvious he couldn't believe it had taken him this long to see it.

"Got to get Lily on the telephone," he gasped, as Diana struggled to get both him and the chair upright. "Got to tell her -- she needs to look closer to home."

• • •

"Our newest, our latest, and our best theory of the case," Lily announced, hanging up from the conversation with her father.

"Lay it on us," Megan said excitedly.

"Jason stumbles out of the bar a little before midnight, tosses the garbage into the dumpster, and heads for his box. Dale and his killer come into the alley, fight, and Dale gets shot. The killer spots Jason in his box, is afraid he might have been seen, so he follows him. Then he realizes that Jason is drunk and passed out, so instead of killing him, he decides to frame him. He puts Jason's hands around the gun to get his prints on it, and fires the second bullet into the bed to get the GSR all over him. Then he replaces the spent shot with a fresh one, so the cops won't go looking for it, tosses the gun into Jason's box, and takes off."

"It's a great theory," Megan said, "but how will you ever prove it?"

"I may not have to prove it," Lily told her. "I may just have to muddy John Henry's waters a little."

"Actually, it *is* a pretty good theory," Joe said. "Remember what Jason told us about his dream -- that the last thing he remembered was hearing the bell go off so loud?"

"I remember," Lily said.

"Still, that leaves us with one question left to answer," Joe said. "Where did the replacement bullet come from?"

Lily nodded. "The very same point my father just raised."

"Okay, what am I missing?" Megan inquired.

"Only one bullet was missing from the magazine," Joe explained. "That means there were twelve bullets, eleven accounted for. Someone replaced the second bullet. So where did it come from?"

"Doesn't every officer carry a backup magazine with him?"

"When he's on duty," Joe replied. "But I checked. Dale didn't have his backup on him. It was in his car, parked a block away, and it was full."

Suddenly, Lily was staring at the investigator, because the whole thing now made perfect sense. "That's it, isn't it?" she breathed. "It's been there all the time, right in front of our noses, and we just didn't see it."

"See what?" Megan persisted.

Lily didn't respond. Instead, she was searching through the files in her briefcase, plucking out the one she wanted, opening it, and flipping through it until she found the page she was looking for. Then she grabbed a pen, circled something on the page, and handed it to Joe.

"Find out who that really was," she told him.

• • •

"Defense recalls Fletcher Thurman to the stand," Lily declared at nine o'clock on Friday morning, and the Washington State Patrol Crime Lab analyst returned to the witness box yet again.

"Mr. Thurman, you previously testified that a gunshot residue test had been performed on the hands and clothing of the defendant, is that correct?"

"It is."

"And the results were positive, indicating that Mr. Lightfoot had indeed fired a gun within a few hours of the test?"

"Yes."

"Can you tell us what the results were for the blood spatter test?"

"I wasn't asked to perform a blood spatter test." Thurman said.

Lily feigned surprise. "You mean, you were asked to test the defendant's hands and clothing for gunshot residue, but you weren't asked to test his hands and clothing for blood spatter?"

"The investigating officers did the GSR test. I simply confirmed their results."

"Well then, did the investigating officers run a blood spatter test?"

"Not that I'm aware of."

"So, there was no blood spatter test done by the investigating officers," Lily clarified, "and you were never asked to run one?"

"Yes. I mean, no."

"Didn't that strike you as a little odd?"

"Objection!" John Henry cried. "The personal opinion of the witness is not relevant here."

"Sustained," Grace Pelletier declared.

"My apologies, Your Honor, let me rephrase," Lily said. "Mr. Thurman, is it customary, in gun-related homicides, to test for gunshot residue, but not for blood spatter?"

"No, they pretty much go together, unless the shot was fired from such a distance as to render the analysis unnecessary."

"Will you explain that for the jury?"

"When a bullet is fired into a living thing," the analyst said, "a certain amount of blood sprays from the entry wound. If the shooter is within a certain distance, some of that blood spray, or spatter as we call it, will deposit on the shooter, or on the shooter's clothing. If the shooter is beyond that distance, a blood spatter test would be meaningless."

"And how far away would the shooter have to be, for the blood spatter test to be considered meaningless?"

"At least six feet."

"And how far away from Dale Scott was the person standing who fired the bullet that killed him?"

"Judging from the amount of gunpowder residue at the site of the wound, I would say no more than two feet."

"So, would you expect that, at that range, the shooter's clothing would have tested positive for blood spatter?"

"Definitely," the analyst said.

"And would you consider such a test to be a rather important link in confirming the identity of the shooter?"

"Every link is important. A positive GSR result combined with a positive blood spatter result would pretty much clinch the deal."

"And yet a blood spatter test wasn't requested?"

"No, it wasn't," Fletcher Thurman confirmed.

"Thank you." Lily said with emphasis. "I have nothing further."

• • •

A hurried conversation went on at the prosecution table for a moment before Tom Lickliter stood up.

"Isn't a positive result for gunshot residue the primary indicator that someone has fired a gun?" he inquired.

"Yes," the analyst conceded.

"So, do we really need to read a lot into the fact that a blood spatter test wasn't requested in this case?"

"I was asked if it was an important link, not if it was essential," Thurman replied.

"Thank you," the deputy prosecutor said. "I have nothing further."

• • •

Although she was sorry it had come from the new guy, Lily had been hoping for just such an opening.

"Mr. Thurman," she said on redirect, "is there any way to get gunshot residue on your hands other than by firing a gun?"

"I suppose if you picked up a gun that had just been fired, that might result in some GSR being deposited on your hands, but it wouldn't be in the same pattern or amount as if you'd actually fired the gun."

"And the pattern on Jason Lightfoot's hands?

"He clearly fired the gun."

"All right then, is there a way to get gunshot residue on your hands by firing a gun from no more than two feet away, as in the case of Detective Scott, and not get blood spatter on your clothing?"

"I'd have to say no."

"Hypothetically then, suppose a person fires a gun that kills someone, and then shortly thereafter, that person takes the same gun, wraps someone else's hands around it, and fires it a second time -- what would be the result?"

Thurman shrugged. "Assuming the gun wasn't fired close to anything living," he responded, "the person whose hands were wrapped around the gun would test positive for gunshot residue, but negative for blood spatter."

"And in that case, would the results of a blood spatter test become even more significant?"

"Certainly."

"Thank you. Nothing further."

• • •

Joe was driving west again, heading toward Trent. He had as good as promised Mary Pride that he wouldn't come back, but he had no choice. One last piece of the puzzle needed to be put in place.

He pulled into the hospital parking lot a little after two-thirty. He didn't know if she would be there, if she had changed shifts, or if it was her day off. But it didn't matter -- he knew he would wait all afternoon, all night, all weekend, if he had to. He didn't have to. At five minutes before three, he spotted her Dodge Ram coming into the lot.

A look of sheer panic flooded her face when she saw him. "I told you not to come back," she cried.

"I know, and I'm sorry," he said. "But I had no choice."

"I can't do this," she told him. "I need this job."

"The file you gave us -- it shed a whole new light on the case," he said. "But this may mean the difference between Jason living or dying."

She looked around hurriedly, and then pulled him back between the cars. "All right, what is it?"

"In the file, it says she was brought in by her husband -- did you see him?"

Mary nodded. "Sure, several times. He was actually very nice, and he seemed very concerned about her. It's hard to believe, sometimes, what people can do to people and then act as if it wasn't them."

Joe handed her a photograph. "Is this the guy who brought her in?"

Mary peered at the photo for a moment, and then shook her head. "No, he's nice looking, for sure, but he's not the one who came in with her. That one was good-looking, too, but younger, thinner, lighter-haired."

Joe nodded, and reached into his pocket. He had a hunch, actually one he'd had for a while now, with no way to prove it, until maybe this moment.

"How about him?" he asked, handing her a second photo.

"Yes, he's the one," Mary said immediately.

"Are you sure?"

"I'm sure."

"Look again," Joe insisted. "I need you to be sure."

"I'm sure," the nurse said. "The times when I was on duty and she came in, that's the man who brought her."

"Thank you," Joe said. "Thank you very much. And this time, you have my word, I won't be coming back."

"Have I really helped Jason?" she asked.

He smiled. "More than you know," he said.

• • •

"Defense recalls Ben Dawson to the stand."

Like just about everyone else in the police department, the senior crime scene investigator had been following the progress of the trial, and was therefore not surprised when he was notified that he would be required to give further testimony.

"Officer Dawson," Lily began, "when did you first hear about the death of Detective Scott?"

"I heard about it on the morning after it happened," Dawson replied.

"The morning of February 10th?"

"Yes."

"Can you recall what time it was?"

"I believe it was around six-fifteen."

"And where were you when you heard about it?"

"I was at home."

"And how did you hear about it?"

"I had a call from Detective Hitchens. He told me that someone had been killed, and requested that my partner and I get over to the alley as soon as possible."

"Defense 29, Your Honor," Lily said. She took a sheet of paper up to the clerk to be entered as evidence, waited while the judge perused it and accepted it. Then she showed it to John Henry, and finally handed it to the witness. "Will you tell the jury what it is that you're holding?" she requested.

Dawson looked at the sheet. "It's a copy of the police call log for February 10th."

"Will you read for the jury what the highlighted line says?"

The crime scene investigator looked at the paper, and then looked up at Lily. "It says the 911 call from the garbage truck guy who found Dale's body came in at six-fifteen."

"Defense 30," Lily said, going through the same routine with another sheet of paper. "Officer Dawson, will you tell the jury what you are now holding?"

Dawson glanced at it. "It's a copy of my cell phone record for February 10th."

"And will you read the highlighted part?"

"It says the call made to me by Detective Hitchens came in at six-sixteen."

"It shows that Detective Hitchens called you exactly one minute after the 911 call was made by Martin Grigsby, is that correct?"

"Yeah, I guess so."

"Will you tell the jury again what time it was that you and your partner arrived at the scene?" the defense attorney pressed.

"We got there a little before seven o'clock."

"And who was at the scene at the time you arrived?"

"Officer Stiversen and Officer Cady were there, with the defendant, and Detective Hitchens pulled in just a few minutes behind us."

"And who was in charge?"

"Detective Hitchens was. The chief had put him in charge."

"And did Detective Hitchens tell you and your partner what he wanted you to look at?"

"No. He just told us to do a thorough job with the scene."

"Did the scene he told you to do a thorough job with include the box in the alley that Jason Lightfoot lived in?"

"As I remember," Dawson said, "he told us not to worry about the box, because it wasn't part of the actual crime scene, and just to do the GSR test on the Indian's hands and his clothes, and take his DNA."

"Thank you," Lily said. "I have no further questions."

• • •

John Henry and Tom Lickliter looked at each other. Neither had the faintest idea what this was about. They knew Lily was going somewhere, they just didn't know where, and they realized there was no point in cross-examining the witness on an issue they didn't yet understand.

"We have no questions at this time," John Henry told the judge.

. . .

"Defense recalls Martin Grigsby to the stand," Lily said.

The garbage man strode down the aisle, looking far more comfortable this second time than he had the first.

"I'm sorry to have to drag you all the way back in here, Mr. Grigsby," Lily said. "But I find I do have a question for you, after all."

"That's okay, Ma'am," Grigsby said. "It's real hot out there, so I don't mind takin' a break."

Members of the jury smiled. So did Lily. "In that case," she said, getting right to the point, "when you placed the 911 call on February 10th, after finding the body in the alley, did you tell the operator anything about how that person had died?"

"No, Ma'am," Grigsby replied, looking startled. "I couldn't have. I could see there was blood, but I'm no doctor -- I didn't have any idea how he died. I just told 911 there was a dead guy."

Lily beamed at him. "Thank you," she said.

. . .

This time, John Henry had a pretty good idea where the defense was trying to go, but he was at a loss to understand why.

"No questions, Your Honor," the prosecutor said casually, but he was beginning to worry.

• • •

"How did I know you'd be back," Arnie Stiversen said with a sigh, as he saw Joe Gideon coming around to the deck at the back of his house on Saturday morning.

"She's got almost all of it now," Joe told him. "She's running me all over the place, tying up loose ends."

"Am I a loose end?"

Joe shrugged. "I don't know -- you tell me," he said. "I think you've been wanting to tell me for quite a while now, haven't you?"

The police officer stared at the private investigator for a full minute before he replied.

"Yeah," he said finally. "I guess I have. And it looks like I'm going to get the chance, doesn't it?" The subpoena had already come. "It's not that I was trying to hide anything," he wanted his former mentor to understand. "I really thought the Indian did it."

"I know you did," Joe assured him. "To be honest, we all did."

"He was there, he was drunk, he had motive, and he fired the gun."

"Yeah."

"Then I thought someone else would come forward. Or maybe it was just wishful thinking on my part -- maybe I was just hoping it wouldn't have to be me."

"You saw him that night, didn't you?" Joe prodded softly.

Stiversen looked past his friend's shoulder, and out across his yard. "Yeah," he said. "Getting into his car in front of Gilhooley's."

Gilhooley's was a rough and tumble bar about ten miles east of town. It was patronized mostly by bikers, by people from the trailer park just down the road, and by residents of the nearby Shaw River Reservation.

Joe nodded. "What time?"

"About half past eleven."

• • •

For Carson Burns, the most irritating part of his having fallen victim to a stroke was his inability to get up and pace. It was how the former Jackson County Prosecutor used to think, how he used to work out problems with his cases, on his feet, covering the expanse of his corner office in five strides, over and over again, until whatever thorny issue on his mind was resolved. It was no longer his office, of course, and no longer his job. He wondered what his daughter did, when she needed to think things through. Oddly enough, he had never asked her. But he wasn't worried. He wasn't even defending Jason Lightfoot, and yet he could see the holes in this case -- holes that were growing bigger by the day, and he knew his daughter was also seeing them.

"Got it all figured out?" he asked on Sunday night.

"Pretty much," she replied, Arnie Stiversen being the last piece to fall into place. "Thanks to you."

"No, you knew where to look," he said. "You didn't need me. You were getting there all on your own."

"Maybe," she said. And maybe she would have, she thought, if the bomb hadn't blown up her brain.

"All the ducks in order?"

"I think so."

"Don't take it too far."

She sighed. "I won't," she promised. "I want to -- this whole thing infuriates me that much -- but I won't."

Carson smiled, his crooked left-sided smile. "I know," he said. "You'd take on the whole county, if you could. But you can't. And I have a sneaking suspicion you're not going to have to. Just remember, though, what you *are* going to have to do, and that is -- work here, in this town, long after this case is over."

Eleven

Then it was Monday morning, the second week of November -- the last week of the trial, and Lily felt renewed. For one thing, the heat wave had broken, temperatures had dropped down into the sixties, and the courtroom was almost comfortable. For another, a case she had first thought totally unwinnable now had a real chance of ending in an actual acquittal.

"The defense calls Officer Arnold Stiversen," she said.

The police officer made his way down the aisle, swore to tell the truth, and took the witness stand. This was nothing new to him. He had testified many times in his career. But this was one time he wished he didn't have to.

"Officer Stiversen," Lily began, "will you tell us where you were on the morning of February 10th of this year?"

"I was responding to a call about a body that had been found in the seaward alley off lower Broad Street."

"How did you hear about that body?" Lily asked.

"It came in through a 911 call."

"All right, now will you please describe for the jury how Jason Lightfoot appeared the morning of his arrest?"

"He appeared to be hung over, not too steady on his feet, and he seemed confused. His clothes were filthy. His breath stank."

"Did you notice any blood on his clothes?"

"No, I did not."

"His body -- his hands and arms and his face, did you notice any blood on them, any wounds, any bruises?"

Stiversen took a deep breath and looked right at Lily. "No, I did not."

"None at all?"

"As far as I could tell, he didn't have any bruises on him, that is, not until he tried to resist arrest."

"All right. At about half past eleven on the night Dale Scott was murdered, where were you?"

Stiversen sighed. "I was in my car, with my wife," he said. "We were driving home from a friend's house on the Shaw River Reservation."

"And did you have occasion to pass a bar called Gilhooley's on your way home?"

"I did."

"Will you tell the jury what, if anything, caught your eye at the bar?"

"There was a red MG just leaving the parking lot, in a big hurry."

"Thank you," Lily said with a nod, having all she needed for now. "Nothing further at this time."

• • •

Neither John Henry nor Tom Lickliter had any idea what the significance of the red MG was, nor did either of them want the jury to know that. So it hung there, dropped like a hot potato.

"Officer Stiversen," Tom inquired, "what time was it when you encountered the defendant in the alley?"

"It was a little after six-thirty in the morning," the officer replied.

"A little after six-thirty in the morning, in the middle of February -- and what were the conditions?"

"It wasn't exactly light yet, and the marine air was pretty heavy."

"Is there any chance you missed seeing the bruises?"

Stiversen hesitated for a few seconds. "I don't think so," he said finally. "I was practically right on top of him. And I had my flashlight on him. I don't think I would have missed the kind of bruises he would have had if he'd been in a fight with Detective Scott."

"All right, let's talk about his clothing. Are you sure there was no blood on it?"

"I didn't see any."

"You are aware, aren't you, that blood spatter can sometimes be so small the eye wouldn't necessarily catch it?"

"Yes, sir, I'm aware of that. And I didn't say there was no blood on his clothes. I just said I didn't see any."

"Thank you for your preciseness," Tom said. "I have no further questions."

"Redirect, Miss Burns?" the judge inquired.

"No, Your Honor."

"In that case, the witness is excused."

Arnie Stiversen beat a hasty retreat out of the courtroom before she could change her mind.

• • •

"The defense recalls Detective Randy Hitchens to the stand."

The police detective stalked almost defiantly down the aisle. He was not here by choice.

"I remind you that you remain under oath, Detective Hitchens," Grace Pelletier told him.

"Yes, Your Honor," he said as he took his seat.

"Permission to treat the witness as hostile," Lily requested.

"Proceed," Grace Pelletier said.

Lily turned to her witness. "Detective Hitchens, as you have previously testified, you were in charge of the investigation into the death of your partner, Dale Scott, were you not?"

"I was."

"And will you tell us again how you came to be in charge?"

"Chief McAllister put me in charge."

"Under what circumstances?"

"It was just after he came in that morning, and I told him that Stiversen and Cady had found Dale, and that I had notified the M.E. and the crime scene boys."

"And he just put you in charge?"

"Yes."

"And if I recalled Chief McAllister to the stand, would he say that it was his idea to put you in charge of the investigation into your own partner's death?"

Hitchens shifted in his seat. "I don't know what he would say. I'm just saying that's how I remember it."

"And if Chief McAllister were to testify that you all but demanded to be put in charge of the investigation, what would you say?"

Hitchens shrugged. "I'd say I don't remember it that way. But what difference does it make? Dale was my partner, and he was dead. And I wanted to make sure everything in the investigation was done by the book, so that no shyster lawyer would be able to come around after the fact and get my partner's killer off on a technicality."

Lily ignored the remark. "At sixteen minutes past six, you called Officer Dawson and told him that someone had been killed in the seaward alley," she said. "How did you know that?"

"I didn't know. I just told him a body had been found there."

"Well, what if I told you that Officer Dawson has already testified that he remembers you telling him someone had been killed in the alley?"

Hitchens shrugged. "Well, someone *had* been killed in the alley."

"Yes, but how did you know that? Officer Stiversen didn't call that information in until after six-thirty."

"From the 911 call, I guess."

"I don't think so. The man who made that call reported that someone was dead -- but he had no idea how he died."

"Well, I might have misunderstood, or jumped to a conclusion," the detective said with a shrug.

"Or had prior knowledge, perhaps?" Lily suggested.

Hitchens glared at her. "I don't know what you're talking about."

"You didn't have to look very far for your suspect, did you?"

"No, we sure didn't."

"He was conveniently right on the scene, with the gun practically in his hand and no memory of what had happened."

"I don't know how convenient it was, but yeah, he was right there on the scene."

"At least, you thought he had no memory of what had happened, didn't you?" The pale eyes looking back at her widened just a bit. "But as it turns out, that's not exactly accurate."

"So, he's made up some cockamamie story at the eleventh hour to try to save his neck," the detective said. "It wouldn't be the first time a defendant tried that."

"True, but let's not worry about that just now. Let's go on to something else. It would make sense, wouldn't it, that you would want to be as thorough in your investigation as you said you did, to head off -- how did you phrase it -- some shyster lawyer coming in and getting him off?"

"I tried to be."

"Did you? And yet you didn't bother to test my client's clothing for blood spatter. Why was that?"

Hitchens was prepared for this question. "In hindsight, it's clear I should have," he said. "But at the time, I guess I wasn't thinking about hindsight. We have a pretty tight budget in our department, and since we had a positive GSR result, it was obvious we had the right man, and I didn't think it was necessary to spend any extra money just to put icing on the cake."

"You're sure that was the only reason, Detective Hitchens?" Lily asked. "You're sure there wasn't another reason?"

"I don't know what you're talking about."

"I'm talking about the very real possibility that there was no blood spatter on Jason Lightfoot's clothing, and you knew it, and that's why you chose not to request the test."

The witness's body stiffened and his pale eyes flickered ever so slightly. "I still don't know what you're talking about."

"What do you think happened to that clothing, Detective?"

"I have no idea," he replied. "I assume it got disposed of at some point."

"Well, what if I were to tell you that it didn't get disposed of -- that the clothing Jason Lightfoot was wearing on the night your partner was killed is sitting in a paper bag at the Jackson County Jail, and has been sitting there since three weeks after it was originally collected?"

Hitchens hesitated for perhaps a second or two, not necessarily long enough for the jury to notice, but definitely long enough for Lily to notice, and for Tom Lickliter to notice, as well.

"I'd say it should be tested immediately," he said. "But of course, that's assuming it can be proven that the chain of custody hasn't been broken."

"Very good, Detective," Lily said with an appreciative nod. "After all these months, chain of custody would definitely be an issue. So, that leaves us with an interesting question, doesn't it? Would a blood spatter test performed on Jason Lightfoot's clothing immediately after his arrest for Dale Scott's murder have incriminated him -- or exonerated him?"

Hitchens shrugged. "I guess we'll never know."

"You're probably right," Lily conceded. "Especially when you consider that the clothing isn't really sitting in a bag at the jail, is it? It was signed out of police headquarters two days after Jason Lightfoot's arrest, and hasn't been seen since. Would you have any idea who signed it out?"

"No idea at all," the detective said.

"That's odd," Lily said, "because I do have an idea. It was signed out by an officer named Sheila Burton. Are you acquainted with her, by any chance?"

"Sure. She used to work for the department."

"Yes, she did. And now she's moved to Idaho, I believe. Do you know under what circumstances she left the Port Hancock Police Department?"

"No, I don't."

"Do you know why she would have had reason to sign Jason Lightfoot's clothing out?"

"She might have thought she was helping the case in some way," Hitchens offered. "I don't know."

"Are you sure about that, Detective? Because I can have Sheila Burton come here to testify. And I think you know what she'll say -- that you and she were having an affair at the time, and that she signed the clothing out at your request."

"Objection!" John Henry declared. "Assumes testimony not in evidence."

"Rephrase, Miss Burns," Grace Pelletier said.

"Yes, I'm sorry, Your Honor," Lily responded before turning back to Hitchens. "Hypothetically, Detective, if I were to call Sheila Burton to the witness stand, and put her under oath, would she testify that she had signed the defendant's clothing out at your request?"

"She may say that," Hitchens said smoothly. "But I don't recall making any such request."

"That's certainly possible," Lily conceded. "She could have been acting on her own. But there's something about this case that just doesn't sit right with me, so let me ask you for your opinion. Let's say -- just hypothetically, you understand -- that on the night of the murder, Jason Lightfoot comes out of the bar drunk, as we already know he was, and stumbles into his box, as we already know was his habit. And, just for the sake of argument, let's say that Dale Scott meets his killer in the alley and they get into a fight. Perhaps the killer has no choice but to pull the trigger, and after he does so, he realizes that Jason may have witnessed his crime. So he follows Jason into his box, intending to dispose of this witness, only to realize that Jason is passed out, and likely has no idea what just happened. So instead of killing him, he hits on a better idea. He wraps Jason's hands around the murder weapon and fires it into the bed, assuring that there'll be gunshot residue all over Jason's hands and clothing. The police then investigate, find the gunshot residue -- but not the second bullet, and just like that, they have themselves a killer. Would you say that's a reasonable alternative?"

"Maybe, if I was writing fiction," Hitchens said.

"Oh, you don't think much of my theory?" Lily inquired.

"No, not so much."

"All right, let me ask you something else then. The night after the murder, after all the evidence had been gathered at the crime scene, and the yellow tape had come down -- actually, it was pretty late that night, past midnight, I'm told, didn't you come back to the alley, looking for Jason Lightfoot's box?"

The detective's mouth was suddenly very dry. "So what if I did?" he said.

"So, I'm just curious -- why?"

"I wanted to make sure everything relevant had been collected."

"Even though, as Officer Dawson has testified, you told him he could ignore the box?"

"Well, that's why I went back -- I had second thoughts."

"I see."

"I didn't think there'd be anything there, but I wanted to look around, just to make sure."

"Are you sure you didn't know exactly what you were looking for, Detective Hitchens?" Lily inquired. "And weren't you beside yourself when you found the box was gone?"

"I don't know what you're talking about."

"I'm talking about a bullet, Detective. A second bullet that was fired into Jason Lightfoot's bed that night. That's what you were looking for, wasn't it?"

"Of course not," he declared. "I had no idea a second bullet had been fired. Besides, there's no way to prove it was fired that night."

"Or to prove it wasn't," Lily reminded him.

"It was a good arrest," Hitchens declared, although there was no question pending. "I had a good faith belief that the Indian had killed my partner. And apparently, so did the two officers who brought him in. Now you can twist it anyway you like, but the facts are the facts."

"Did you like your late partner, Detective?" Lily asked abruptly.

"I liked him okay, sure."

"Didn't you find his increasing violence to be of concern?"

"He had a temper. I wouldn't necessarily call him violent."

"You wouldn't?" Lily crossed to the defense table and picked up a file. When she returned to the witness box, she casually positioned the file on the edge of the witness box, so that he could clearly see the label. It read: Margaret Dean. "Are you sure about that, Detective?"

Hitchens' face went ashen. He stared at the label for a moment, and then looked up at Lily. "I suppose some might have considered him volatile," he said reluctantly. "As I said, he had a temper. I suppose he might have gone over the edge once or twice."

"He put his wife in the hospital eight times in three years, and you think he might have gone over the edge once or twice?"

"Objection!" John Henry exclaimed. "Counsel is stating facts not in evidence."

"My apologies for getting ahead of myself, Your Honor," Lily said, handing Margaret Dean's file to the court clerk. "Defense 31."

The clerk took the file and passed it up to the judge. Grace Pelletier glanced through it, doing everything she could to prevent the shock she was feeling from showing on her face. Finally, she closed the file, nodded, and directed that it be placed into evidence and then returned it to Lily who promptly handed it over to the prosecutor.

"Proceed," the judge said.

"I repeat, Detective, would you not call someone who put his wife in the hospital eight times in three years violent?"

"What went on between him and his wife was between him and his wife," Hitchens said.

"Really? You weren't involved? Not in any way?"

He paused, clearly weighing his answer. "Not in any material way," he said finally.

"Detective Hitchens, please consider your answer carefully. I can produce a witness to testify that you brought Lauren Scott to the Trent Community Hospital on at least five separate occasions, passing yourself off as her husband -- do you really want me to do that?"

Lily had no intention of compelling Mary Pride to testify, but she was counting on him not to know that. And to her relief, the bluff worked.

"No," he said with a heavy sigh. "You don't have to do that. Yes, I drove her to Trent. Somebody had to -- she couldn't drive herself. And she wouldn't go to the hospital here. She was afraid someone would recognize her. She was afraid, if it got out, he'd get in trouble at the department, and then he'd really kill her. He threatened to often enough. He used to tell her how he could make her disappear -- make her vanish into thin air -- and then tell people that she had just up and left him for another man, and no one would ever be the wiser. And she believed him."

"Your Honor," John Henry protested. "While certainly illuminating, I fail to see the relevance in any of this."

"I was just about to get to that, Your Honor," Lily said.

"Objection overruled," Grace Pelletier said. "But do get to it, Miss Burns."

"What really happened in that alley on the night Detective Scott died, Detective Hitchens?" Lily inquired softly.

The police officer sighed again. "I knew he was meeting his supplier there," he said. "So I went to try to talk some sense into him. It was starting to affect his work. I told him I couldn't cover for him any more. We had an argument. There was a fight. I left."

"And the second bullet?" Lily asked softly.

He nodded. "I went back about an hour later. I assumed Dale would be beat up, but alive, and I'd have to take him to the hospital. But when I got there, I realized he'd been shot and he was dead, and I saw his gun just lying there beside him. I didn't know who had shot him, so I panicked and did something stupid. The Indian was passed out, so I did what you said -- I put his hands around the gun and shot into the bed. Then I replaced the second bullet from Dale's gun with one of my own. Afterwards, I realized what would happen if someone found it, so I didn't let anyone look. I waited until it was late, but I was too late. The box was already gone."

The spectators packing the courtroom gasped. The members of the jury tried not to.

"When you're off duty, what sort of car do you drive, Detective?" Lily asked, changing the subject.

He was confused. "An MG," he replied.

"What color?"

"Red."

"I have nothing further," she said.

"Are you anticipating a lengthy cross-examination, Mr. Morgan?" Grace Pelletier inquired.

A flustered John Henry looked at Tom Lickliter, then at the witness, and then back at the judge. "I'm not sure yet, Your Honor," he replied.

The judge looked at him. "All right," she said, and turned to the jury. "We will stand in recess until two o'clock."

. . .

"Is what just happened in that courtroom what I think just happened?" Joe wanted to know.

Lily and Megan and Dancer had come back to the office, and they were sitting around the table in the conference room. The television set was on, with the sound muted, and they were staring at each other, as if afraid to say what they were thinking.

"I do believe so," Lily said with a tentative smile.

"Why did you stop?" Megan asked. "You got him to admit about the bullet. You were one step away from nailing him for everything."

"I wasn't going for a Perry Mason moment," Lily responded. "I got what I needed out of him, and made sure the jury heard it."

"And I bet the jurors weren't the only ones listening," Joe said.

As if to punctuate his words, Wanda stuck her head in the door. "Tom Lickliter's on the line," the receptionist said.

"Now what do you suppose is on his mind?" Lily murmured with a little smile, reaching for the receiver.

"Can we meet?" the deputy prosecutor asked.

"Before cross-examination?"

"Yes," he said. "John Henry and I think we should meet. It would be in everyone's best interests if we meet."

"Okay."

"Our house. Half an hour?"

"I can do that," she said.

• • •

They met in the prosecutor's office.

"Tell me, how far are you prepared to go with this?" John Henry asked.

"As far as I have to go, to see that my client is fully exonerated," Lily replied.

"What if you ask for a dismissal of all charges, and we don't oppose it? Will that satisfy you?"

Lily barely managed to hide her surprise. "It may satisfy me, but why would it satisfy you?" she asked. "Do you know something I don't?"

"We were in court today," John Henry said pragmatically. "We heard Hitchens' testimony. You tied him to the second bullet. And whatever we might do on cross, I have a feeling you're going to try to nail him for the murder, too. I just thought we'd save you the trouble."

"Are you saying I've established reasonable doubt?"

"Whether you have or not," the prosecutor told her, "this isn't the time to gamble, it's the time to be practical."

"You're not going to be able to sweep this under the rug, you know," she said.

"I don't intend to," John Henry snapped, because that was exactly what wanted to do. "I'd just like to minimize the black eye we're going to get, if I can. So, would you be willing to stipulate that my office was in no way complicit in this -- that we knew nothing about any of it, not until we heard Hitchens on the stand this morning?"

John Henry wasn't the smoothest lawyer in town, but as far as Lily knew, he was an honest one.

"I can do that," she said.

"All right then," the Jackson County Prosecutor declared, "we'll ask for the dismissal."

• • •

The discussion in chambers was held out of earshot of jurors, spectators, and cameras. There was just the judge, the defendant, the three attorneys, and the court reporter.

It took the better part of an hour to hash everything out. When they returned to the courtroom, the judge thanked the jurors for their service and declared the case dismissed with prejudice and the proceedings over. No bang, no pop, not even a whimper.

"What does that mean, it's over?" Jason asked, as the deputy who had been escorting him to and from the jail every day for a month slapped him on the back and wished him luck. He hadn't really understood much of the conversation in chambers.

"It means all the charges have been dismissed, and you're free to go," Lily told him.

His jaw dropped. "What happened?"

"I guess, given the turn of events, the prosecutor was no longer confident he could get a conviction," she said. "And if I were you, I wouldn't argue."

"I ain't gonna," Jason declared. "Does this mean they don't believe I killed the cop anymore?"

"Not exactly. It just means the prosecutor no longer feels he has sufficient evidence to prove you did."

The Indian frowned. "So people could still think I did it, even if I didn't get convicted for it?"

"Some people might," Lily conceded, "but I wouldn't worry about them. Besides, I doubt any of them would be the people you care about."

"Do *you* still think I did it?" he asked.

Lily smiled "I don't know," she said honestly. "But there's enough evidence to suggest that you didn't."

"But the cop is dead, and someone has to pay for it, right? If they can't find someone else to blame, can they change their minds? Can they come after me again?"

"No, they can't," she assured him. "There's something in the law called double jeopardy, which means you can't be tried twice for the same crime."

"Are you sure?"

"I'm sure."

Jason stood up, and took a few tentative steps, almost expecting a hand to reach out and pull him back and slap the cuffs on his wrists, but none did.

"If I'm really free, you know the first thing I'm gonna do?" he said, a mischievous grin breaking out across his face.

"Head for the mountains?" Lily inquired.

"Nope, that's the second thing," he told her. "The first thing -- with all due respect to you -- the first thing I'm gonna do is dump this suit!"

• • •

The analyst on the local cable channel, who had been reporting on the trial from the very beginning, was at a loss for words as he tried to explain to his viewers what they had just seen on their television screens -- or to be more precise, what they had not seen. The editor of the *Port Hancock Herald* pored over legal tomes in an effort to construct reasonably informed sentences to enlighten his readers. And talk radio was overrun with callers from both sides, wanting to know what the hell had happened.

Tongues wagged for hours over telephones, across back fences, on street corners, at the supermarket, the pharmacy, the hardware store, and the beauty salon. The Internet's social media outlets were flooded with exclamations of both outrage and delight. And the patrons of hangouts from Old Town to New Town to out-of-town weighed in with their opinions on the totally unexpected turn of events.

"So, did he do it, or didn't he?" was the most often asked question.

"I guess we'll never know," was the most frequent answer.

"I knew he didn't do it," some said.

"The son-of-a-bitch got away with murder," others declared.

"Which son-of-a-bitch?" several couldn't help but inquire.

"It's nothing but another damn liberal bleeding-heart cover-up!" a few asserted.

"It sure is," came the inevitable response, "when you try to railroad an innocent man just because he's a minority."

"What kind of country are we living in," still more chimed in, "when you can't tell the cops from the crooks?"

Even the jurors were speaking out.

"I have no idea why the case was dismissed," veteran juror Julia Estabrook declared. "I'm sure we could have come to the right verdict."

"The state made a pretty good case," John Boyle confirmed. "But the defense was making a pretty good case, too, so there's no point in asking whether we'd come to any decision."

"Is this the way our justice system really works?" Eileen Wolcott wanted to know. "That's my question."

But the question that was on the minds of most people, as they went about their daily lives that day and the next and the one after that, was the same as Jason's -- what had happened?

• • •

The fallout was immediate. Demands for Kent McAllister's resignation could be heard all across the city. Demands for John Henry Morgan's resignation could be heard from every corner of the county.

"As it turns out, we didn't have the evidence we needed," the prosecutor tried his best to explain to a large crowd that gathered outside the courthouse the next morning. "So we did the right thing -- we asked to have

the charges dismissed. What would you have had us do --
convict an innocent man just because the community
wants closure?"

"If the Indian didn't kill Scott," a veteran reporter
from the *Port Hancock Herald* called out, "then who
did?"

"We may never know."

"Will you reopen the investigation?" the TV analyst
asked.

"Certainly."

"Do you think that other cop did it?" a talk radio
host cried. "The one who admitted to firing the second
bullet?"

"We are reopening the investigation," John Henry
said, promising himself, if he still had anything to say
about it, that the Lightfoot trial would be the first and the
last to have cameras in the courtroom. "When we have
something to report, you'll be the first to know."

"I want everyone working on this," he told Tom.
"If Hitchens did it, I damn well want to nail him for it."

• • •

"There's someone to see you," Wanda said.

Lily was at her desk, taking care of the odds and
ends of the Lightfoot case. She looked up at the knock on
her door, in time to catch a strange expression on the
receptionist's face.

"Yes, who?" she inquired.

Wanda stepped aside, and Randy Hitchens came into view. "I think I need a lawyer," he said.

"Yes, I expect you do," Lily replied. "But you've come to the wrong place. I can't represent you."

"Why not?" he asked. "Your case is over. Your client is free."

"No thanks to you."

"Okay, I admit it, I didn't do a very good job of investigating the damn case," Hitchens said, his pale blue eyes looking directly into her hazel ones. "But I didn't kill my partner."

"And I'm supposed to believe you because -- ?" Lily inquired.

"Okay, so maybe I didn't like him very much. I guess you could even say I despised him -- especially after I found out what he was doing to Lauren -- but that doesn't mean I killed him. I didn't kill him."

"I know," Lily said. "You didn't kill him, and you didn't plant the bullet, and you were at home all that night with a head cold, too."

Hitchens sighed. "All right, look, I'm not going to lie to you anymore, whether you'll represent me or not. I messed up. I got in over my head and then I didn't know how to get out. Yes, we had a fight that night. Yes, I planted the bullet. But I swear to God I didn't kill him."

"No, of course not, and now I suppose you're going to tell me that you were only trying to --" Lily stopped abruptly, because, suddenly, it all made perfect sense. "Of course you were," she murmured.

He shrugged helplessly. "So tell me -- what else could I do?"

"Sit down," she said.

. . .

At exactly the same time that Lily was meeting with Randy Hitchens, Maynard Purcell came wandering across the lawn of his Morgan Hill home and onto his next-door neighbor's patio. Diana Hightower had wheeled Carson outside to get a breath of fresh air while she cleaned the library.

"Beautiful day, isn't it?" the physician said.

"Sure is," Carson agreed. "Never thought I'd ever yearn for the weather to go cool."

Purcell nodded. "But it was nice while it lasted."

"What -- you mean the Indian Summer?" Carson asked.

The physician chuckled. "Ironic, don't you think?" he said. "All things considered."

"Ironic, indeed," the former prosecutor agreed. "So what are you up to -- taking the day off?"

"I guess so," Purcell replied. "Thinking about maybe taking the rest of my days off."

"You're going to retire?" Carson was truly surprised. The physician was in excellent health and ten years younger than the seventy-four-year-old former prosecutor.

"Maybe."

"Never thought I'd hear you say it. Always thought the heavenly angels were going to have to carry you out of your examining room, kicking and screaming."

"Things change," Purcell said. He looked up at the trees that ran between his property and his neighbor's, and sighed deeply. "Look, can I talk to you -- about a matter?" he asked. "I mean, in confidence?"

"A legal matter?"

"Potentially."

"Sure you don't want to talk to my daughter? She's the lawyer in the family now."

"It might come to that," Purcell said. "But right now, I'd just like to talk to you, friend to friend, if that's okay."

Carson eyed his neighbor thoughtfully. He could sense a fair amount of stress, and perhaps something else, lurking just below the surface.

"Sure," he said.

• • •

"You'll never guess who came to see me today," Lily began the dinner table conversation that evening.

"That wouldn't be a certain Port Hancock police detective, would it?" Carson suggested, hazarding a guess, but not a far-fetched one.

Dancer smiled.

Lily blinked. "How did you know?"

Her father crunched the left side of his body in what nowadays passed for a shrug. "After court yesterday, it seemed likely the young man would be looking for an attorney."

"He says he didn't kill Dale," Lily reported. "And you know what? I'm inclined to believe him."

Carson nodded slowly. "I think we may just have found ourselves in an interesting predicament," he said.

"What do you mean?"

"Maynard came to see me today."

"Why? Is he upset that Jason isn't going to hang for killing his son-in-law?"

"Not exactly," Carson said.

"Oh my God," Lily breathed. "I was right."

"Right? About what?"

"I got the feeling Randy was protecting someone. I think he wanted to tell me, almost told me, but stopped just short. And now, with Maynard getting into the picture, it's getting clearer."

"Maybe not as clear as you think," her father said.

"Why?"

"Maynard is willing to say that he killed Dale -- beat him to a pulp and shot him in the head."

"That's nonsense," Lily declared.

"You know it, and I know it, but that's what he's prepared to say."

"And Randy is willing to say that he covered it all up, but that he didn't kill Dale, and won't implicate who did."

"And if we believe that," the former prosecutor said, "then we're left with only one option."

Lily nodded. "Two men trying to save one woman."

"Which means there may be a little more to the detective's relationship with the widow than simply transporting her to and from the hospital."

"So what do we have," Lily wondered, "three lives ready to be destroyed over one bad cop?"

"I don't like those odds," Carson said.

"I don't, either," his daughter agreed. "But I guarantee you John Henry won't let it go. He took too big a hit over Jason."

"That's the least of my worries," Carson declared. "But I have an idea."

"What sort of idea?"

"One that might just take care of everything," her father informed her. "We're going to have a small dinner party. Right here. Tomorrow night. You issue the invitations. I'll tell Diana."

Dancer listened intently, but said nothing.

• • •

It was an odd group that gathered round the dinner table at the Morgan Hill home on Tuesday evening -- the physician and his wife, their daughter, the detective.

The bodyguard was absent. His job was over, and it was time for him to head back to Spokane. He wanted one last night to say his goodbyes to the part of the community that had welcomed him in, and done their best to make him feel at home.

Diana served a shrimp creole over steamed rice with a garden salad and fresh corn muffins dripping in butter. Carson opened a prized 1968 Chateau Margaux. The guests ate and drank and made small talk, but weren't sure what they were doing there. There had been few dinner parties at the house since Althea died, and certainly none like this one.

"We seem to have ourselves a bit of a dilemma," Carson said as soon as the chocolate mousse had been served, and the coffee cups filled. "We have one dead police detective, and three potential perpetrators."

Maynard Purcell, Randy Hitchens, and Lauren Scott all stared at their host, and then at one another.

Helen Purcell, Maynard's wife and Lauren's mother, just look confused.

"Now just a minute," Purcell began, as his daughter opened her mouth to speak.

"I don't know what you think you know," Lauren exclaimed.

And Randy Hitchens slumped in his chair and wondered if this was an ambush.

"Just settle down, all of you," Carson advised. "It should occur to you that Lily and I invited you here for a reason. Maynard, you came to me. Randy, you went to Lily. And Lauren, well, it was only a matter of time before you would have had to talk to someone. Now we think we just might have a way to deal with this mess, and we think you should listen."

Three of the guests said nothing.

"I don't understand what's going on," Helen Purcell declared.

"Never mind, Mother," her husband said. He turned to his host. "All right, we're listening."

· · ·

"Did you and your father get it all worked out last night?" Dancer asked the following morning. He was all packed up, he had filled the 4-Runner with gas, he had said his goodbyes to Carson and to Diana, and he was ready to go.

"Most of it," Lily told him.

"And do you think you've figured out what really happened?"

"Oddly enough, I think I have," she said.

"Can you fix it?"

"I can try."

The man from Spokane smiled. "It's been a pleasure knowing you," he said.

"That goes both ways," Lily said, and meant it.

"Well, if you ever stick your nose in another thorn bush, and need a shadow again," he told her, thrusting out his hand, "keep my card."

Lily ignored the outstretched hand and instead threw her arms around him in a big bear hug.

"You know I will," she said. "In spite of all my efforts, you've been in my face, in my way, and in my corner, and I'll never forget it. I'll probably be looking over my shoulder for you for months, and each and every time, I'll be disappointed that you're not there."

John Dancer didn't embarrass easily, but his face felt suddenly warm. He knew she wasn't going to mention the Jansen cottage, and she knew he wouldn't, either.

"I could've done better," he told her, "but I'm glad it all worked out."

• • •

It was drizzling as Lily drove herself to the courthouse, which would later be noted by the statisticians as the first official rain of the season. Temperatures had receded into the more normal fifties. The air-conditioning had been turned off. Summer clothes had disappeared.

In a navy wool gabardine suit and high heels, Lily made her way into the courthouse and up to the third floor. Her appointment was for ten o'clock. She knew how John Henry liked punctuality and, on this occasion, she intended to be right on time.

"This must be important," John Henry said, rising as Lily entered his office. He gestured her to the chair in front of his desk, and then sat back down. Tom Lickliter was there, too, standing at the window.

"It might be," Lily responded. "And in case you're wondering why I asked for this meeting, I'm here to give you official notice. As of nine o'clock this morning, I am representing Randy Hitchens, and therefore any future conversations you might wish to have with him will not take place without my being present."

John Henry had indeed been wondering why she had requested this meeting, but to tell him she was representing Randy Hitchens had never entered his mind. "I see," he said, to cover his surprise.

"Are you planning any such conversations?"

"Let's not beat around the bush, Lily," the prosecutor declared. "You know damn well we're looking hard at him."

"That's what I thought," she said. "Which is why I'm here."

"I'm listening."

"And I'm talking -- as long as it's understood that every word spoken from this moment on is off the record."

John Henry glanced at Tom, who shrugged. He looked back at Lily. "I'm still listening," he said.

"All right then, I'll tell you a story," she began. "A story of three people who are ready to go to the gallows, if necessary, to protect one another. The first is a woman who, for years, suffered incredible brutality in her own home, at the hands of a man she was supposed to be able to trust. The second is a police officer who befriended her, realized her predicament, and tried to help. The third is a respected patriarch of this community who, among many others, brought *me* safely into this world and, I suspect, has been waiting patiently for me to somehow return the favor."

"Maynard Purcell is involved in this?" John Henry breathed.

Lily ignored the question. "Just for argument's sake," she continued, "let's say the woman's husband is a cocaine addict, an addiction that makes his behavior totally unpredictable, one minute calm and the next violent, with the result that she lives in constant fear for her life, and the lives of her children. And one night among many -- let's say, one night in February -- the husband goes off the deep end, beats her viciously, and tells her that if he ever lays eyes on her again, he'll kill her, and no one will ever be the wiser."

John Henry sighed. Tom Lickliter nodded to himself.

"He can't get enough cocaine into his system to keep him as euphoric as he once could, and she believes him," Lily went on. "So she makes two panicked telephone calls. The first is to the police officer friend, who's at a bar on the outskirts of town. The second is to her father, who's already in bed. The friend leaves the bar, jumps into his car, and heads back to town to look for his partner. The father jumps out of bed, pulls on his clothes, and tells her he's on his way. Now, I suspect you're about to charge my client with Dale Scott's murder, so I feel obligated to tell you that one of these three people is prepared to admit that, after finding Dale in the alley and trying unsuccessfully to talk him down, he lost his temper, and did indeed beat the crap out of him. The other two are prepared to say that, at one point or another, they were there, in that alley, too. And all three of them are prepared to confess, under oath, that they shot and killed Dale Scott."

Lily sat back in her chair and waited for comment from the prosecutor and his deputy.

"That's quite a story," John Henry said.

"Isn't it?" she agreed. "All three of them had means, motive, and opportunity. And all three of them will testify against themselves and for each other. You know as well as I do what that means -- you've been a lawyer longer than I have. You'll never get a conviction."

The prosecutor scowled. "I can charge one for the murder and the other two as accessories, you know," he threatened.

"Yes, you could," Lily conceded. "But which one, which two? How are you going to prove who actually pulled the trigger?"

Tom Lickliter smiled a genuine smile of admiration. "I think she's got us, John Henry," he said.

"So, whoever it is who did it -- he or she -- is going to get off scot free for a cold-blooded murder?" the prosecutor exclaimed. "Where's the justice in that?"

Lily shrugged. "Where's the justice in a woman being used as a punching bag for years on end? You saw that hospital file. You know what he did to her. That heavy veil she wore at the funeral, it wasn't to hide her grief -- it was to hide her injuries."

"She could have left him."

"Maybe," Lily said. "But after you're told long enough and often enough that, if you leave, he'll hunt you down and kill you, and no one will ever find you, and he's a cop who could do it and know how to get away with it -- for some people, it's just not that simple. And she had two children to worry about."

"So what am I supposed to do? Just drop the whole thing?"

"I certainly would never presume to tell you what to do, John Henry, " Lily told him. "But if I were you, I'd call a little press conference to say that the case will remain open, that you aren't going to rush into anything, and that as soon as enough evidence is obtained to enable you to make a charge that will stick, you'll make it. Then I'd leak a little drib and drab here and there about what kind of person Dale Scott really was, and in time -- I suspect that most people won't care if his killer is ever brought to trial."

John Henry thought for a moment. "It doesn't seem entirely fair, though," he said at length. "After all, the three of them were ready to let an innocent man go to the gallows, weren't they?"

"It looks that way," Lily conceded. "And what I said was, you wouldn't get a conviction -- I didn't say they were honorable."

The prosecutor drew a deep breath and nodded. "All right, Lily, I'm going to go along with you on this. I have no choice, really. I've already gotten one black eye from this mess. I don't need another. But I'm curious -- do you know which one did it?"

Lily shrugged. "I have my suspicions. But to tell you the truth, I don't think you really want to know."

"I still think it was Hitchens," John Henry declared. "I could have made a pretty good case against him."

"Not good enough," the defense attorney said.

"Which means the whole thing will just languish for a while and then fade away."

"And maybe, twenty or thirty years from now," Tom interjected, "when we're retired, someone will pull the file out and wonder why the case was never solved."

John Henry nodded. "I guess I don't really mind so much. Scott was a dirty cop. He probably deserved what he got."

"Thanks for seeing it that way," Lily said, rising. "I'll tell my client."

Tom walked out with her. "That was nicely done," he said.

"I'm afraid I can't take much of the credit," she responded. "The idea wasn't mine. It was theirs, with a little help from my father."

"Why am I not surprised?" the deputy prosecutor said. "The profession lost a lot when it lost Carson Burns."

Lily smiled. "Thanks," she said. "I'll tell him you said that. I know he'll appreciate it."

"Look," Tom said, feeling both bold and tentative. "The case is over, which means there's no issue of impropriety here. So I was wondering if maybe, sometime, you might like to go out for dinner?" It had been way too long. He felt totally clumsy.

For her part, Lily felt her face grow warm. "I anticipate we'll be facing each other over many more cases in the future, but I don't see why that should be a factor," she replied, wondering why her legs suddenly felt a bit wobbly.

"Should I take that as a yes?" he asked, trying not to sound too eager, because things like this couldn't be rushed.

"I think you can interpret that as a yes," she confirmed, hoping she didn't sound too eager, because things like this needed to go slowly.

• • •

Lily sat in her office long after Megan and Wanda and Joe had left for the evening. It was quiet, and she could think her thoughts without having to worry about sharing them with anyone. Because, of course, she couldn't share them. She would never be able to share them. It was part of the job. She sighed. It had been a tough nine months -- tougher than she would ever be willing to admit. From the moment she had walked into Grace Pelletier's office to the moment she had left John Henry's. So many things had happened during that time -- not the least of which was that her whole world had been turned upside down by a pair of idiots in an airplane. Which was probably why the pieces had taken so long to come together. But who knew? Perhaps that was just the price she had to pay.

She meant what she had told John Henry. She didn't think he wanted to know who had really killed Dale Scott. To be honest, she would have preferred not knowing herself. But of course, that was irrelevant now.

She got to her feet and snapped off the light, then walked down the stairs and out of the Victorian, into the cool night air. It had been a long journey to the truth, with one theory dissolving into another, which in turn morphed into yet another. So many times that she had lost count. She wasn't sure she would ever understand it completely. She was certain no one else would.

Well, maybe there was one person who would. One very wise person who had gotten it from the beginning, had tried his best to tell her, and then had tried his best to steer her in the right direction. Maybe, if her brain hadn't been so messed up, she would have seen it sooner.

"Everyone has his breaking point," he had said. "Maybe it had nothing to do with Dale Scott at all. Maybe it was about something else entirely."

It wasn't clear what that something else might have been, but it really didn't matter. It was over, and to be honest, she actually did think it had turned out pretty much the way it should have. The proof of that, if she needed any, was Randy Hitchens. She would never have been able to go after him in court as she had, or agree to represent him, for that matter, if she hadn't known, beyond any reasonable doubt, that he was telling the truth.

• • •

Jason Lightfoot had become something of a celebrity in Port Hancock. The small cadre of people who never stopped believing in him was soon bolstered by a significant part of the community. Good people all, they wanted to right a wrong. If they had unjustly accused him of a crime, they now wanted to make up for it.

A local matron offered him a cottage on her estate, free of obligation. Odd jobs came pouring in from all over, some even from people who could afford to pay. And offers of fulltime employment were tendered -- from a building contractor, the local dairy, and the city's largest building supply store. And those who had always known the quality of Jason's work smiled to themselves.

"It's your time, my boy," Billy Fugate told him. "Make the most of it."

Jason thought it all over. Then he turned down the offer of the cottage, because it was too far out of town, but he agreed to take a room at Miss Polly's, in exchange for maintenance services. It was a room with a bath over the garage, actually, detached from the house itself, and he figured the measure of privacy he would have out there more than made up for the flight of stairs he would have to climb.

He liked doing odd jobs, but he liked the idea of regular employment even better. Because of his knee, he accepted the offer from the building supply store. The store was about two miles from the boarding house, and the storeowner offered him the use of a secondhand Honda so he could get to and from work without having to rely on the bus. For the first time in his life, Jason got a driver's license. Ironically, it turned out to be a sweet deal for the building supply store, too. Just the fact that Jason was there brought in a lot more business than it lost.

And, too, now that he had reliable transport, he had no excuse for failing to show up at his uncle's home for Sunday dinners.

As bits and pieces of Dale Scott's life and work were carefully leaked to the media, the community reacted much as Lily had predicted, and even those who still believed that Jason was a murderer were willing to consider that there might have been mitigating circumstances.

In a matter of weeks, Jason had gone from accused cop killer to hero. He had money in his pocket and he had something else, too -- something he had never had before -- respect. But he didn't let it go to his head, and he didn't forget his friends. In the evenings, he could still be found at The Last Call, having dinner and even cleaning up the place. Which was exactly where Lily found him just before Thanksgiving.

He smiled broadly when he saw her. "Hey there, Lady Lawyer," he greeted her.

"Hey, Jason," she returned. "Had a feeling this was where I'd find you."

He dropped down onto the barstool beside her. "No place like home," he conceded. She nodded. She understood. "I thought you said it was all over," he said, wondering why she had come.

"Yes," she assured him, "it is."

"Good," he said, relieved. "Although it wasn't all bad, you know. Ten months and Greg Parker, and I still ain't gone back on the rum."

"I'm glad."

"In addition to everything else you done for me, I got you to thank for that, too, you know," he told her. "Well, you and Parker, and I guess, in a way, my mother."

"Then maybe it all happened for a reason," she suggested.

"You think?"

"Well, it doesn't seem to have done you any harm. As far as I can tell, you're the toast of the town these days."

"Yeah, well, I guess life is funny sometimes," he conceded.

"It certainly is." She eyed him thoughtfully for a long moment. "When did you remember?" she asked finally, her voice deliberately soft enough so that only he could hear.

He looked at her sharply, and then he chuckled, because it didn't matter. She had told him it didn't matter. She had as good as told him he could shout it from the middle of upper Broad Street, if he wanted to, and it wouldn't matter. And now he knew why she had come.

"In the mountains," he said, because he guessed he owed her at least that much. "Somethin' about breathin' in all that fresh air -- it really does clear the brain." He sighed. "I didn't wanna kill him. I just wanted him to shut up, so I could sleep. But he was screamin' and actin' all crazy like. When I saw how bad he was hurt, I just wanted to help. But, when I tried, that's when he pulled his gun on me -- and then what was I supposed to do? He was outta control. I knew it was gonna be me or him, and I guess I didn't want it to be me."

The attorney nodded slowly, because it had gone down pretty much the way she figured it had.

Jason cocked his head. "How'd you know?"

Lily shrugged and then she smiled, because true honor was indeed a rare thing in this world.

"You came back," she said.

Made in the USA
Charleston, SC
28 November 2014